LAST OF THE
NIGHTHAWKS

A MEMORY OF ANSTRACTOR

GREG DRAGON

LAST OF THE NIGHTHAWKS

This is a work of fiction. Names, characters, organizations, places, events, and incidents are either products of the author's imagination or are used fictitiously.

Cover Art by Tom Edwards

For more books by the author
GREGDRAGON.COM

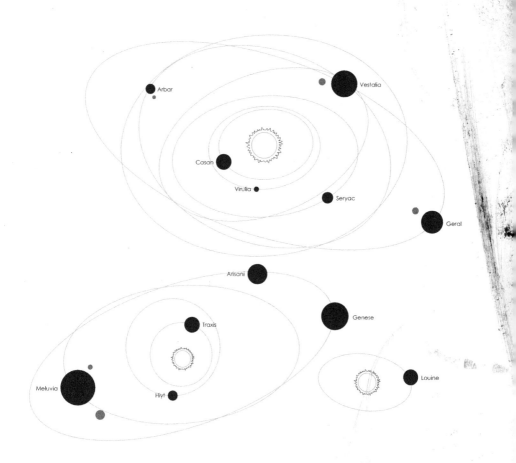

The Galaxy of Anstractor

1

Helga Ate kept her body steady by gripping the sides of the bench while she used her upper back as a form of anchor. This was not what she expected after receiving a formal invitation to the glorious Nighthawks, the first Special Forces squad on the battleship, *Rendron*, and third in the galactic Alliance military.

Two spacemen worked at pulling on her second layer of protective gear but it didn't help that it was a size too small. Though she was small in frame, the *Rendron's* outfitters couldn't find a 3B XO-suit in her size.

"May I suggest a diet, Ate?" said the man on her right leg, an E-4 named Adan Cruser who she knew from the academy.

She made a face at him, something between amusement and frustration, but they made progress and suddenly she was up to her waist in an ill-fitting pressure suit.

"See Cruse, you got it," she said, exhaling, as if from some relief. "Here you had me worried that I'd have to cut back on that delicious protein paste."

"First time?" said the other man, who didn't seem amused by her joke.

"Hey, you have your hands on my legs and that's what you choose to ask me?" she said, forcing her face into a scowl. "I'm ready enough, if you perverts could just get me into this suit—sheesh! I can't believe that they don't have a size smaller than a three."

"You may want to take this serious, ma'am," the man said, unamused by her humor. "You're about to fight real lizards, not simulated ones on our machines. I don't know if they told you this, but women your size don't make it back too often."

Cruser shot him an angry look. They were up to her torso now, strapping her in, and Helga saw him mouth a string of expletives at the giant.

"Don't mind Nanda, Ate. He's just giving you *schtill*. Plenty of our women do fine—just like the men. Even the tiny ones." When he said tiny, his eyes shot up to Nanda, who she swore looked frightened of the shorter man.

Though she didn't like it, Helga still had to wonder about Nanda's words. He didn't say much, and it had taken all this time for her to catch his name. Experience told her that the quiet ones were always the most sincere, and he really didn't have to volunteer that information.

When she was strapped in, they backed away, and she looked down at herself and then up at Cruser. It was all so tight that her skin was screaming, and she struggled against demanding that they pull the thing off. "It's okay," he said, as if he could read her mind. "It's okay, just give it time."

Helga got up off the bench and tried to walk around the locker room. It was so tight that it stung, as if she'd been squeezed into a leather tube. "How am I supposed to fight while wearing this thing?" she said. "Here's a better question. How do I use the *thyping* bathroom?"

"Work out your limbs and let it get used to you," Cruser said. "The fabric is alien, so you can't treat it like any of our stuff. It's tight now but keep on moving, you won't even notice it after a while. As to the bathroom, it's alien." He gave her a wink. "Mess your drawers all you want. It'll be absorbed and repurposed."

"Gross," Helga said, trying to imagine how it would feel. "Gross! What? Are you being serious?"

"I am, but it's okay, Ate, you'll figure it out," Cruser said, laughing. "Now, we're going to go help the others get their 3B suits on. When you feel comfortable enough, step into your armor. Then come join us in the ready room."

Helga was still processing the bathroom logic, as in how would it repurpose her waste. "Thanks, Cruser, and thank you, Nanda," she said. "I'll just jump around and get used to these pajamas." The two men waved and walked outside, but not before Nanda shot her a cautionary glance. "Geez, what's your problem?" she mumbled, then brushed it aside to continue swinging her tight arms.

It was hard to convince herself that the suit would be okay, being that her body wanted nothing more than to peel it off.

She looked down at her wrist comms lying on the bench and saw that there was a little under thirty minutes to go. Forgoing the workout, she walked over to her powered armor suit (PAS), which was a close-fitting Frankenstein of more alien material and metal.

Seeing the black-clad mannequin before her brought a smile to Helga's face. She was about to be dressed like a true Alliance ESO—Extraplanetary Spatial Operator. She had flashbacks of a childhood spent watching men and women wearing this armor. How badly she'd wanted to be one of them, a hero of the *Rendron*.

Now here she was, one step away from being an inspiration herself. She spun the mannequin and began removing the armor piece by piece. Helga was surprised by how malleable the plates were. They felt like hard rubber and bent just like it, too.

The PAS fit like it was always meant to be hers. She dressed quickly, then walked over to a mirror, surprised by how easy she could maneuver.

When she saw herself she almost cried. Her face was still what it had always been—a tanned mélange of human and Casanian features—but her body was now a sleek, black fighting machine. Looking around to make sure she was alone, Helga performed a little dance of celebration.

After pulling on the helmet, she no longer recognized herself. Helga Ate had transformed into Ensign Helga Ate. She made a mock salute, then hoisted an imaginary auto rifle, but then her comms beeped and she knew she was out of time.

Removing the helmet, she slipped it beneath her arm, then grabbed her rucksack and marched out of the locker room. As she walked through the spaceport, she saw the eyes of the cadets looking on with envy. It lifted her spirits—as if they could get any higher—and she felt like a giant, off to do giant things for the little people.

When she entered the dock, a host of hard eyes fell on her, so she checked the time and was surprised to find that she had five minutes left to spare. Still, they stared at her as if she had walked in late, and as she took her place she realized why. "Thype me," she whispered under her breath. "Why am I the only woman?"

There were seven men, dressed in armor like hers, but theirs showed the scars of numerous battles. Some regarded her warmly while others seemed annoyed, and one went out of his way to make her feel uneasy. As the high she'd once felt drained out of her pores, Helga got a smile from a female mechanic as she slid out from under an X-23 fighter.

She returned the smile. *At least someone appreciates me being here*, she thought, then looked over at the ship that would take them to their destiny. The vessel was a Britz SPZ, a tiny beetle-shaped ship with an FTL. From what Helga could remember from her studies, it had just enough room to hold ten average-sized spacers.

The thought of being trapped with these men made her hairs stand up. Plus, outside of Cruser—who waved at her—she didn't recognize any of the other ranks. *Rendron* was a large ship with hundreds of spacemen, but it frightened her that she was the sole female being deployed on the mission.

The man nearest the Britz removed his helmet and she recognized him as Lieutenant Cilas Mec. Like Helga, he was a superstar cadet who had been drafted into the formal Navy. And upon seeing him, she understood why she had been chosen.

Cilas walked out in front of them and raised a remote, which projected several screens in front of him. The screens showed a dark grey moon and a photo of a settlement. There was also a stream of readouts but they were too small for her to read. He froze them in place and then waved the remote again. This time it showed a humanoid creature with a mouth full of razor-sharp teeth.

"Nighthawks," he said, "Our mission is to rescue civilians trapped on a moon called Dyn, orbiting Louine." Several sounds of disapproval came from the group of men, but Cilas didn't seem fazed by it and continued to read their instructions.

"The colony of Abarion is made up of several families that are refugees from our planet, Vestalia," Cilas said. Upon hearing "Vestalia," which was the human's ancestral planet, the noisemakers quickly grew quiet. The Louines were a reclusive race that had remained neutral in the war, so Helga understood the objections when they assumed the mission was to help them.

Cilas continued. "Over the last few months, communication with Abarion has gone silent. We can contact the Louines, but they aren't helping. While they allowed the colony to settle on their moon, they haven't been monitoring them. We'll be in the dark out there, Nighthawks. No support, and little chance of rescue."

"That's how we like it," someone shouted, and the others grunted their approval.

"Now, if you pay attention to this vid that I'm about to play for you," Cilas said, seemingly unfazed by the interruption, "you will see why our group has been tasked with this mission."

4

He waved the remote in the air and a new screen materialized in front of him. There was surveillance footage of the colony, which would have been a clear picture if not for an occasional glitch showering the video with static.

The place looked unoccupied, though there was some evidence of life having existed there. Transparent atmosphere bubbles covered schools, temples, and businesses. Inside the farm grew a number of plants that were still alive and well.

"From this footage you can see that the people are missing. Command suspects that they're in a bunker, hiding from the Geralos," Cilas said.

"Geralos," Helga repeated.

"Yes, Geralos, Ensign Ate," Cilas said.

"Then it's too late," said the loud ESO from before, who looked around at the other men for support. "If the lizards are there, those people are dead, and the most we'll be able to do is collect their bones."

Cilas walked past the screens, pointing to the image of the Geralos. "It isn't just about rescue, it's about territory, Wyatt. If the Geralos are on Dyn, they can eventually move on Louine. Now, aside from Ate, we all have fought with the lizards before. You know how they move, you know what motivates them—so I don't have to remind you that speed is our best ally."

"Hey, Lt, quick question," said the man, whose mannerisms kept Helga on edge, nervous. "What is she doing here?"

Cilas shot him an impatient glance. "The Ensign is here because of her record in the academy, and due to our need for a backup pilot. Need I remind you that we lost Ahmad? Did that slip your mind, Wyatt?"

"No, sir!" the man said, sitting down quickly.

"Idiot," whispered a bigger man with massive, tree trunk arms, and Helga had to hide her smile when she saw how Wyatt regarded him.

"So, she's just a pilot then?" Wyatt said under his breath, giving her a condescending grin.

"You see this area?" Cilas continued, and waved the remote again, this time producing a large hologram image of Dyn. "Based on our time of departure and where the moon will be in its orbit, we expect to make touchdown in this region, south of the colony. I'm told that once we're in cryo-sleep it will take us three days to arrive. There will be about fifteen hours of drop time once we're all thawed out, then we'll discuss further details on the moon."

The large man from before raised his hand and Cilas motioned for him to talk. "Do we know what to expect there, Lt? Will the lizards see us coming, or was our LZ chosen to maintain secrecy?" he said.

Cilas seemed to think about his answer, buying time by manipulating the screens. "You all know I blame myself for what happened to Ahmad. I don't intend to have us flying blind into anything again," he said.

"Now, as far as we know, the lizards are inside the colony itself. We aim to slip in silent, cut their throats, and jump back here, victorious," he said. "Now, gather your gear and let's get moving. We have one more hour until takeoff. If you haven't called family do so now, since you will be out of contact for weeks."

He gave them leave and walked away towards the Britz. Helga glanced around one more time before following him inside. Her only family was her brother and they hadn't talked in years. She didn't need to make any calls since there was no one to really care. There was her ex, Oren, but he was now married to an Ensign that worked on the bridge. She was pretty and had a bright career ahead of her, all of the things he wanted in a mate.

The memory of their last fight brought up old, uncomfortable pains, and Helga stopped to check her thoughts before they drove her into a rage. "Be tough, big girl," she said to herself, repeating those words of encouragement that her mother used to say.

She gripped the handle of the ladder leading up in the ship and looked down at her armored gauntlet, still in awe that it was hers. *Several million credits in military equipment, all entrusted to me,* she thought proudly. *And yet I'm here worrying about a loser like Oren.*

Climbing the ladder, she stepped inside and stopped to take it all in. It was larger than she anticipated, with each seat occupying a good amount of room. There were racks for gear, hooks for armor, and the cryo-tech was built into each of the seats. She squeezed through the narrow aisle to gain the cockpit and saw Cruser already seated, running through some checks.

"You ready to *thype* up some lizards?" he said without turning around.

"More than ready, if I actually get to see some action," she said.

He motioned to the copilot's seat, and she sat down inside of it. The material was soft, and she leaned back with a sigh.

"Missions like this look good on your record, Helga," he said. "Especially if you want to earn your way onto the Captain's bridge. Trust me, they won't need you out there when they go for the lizards. This team has been doing it together for a long time."

"Are you assuming that I joined you men to get a nudge towards a commission on the bridge?" Helga said. "That's messed up, Cruse. I didn't expect that from you. What, a girl can't serve her starship for honor and all that stuff?"

"Am I wrong?" said Cruser, stopping his checks to look at her.

"Well, not exactly, but you don't have to throw it in my face, okay? Look, I fully expect to fight. That's why I answered when I was called," she said.

"I know," Cruser said. "They don't pick just anyone to be a Nighthawk, but since you're going to be my backup, let me see what you can do. Have you ever flown one of these before?"

"No, but isn't it built from a Wyman's parts? The HUD is the same, and I've flown Wymans before," Helga said.

Cruser nodded. "Good. So you're used to the controls. That makes me feel a little bit better. You may actually be of some use. The thing you need to be careful of though is that this is still not a Wyman. This bug is smaller and doesn't maneuver as well, and we will be dealing with the atmosphere on the moon. These drops are nothing like what you simulated at the academy, and only experience will get you through."

"I understand, Cruser, it's not like I haven't flown before. Maybe not on moon drops or combat sorties, but I've handled transports and dealt with emergencies," Helga said.

"That's good," he said. "Well, welcome aboard. It will be interesting to see how well you can handle the controls. Now, strap in and run some diagnostics, will you? Get yourself acclimated with the old girl while I go have a talk with the lieutenant."

2

When the Britz had been cruising for little over an hour, Cruser told them that it was time to prep for cryo. Helga didn't understand why they'd been forced to get fully dressed just to sit on the ship for a short time period before stripping down again.

Changing inside of the tiny ship would be challenging, especially since she would need help in order to remove her XO-suit. Helga turned in her seat to see what everyone was doing. The men were already changing out of their armor. There was little care for privacy as they prepared for the cryo-sleep, and some of them were as naked as the day they were born.

Helga looked over at Cruser, who was now down to his underclothes. He placed his suit and armor inside one of the lockers near his chair. She checked the wall on her left and saw that there was a locker there, so she swallowed her pride and got up out of the seat.

Removing the armor was simple enough, so she placed her helmet and gauntlets inside of the locker. She couldn't get past the cost of the PAS, so she took her time and stacked the pieces carefully.

When it came time to remove her XO-suit, the near-naked Cruser helped her out. She thought about where she was—inside of a tin can with dangerous men—and though she trusted Cruser, she couldn't help but feel anxious and vulnerable.

"Do I have to take it all off?" she whispered to him. "I know it's cryo, but I ... I don't know these men."

He gave her a look that she read as concern, and then positioned himself so that he could block her from the others. "You'll be alright," he whispered, and helped her pull the suit off. Helga quickly threw it inside the locker, then covered her breasts with her hands.

"I don't mean to be a bother ... paranoid and, whatever. Thanks for your help, Cruser," she said. "I owe you one."

As he left her side to prep his chair for cryo, she saw that several of the men were looking her way. She was one of the few mixed-race aliens on the *Rendron*, and she knew that her appearance was a curiosity.

This was a lifelong curse that kept her on edge. She couldn't tell if the staring was because she was female or curiosity due to her unique features. She didn't see the big deal. She had a human body, all developed and built up through a lifetime of training. The *Rendron* was a military ship, so her fit body wasn't out of the ordinary. The spots on the sides of her face, however, led people to believe she had more on her body.

Cryo required complete nakedness, and she knew this coming in. But she'd assumed wrongly that there would be private compartments for them to change in.

A panel above her shifted to the side and a glass attachment descended from it. When it touched the chair it slid forward with a hiss, sealing her inside. Metal restraints came out of the chair and wrapped around her arms and legs. This was disconcerting. She felt helpless and claustrophobic. Then she felt the pinch of a needle shoot drugs into her spine.

She felt her body go limp, and she began to have trouble focusing. She no longer cared that she was restrained, or that she was naked next to Cruser. All she could think about was the pretty blue glass, this chamber that would be her home for a couple of days.

She tried to focus on the mission but that didn't work. "I'm about to go into combat wearing powered armor," she whispered. The thought made her smile, and she forgot where she was. Soon she was asleep and dreaming of happier days.

After several days at faster than light travel, the Britz SPZ slowed itself to orbit the moon of Dyn. First the computer came online, and then the lights as the cryo-pods came back to life.

Helga's eyes flew open, and the glass was gone. She saw the panel close above her station and felt the restraints open on her limbs. She rubbed her wrists and moved her legs, stretching painful joints. When she looked over at Cruser he was already on his feet, jumping around and flailing his arms.

The pilot was still naked and she caught herself staring, so she quickly averted her gaze and rubbed the life back into her arms. Reaching into the locker, she grabbed her underclothes, dressed quickly, and then pulled out the 3B XO-suit. To her surprise it maintained her form, and she could pull it on without anyone's help.

When she was back in her armor, she could move around effortlessly, and in time the stiffness went away.

"There she is," said Cruser, and Helga made to say hello, but then she saw that he was referring to the moon of Dyn. It didn't look like much, just a lifeless chunk of rock, but when she consulted her computer, she learned that it had enough gravity to support human life.

"I can see why the settlers chose to take a chance here," she said. "What about you, Cruser? You ever think about settling down on a moon like this?"

"Me? Please, it would never happen. I was born and raised in the black of space, and that is where I will remain. You thinking about putting down some roots down there, Ate?" he said, laughing, and she quickly shook her head at him.

"Computer says the atmosphere is toxic like Geral. Bad for us, good for them. Can't settle down in a place where I'm having to watch my back," she said. "Plus, the Alliance needs me to hunt the lizards."

"What do you know about lizards?" someone said, and Helga turned around slowly to see who it was. She hadn't realized that she was speaking so loud that the whole ship could hear. "You think what they show you in vids has you ready for the enemy? You're going to get educated real fast. They like Vestalian women, even the ones with spots. You will be a special kind of dish for them. If I were you I'd stay onboard and hope that we kill them all. As soon as they get a whiff of you, woo-boy, you will wish that you'd never put on that armor."

Helga stood frozen, staring at the man. She was so blindsided by his words that she didn't know what to do. He had hit her with a trifecta of insults, hitting on her race, sex, and newness to the war. "Why don't you worry about yourself?" she said, instinct kicking in to make her defend herself. It felt like the cadet academy all over again, and she would have to prove herself the way she did back then.

"Sure, if it was just about you I'd let you walk into hell," he said. "But you're a liability whether you like it or not. Talking tough don't mean schtill. Our commanders know all too well that the lizards want our women, yet they allowed you to come out here where they've set up shop—"

He shut his mouth as soon as Cilas Mec walked over to where he stood. The lieutenant whispered something to him, and he shot Helga an angry look before sitting back down. Cruser reached over and touched Helga on her arm and when she faced him he gestured for her to sit.

"This isn't the cadet academy, Helga. You need to keep a low profile," he said. "These men are dangerous, and they don't care about you. When things go south—and they always do—you don't want to be on the bad side of your team."

Helga sat down fuming. She couldn't believe it. Here was the same nonsense that she'd dealt with inside of the academy. It was beyond exhausting having to deal with people picking fights with her. Somehow she thought that it would be different in the military, but she was quickly learning that it wouldn't be.

As in all situations where she felt cornered, her mind went to ways to get back at him. One day he would need her, and she would remind him of how he'd spoken to her, and more importantly how she'd felt.

"He's like that with everybody," Cruser was saying, but she only felt herself get angrier.

"Is there anything you need me to do, Cruser?" she said, desperate for some stimulus to calm her nerves.

"You can bring us in." He pointed to the star map. "Just follow the beacon and don't try anything crazy."

"Got it," she said and took over the controls, tracing the beacon leading down to the moon. There was something about piloting that put her mind at ease, and Cruser letting her fly the ship took a weight off her shoulders.

"Ate, you're new, so the guys are going to give you *schtill*. This isn't the cadet academy, kid, but they are rightfully worried that you're not qualified. Our last mission was rough, and we lost a Nighthawk. That was our ninth mission, and we did everything by the book. Everyone was shaken up, Ate. Nighthawks aren't supposed to die. You're here with seasoned warriors, the *Rendron's* best of the best. They know each other's strength and weaknesses, but they know nothing about you."

Helga looked at Cruser, struggling to find the right words. "What happened on the last mission to kill Ahmad?" she said.

"Ghost ship stranded out in deep space," he said, reminding her of a man in his cups, rambling to himself about a past trauma. He stared out at the moon as if he could see down to its surface, and fidgeted with his hands as he spoke. "We were told that it was Alliance, and that we needed to scavenge it before the Geralos did. I could tell it was wrong from the moment we were briefed, but we go where we are sent, Ate. We go where we are sent."

He was speaking so low that she could barely hear, low so the others wouldn't have to relive it the way he did. "Ahmad was first pilot, and a mentor to me. We'd flown together for years, becoming Nighthawks at the same time. I owed him a lot; he'd saved my hide countless times on mission drops. Like I said, though, this one felt wrong. Scant details on why we were searching this ship, and little time to prepare for it," he said.

"Sounds a bit like this mission," Helga said, and she noticed his eyes grow wide.

"Yeah, well you better get used to it," he said, looking around. "We don't have the luxury of asking for details on these drops. Now, this last mission with the derelict ship, we boarded it and—"

"Hey, Cruse," someone called from the back of the ship, and the pilot looked around then got to his feet. It was as if he was relieved to be interrupted from his tale. Helga watched him walk back there and sit with the biggest ESO. At first she thought that he had gotten in trouble for saying too much to her, but soon they were laughing and trading barbs.

Helga, feeling isolated, focused on the Britz's approach. The autopilot could have managed it, but she wanted to be prepared in case of anything.

"How's it going, rookie? You okay?" someone said, and Helga turned around to see who it was.

The man standing behind her was one of the men who had welcomed her earlier. He seemed to be made of muscle, to where even his face looked strong, and though his presence was intimidating, he didn't come across as a brute.

"Thanks, Chief, I am good," she said after looking at his patch to see his rank. "Just ready to get off this bug and walk around."

He walked over and took a seat in Cruser's chair, then stuck out his hand for her to shake it. "I'm Casein, by the way. Casein Varnes. Your name is Helga, right? Helga Ate."

"Yeah," she said. "At your service. Shouldn't you be avoiding the liability like your friend over there?"

"Not my buddy, but he's my brother all the same. He's your brother too, even though you may not like it. Listen, I'm over here because we're on a mission and I need to know who has my back. You're new, and that's alright, we were all there, but when the schtill starts to fly we're all the same. The only thing that matters is the mission and our survival, so try your best to not take any of Wyatt's words personally."

Helga nodded slowly. He was probably right, but she wouldn't be making friendly with Wyatt any time soon. "I'm a boomer kid," she said. "Born and raised on the *Rendron*. My dad was Vestalian Army, and my mom was Casanian. My brother and I are the freaks that they produced. Been a military brat my entire life. I got to second class in the cadets and now I'm here. Sorry, but I don't have any war stories yet. Maybe in a few years if I'm still alive."

"You have a sense of humor, though," he said. "That's kind of a surprise. You should use that wit the next time Wyatt insults you. Show him that you can dish it out. You'll get farther with these boys if you get down in the mud with them. Getting upset will give him what he wants. You're playing right into Wyatt's hands."

"So what's your story, Chief?" Helga said, glad for the distraction and the break from her solitude.

"I'm not formally Alliance. You can probably tell. I'm originally from Virulia, but a military brat just like you. I was recon for the Virulian Army and made a lot of noise against the Geralos. But my unit was defeated and the Vestalian Navy rescued me. The lizards torched our country and ate my people. I am one of the only survivors. The *Rendron* gave me a chance to get some revenge, so here I am with you."

"That's awful," Helga said, wanting to say more but unsure if it would be appropriate.

"What do you know about the Geralos, Ate?" he said, his right hand fidgeting with the pilot's controls.

"Not much, but can you please stop doing that?" she said. "If you trigger a thrust you'll knock us off our timing, and we really need to make the LZ."

"Oops, don't want to do that," he said with a nervous smile. "Guess I have nerves now that we can actually see the moon."

"I've seen vids of the Geralos, and illustrations of course, but I don't think I've ever seen one in person," she said.

"That's a no then," he said quietly. "The first time you see one you won't forget it. I still have nightmares about them and I've been fighting them for years. They're animals, Ate. Vicious, but intelligent. If you let your guard down they will harvest you quickly." He made a snap with his armored fingers and it made her jump. "You're a woman, so they will want to eat your brains."

"I know about that," Helga said. "Hell, that's all they teach us about them. If you're caught, kill yourself; it will be better if you do. The lizards think we have powers so they eat our brains. Women are a delicacy, so they mainly target us. It's funny, I never believed the stories. I always thought it was propaganda to keep women out of the military."

"There are millions of Vestalians that prove it's true, Ate. Women rotting inside of Geralos camps waiting to be eaten. The things you heard were true; do not assume you know better. The minute you underestimate them, that's when you become their food."

Helga thought about Wyatt's words from earlier and how he called her a liability. With everything that Varnes was saying she was beginning to think that it was true.

"I won't put myself in a position to get caught or to endanger the team," she said. "I'm here to backup Chief Cruser, and to get us in and out of there."

"How old are you, Ate? About eighteen?" he said.

"Seventeen, actually, but don't hold it against me," she said. "You had one hell of a hard life leading up to here, Chief. Why aren't you an officer, given everything you've done?"

"That's a complicated answer, but I am happy where I am. Plus, after Virulia, I wanted to be back in the fight, not commanding men to do it for me. Anyway, I better get back to my seat before they think I'm over here chatting you up," he said, winking. "We'll talk later, Ate. Just remember what I said, and don't let Wyatt scare you. You're one of us now."

3

As the Britz began its descent on the moon's surface, Cilas Mec stood up and addressed the Alliance ESOs.

"Welcome to Dyn, Nighthawks," he said. "Now that you all have gotten some sleep, I can make the proper introductions. Master Chief?"

He gestured to the biggest ESO who was holding up his hand, and the man stood up and saluted.

"Sorry to interrupt you, Lt, but why all the secrecy? I get that we're going to rescue civilians, but we're in a different system above a neutral planet. I didn't hear anything about support, evacuation time, and the standard details of a mission like this. Are we really going in blind, sir?"

When he took his seat Cilas stopped to think. He appeared to have had the air knocked out of him, but then he faced them again. "Blind is an understatement, Hem. I was briefed exactly one hour before sending out the orders to assemble. Like you said, this is a different, and if I was to guess, the sparse details was necessary, since the Geralos have spies everywhere. We need to be professionals about this, Nighthawks. This could turn out messy if we're not on our game."

Helga could feel a new tension come over the men, and she wondered at Cilas's words and what they truly meant. A few more men asked detailed questions that the lieutenant couldn't answer, and it became obvious that whomever gave him the order knew little about Dyn.

"We all know one another, right?" Cilas said.

"I don't know this man," Wyatt said and tried in vain to push the Master Chief, who took his fist and slammed it into his chest. Wyatt doubled over, coughing and raising a hand in surrender, and the big man smiled with satisfaction, not taking his eyes off the lieutenant.

Cilas stopped to give Wyatt a stern look, then went back to jovially pacing the deck in front of them. "We know each other, we've bled together, and we've raised enough hell to be recognized across the Alliance," he said, and the men showed their approval in a loud series of shouts. "But we have a new recruit that needs to catch up," he said, staring at her.

Helga could never meet his eyes without looking away, embarrassed. It was one of those things when you find someone attractive, was worried that they would read it in your eyes, and feared that it would make them think less of you. She glanced down at her hands, chancing a glance or two up at him until he broke his stare to scan the room.

She was never good at the whole eye contact thing anyway, so she exhaled happily when he continued. "Just raise your hand when I call your name, so Helga—over there—can put a name with the face."

The rest of the men turned to look at her now, and she dared not look away. Unlike Cilas, who she knew from the academy, these men were strangers and she needed their respect. She saw a few warm glances, but most were cold, and when she focused in on Wyatt, he blew her a kiss.

"All right, Ate, stand so they can see you," Cilas said. "You can't hide in the pilot's seat forever, you know." Helga stood up quickly, still facing them, but she chose to look directly at Cilas's chest in order to avoid Wyatt's glare.

"Men, this is Ensign Helga Ate, a second class cadet that just graduated from the academy. Helga is one of the only cadets to score perfect marks on the combat exercise. This will be her first official dance outside of simulation, so we should aim to break her in properly. Right?"

The men shouted their approval in unison, even Wyatt, who gave her a genuine smile. Helga didn't know what it meant, but she wasn't ready to forgive him, not until he gave her a formal apology.

"Now, Ate, let me introduce you to the Nighthawks. First, we have Master Chief Stargunner, Cage Hem. The Master Chief is a true veteran of this conflict, having led men into battle on every Alliance planet, and several remote moons. If you need a role model, Ate, look no further. MCS Hem is your prototype," Cilas said.

Helga saw that Cage was the same man who had asked Cilas if the lizards would be ready for them. He was a silent giant, dark and beefy, who appeared to be in his mid-thirties. He gave her a friendly nod and she returned the gesture, hoping that he was as nice as he looked.

"You know Chief Adan Cruser, but it goes without saying that he is the best space to surface pilot that the *Rendron* has ever seen. You also met Chief Casein Varnes, a former Virulian Ranger. He's now a valuable asset to our little company," Cilas said.

He then introduced Chief Horne Wyatt, a former planet buster. That was all Helga needed to hear in order to know what he was. The fact that he bore no scars on his face spoke to his skills with surviving, or his extreme luck.

When Cilas was finished, Wyatt merely stared at her, and Helga returned his glare hoping he'd see that she wasn't afraid of him.

While Wyatt was the definition of hard, the man next to him was the extreme opposite. He was pale but dressed in a tight black outfit that looked nothing like the armor they wore. Helga wondered how it was that she hadn't seen him until now. She didn't recall him being there when they boarded the Britz.

He was thin, sinewy, and never made eye contact. There was something about him that made her feel nervous. This man was introduced as Lamia Brafa. He was a Virulian spy who joined their company to act as scout and CQC master. He seemed out of place, even beyond his dress, and when Cilas finished his introduction he merely glanced at her.

"Last but not least, we have Petty Officer Brise Sol. Sol is our vehicle operator and engineer. It will be Sol who will help us fortify the settlement once we pull the lizards out. This is his second trip with us, ain't that right, Sol? So you see, Ate, there's hope for you yet," Cilas said, smiling.

"The people on this moon have been here for a period of two years," Cilas continued. "Since then, Geralos intelligence has located them and targeted their settlement as a place for experimentation and human breeding. As you all know, the lizards like to bite into our heads and eat the gooey goodness inside. The things they intend to do with these people will make even the hardest of us lose sleep.

"They aim to make this a farm—a human farm. Where women raise their children for the sole purpose of being food. Our job is to prevent the loss of this settlement to the Geralos and to protect the people who call this place home. Right now there are ten families living down there and they are going to need our help. We're going to land on the lizards, send them on a nice trip to hell, and then we are going to give those settlers the defenses they need."

When the introductions were over everyone retreated to their respective corners to prep for the excitement to come. From the simulations Helga knew that they would have several hours before they'd have to strap in.

She decided to stretch her legs and walk around the general cockpit area. Cruser was in his chair, feet up on the command panel, playing around with a star map on his handheld tablet. "What do you need me to do?" Helga said, walking over to see what he was doing.

"We have several hours before we break atmosphere," he said. "You're going to have to find a way to pass the time. Let's see, you can socialize, but knowing you, that won't happen. Or you can try to sleep. It's what you'll end up doing anyway."

"Very funny," she said. "But I'm good on sleep. We had three days' worth of shut eye if you recall."

"It's a small ship so your options are minimal," Cruser said. "Pull up a book on your handheld, or a game or something. Just figure it out, alright?"

Helga sat back down and checked the readouts. She saw that they had an estimated fifteen hours before reaching Dyn. She was a bundle of nerves, and there was a lot of time left, but her mind was too busy for reading. It also didn't help that she was feeling nauseous, and she didn't know if it was anxiety or the aftermath of the cryo.

She got up again and scanned the ready area to see what everyone else was doing. Several of the men were playing cards in the middle, and Cilas was having a heated discussion with Cage Hem.

Helga walked over to the card game and all eyes turned to her. "What are you all playing?" she said to them.

"Wild Nines," said Wyatt. "Nighthawks only. Sorry you can't play. Only lizard-killing hands get dealt into this game, not future food." Then he bared his teeth and bit at the air.

"Oh yeah?" Helga said. "Sounds to me like you made that up. What? Are you scared I'll win and embarrass you in front of your boys?"

When he gave her a wink instead of a counter, Helga didn't know what to think. "Looks like the lessons start early," he said. "Lizard food wants to play. Deal the lady in, Chief, and let's see what she got. Now remember, fellas, Helga Ate is a second-class cadet. We don't want to get on her bad side, so go easy this first game."

"Are you ever going to stop?" she said, sitting down next to Varnes. "Anyway, what's the ante? You boys playing for real credits or what?"

"Looks like we got us a gamer!" shouted Brise Sol, and Varnes began to laugh hysterically.

"We'll see about the gamer," Wyatt said, seeming annoyed. "The ante's ten credits, lizard grub. Just do me a favor and don't go crying to the lieutenant when you're broke."

After several long hours of cards and conversation, Helga felt better about the company and the mission they were on. Though she lost a lot of money, she won enough games to break even, and even Wyatt seemed to warm up a bit when she matched him with the insults.

They mostly swapped stories and gossip, which helped make the time go by quickly, and before she knew it eight hours had passed and they decided to call it quits.

Helga went back to her seat and pulled the foil off a hard meal ration. She ate it slowly as she watched the grey moon grow closer, and washed it down with a supplement. Once her hunger was sated, she reclined her seat, then placed her feet up on the console. Cruser was asleep in his seat with the tablet resting on his lap. Helga followed his lead and closed her eyes.

"Alright, we're in the pipe now," Cruser shouted, and a flurry of activity took over the ship.

Helga opened her eyes. She didn't know how long she had been out, but the large grey moon was now all that she could see.

"Armor on, check your gear, and let's get ready to *thype* some lizard tails, Nighthawk!" Cage shouted. Helga gave him a look of surprise. The stoic Master Chief had been replaced with a rowdy, backslapping leader. His gusto was met with approval from the men as they pulled on their armor and checked their weapons.

Helga looked over at Cruser and he was gearing up too, but when their eyes met he frowned at her. "Did you not hear the Master Chief?" he said. "I have the bird in a descent, Ate. Stop sitting there looking dazed. You need to get up and get moving. Now."

Helga realized that she was still in her seat and she jumped up to pull on her armor. It had been hours since cryo, but it felt a lot shorter, and now the reality of the mission was the looming grey in front of her.

Numb fingers fumbled with straps, but she did her best to keep moving. After what seemed like an hour, Cruser was on her side, pulling down her breastplate and locking it in. "You were a second class cadet, Helga. They prepared you for this," he whispered. "Push that fear to the side and ready your *thyping* gear."

She inhaled deeply to calm her nerves and then took command of her body. It didn't take much; she was conditioned for this. She reached into the locker, grabbed her helmet, and then pulled it over her head.

Cruser adjusted it from behind and it snapped into place, and the HUD suddenly appeared before her eyes. It showed her heart rate at 108 bpm, and a green paper doll with the condition of her armor. An empty gauge floated at the bottom of her vision, and another gauge wrapped around it all, showing how much fuel was left in her booster.

This was the first time she'd seen the inside of a PAS, though she'd simulated wearing one no less than a hundred times. All the ESOs were in their armor as well, including Lamia Brafa, who wore something sleeker with red highlights.

"Strap yourselves in, this moon is not playing," Cruser shouted, and Cage picked up his command and screamed at them to get strapped in.

Helga jumped into her seat and pulled her straps tight, then looked over at Cruser who was working the controls.

They began to vibrate, as if a giant had grabbed the dropship and was attempting to shake them out. Helga felt as if her guts were being pushed up into her throat and then they were past it and she could see the surface of the moon.

Suddenly her HUD began to scream in red text. She could make out "breech," and atmosphere warnings, so she looked to Cruser for help. The chief was slumped over in his seat, with a hole in the place where his face used to be. Now she heard shouting from the men behind her.

"*Thype* me," she whispered. "Adan, please don't be dead." She made to scream but caught herself. He would want her to be strong. Fumbling for the release on her arm restraints, she leaned forward to take over the controls. Two blast doors slammed down in front of Cruser, protecting the ship from the breech. Helga heard more shots against the hull, then cannons exploding everywhere.

"Ate, what are you doing? Put us down," Wyatt yelled, and that was when her anger took over. *Put us down?* No, they had killed her friend. She wasn't going to land without putting up a fight.

She righted the ship and found her attackers. They were Geralos zip-ships flying circles around the Britz. Helga thought back on her training, flying a Wyman into combat, and her muscle memory found the controls needed to arm the Britz.

When she activated hardpoints, an echo of cheers came to her ears, and she timed the flyby of one of the ships and let out a barrage of machine gun fire. Clipping the aft of the nearest ship, she watched it dip and then crash. The other ship disappeared so she scanned the radar, and was pleased to see that it was flying away.

Helga looked for a good place to land the Britz, somewhere safe enough to stave off an ambush. Her answer came by the way of a ravine which dipped deep into the moon's surface.

When she flew into the chasm, she saw large rocks and outcroppings, no ground stable enough to set the bulky Britz down. "Land the thyping bird, rookie!" she heard Varnes shout. So she chose one of the clearest areas and put the dropship down.

She stared at Cruser for a very long time, ignoring the men as they rushed about the cockpit. The pilot's face was now a vacant, bloody hole, and a part of her felt guilty, even though that made no sense. *Looks like we may have gotten here a tad bit late,* Helga thought, and she looked back to see what Cilas was doing.

She saw that the lieutenant was seated on the floor, with a hole in his armor from where he had been shot. Varnes and Brise Sol were tending to his wounds while the rest of the men were scrambling around. "Let us the *thype* out of this thing, Ate," Wyatt said.

"Cool your jets," said Varnes. "I need to patch up this hole."

Shots rained down on them from above, and continued relentlessly as Helga struggled to release the door.

Cage Hem began unscrewing an airlock that he found on the floor of the Britz. "We're going to be exposed if we don't do something soon!" Varnes yelled, and as if on cue, Hem pulled up the giant lid to reveal the surface of the moon.

The big man jumped through and then motioned for them to hand him Cilas. "Give me the Lt, I need to get him secured. The rest of you hawks quit screwing around. Get out here and raise hell," he shouted through the comms.

The gravity allowed for them to carefully drop Cilas's body, and Cage laid him down behind a pair of rocks. One after another, the men jumped through the hatch, but when it was Helga's turn she took one last look at Cruser. "I'll make it count," she said, after shutting off her comms.

She picked up her rifle, synced it to her suit, then stepped into the vacant hole and dropped.

4

When they were all outside, they huddled beneath the Britz and Cage began to bark out orders: "Alright, listen up, we're covering Brafa, that's the plan right now. Sol, stay inside the bird and figure out what you can. Ate, get over here. I need all guns on deck. Stay by my side and act like you've been here before. You got it?"

"Got it," she shouted and readied herself for action. Both Cage and Wyatt ran below the wing of the Britz and started shooting into the air at their attackers. Varnes followed close behind and started doing the same with Lamia Brafa at his side.

Helga made to run out but the Geralos vessel shifted positions. It started firing on the area right in front of her. The rocks exploded from the gunfire, and she pressed up quickly against the landing gear. The bullets had her PAS going ballistic as the computer tried in vain to find her some sanctuary.

It took everything within her not to pull her helmet off. The readouts obscured her peripheral vision and only added to the chaos. The Geralos fired a weapon that she was not familiar with, and though she couldn't hear the bullets ricocheting off the Britz, she knew that it was all around her.

A voice was in her ear, screaming for her to move, and she recognized that it was Casein Varnes.

"Shield," shouted Cage through their comms. Wyatt got behind him and threw up his hands. A large translucent disc formed from the device he thrust in the air. It shielded the Geralos bullets, allowing the Master Chief to mount his stargun.

Once it was in place, Horne Wyatt shifted positions, holding the shield at an angle while Cage brought his fire down on the Geralos zip-ship.

"Anytime now, Ate," Varnes shouted at her again, but as much as she wanted to leave the wing, the Geralos wouldn't let up. She looked over to where the Nighthawks were and saw Lamia Brafa touch his wrist. She thought that her helmet had a glitch because it looked as if he disappeared.

"Ate, come on, you have to move. They're circling around," Varnes said. Helga gripped her rifle and pulled it into her body as if it would provide her some protection. She waited for a break in the Geralos fire then dashed from under the Britz. Her PAS picked up the motion and the rockets came on, both in the soles of her boots and on the backpack that she wore.

She floated forward and into the air, not knowing how to stop the boost. Wyatt saw what was happening, jumped, and plucked her out of the air, pulling her down below his shield.

"What the hell just happened?" Helga said when she could finally catch her breath.

"Suit reacts to your thoughts," Wyatt said, while urging her to get behind him. "Didn't they teach you this stuff back in the academy, second class?" he said, and she resisted the urge to punch him in the back of his neck. He had risked his life, pulling her down from that fatal jump, so she took it on the chin and saved her anger for the Geralos.

When Helga finally could see what it was that they were fighting, she was quite surprised that it wasn't a zip-ship. If the Britz was a beetle, this vessel was a mosquito, with a pair of rotors for wings. It flew out from above the Britz, maneuvering to get around the shield, but Wyatt was brave and stood his ground.

Some of Cage's shots finally clipped one of the shooters, who hung from the side of the thopter shooting down at them. The creature fell from the craft and was impaled on one of the rocks. This caused the pilot to panic, and attempt to fly them out of the chasm.

Varnes took advantage of their hasty retreat and began firing at the exposed men. Helga lifted her auto rifle and sprayed the sides thoroughly, hoping to hit one of the Geralos hanging out on the edge.

Suddenly a thin line of light flashed through the cockpit of the thopter. Helga recognized it as an impact laser, fired from the upper portion of the rocks. She knew that it was friendly, but wondered at its source. The thought of a sniper—possibly from the colony—hiding out near the chasm crossed her mind. Those settlements had all sorts of people, some with military histories, and all kinds of skills.

The thopter began to spin out of control and she knew that the pilot had been hit. The Geralos onboard tried to jump for safety but one got caught inside the rotors and was brutally cut to shreds. Another lost his footing and swung around with the vessel as it hit one of the rocky walls and then crashed into the ground.

"That's what I'm talking about. Hell of a shot, thin man," Wyatt shouted. Then Helga saw Lamia Brafa descending from the rocks. In his right hand was a laser rifle, which she didn't recall seeing him have before. He took his time, the essence of confidence, using his boosters to slowly glide down to the floor.

"They had no shield around that thopter," he said, as he walked over to where they stood. "It was easy enough to just pick off the pilot. They're not used to humans fighting back."

"I heard about you Jumpers when I was back on Virulia," Varnes said. "But, brother, what I just saw you do blows all those stories to bits."

"Lamia's our secret weapon," Cage Hem said, and Helga could tell he was smiling when he said it. He led them over to the wreckage to make sure that the Geralos were dead. Helga felt queasy when she saw one up close, this being her first time seeing one in the flesh. She couldn't understand why the humans called them "lizards" but assumed that it was due to their rough, scaly skin.

From what she saw lying broken in front of her, the Geralos were very much a humanoid race. Their faces were flat, and they had holes instead of noses, but they did not look like "lizards" at all. She knelt next to one and pushed back his lids. The eyes were recessed, giving him a menacing appearance. Next she studied the mouth, which hung open. The sight of the teeth sent shivers all along her spine.

"Nasty *cruta*, isn't he?" Varnes said as he walked over. He shoved the body violently with his boot. "I think this one here is the leader of their party." He began searching the body as if he knew it held something he wanted.

"How we looking on the repairs, Sol?" Cage said through the comms. "There's bound to be more coming back, and I don't want to be down here when they show up."

"It's not looking good, Master Chief," he said. "The engine was hit several times and it's fried beyond repair. The system works, so it could provide us some shelter, but the Britz will never fly again, sir."

Cage growled with frustration, and marched off in the direction of Cilas. "I'm going to check on the lieutenant. You all can finish up down here," he said. "We're not taking hostages. If lizzy moves, lizzy dies, you hear me? Stack their bodies inside of that...thing, and then move before we find ourselves freshly *thyped*."

When he gave them this directive, Varnes quickened his search of the leader. "Expecting to find something on him, Varnes?" Helga said, genuinely curious as to what he was doing.

"Geralos leaders carry those awesome swords," he said. "Hey, Brafa, can you show Ate your sword? I don't think she's seen an actual las-sword before."

As Lamia floated over, he reached behind his back and withdrew a long black sword. "This is a spectacular weapon that was created by the ugliest of people," he said. "The Geralos are the only ones with this technology, so we take it from them when we can."

When he got close enough for her to see the details of the sword, she saw how it glimmered in the starlight. It was about 90 cm, and was built from a metal that Helga didn't recognize. There were grooves and runes from an alien language running all along its length.

Lamia did some fancy tricks and the edge of the blade came alive. White fire ran along the sharpened edge, and Helga backed away from it slowly. There was something unnatural about this weapon. It made her even more petrified of the Geralos that they'd fought.

She imagined that the cost of one of these weapons was enough to secure a fighter, or a luxury apartment on the *Rendron*. Fight enough Geralos and she could collect two or three. That could get her a home on Casan and an early retirement from the military.

"I need to get my hands on one of those," she said out loud, and Lamia cooled the blade and then handed it to her, hilt first. She studied it carefully then touched the button near the hilt. That was when she heard a hum and saw the edge grow white.

"That hot edge can cut through anything. Our PAS, stone, even the hull of the *Rendron*," Lamia said. "I've used it on over 35 missions, and it still hasn't let me down. By the time we make it out of here you may end up with one, Ate. It just depends on the Geralos that we're fighting."

Helga tried her hand at wielding it, swinging it wildly around her body in arcs. "I think a lesson may be in order, before you take off your own leg." Lamia laughed.

"Hurry your schtill!" Cage shouted through the comms, and Helga powered down the las-sword and handed it back to him.

"I think I'll stick to fighting in the air," she said, not knowing whether to be impressed or horrified by the weapon. She had learned so much in school about the Geralos, but out here she realized that she didn't know much at all.

Now that they had a break, she tested the movement of the PAS as they worked their way over to Cage. She found that the boosters worked with gestures and motion. Move quickly in any direction and it assisted your velocity.

Crouching while you clenched your fists would activate the boosters, causing them to overheat in preparation for a high jump. Launching from that crouch would literally make you fly. Walk with your arms slightly behind, and the rockets would pulse, allowing you to float.

They found Cage near the lieutenant, who was propped up against a rock. His face looked pale beneath his mask, but he was breathing and conscious.

"Get what you can from the Britz. We're going to have to relocate," Cage said, and then hoisted Cilas up onto his shoulders. Brise Sol jumped down from the Britz's hatch with a large sack tied to his back.

"Good flying, Ate, but she couldn't be saved. Not unless we can salvage some parts from the settlement," he said. "Hopefully they haven't stripped their dropship, but I wouldn't hold my breath. If they still have it there, we can borrow it to go home."

"Here's hoping," Helga said and fell in next to Cage. None of them spoke as they marched along.

Helga found that she was still haunted by the image of the Geralos. Despite the numerous images, videos, and simulations in her training, it still hadn't prepared her for what she had seen. She looked forward to addressing this when she returned to the *Rendron*. Updating the codex for all of their future cadets.

The HUD of her helmet reflected the time, and she realized that they had been walking for well over an hour. Surprisingly the gauge on her PAS read full on her display although she had been using her rockets to drift along. The more she used the armor the more impressed she was with it. She wished that she could wear it all the time.

Cage pulled them up short and Helga floated up to see. There was a hole in the rock wall next to him, big enough for them to walk through. "This looks promising," he said. "A cave where the lizards won't be able to track us. We can set up camp here, and see to the Lt. Then get back to the mission afterwards."

"We should put detectors here, and traps over there," Wyatt said. "Then one of us can cover the entrance in case the lizards come back. I'll take first watch if that's alright with you, Master Chief."

"Yeah, you got it, Wyatt," Cage said, as he placed Cilas down by the wall.

There was a slight vibration in the ground below their feet, and Helga had to double check to make sure that it wasn't her boots. Lamia Brafa stretched out his arms and moved them away from the hole. "Get away from the cave," he shouted, and the company complied, except for Cage who wouldn't leave Cilas's side.

Suddenly a large shape burst from the hole, revealing a maw so large and horrible that Helga jumped back several meters. As she drifted up and away, she saw what it was, the monstrous head of something large and serpentine. Its mouth was lined with several layers of chipped up teeth, and its forked tongue probed the atmosphere trying to find its prey.

Cage deployed his stargun, firing as he stood his ground, close enough for the creature to devour him. But it seemed to know pain, so it thrashed about, tried to consume Cilas, but then retreated instantly.

"What in the worlds was that?" said Wyatt.

"That was a dredge," said Lamia. "Now we're going to have to kill it or it will hunt us down forever."

"Whoa...whoa...whoa, we're not killing anything. It went back into its hole, after Master Chief lit it up," Wyatt said. "I would take that as a sign that we need to keep it moving."

Lamia shook his head at him. "Dredges have long memories. Either we kill it now or we will be ambushed later, at which time we lose the advantage."

"Get your rear end in line," Cage said suddenly, as he peeked inside the cave. He reached down and unclipped a flare from his belt, then tossed it into the darkness.

Lamia Brafa walked past the big man to take point and led them into the cave. Helga swallowed against her fear and fell in behind Brise Sol.

A private comms came in to her then. She wasn't surprised that it was Varnes. "How you holding up, rookie?" he said. She hated that he kept calling her that.

"Well," Helga said, "so far, I've managed to not wet my pants."

Lamia stopped and raised his right fist. "Mute the chatter," he said. "You all need to be ready for anything. This path splits, but I saw it move to the right. But we can't know if it has a way to circle back to the left. Dredges are large, but they can twist their bodies in any direction. I suggest we leave the lieutenant here with someone while the rest of us split up to investigate."

Cage Hem touched Wyatt's shoulder and he pointed to Brise Sol, but the Master Chief shook his head and beckoned Helga over. "Sol, stay with the Lt and watch the entrance there for lizards," he said. He then walked over to the young ESO and handed him his stargun.

5

"So listen up," said Lamia, "the Dredge is only about 24 meters long—"

"That's it?" said Wyatt.

"Clear the channel, Wyatt, this ain't the time or place, copy?" Cage said.

Lamia let them finish. "There is a chance that there are a number of them. We're seeing blood stains from the wounds it took, but it seems to be moving at a rapid pace. This means that there's bound to be more inside of here, possibly a nest that we will need to destroy."

The comms grew silent and Helga knew that they were all thinking the same thing. Why would they be pursuing this dangerous behemoth into its lair to fight more like it?

"It's either we do this now, or risk the surface where the lizards have us outnumbered and outgunned," Cage said, as if he could hear her thinking and wanted to explain.

"Aim for the mouths; it's their weak spot. They have a metal-like exoskeleton, tougher than a ship's hull. There's no point in overheating your weapons trying to penetrate it," Lamia said. "They are highly intelligent creatures, so please don't make the mistake of underestimating them."

Helga's mind went back to Lamia's las-sword. *I bet it could cut one of those things in half,* she thought. Were there las-guns and las-bullets that the Geralos had in their arsenal? She thought about the futility of going up against ordinance like that, and she hoped that the tech was restricted to melee weapons.

After they started to move the cave opened up, spreading out to give each of them a clear line of fire. Cage was in the center leading them through, while Wyatt hugged the right wall close to him. Helga hung back with her auto rifle raised and her rockets pulsing steadily. She liked this mode of travel since she exerted no energy doing it, but when she saw that she was the only one floating, she quickly turned it off.

The HUD of her helmet mapped the cave, utilizing the synced data from each of their vantage points. The fork had divided them, but it converged further ahead where she saw the two green blips of Varnes and Lamia Brafa.

"We got contact!" said Varnes, and she could hear auto rifles over the comms. The Master Chief picked up the pace, charging forward, and they followed him, pushing through.

As they ran to keep up with Cage Hem, Helga chanced a glance behind her. She saw a hole in the ceiling that they had somehow missed and her heart jumped out of her chest and into her throat. Silver ridges and monstrous coils dropped down to their level, then teeth reflected her PAS's light and it came for her. She took a step back and squeezed the trigger, pulsing her shots to keep her weapon from overheating.

"Contact on our six, Master Chief," she shouted, but no one seemed to hear her.

Kinetic rounds ricocheted off the monstrosity as it twisted towards her through the tunnel. She felt a presence on her side, and Wyatt ran up, adding his gunfire. He was using one hand to shoot while using the other to urge her away from it. Together they drifted backwards using their rockets while the dredge kept coming with its mouth closed.

"Damn it," whispered Wyatt. He pushed her back. "Get ready to shoot when it opens its mouth."

Helga didn't understand, but kept on retreating. Then she saw Wyatt raise his hands. "Shields!" he shouted, and the translucent disc formed on his forearm. He stood his ground and thrust it forward as the dredge wrapped its coils around his legs. Helga's knees felt weak as she saw it raise up and open its mouth to devour him.

"Ah!" she screamed as she squeezed the trigger, allowing for a fully automatic stream. Most of it caught the outer skin, bouncing off harmlessly, but a few managed to find its mouth. The dredge seemed to ignore the pain and bit down on Wyatt's head.

Helga saw that she'd failed but she kept on firing, but then the creature stopped and slumped to the ground. Wyatt emerged with his auto rifle smoking and his PAS dripping with the dredge's slime. She ran over to check on him to see what happened, but he didn't seem to have any injuries.

"Woo!" he screamed over the comms. "Looks like their teeth can't penetrate our armor. Lucky for me since Ate can't aim for *schtill*, but now we know," he said, laughing.

Helga felt worse than she had ever felt in a long time, but he patted her on the shoulder as he walked by. Not only was it embarrassing that she'd let him down, but she knew that he'd never let her live it down.

When they caught up with Cage he was standing next to Lamia and Varnes. Before them were several dead dredges, piled up into a heap. "Where were you two?" the Master Chief said without turning to look at them. Wyatt proceeded to tell him how they'd been flanked by one of the dredges.

"Nasty creatures," was all he said, then turned to glance back at the tunnels they had come through.

"We should place motion detectors here, as well as under that hole where yours came from," said Lamia. "You never know with these creatures, though I believe that they're all dead."

"Can they eat through the rock?" said Helga.

"Yes, but it takes them a long time to make tunnels like this. Their digestive systems are capable of breaking down anything, but with the rocks it takes days, which is why they do it as a group," Lamia said.

"So why don't we just collapse the tunnels?" said Helga. "Then we can camp here without worrying about any secret holes."

"I like her idea. Put a wall between us and them," said Wyatt.

Cage Hem regarded her. "Good thinking, Ate. Now, let's blow this *schtill* hole and get back to the lieutenant."

Seismic charges planted at the entrance to the forked tunnel collapsed it in a matter of seconds. Lamia Brafa installed sensors in the deeper regions of the cave so any movement would be tracked.

Helga didn't trust camping inside the tunnels. It was reassuring that their armor could withstand the bite, but the sight of those numerous teeth would give her nightmares, forever, even after a long career of similar fights.

She sat next to Cilas who was finally conscious, and the two of them looked on as the men set up camp. First they used rocks to conceal the entrance, but left enough space for one person to squeeze through.

They decided to take turns on watch outside of the tunnels, since the cave walls rendered the radar useless. Normally this wouldn't be necessary with a flobot surveillance android, but they had traveled light and were short on equipment.

"If we're stuck here for long then I'm going to be ripe," Helga said to no one in particular, and got a few chuckles from the rest of the men.

A private call came through, and it was Cilas. He was reclined with his hands covering the hole in his armor. "We're hiding in a cave built by aggressive giant worms and you're concerned with how bad you smell," he said.

"No, Lieutenant. I mean, yeah, it's not the greatest of my concerns. But it has crossed my mind that I will be stuck inside this suit," she said.

"Come on, Helga," he said, annoyed. "Are you seriously sitting here, worried about a shower? How about staying sharp and watching the entrance so that we can do what we came here to do?" he said.

"I will, Lt, I'm just thinking out loud. I tend to run my mouth, but you know that," she said.

He placed his hand on top of hers and she looked down at him. "Do you know how many cadets qualify for a tier as high as second class?" he said.

"I don't know, about twenty percent?" she said.

"Five percent, Helga. You're a five-percenter. Not many ESOs have this distinction. We stand apart from anyone else. Look, I get it, you're a young woman, stuck in the company of hardened men. It's intimidating as hell, and again you're a rookie, so you want to say and do things to make it okay. The thing is, this isn't a simulation.

"This is the real thing, life or death. All we have out here is each other. And the little jokes you tell? It makes them respect you less. You're a five-percenter, just like me, and the fraternity of officers on the *Rendron*. Now I want you to say it so I can hear it, Ate," he said.

"I'm a five-percenter," she said, feeling embarrassed.

The last person she wanted to get a lecture from was Cilas, who she saw as a big brother of the academy. It was so different out here on the field. Everything was brand new and kept her on edge. Had it been a simulation where she had the shot on that dredge, she would have killed it easily and Wyatt would respect her.

She began to wonder if they saw her as a goof, and a liability like Wyatt said. She had been so focused on proving him wrong that she had managed to forget herself.

Where was the Helga who'd made second-class in her unit? The tough half-breed Casanian who defied all the odds? She had graduated with honors from officer school, and was given the rank of Ensign, not to mention she was invited to be a part of the elite Nighthawks.

"I'll tighten up and get it together, Lieutenant. You can rely on me to make you proud," she said. "Can't promise that I won't say anything else that's inappropriate, though. It's kind of a tic, if you know what I mean."

Cilas laughed, and it helped. She felt a tremendous weight lift up off her chest. For a few minutes there, she had been convinced that she had managed to let him down.

Brise pulled out several rods from the pack he was carrying, then connected them in such a way that they formed a cross about two meters wide. Helga watched as he walked to the middle of the cavern and placed it on top of a square base, where it levitated till it touched the ceiling. Beams of light arced down to the floor, forming an illuminated dome.

"It's good," he said, and Varnes gave him a nod, then lifted the lieutenant up and placed him inside. They removed all his armor, carefully, and then Varnes knelt next to him, working on his wounds with an artisan's care. "It's safe to take off your lid, Ate," he said. "This is a Vestalian atmosphere generator, you can breathe the oxygen in here. Stay within the light and you will be alright. The air's good, it's just a tad bit rank."

They huddled around him as he worked on their leader and Helga reached up and removed her helmet. She felt brave for doing it. The moon wasn't meant for human beings, but she was happy for the chance to see with her own eyes. The armor she didn't mind; it kept her warm and right, plus it allowed her to float around and conserve her energy.

"Sol get over here, I need you," Varnes said suddenly. "Pull off your layers and spray your hands." Brise did as he asked and walked over to the makeshift operating table, removing both his PAS and 3B

XO-suit. "He should be out cold, but I'm not taking any chances. Hold him steady while I clean his wounds."

They worked for an hour as the rest looked on in silence. They had already lost Cruser, which was still fresh in Helga's mind. The thought of losing Cilas was a bit too much to bear. She recalled her days as a cadet when he first visited them during one of the assemblies. He had worn his armor, all decked out in medals, and they'd watched in awe as he addressed them.

Being both an orphan and part Casanian had made for a tough childhood on the *Rendron*. Being one of the star cadets made it even worse for Helga, but she had pushed through with silent perseverance. Lieutenant Cilas Mec had called her name that day and praised her accomplishments in front of everyone. She had been so happy that she'd almost floated, and from that day on he had been a hero to her.

The Geralos bullet had struck his abdomen, boring its way through the armor, but according to Varnes—who spoke as he worked—it didn't do much damage to his internal organs.

Helga felt guilty for Cruser's death. It was a numbing, debilitating feeling. She couldn't understand why he was gone and she was still here, alive.

The shooting of their two most important members was hard to accept as a coincidence. She wondered if they had been compromised—there had been rumors that the Geralos could take over minds—but how, and who could it be? Every one of them had fought like demons when Cage led them out from the Britz.

"He'll need to stay here for a Vestalian day before he's ready to move again," Varnes said. Cilas was sedated and propped up on several rolls, but his face looked peaceful despite the bandages around his abdomen.

"Where did you learn to fly like that, Ate?" It was Lamia Brafa asking the question.

Helga started to give a sarcastic answer but remembered what Cilas said. "As a cadet, for as far back as I can remember," she said, "I spent most of my free time running simulated combat. When I made second class, there was a huge demand for pilots and because of my reputation I was allowed to—is there something on my face?"

Lamia had chuckled and looked down at his sword, and she thought that he was making fun.

"Don't mind me, I was just laughing at your enthusiasm. You stepped up when we needed you, and that's a testament to your instincts. Training only gives you the know-how, Ate. What you do when it's inconvenient, that's what sets you apart. You didn't cry for Cruser and you didn't freeze up. You grabbed the flight stick and you saved our lives."

"Adan was my friend. He taught me a lot," she said, fighting back tears. "I'm not as good as he was, but I want to be. I was hoping to learn more from him when we completed this mission. Now I just want to get back to the *Rendron* so that we can send him off with a hero's honor."

"Focus on the now," Cage Hem said, standing up. "Start to think too far ahead and you'll miss the lizard right in front of you. At any minute those lizards could come back and we need to be ready to go."

6

On *Rendron*, none of the spacers ever talked about the fighting and Helga never understood why. Sure there was the occasional big mouth who would brag about killing lizards, but most of the time it was only hot air – said badass hadn't even seen a firefight.

The Geralos was the stuff of legends, something you knew existed but the men and women who survived encounters never talked about it. Helga thought about the fights she had been in since landing on the moon, and wondered if she'd be willing to talk about it when she returned.

Of course she would. She'd survived a giant worm, not to mention seeing one of the lizards up close. She had traded shots with them, and survived. What cadet wouldn't want to hear about that?

But as she stood in the circle of men listening to their stories, she couldn't help but notice that they avoided the subject. Varnes talked about his family, and Wyatt his multiple girlfriends. Cage—when he was chiming in—spoke of an exotic beer brewed on Traxis.

All of it was interesting to her, but she was itching to talk about their encounters. "Have you all ever been in a situation like this?" she finally said, the words spilling out before she could check them.

"What do you mean, Ate?" Varnes said, and she froze when they all turned to look at her.

"The crash, and all of this craziness," she said. "You all have been through everything, it seems, so I want to know how bad this is."

"It's thyped up," Wyatt offered, and they all grunted in approval. "It's like this time back on Meluvia, when I was with that girl I told you about." He started grinning and nodding like an idiot. "You ever had a Meluvian, Sol? Oh brother, you haven't lived—"

Helga tried her best to tune the rest of it out, not missing the fact that he had changed the subject. They were all so relaxed; helmets off, some even had their weapons on the ground. Lamia Brafa stood apart.

This was not surprising, but when she found his face she realized that he was still looking at her.

She knew the look, or thought she knew. It was the look of curiosity—one she was familiar with. It was the look that people would always give when trying to figure out her racial background.

"I'm Casanian and human," she mouthed at him, smiling to herself when he looked away. But then he looked at her again and nodded slowly. *Of course he can read my lips*, she thought. *The man can scale cliffs and make himself disappear.*

"For Ahmad," said Cage, and they all grew quiet. He made a sign in the air, and they all did the same. Helga imitated it, not knowing what it meant, and the Master Chief caught her attempt and repeated it slowly so that she could see. "It's a Vestalian ritual, Ate. We honor our fallen. Everyone has their methods, but this is ours," he said.

The rest of the men grunted their approval, and Helga repeated the movements exactly the way that Cage showed it. She held her right hand above her head, tucked in her thumb, then brought it down in a vertical chop. Stopping when her arm was straight in front of her, she turned her palm down.

"Perfect," said Varnes. "I think that Ahmad would approve."

"Master Chief," Helga started, regretting her words before she spoke them. She felt closer to the group now than she'd felt since joining and her mouth took on a life of its own. *Shut up, stupid girl,* she thought, but the words were already out.

"Yes, Ate," he said, sounding like a parent whose patience was wearing thin.

"How long have you been fighting the Geralos?"

Cage looked over at her, as if trying to read her face, and the rest of the men grew quiet. "I would say a little over twenty years, Ate. I've been fighting them all my life, even before I joined the military."

"I don't understand," she whispered, and finally found the strength to shut her mouth.

"Speak your mind, Ate. Get it out of your system," Wyatt said. "You've been obsessing over the lizards since we landed on this rock. All of us have been up close and personal with the lizards, so what do you want to know? Schtill, just spit the question out."

"Okay," she said, "here it is. Do you think we will ever win Vestalia back?"

Cage flashed her a glance that made her flinch, then caught himself and took his gaze across the rest of the men. When he finally spoke, he did so mechanically. It was almost as if he'd rehearsed this speech to give it to anyone that asked.

"The Alliance has been fighting lizards for over 100 years, Ate. Much of that fighting has been in open space, on allied planets ... on our own ships." This last bit made him pause, and he reached down and picked up some of the loose rocks. "I can't even tell you what Vestalia looks like from the ground, and there are very few people in this galaxy who can. That being said, we cannot give up on fighting for what is ours. In the old wars of Vestalia that our ancestors were in, they fought each other over territories, countries ... their homes.

"Now we are out here in the great void of space, fighting for our stolen planet. It's hard to see a happy ending, especially stuck in here, hiding. But you need to focus on the now, Ate, or you'll drive yourself crazy. Even if we manage to run the lizards away from our world, there will still be wars to fight. This reality of ours is war after war, and with Vestalia won you better believe that there will be more."

"Hold," said Casein Varnes suddenly. "We've got movement outside." He was staring down at the computer on his wrist and poking at the interface with his other hand. "Lids on, we got incoming," he said before pulling on his mask.

Helga jumped up and smoothed back her hair. *Here we go*, she thought. After emerging from cryo it had grown significantly, and she had to pin it back before donning her helmet. Once it was on and sealed securely, she reached down and picked up her auto rifle.

If the lizards were coming she wanted to be effective, not fumbling around like a rookie. Wyatt—who had been her biggest critic—had given her a shot with the dredge. That had been her chance to prove to him that she wasn't a "liability," but she'd missed the shot and a chance at proving him wrong.

Casein Varnes touched the base of the generator, and the lights of the dome went out. He collected the parts, placed them into his pack and then hoisted it onto his back. Cage was at the entrance of the cave talking to a hunched over Lamia. She saw him give a quick salute and then slip out through the cracks.

Cilas was up, looking around, and Sol was helping him into his armor. "Stay off comms," Cage said. "Use hand signals only. They can pick up our chatter and track our location. Brafa's on recon. He's going to give us a signal. When it happens, get ready to fight."

They stood in the darkness, silently waiting, but Helga could hear her heart pounding in her ears. She wanted to be ready, but her throat was dry, and all she could think about was her brother, Rolph. They hadn't spoken in ages but they were twins, and deep down she knew that he was okay.

What would Rolph feel if I was to die here in this cave, on a moon orbiting a planet light years away from the Rendron? she thought. *Would he feel anything? Would he even know?*

Motes of light floated through the entrance, surfing on a beam of starlight. Without the Geralos threat she would have considered this peaceful, the only sound being Cage, breathing hard on their comms.

There was a disruption in the light and a silhouette appeared, large and looming. Someone had walked up and was looking inside. Another shadow merged with it, and the first shadow shuddered, then black blood spattered across the rocks.

Lamia Brafa pulled the hot blade out of the Geralos's back and motioned for them to come outside. Cage led the charge, then Wyatt, and Varnes. Helga fell in after Brise, carrying the lieutenant. In a single line they poured out of the cave, staying off comms as instructed by Cage Hem.

In the front Lamia was gesturing wildly to Cage, who glanced back at the party and pointed up. Suddenly he jumped, his rockets guiding him up and out of the ravine. Lamia followed closely, then Wyatt and Varnes.

Brise, still clutching the lieutenant, squatted down hard and then jumped, pulling Cilas up into the air with him. Helga followed suit, squatting then jumping up, trusting her rockets to activate. They did not disappoint.

When they were out on the moon's face, they started running towards some rocks. Lamia Brafa led them with Cage Hem in tow. Helga used her rockets to pulse quickly after them, scanning the black horizon for movement. As they neared the rocks Lamia forced them to the left, and it wasn't long before Helga saw why. A thopter was behind them, firing off a cannon strong enough to make small craters in the surface.

"Find some cover!" Cage shouted, as they dove for the safety of a hill. Helga pulled out her auto rifle and fired on the thopter. It responded with a shot that exploded in front of them, throwing her back into a small depression.

Cage Hem was on a slope of rocks, wedged up behind a natural barrier. He locked in his stargun as Wyatt threw up a shield.

"Rifles on the lizard, I've marked your radars on their locale," Lamia said, but Helga couldn't hear him over the ringing in her ears. She was covered in rubble, and she felt dazed and confused. She could see the pilot and he was all that mattered. She needed to shoot him to bring down the ship.

"Wyatt, keep your head, idiot, do you not see that they have a heavy cannon on that thopter?" Cage shouted through comms. "Ate, get your rear over here! What part of stick next to me are you *thyping* misunderstanding?"

Helga barely heard him as she began again to fire up at the thopter. "On my way," she managed, as she slipped down behind a rock and checked her weapon's heat-gauge. "Thype me, it's on orange," she mumbled, then scampered over to where Cage was positioned.

"You had one directive, *thyping* follow it," Cage barked as he gripped her by her rucksack and shifted her to his right. Too confused to feel humiliated, Helga got back on her gun, but Cage grabbed her arm and pointed in front of them. "Stargun on the thopter. Rifles on the lizards," he said. "What are you doing? Get your head out of your rear. Keep the thyping lizards off us!"

He went back on his stargun and the thopter began to buckle, evidence that he had finally managed to rattle the pilot. Helga poked her head around one of the rocks to see where the foot soldiers were located. A bullet smashed into her helmet, sending her sprawling backwards.

"Ate," she heard Cage scream, and she quickly signaled that she was good. But Varnes was next to her, pulling her up to another set of rocks on her left. Helga tried to ignore the red text running all across her HUD. She couldn't shake the fact that she had been shot, and Varnes had somehow saved her life.

Lying on the rocks staring up at the stars, she finally focused on her readouts. Everyone's status was in the green, except for Cilas's which was on yellow. Hers on the other hand was bright red, as the computer tried desperately to repair her shields.

"You don't move from there until you see yellow, Ate," Cage said, but Helga was over feeling worthless.

She rolled to her stomach, then crawled forward and peered through the cracks at the Geralos thopter. It had strong shields and was sealed on all sides, unlike the one they had destroyed near the

Britz. Its only attack came from a mounted cannon that sat below the front rotor.

This will go on forever, she thought, realizing that their weapons would overheat before the thopter's shields would go out. With attacks on all sides, from both foot soldiers and the thopter, it was only a matter of time before they were overrun.

Does Cage realize that this is futile? she wondered, but knew better than to ask. *We're thyped*, she thought and glanced over at Cilas. He was wedged between two rocks, with his arms by his side as if he was merely reclining.

She could hear his voice reminding her that she was a "five-percenter," and it gave her strength amidst the chaos. Her shield gauge was orange, and fading towards yellow, but she saw that Wyatt's gauge had suddenly gone red.

"*Schtill*, where is that coming from?" Cage shouted into the comms. "Wyatt, don't be a hero. Get down so your shields can recharge."

Wyatt did as he was instructed and Cage slid behind the rocks, sitting so that the heavy gunfire would have no chance of hitting him. "Anytime now Brafa," he growled with desperation, and Helga glanced back to where Brise and Varnes were.

A white line appeared, thin and mysterious, slicing through one Geralos and then another. Suddenly their firing slowed, as they struggled to figure out what was killing them.

"Now," Cage screamed, and Helga hopped up to her feet, slammed the auto rifle on top of a nearby rock, and fired on a Geralos that was trying to run. Two shots found his back and he toppled over, motionless. It was a surreal moment, and she couldn't believe what she had done. "T-target down," she whispered, confirming her first Geralos kill.

Cage was back on the stargun, lighting up the thopter—who had made the mistake of trying to aim at Lamia. The spy was cloaked, invisible to the naked eye, but the angry pilot kept on firing on the area where he'd first appeared.

"*Thyping* Lamia Brafa," Varnes said, laughing. "I bet the last thing the lizards expected was a, Jumper."

"They never do," Brise Sol offered up cheerfully. "Now let's drop this bird before it escapes."

"Clear the comms. What did I tell you?" Cage said, his massive gun spitting out row upon row of bullets into the shields.

The rest of the company joined in with his stargun as the thopter tried in vain to escape. But the shields gave out and their bullets struck glass. The vessel tipped and careened off to the right.

"Stop!" Helga shouted. "The pilot is dead. That thing may be our only chance to get to the settlement." The thopter drifted down, crushing its landing gear, but from what she could see, it was still whole.

"All contacts are nullified," she heard Lamia Brafa say before uncloaking within their midst.

He led them over to the thopter, where they pulled out the dead pilot, so that Brise could examine the state of the vessel. Helga, who should have been with him, found herself walking towards the Geralos she'd shot.

"Ate, what the thype do you think you're doing?" Cage said.

"Sorry, Master Chief, it was my first kill," she said. "I just wanted to make sure he was dead."

7

"So, do you think you can fly it?" Brise said as Helga walked up to the front of the thopter's cockpit to look at the controls.

"I don't know," she said as she glanced over the panel that was splattered with a combination of Geralos brains, glass fragments, and a thin layer of black dust. "We'd have to repair this glass before anything else. Is that even possible? Wait ... we may be alright if we fly slow and stay low enough so we can bail if we get attacked. I know the shields are fried so we won't be able to fight from it."

She glanced down at the dead pilot, who was still strapped in. She unclipped his belt and pushed him to the floor. Brise had done what he could with looking under the hood, but decided that it was too alien and had promptly given up.

Helga, feeling obligated—since it was she who had suggested they use it to fly—looked over the panel to see if she would be able to figure it out.

The thopter's controls were minimal, but this too proved to be intimidating. Unlike the Britz, which had a button for everything, the console had a round screen with strange glyphs on its face. Each of these symbols danced around, taking on different shapes and sizes.

"What does that do?" Brise said, as he sat down in the co-pilot's seat. He reached out with one of his hands and put a finger on the glass.

"Don't touch that," Helga shouted at him. "You're going to blow us up. Can I get a few minutes to figure this all out? I'd be more comfortable if you weren't in here with me."

"You sure?" he said.

"Very," she replied. "Plus you're next up to deck if I explode or something."

"That isn't funny. Master Chief would flip his top. All of that work he did to keep you alive, just for you to explode with this thing."

"The irony would probably cause him to laugh," Helga said.

"Cage Hem laughing? I'd pay real credits to see that happen," Brise said. "Alright, I'll leave, but don't do anything stupid. If we need to be on foot again, I don't think any of us would mind. Just be careful, Ate. I'm being serious. You can't die. We've lost enough already on this mission, and I don't see us getting back home without you."

Helga appreciated him saying this, but it did nothing to help her confidence. Her flying them away would give them an opportunity to build a camp and properly attend to the lieutenant. They needed time for Cilas to heal, and to make a call to the *Rendron* to report their situation.

The communication itself would be a complex science, and the equipment they needed was back on the Britz. This meant that they would have to make a call to Louine, and beg them to transmit the news to *Rendron*. They wouldn't be able to do this while they marched on foot, with one of them carrying Cilas.

Helga and Cage Hem were of the same mind on this, which was why he'd allowed her to try the thopter. A long trek across the moon wouldn't get them to the settlement. It would just leave them open to more Geralos attacks.

The thopter had to fly, this was what she told herself. So she tried to think of a way to make the controls work. In her training she had been made to fly a myriad of different spacecraft. Her choices had ranged from Vestalian strike ships to the slow Meluvian frigates with no hardpoints.

Each one of these vessels was unique in its own way, and with ships from Meluvia, Louine, and Genese, there was a language barrier that she'd had to overcome. Only once had she been made to try a Geralos ship, and it was in a simulation, with a situation just like this.

Helga had failed the exercise at first, relying on her instincts with flying alliance ships. It taught her that the Geralos were in fact quite unique' their ships relied on the AI to be synched with the pilot.

Remembering this now, she removed her gauntlet, and placed her palm on the glass. She closed her eyes and cleared her mind, letting the computer synch with her thoughts. When it accepted her as the pilot, she could feel it in her head. The sensation was alien, and frightening. It was as if another person was sharing her brain, but now she knew the thopter as if she were part of it.

The glass lit up and she opened her eyes, removed her hand, and grabbed the controls. It would only fly for her now, and she had total control. She put aside her doubts and brought it up to hover.

The rotors came alive, and the thopter began to shake. Then it grew steady and rose up from the surface. Helga liked how responsive it was to her every move. She tilted it forward and flew past the men, circled around the perimeter, and then brought it down in front of them.

When she opened her comms she could hear them cheering, and the weight on her shoulders fell off. She had frozen during their first skirmish and missed her shot on the worm, but here in the cockpit, they could rely on her to do well.

She placed the thopter near the ground, remembering that she had no landing gear, then opened the doors to let them in. Lamia Brafa was first, jumping in with little effort. He grabbed the overhang with his left hand and pulled aboard the bulk of their heavy equipment. Next came Cilas, who he strapped in next to Helga, while the rest of the team quickly boarded.

"Stargun is mounted. You can fly us out, Ate," Cage said. "Find us a good location, preferably one without worms."

"Aye aye, sir," she said, and took them up a little ways before tilting the stick forward and exhaling with relief.

Cilas touched her arm to get her attention. She was surprised that he was conscious, so she looked over to check on him. "This is stupid," he said. "What have you done? They will locate this vessel and shoot us down."

"How will they know that we're different from their own?" she said. "Plus, we have the same radar they use. Besides, if they come for us I have a plan. You all will abandon the thopter, using your PAS, and I'll lead them off while you make your escape. Since we can track one another, you can come for me later on, once I've rigged this thing to fly auto, while I jump and—"

"Planets, Ate, shut up," Cilas said. He slumped down into his seat and threw up his hands. "You don't know anything about our enemy. How they can literally smell you, and track your armor. Do you think that their finding us in the cave was just a mere coincidence? Cage knew they would come, but he wanted me to be safe. Have you not been paying attention? The only way to stop the Geralos is to kill them, dead. That is why we're here. It is what we have to do."

Helga stared forward, stunned, not knowing what to think. Everything she'd tried to do had turned out to be wrong. "What's your order, sir?" she said, frustrated to the point of giving up. If she couldn't get this right, this area of her expertise, then she'd just reserve herself to being a brainless puppet.

"We're already in this thing, so let's take advantage of it," he said. "Turn around and take us here." He brought up his wrist comms and gestured across it. A detailed map of Dyn's surface appeared on her helmet's HUD. There was a red circle around an area on the map, north of the rocks where she'd flown them from.

"That's the colony of Abarion and the mission we were sent to do," Cilas said. "Take us in, keep her low, and watch that radar closely. On contact we're not bailing like that boneheaded idea of yours. What we will do is engage the enemy, and you're going to fly the way I know you can fly. Am I making sense to you, Ate?"

"Yes, sir," she said and turned them around. She banked the thopter slightly, flying a wide, low arc back the way they had come. When she steadied it, Cilas stood up, touched his wound, and walked to the back. A few minutes later he was over the comms, thanking them all for saving his life.

Helga barely listened, still stinging from his words and doing as she was instructed. As he made what would probably be remembered as a great speech, her mind drifted to days when she was a cadet on the *Rendron*.

Back then, there was always someone asking her about her parents, and whether or not they were people of note. The spoiled offspring of rich Vestalian opportunists took great pride in making her feel unwanted. The older girls were the worst: they would say the nastiest things to her, especially when she wouldn't play along.

Most of them were human or Meluvian, so Helga's Casanian heritage was often brought up in mockery with some inference to her mother being a prostitute. The cadet academy felt like a prison sentence that she was made to endure. But there would be glory upon graduation; this was what the cadet commander, Loray Qu, would often tell her whenever she would go to her office to complain.

One day while eating noodles inside of her tiny compartment within the barracks, a buzzer alerted her to someone at the door. It was past curfew, but the cadet commander would often make unannounced visits to check if they had contraband or fellow cadets inside their compartments.

Helga still found the buzzer odd, since the commander had access to all of their compartments. She had picked up her pistol—which she had stolen to protect herself from her bullies—checked the charge, and slid it into the small of her back as she walked up to see who it was.

"It's a bit late, don't you think?" she had said, annoyed at the possibility of someone playing a prank at that late hour. Having been jumped a few times by angry groups of girls, Helga knew that she had to be ready for anything.

Cutting off the light inside her compartment, she'd touched the panel to unlock the door. But when it slid open, she'd seen that it was a man; tall, bald, and poised to attack. Helga's training kicked in and she'd pulled him inside, twisting her body in a way to throw him into the table.

As he scrambled to his feet with vicious intent, she had jumped back quickly and shot him in the chest. Blood had burst from the wound as he went down and all she could manage to do was just stand there shaking. It was the first time she'd shot anyone outside of a simulation, and all she could remember now was just how frightened she felt.

Helga couldn't recall if her fear was for the possible repercussions, or for what the man would have done if she hadn't been armed with that weapon.

When the cadet commander came in with an MA in tow, she had fully expected to be kicked out of the academy. But the commander protected her from expulsion, even though it was unforgivable for cadets to have a firearm inside their compartment.

She had loved Loray since, the way she imagined people loved a big sister. She remembered her words as clear as if they'd been uttered the day before.

"You are a first class cadet, Ate. I don't care if nobody else sees it. What you did here tonight shows that you have sand. And girl, that means no matter what life throws at you, you're going to be ready to shoot it in the chest."

Those words were her anchor when the bullies would come, and she remembered them whenever she had to make a hard decision. Taking this thopter had been a hard decision, just like speaking up to this company of seasoned warriors. It had stung to be scolded by the lieutenant, but when they needed her, she had managed to step up.

The memory was painful but it reminded her of who she was. She was a new recruit that had been given the privilege of becoming a member of the Nighthawks. Being insecure was natural when placed in a company like this, but hadn't she proven herself time and time again as a cadet? Did she not belong with the *Rendron's* elite team?

The memory helped and she was able to focus and catch the end of Cilas's speech. It was something about getting home and honoring Cruser's sacrifice, which brought hot tears to her eyes.

The thopter's glass had shattered when they killed the pilot and now the diminished shield was her only protection up front. A well-timed shot would kill her the same way Cruser had been killed, and Helga couldn't help but think about him.

"Anything yet?" Cilas said through comms as he walked up to retake his seat. He placed a reassuring hand on her shoulder, giving it a squeeze before sitting.

"Nothing yet, Lieutenant, just dunes and craters," she said.

"Good," he said. "Either they are looking for us in the wrong place, or they haven't realized that we're on our way back. These lizards have a way to communicate without the need for comms. There was one time when we thought that they were all part of a hive mind. Turns out that they have empaths, special soldiers who can read minds, communicate telepathically, and even take over other minds."

"I've heard of those," Helga said. "It's the scariest thing about them. How do they do it, do you know? Why don't they just take us all over and end the war?"

"From what we know it's too much of a sacrifice. The parasite is unable to return once he jumps inside a new host. Basically the lizard becomes you in every way, and while it does its actual body withers away. Not all of them are okay with this, as you can well imagine. Only the fanatics, but they have a lot, so every time we face them we face that risk."

"Thype," Helga whispered, thinking of what would happen if one of them got flipped.

"This is why we don't allow you to salute during war. As soon as a lizard knows who's in control, you run the chance of being compromised."

"Makes me regret being an officer," Helga said.

"Now you know why men like Varnes refuse to take command," he said. "They want to fight, but they fear the head games. Do you think that it doesn't haunt me every waking hour? I keep a low profile, and you will need to think about this as you climb the ranks. Never lead from the tallest horse, Ate. Stay on the ground, and keep it low key."

"They won't be able to get into my mind if they're too busy watching their six, Lt. I don't plan to be on the ground much. I want to be in a cockpit lighting them up," Helga said.

"Never heard of any pilots being made into puppets, so I can see your point," he said. "But it can happen to anyone, at any time. Let's hope that we're spared that nightmare."

8

When the enemy thopter appeared behind them there was no warning from the radar. Cage had the portside door open, and it was only when he started firing that Helga realized that they had been ambushed.

Time went still as the Nighthawks scrambled for their weapons. Two shots from the enemy caught the aft rotor and sent them spinning. Helga adjusted to stop the spin, taking evasive maneuvers. She dropped the nose and flew them into another ravine.

The Geralos followed as she took them through a narrow gap, then climbed into a vertical rise once she was past the rocks.

"Ate, what are you doing?" Cage shouted. "Position us where we can kill these *thypes*."

"There's another one cloaked just over the rise," she said. "If I slow down they will cut us to pieces."

She ignored his objections and flew the way she'd been taught on the *Rendron*, trying to avoid being caught between the two enemy thopters.

After a few minutes of this, Cage seemed to give up and barked out commands for focused fire. He and Varnes aimed at one, depleting its shields immediately. But instead of evading—now that it was vulnerable—the Geralos fired back at them. Helga saw it coming, and dodged as best she could before firing back at them with the thopter's gun.

The Geralos thopter rocked violently as one of the rotors went out, and that was when its pilot made an attempt at escape. Helga smelled blood in the water and turned on it with relentless fire, but now the other thopter was onto them, trying desperately to pull them off.

"Stay on that cruta, Ate," Wyatt shouted from the back. "Do not let those thypes survive."

His words resonated when she heard them, her biggest critic egging her on. She growled with fury as she stayed after the thopter while simultaneously dodging the other. As her bullets found home she saw the thopter begin to sink, and one by one the Geralos started jumping to the surface below.

Eventually their thopter stalled and crashed into a rock, and Helga went into defensive maneuvers to evade their new attacker. But her shields were falling, and they were too close to shake. Cage Hem was still screaming for her to stabilize to give him a shot.

"Ate, I am not going to tell you again," Cage said. "Level this cruta and let us do what we do," he growled.

"Do as he says, Ate. He knows what he's doing," Cilas said, and she noticed for the first time that he was no longer sitting beside her.

Against her better judgment, Helga obeyed, and leveled off the thopter with their pursuer. Cage Hem opened up with little care for overheating his gun. Back and forth they fired on one another and then the enemy's shields went out.

Helga gnashed her teeth as she braced for impact. She could feel the vessel rocking as their shields gave out. But Cage kept on firing despite the danger, and to Helga's surprise the Geralos turned around.

Taking the cue to pursue and finish them, she engaged the thopter's thrusters and aimed for the enemy's rotors. The fleeing vessel became a fireball as the Nighthawks cheered through the comms. And just like that it was quiet again, and they were the only thopter remaining of the three.

Helga felt as if she'd been underwater and had finally come up for air. Blood rushed to her head as the adrenaline lifted and she screamed in victory and pumped her fists. It felt good to win and survive an attack that for all intents and purposes should have been their undoing. But she was with a team that excelled in the impossible, and a Master Chief whose stargun was the stuff of legends.

She leveled them out and pushed forward on the control stick to tilt the nose down as she increased the thrust. Cilas struggled over to his seat and sat back down, throwing back his head in what appeared to be relief.

"Very impressive, Ate," he said. "I knew you were capable. But now the rest of these men know it too."

::

After another hour of flying, the domed tops of Abarion appeared on the radar at 80 km out. Helga looked over at Cilas and assumed that he was sleeping, since he had been sitting still with his mask inclined.

"Lieutenant," she said and he turned slowly to look at her. "The settlement," she said, pointing off towards the domes.

"Oh ... Well, put us down in that crater over there," he said.

She did as she was instructed and took them down inside the crater. Without any landing gear, she hovered close enough to the ground for them to jump out.

"Good job, Ate," she heard Cage Hem say before exiting the vehicle with the rest of the men. Cilas remained behind and Helga wondered if he was okay. When he didn't move, she reminded him that the landing gear was damaged, and that he would need to jump out soon.

"Once I'm out, I want you to fly this thing over to that rock formation," he said, pointing at an area on the radar. "It looks to be about a klick off to the Louine side, so it should be relatively easy to get back. Do you understand?"

"I do, Lieutenant. I'll fly to the rocks, put the thopter down amongst them, and then rendezvous back here." It made sense to hide the vessel, just in case the Geralos came back. She hadn't thought about it when they approached, but now it seemed like common sense.

Cilas nodded and then stood up, touching her on the shoulder again. Helga had learned that this was his way of letting her know that they were good. He was so much her senior in rank, and she had stumbled since joining the group. She had been scolded, yelled at, and even insulted, and none of the men were going to apologize. The squeeze was Cilas being Cilas, supportive to the end. It let her know that none of it was personal, they just wanted her to catch up.

He walked slowly to the back, held his wound, and jumped out. Helga lifted the thopter out of the crater and turned it towards the mountain of rocks. They ended up being a little farther away than she had estimated, but upon approach, she saw that they were ruins from an old building.

"Thype me, this isn't happening," she whispered. "I thought that no one else had settled this moon. Now, this is troubling. What have we stumbled onto?" She flew a tight circle around the ruins, taking in the view. "Um, Lieutenant," she said, touching her comms. "I thought you said that Abarion was the first settlement here."

"That's correct, Ate. What's the situation?" he said, switching their comms so that they all could hear.

"This rock formation, where I'm trying to land...it's actually an old human building. More than that, however, this entire area looks to have had several buildings at one point. These aren't the Geralos style of architecture, Lieutenant. These are human built. I'm sure of it."

Cilas was quiet, but she could feel his confusion, and it was Lamia Brafa who finally spoke. "Abarion was the first colony that was given permission to be here, Helga. There have been several groups in the past who jumped in to Louine and got turned away. Most didn't have the fuel to return, so they set up communities on this moon.

"Without the Alliance and the Louines knowing they were here, they ran out of resources, and ... many died off. The Geralos would have harvested them, but most would have died from extended exposure. It's not something widely known, and I hope you all understand that we are to keep it this way."

"That makes my blood boil. You knew about this and didn't bother to share?" Wyatt said. "If you knew about it, then our leadership knows about it too. How many people were left to feed the lizards, Brafa?"

"Wyatt, am I going to have to tape that ass in your face shut?" Cage said. "You seem to have a permanent case of diarrhea, and I'm about tired of handing you wipes. We get it, Lamia; I don't like it either. But we came here to do a job, and that's what we aim to do. Nighthawks don't gossip. We're too busy winning the war. Aye?"

"Aye," came the resounding agreement from the other men.

Helga rolled her eyes, frustrated. Who would she tell that would actually believe her, anyway? The cadet commander? Even she would not know what to do with the information. Gossip was the right word, since it would be treated as such, with all the important people cupping their ears.

"Just wanted to make you all aware," she said. "I'm going to park the thopter and make my way back." She closed the channel and placed her helmeted head inside her hands. There was something stinking about this mission, and she wasn't thrilled to be left in the dark.

Landing without landing gear was more of a challenge than she anticipated, but she took her time and put it down. When she was out, she took a brief tour of her surroundings, using her rockets to stay off the ground.

There was evidence of a fight that had been largely one-sided. The settlers had been ambushed, and then put to the flame. There was old burned-out furniture buried under the rubble, and other things that told her that the people living there had been thriving before the ambush.

This is so sad, she thought. *All these lives lost and forgotten, as if they never existed.* She looked off towards Abarion. *Is this the fate that awaits the settlers there now?* This last thought spurred her on to make her way back towards the crater.

The PAS picked up on her need to move fast and the rockets in her boots came on. Soon she was zipping along the surface towards the dark expanse of the crater, watching as her fuel gauge throbbed below 50%. It took only fifteen minutes for her to make it back, and she saw that they had already set up camp.

As she grew close to them, Lamia Brafa waved her over, pointing to an area on his makeshift bench that he had apparently saved for her. "Come catch your breath, Ate," he said, giving her a smile. She walked over and sat down but she kept her helmet on. The rest of the men were having an intense discussion that made her feel left out and suspicious.

Was Cilas's last directive a ruse to get me away? she thought. She was so incensed that she almost missed what Lamia was saying.

"Don't take it personally, Ate. You are here to help with this mission. But like me, you are an outsider. Not quite a Nighthawk. You have an important job, and they have to rely on you. Focus on that now, and not the betrayal you feel inside."

She looked over at him, trying to read whether or not he was being genuine. She felt angry at herself for being hurt by the exclusion. What was she to expect? She'd been excluded here entire life. This feeling was one that she had been enduring since her Casanian mother died, and left her in the capable hands of the *Rendron* military. She would accept this reality, just like she'd accepted it back when she was a cadet, but for some reason it hurt just as badly as it did back then.

"You said that you're half Casanian. Have your ever visited the planet, or talked to other Casanians about your heritage?" Lamia said.

"Nope," Helga said, as she chewed on her bottom lip. It was her way of dealing with the pain and stopping the tears from coming. She would swallow her pride, push it down inside, and then tell a joke or two. Chewing her lip had always helped to make it easier, though she couldn't bring herself to joke.

"How do you disappear the way you do, Lamia?" she said and the Jumper spy smiled as if he had anticipated her asking.

"I could tell you, Ate, but then my order would make me kill you. And then they'd kill me for sharing our secrets," he said. "The most I can tell you is that it has little to do with technology. But that is all I'm allowed to say."

Helga studied his face to see if he was lying, but he'd answered her as evenly as if she'd asked him about the weather. "Do your skills with that lizard sword come from the order as well?" she said.

"It does, and it is the preferred weapon of the Jumper network."

"So how does one become a Jumper?" she said. "You single-handedly wrecked the lizards in our fights here. I'm wondering why the Alliance doesn't just send a hundred of you all down to Geral to end the war."

Lamia Brafa laughed. "That would be convenient, wouldn't it?" he said. "If only there were twenty of us, let alone one hundred, to deploy. We make great sacrifices to become Jumpers, Helga Ate. You give up your past. All affiliations. Family, friends, lovers ... all of it. You commit to the order and become reborn. This is why it isn't a thing that you sign up for or get born into. They choose us carefully, and when called you have to go."

"It sounds so sinister," Helga whispered.

"I guess it does, doesn't it? But then you get to disappear and wield las-swords," he said, winking.

"They could recruit me. I only have one family member, and he wants nothing to do with me," she said. "I could make a difference in the war. A real difference beyond this. Can you imagine all of the naughty things that you can do if you could disappear?" she said, laughing. "Well, of course you can, you probably did them already. I'm going to have to keep an eye on you."

"It doesn't work that way, but I can see where your imagination is going. Jumpers are extremely busy, Ate. There is hardly any time for us to play around with our gifts. Most of our work deals with assisting missions like this one, and we move around from starship to starship. Wherever they need our help."

"Do you like it?" she said, noticing the change in his mood.

"Yes ... well, sometimes, maybe?" he said, taking in a deep breath. "There are many spacers who envy our skills, Ate, but as I said before, it comes at a great cost. Remember our talk later on, if you are fortunate enough to—excuse me, will you?" He got up suddenly and walked towards the men.

It was an odd break in his speech, a glitch in the perfect coding that was the mind of one so free of error. Through the mask she'd seen his eyes go from wintery blue to a deep dark emerald. Even his speech had changed when he had turned away. Now he was—Helga screamed when she saw what was happening.

Lamia Brafa, the wise Jumper that had spoken to her, had thrust his las-sword through the chest of the Master Chief, Cage Hem. Time stopped when it happened, and Helga couldn't process it enough, especially when he spun around and cut off the head of Casein Varnes.

Brise dove out of the way of the las-sword, but Wyatt wasn't fast enough and became Lamia's third victim. Time moved slowly as she witnessed this, and she found herself frozen. An unwilling audience member to the betrayal, powerless to lift a finger.

But Cilas Mec grabbed Cage's stargun and fired into Lamia Brafa, overloading his shields and filling him with holes. The time it took for all of this to happen was in the span of five seconds. Helga screamed and fought through the paralysis, but by the time she could move the carnage was over.

9

First came the smoke and then the blackout. It all occurred in a manner of seconds. As Helga ran to help Cilas and Brise, an explosion occurred in front of her, sending up a thick cloud of dust that forced her to stop and cover her face.

When her HUD went dark, it didn't take long for her to realize what happened. They had been hit with a panic bomb. It rendered their PAS useless and disabled their shields. Without powered rockets in their boots, even walking became an effort.

Through the dust and smoke, Helga could make out the shadows of figures all around her. Large figures, armed and looming. She lifted her auto rifle and pulled the trigger, but with her system offline, the weapon would not respond.

Oh no, she thought, as hands restrained her arms and pulled away her auto rifle. She had trouble seeing past 50 cm in front of her, but she could tell that the shadows were Geralos.

A violent shove pushed her forward, forcing her to walk. They had restrained her hands and feet, restricting her movement to tiny steps. Without power to her PAS, it felt as if she was walking through mud, and with every step came another shove, causing her to stumble.

As they escorted her to a waiting thopter, Helga thought back on Lamia's betrayal. *How long had his brain been invaded?* she wondered, trying to recall if he'd been different once the Geralos had attacked. Of all the minds to take, his was the deadliest. *How would they have known so much in so short a time? Could Lamia had been corrupted all this time?*

When they reached the thopter she was thrown in the back, where she landed on top of Brise Sol. He and Cilas were seated on the floor, and they adjusted themselves so she could sit next to them.

Cilas leaned over and touched his helmet to hers. "We're in the *schtill*, Ate, but remember your training. No matter what they do to you, keep your mouth shut," he said. "If we don't get to talk again, I want you to know that you earned your place as a Nighthawk. Before they died, Cage, Wyatt and Varnes pulled me to the side in order to vouch for you. They wanted me to make you official, but..." His voice trailed off and then he stopped.

Helga's tears were out before she could react, and she placed her helmeted head into her hands. All of the speculation she had about them could not have been more wrong. Now she felt a deep guilt to go along with the hurt. Besides that, she couldn't help but wonder if the blame was hers. Maybe if she hadn't been so focused on the buildings, she would have seen the Geralos hiding above the crater.

Everything she'd heard about the lizards had been confirmed on this mission. Even the absurdities that she had assumed to be rumors. They invaded minds, even those of master spies like Lamia, and that was enough to make her wonder how the humans had any chance against them.

There was also the rumor that they enjoyed human brains, particularly that of Vestalian women. She was part Vestalian, but it was probably enough. They would bite into her head and prove Wyatt right.

She wondered if her being a woman was the reason they'd captured her alive. Were she, Brise, and Cilas being taken to some sort of special Geralos lunch?

These questions grew heads and her heart began to race as she thought about the jagged teeth biting into her skull. Even if they managed to escape somehow, their minds could be invaded like Lamia's.

What would she and Brise be able to do against a corrupted Cilas Mec? The thought turned her blood to ice as she contemplated their fate, not realizing that the thopter was now flying towards the settlement.

It was only when the glass domes were visible through the door that she saw where they were headed. *We were too late*, she thought. *The colony is lost*. She could make out a row of thopters parked just outside the settlement.

They landed in an open area, and several Geralos could be seen approaching the vessel. They dragged Helga out by her feet and forced her to stand with Cilas and Brise. They were within the fenced-in perimeter of the Abarion settlement and Helga counted at least 23 Geralos.

Behind their captors were the domed structures that had provided a livable atmosphere for the settlers. There were several squat houses inside of one, and a sprawling farm inside another. Behind these were three large buildings, each with their own individual domes. Running between the domes were glass-covered walkways, and a tall fence that stretched around the perimeter.

Helga scanned the property for a means of escape. The fence was electrified and the Geralos hadn't bothered to power it down. She looked over at the thopters and a thought crossed her mind. If she could steal one of them—the same way she did before—and turn the cannons on the rest, this would leave the lizards stranded within the walls.

She began to grow excited over the prospect of getting out, but her plan did not account for her fellow Nighthawks. If she spoke to them now, the Geralos would know, and there was really no way for her to covertly signal the details of her plan.

The need to act grew stronger within her chest. It was either move now, or be lizard food—her vision went white as something struck her in the helmet, and she found herself staring at the ground. As she reeled from the blow, one of the Geralos grabbed her wrists, slapped on a new set of cuffs, and pulled her back up to her feet.

When he pulled off her helmet, Helga shut her eyes and mouth, afraid of what the atmosphere would do to her lungs. She felt the lizard's hand on her back, violently urging her forward, and then there was a change in temperature as she stumbled over a threshold.

Taking a chance, she opened one eye and saw that they were now inside one of the glass domes. The Geralos that assaulted her was sealing the airlock, and another pair stood before them, guarding the entrance to a building.

When the dome was sealed, he walked over and stripped her out of her armor. The other two did the same to Cilas and Brise, stripping them down to their XO-suits. Helga still held her breath as they worked, but it was too much, so she sucked in some air. It stunk so badly that it was barely breathable, and it reduced her to a fit of coughs.

"What is that?" she said, suddenly. The smell was so bad that she could feel bile rising in her throat.

"Dead bodies. Probably the people they murdered," Cilas said before one of the Geralos punched him in his face. A gargling grunt came from his attacker and was acknowledged by another, who punched Helga in the abdomen.

The smell and the sudden pain caused her to retch, but nothing came up as she gagged. One of her captors grabbed her hair and yanked her up, then forced her to walk into the building.

As they picked up the pace, Helga thought about the breathing, and how it was that they could survive in the same space as the Geralos. The air was due to an atmosphere generator, which they hadn't bothered to stop.

This was confusing. *Why leave it on?* she thought. From what she knew, oxygen was poison to Geralos lungs. She noticed that each of them wore something at the corner of their mouths. *That must be the device they use to make the settlement air breathable*, she thought.

One of the Geralos turned to another and grunted something unintelligible. It must have been a joke because the other one laughed, then came up to her and placed his hands on her head.

If fear had frozen her earlier in the crater, now it completely shut her down. She could feel his rough palms on her scalp and it sent painful shivers down her body. It was obvious that she was the main course that they were looking forward to eating. He licked her forehead, then shoved her ahead to fall in line behind Brise.

They marched down the hallway in a single file line, with a Geralos commando in between. Helga noticed a pistol in the small of his back, and thought about pulling it and liberating his mind.

If her attempt at escape failed, she didn't think that they would kill her, not after the look of excitement she'd seen on their faces. She was an exotic morsel to their flesh-eating palates, so they'd forgive her attempt, even if she killed one of them.

This thought spurred her on and she reached for the pistol. But as much as she wanted to, her arms wouldn't move. "Stasis handcuffs, of course," she mumbled as the Geralos behind her shoved her along. She had missed her chance back at the crater, and now all she could do was observe.

As they pushed her along she saw bodies strewn about on the floor. Innocent victims of the Geralos invasion. She wondered if the Britz had survived the ambush, if they would have made it here in time. But some of the bodies were far gone, which answered her question. The Geralos had been here long before they'd made their jump.

After several hallways littered with bodies, they shoved her and her fellow Nighthawks into an even worse smelling room. There were people against the walls inside, their arms suspended above their heads. As Helga strained her neck to get a closer look, a Geralos threw her up against the wall. He lifted her arms above her head, and when he stepped away she was stuck.

Pain wracked her shoulders as she hung there suspended, using her feet to try and brace against the stretch. Her toes found an outlet that extended from the wall, and she rested her heels on top of it, hoping it would hold her weight.

Now that she was able to focus, she watched the Geralos leave and lock the door. All around her, hanging from hooks in the wall, were people just like them. Helga wondered if any of them were still alive, but their skin had a pallor that was grey. The woman to her direct right seemed frozen in a state of screaming. But when Helga twisted herself to look, she saw the hole in the back of her head.

Her eyes met Cilas's but she couldn't read his face, which was a cross between a look of horror and one of extreme anger.

"Lieutenant," Helga said, her dry throat causing her voice to crack.

"*Yeah*?" he said. "What's up, Ate?"

She could barely see him in the diminished light.

"Are we *thyped*? What's our plan?" she said.

He didn't answer, which frightened her even more.

"We were sent here as food for these *crutas*," Brise said, and Helga wondered what he meant by "sent."

"How does that make any sort of sense, Sol?" she said. "Who would send us across the galaxy just to become food for lizards?"

"Oh, shut it, Ate. If it wasn't for you, we wouldn't be locked up in here," he said. "You made us take that stupid thopter, which they used to track us and get Lamia. I finally was official, and then you came along, thyping things up for us. What kind of cadet training were you given, anyway? Did they not teach you to obey the chain of command? Master Chief said to march, but you wanted to fly, just so you could show off for the lieutenant."

"*Thype* you," Helga screamed. She was so angry that she shook. Her feet slipped off the outlet and her shoulder pain returned. But she did not feel it. All she could feel was rage, and the need to break out of her restraints to punch him in his mouth.

She was about to cut into him about being a terrible squad mate when Cilas finally spoke. "You two finished?" he said. "We need to cut out the blame and figure a way out of here. Judging by the way these bodies have been preserved, I assume that we will be here for a while. They will bite into each one of us, trying to see if we have the Seeker blood. That's our reality, Nighthawks. You need to accept it.

"We will need to work together to get ourselves free, so whatever you feel for one another, just push it to the side and think. Before Lamia attacked us, I sent an SOS to Louine, informing them that the lizards had taken over the moon. We need to be strong, just in case they send help. Keep your wits, even if one or two of us dies. Do you understand me, Nighthawks?"

"Yes, sir," Helga said.

"Of course, Lieutenant," said Brise Sol, but then he shot her an angry glance. He looked as if he wanted to say something more, but kept his mouth in check.

Helga decided that she hated this man, who had been judging her silently since they deployed. At least Wyatt was honest and had given her a chance. She wished that it was Brise who Lamia had killed.

She wept silently as she hung her head and thought about the men that had died. Cruser, who she had considered a friend, who had helped her strap in and adjust to a new life. Varnes, who had been friendly from the very beginning, who had a wife and family waiting on the *Rendron*. His loss above all brought tears to her eyes. He'd lost so much yet managed to still be so nice.

Then there was the Master Chief, Cage Hem, who had done everything to keep her alive. A giant who placed the mission ahead of himself. Even Wyatt had come around to treating her as one of them. He had touched her shoulder when they faced off against the dredge, and that tiny gesture had meant so much.

The chat with Lamia, seeing his face change the way it did – she feared that she could have warned them, if she only knew. Was Brise Sol right? Had her rookie mistakes cost them their lives? Could a more seasoned ESO had recognized Lamia's change? It was possible, she reasoned, someone who'd seen it happen before. The more she thought about it, the more she felt a painful guilt grow inside of her chest.

She had known that she would experience terrible things coming on this mission, but she didn't know that so much responsibility would have been passed on to her. It was like a painful nightmare she could not escape, and she hoped that she would wake soon. She'd awaken in their camp with Wyatt laughing, and Varnes brooding about his wife.

This was not the case as she hung there for a time, slowly accepting her fate. When a mist of cold vapor came down from the vents, she felt her limbs stiffen, and saw Cilas and Brise lose consciousness. For some reason she didn't pass out completely, and she could still see what was going on around her.

The door slid open, and several Geralos walked in. One pointed, and the leader shook his head and then gestured towards another woman. They touched a panel above the woman's head, and her slender, pale body took on a flush of color.

When the thawing was over, she began to move, and the Geralos grabbed her hair and pulled her head down. He produced a knife with a glowing edge, and cut open her head with a quick, practiced move. As the woman began to scream, the leader bit into the exposed brain, and stood that way, with his eyes rolled back.

Helga had always heard that the Geralos ate human brains, but what she was witnessing was something else. Perhaps this important Geralos was in fact eating the brain, but it was in a manner that she had never imagined. She strained her eyes and ears to investigate further, but then her vision blurred and everything went black.

10

His eyes cracked slightly, defying the thin film that covered his face. The pain was gone, but this wasn't a good thing. Pain meant that you still had feeling, and more importantly, that you were still alive.

There had been so many theories about death and what came afterwards that Cilas Mec had resolved to believe that no one really knew. Now he pondered the numerous possibilities. Was he now a spirit, stuck to his frozen corpse, forever tied to this life until it was properly disposed?

That was one theory at least, but there were others. Perhaps this was the afterlife, and he was being punished for a lifetime of killing. At least the first supposition had some hope. Perhaps someone in time would come, find him hanging, and destroy the place.

His lids came open to a dark room, and he could smell the stench of the deceased. As his eyes became focused, he could make out Brise Sol, but Helga's hook was empty.

His heart sunk. *She must not have made it. They bit into her skull and used her up. Why am I awake?* he thought, looking towards the door. He wondered how long he had been out.

He could feel his heart beating now, pounding in his chest, but he couldn't move his limbs. An hour passed as he hung there, wondering. It felt like torture, and his mind was teetering at the brink of the dark abyss of insanity.

Resolved to his fate, he thought back on their mission. Brise said they were sent as food, but Cilas believed it went deeper than that. For a long time since starting the Nighthawks, their missions had been in sync with the standard Alliance Navy. Starships would fight the big loud wars, while he and the boys went after high value targets.

Going after the Geralos command was as dangerous as it came, but he had Cage Hem, and together they made a formidable team. He missed the big man, especially his smile. It was always there to reassure him that "impossible" was just a word.

Four major battles had been won thanks to his Nighthawks: the Alliance's silent assassins. Then Lamia came aboard and they won three more, and that was when things began to change. There were no more covert kill missions, just random drop and fetch. Things that a regular squad could handle, yet they were the ones made to do it.

It felt like punishment, and he could only vent to Cage. Still, it began to be a problem, trying to keep his men motivated. "Go search a derelict ship," or "escort a Genese diplomat to the moon of Traxis." These were their orders after so much success.

Why would you need the Alliance's best for doing things like this? Then this fiasco, this messy mission to rescue settlers on Dyn. Cilas wracked his mind for an incident in the past where he would have offended Retzo Sho. He was always respectful to his Captain, even when he disagreed with the man.

The only thing that made sense was that it went beyond Captain Sho. But why would Alliance Command want the Nighthawks out of the way? That part was even tougher to understand than the theory of having offended the captain. The only thing they ever did was to follow orders to the letter.

He began to feel his body, and as control returned, so did the pain in his upper arms. He felt as if he'd been run over by big barrels of rocket fuel, or had gotten the worst part of a five-man brawl. Still, he could finally move, and that meant that he had a chance. He examined the body next to him and paid careful attention to its restraints.

It seemed that the only thing holding them to the wall were the cuffs, and they were merely draped over a hook. If he could slip the hook, he'd be able to get down, and then he'd be able to help out Brise.

As time ticked by, he worked at weakening the hook by pushing off the wall with his legs. It was metal in stone, and he was heavy enough to make it move when he threw his legs out in front of him.

Between the hunger and the pain in his limbs, this exercise reminded him of BLAST—which was the Navy's Basic Land and Space Training.

For an ESO operator, BLAST was the epitome of hell. Several long months of grueling objectives, ranging from space to planetary survival. Select spacers were put to the test, from simulating exposure in spatial conditions to spending time in a rain forest on the savage planet of Arbar.

All of the Nighthawks had been through BLAST; it was a requirement that he and Cage had set. They were all special, especially

Helga, who he had seen as a copy of himself. He tried not to think about her, since he blamed himself. He had brought her along just to die.

With one big push, his legs came up, and this time they made it over his head. As he reached the peak, he jerked his hands up, and was free for a few seconds before the floor found his back. Struggling as the air rushed out of his lungs, he blinked past the stars to cough up blood.

When he could finally breathe, Cilas got to his feet. "Good job, Nighthawk," he whispered to himself. His eyes found Brise, who still hung in a frozen state. "I have to find a way out and then come back to get him," he whispered. "No use having us both get killed, if the lizards manage to catch me out there."

He limped over to the door, paused, and looked down at his hands. He was still wearing the chained cuffs and would need to get them off. He examined the room to determine what it had been before the Geralos turned it into a prison. He decided that it had been a freezer that started out as a kitchen. The settlers rigged it to store something large, but he couldn't tell what it would have been.

Did they find animals on the moon to kill and store here for food? he thought. If this place where they were hooked was considered a freezer, than the adjacent room had to be a kitchen. They had been led down a hallway, past several closed doors. Which mean that there was a chance that guards were standing outside that door.

But wouldn't the lizards have heard me fall? It was loud enough— unless they were deaf. He cracked the door, and something moved. Without stopping to consider who it was or what, Cilas acted on instinct and grabbed him. He wrapped his left arm around his neck, pinned his gun arm, and kicked the back of his knee.

The Geralos fell forward, dropping to his knees, and Cilas threw his chained cuffs around his neck. Wrapping his legs around his waist, he hooked in his feet and fell backwards. Gurgling as he thrashed about, fighting for his life, the Geralos reached up to pull the chain away from his throat. But Cilas was desperate, despite his weakened state, and pulled the chain tight, using his legs for leverage.

After what seemed like an eternity, the Geralos went limp, but Cilas kept pulling just in case it was a trick. When his energy was spent and the movement had stopped, he accepted that his enemy was dead.

He listened down the hallway to see if any more would come, but the place was quiet, and the doors stood closed. *Maybe they can't hear,* he thought as he got up. He searched the guard for the keys to his cuffs, and found them almost immediately.

Cilas grabbed the Geralos and pulled him into the room where the rest of the humans were hanging. Before waking Brise, he wanted to make sure there was a clear path of escape. He took the Geralos's handgun and leaned him up against a wall, then went around and unlocked all of the cuffs.

After checking their vitals, he found that Brise was the only one still alive. Most of the others had already been bitten, but some had simply starved to death. He slipped back into the hallway and tried the next door. It was a kitchen just like he imagined, with five Geralos asleep inside. Cilas slid the door shut and destroyed the locking panel, standing with his back to the wall trying to catch his breath.

"I can't do this alone," he whispered to himself, and went back to the first room to wake up Brise. He stepped over the bodies to find the Nighthawk, and rubbed the frost from his face with the blade of his hand. "Sol," he said, then slapped him in the face. "Brise Sol, wake up!"

"Lieutenant?" Brise said.

"Yes, it's me, wake up. We're breaking out of here," Cilas said.

"I can't feel my legs," the young man said, his voice sounding frightened.

"It's okay, you're not paralyzed. This is just part of the process. Whatever the lizards froze us with shuts off the mobility to our limbs." He thought he heard a noise. "Sol, I have to go. There will be lizards storming this building. I'm going to buy you some time out there. When you can finally move come join me."

"What if you die?" he said. "You can't take them all by yourself."

What's wrong with this kid? Cilas thought. *He should be better than this.* "You're a Nighthawk, Sol, how about you act like it? What if I die? Don't ask me that, *schtill.* If I die you fight on, because that is what we do."

Why did I bother? he wondered, then stepped back out into the hall. There were three more closed doors before the main entrance and he needed to know what they were.

The first door he took his time opening, and hid behind the wall. He listened to hear if anyone moved, but it remained quiet inside. He chanced a look. It was empty and dark, except for a solitary figure in the back. It was a female form, which looked like Helga, but the idea seemed absurd.

She had been the sole female with them, but why would they choose to isolate her? He'd heard numerous stories of the Geralos experimenting on humans. Helga was part Casanian and they would have found out the hard way, since Casanian blood was toxic to them.

He'd expected on discovery that they'd kill her outright, not wanting to risk more casualties. But perhaps they were seeing if they could dilute her blood, to make her brain safe for eating. He took a few steps in and examined the form. It was definitely Helga, but she had no clothes.

"I'll come back for you, Ate," he said, backing out. He wondered why she was naked, and assumed the worst. *Poor kid*, he thought. *Whatever they did, I'll make them pay*. With both Brise and his pilot, he was liking his chances of finding a way off this moon.

Cilas checked the next room and found it empty, so he made his way to the final door. A commotion outside the main doors grabbed his focus, he was about to be overrun. He clutched his pistol and brought it up, walking slowly towards the main doors.

"Steady," he said to himself, as he stared down the pistol's sights. He was determined not to miss when they came rushing in. They had the numbers, but he was a Nighthawk, and the steadiest aim always wins.

The doors slid open, and he pulled the trigger twice, hitting the chest and abdomen of the Geralos who came in. The lizard went down, but he kept on firing, dropping another as the first fell back into him. But the Geralos that followed didn't rush him like he expected. They shut the door and took off running, which left him feeling a bit confused.

Cilas lowered the pistol and eased his breathing. He was alive after committing to die. Second chances came with confusion, and a lot of adrenaline, so he didn't really know what to think.

Why had they run? It made no sense; he was but one man with a gun. Even if he managed to keep on shooting, the pistol would've overheated and ceased to function. He'd get at least five, but then they would have him ... every ESO worth his uniform knew the limits of a gun.

Their running only meant one of two things had happened. They'd either set a trap, or something more pressing was happening outside. Cilas checked the last door, holding the pistol up and ready. It was a closet full of gear that the settlers had used for traveling outside.

He slipped inside this closet and locked the door, waiting for the inevitable explosion, or the Geralos rally. Neither happened as he stood in the dark waiting, his mind going through an endless sequence of different scenarios.

One had them opening the door and disarming him instantly, then torturing him and Brise for hours before allowing them to die. Another had them shutting off the oxygen, and he would wake up on the hook freshly frozen.

When it had been over twenty minutes, he donned one of the suits and pulled on the mask. He stepped back out into the hallway and slowly walked towards the main doors. As he grew close, they suddenly opened, and Cilas lifted his pistol, preparing to shoot.

But he paused when he saw what it was that was waiting, an armored figure too tall to be Geralos. Behind him were the dead bodies of the Geralos that had fled when he shot the first two. There were also lights that he didn't recognize, and other armored strangers within the dome.

They regarded one another, and Cilas lowered his pistol. The enemy of his enemy was definitely his friend. It didn't matter who this was; what mattered was that he wasn't Geralos. He lifted his free hand and gave the universal sign of peace.

"I am Lieutenant Cilas Mec, of the starship *Rendron*," he said. "Man, are you a sight for sore eyes. I was sent here to rescue these poor settlers, but they took us prisoner and—wait, can you understand what I'm saying, friend? There are humans here who need your help."

The man didn't move, so Cilas became concerned. Was he wrong to trust this stranger? He didn't recognize the armor, but he noticed that the mask was similar to the ones they wore. If this was some trick by a mysterious Geralos, he would drop to the floor and pull the trigger.

"Who are you, friend?" he asked again, double-clutching the pistol and raising it up.

The man held up his fist, then removed his helmet. His face had the features of a Louine.

11

When Helga regained consciousness, she felt a sharp pain in the back of her neck. She tried to move but couldn't and this sent her mind spiraling through a variety of awful possibilities. Had the Geralos already cut out her skull, and was her brain exposed to the atmosphere? Did they bite her and realize that she wasn't psionic? Was her Casanian blood the culprit?

She felt cold and numb and her vision was blurry, but she was still alive and her mind was intact—at least that's what she assumed. She opened and shut her eyes several times, trying to focus her vision, but even this was painful, so she stopped and decided to keep them closed.

A long time passed as she slipped in and out of consciousness. Time was a mystery as she faded in and out, but she dwelled more in the land of dreams than in the cold dark reality of the Geralos prison.

In the land of dreams she was in her childhood, watching her brother play with a kite. She followed the elaborate paper construct with her eyes as it dipped and climbed in the wind. Rolph, her brother, was tugging on the string, pulling it one way and then another.

Helga smiled as she watched. This was the Rolph she remembered, young and innocent but always in control. The kite continued to perform tricks while magically staying aloft, and it reminded her of the fighters that the *Rendron* would deploy.

They were on a hill in the northern Alps of Ferce on a planet known as Seryac. It was summer time, and Helga was in the birthday dress her mother had bought. They were always with their mother since their father was a Marine, and was actively fighting in the war.

As she looked around the grassy field, she spotted her mother on a bench. She appeared to be watching Rolph, but Helga recognized her expression. She remembered this day, and her mother's face, masking the pain that she hid from them. She had just learned that her husband was dead, his dropship destroyed by a Geralos cruiser.

Why was she dreaming this? Why this memory? After this day her mother would join her father after losing her battle with depression. She and Rolph would be sent to the *Rendron*, orphans to strangers not fit to be parents.

This was the wake before the pain, and the dream kept every single detail. Helga was lucid yet stuck in her younger body, unable to escape. She recognized that she had been dreaming for an extremely long time, and she worried that she was actually dead and this was her version of an afterlife.

She got up off the ground, dusted herself off, and walked over to where her mother was seated. It felt good seeing her again, her Casanian half, and she could see that she got her lips from her. Unlike Rolph, whose features were more Casanian, Helga had a thick crop of hair, and her father's sun-browned complexion.

As Peraplis, her mother, raised her wet eyes to meet hers, the dream began to fade to darkness. Helga's eyes opened again, and though it was painful, she found that the blurriness was gone. When she looked around the room, she realized with some surprise that she was the lone person hanging.

A number of uniformed Geralos were on the far side, speaking in their gargling language. There was one staring at her, and when she saw him glaring, she closed her eyes to pretend that she was still in stasis. But she could hear him, laughing, and the others joined in. Then she heard them approach her body and felt hands on her head.

She felt the cold pressure of a knife being pushed down against her scalp. She tried to scream, but what came out was a cough, as her dry throat and heavy tongue reacted to the atmosphere. A new Geralos rushed in and screamed at the ones around her, and they backed away immediately.

He pointed at her face, then pointed towards his own, and made a gesture as if he was gasping for air. His violent sign language culminated with spit that smashed into Helga's forehead and dripped down slowly past her nose.

The Geralos that meant to bite her walked out of the room quietly, followed by the one who had warned them off. Helga was stunned, trying to grasp what had happened between them. What had he told them to scare them so much, and why did he spit on her? That seemed unnecessary.

The mist didn't appear to be making her tired, but she still felt paralyzed from her neck down. She could feel the spittle freezing in place on her face. *Where are Cilas and Brise?* she wondered, knowing somehow that they were dead. Was she the last survivor? Why hadn't they bitten her first? Were they saving her for someone important, or to use as leverage somehow?

She noticed that the room was different from the one before, even though the mist had obscured everything within it. *Maybe they moved me and the guys are still alive,* she hoped. Tears mixed in with the Geralos spit, and her face felt stiff as if it held a thin layer of ice.

After a time she closed her eyes, hoping to pass out. She wished they had bitten her and rid her of her life.

When she fell asleep again, she was back in front of her mother, but this time they were inside their house. She was in front of her tools working on some plans, drafting up the layout to a house. She didn't seem to notice Helga standing there, and she paused to play with a locket around her neck.

"Mom," Helga said, getting her attention. She was startled to hear that her voice was not the eight-year-old version.

"Look after your brother, Sweet Pea," she said in response, and Helga could see the tears rolling down her mother's cheeks.

"Mom," she tried again. But there was no answer as her mother's head slumped down on the desk. It was the same way she'd died, when Helga found her so many years ago. Face down on the blueprints of a newly designed home, her teacup stinking with a potent Casanian poison.

It hurt as much now as it did back then, just less confusing and surprising. It would follow with her telling Rolph and him blaming her for everything. She hoped that her dream would let her escape before she got to that part.

"I wish that you would have given us a chance, Mom," she said, leaning down and hugging her mother close. "We did great things with our lives, despite the odds. Rolph, I don't know, we haven't been in touch, but I became a spacer ... just like dad. If you were here it would give me someone on the *Rendron* to fight for. Someone who would care if I'm stuck in this place forever. But your heart was broken, and you were lonely. I understand now, more than ever. Rest easy, Mom. Maybe I will be seeing you soon?"

This time when Helga opened her eyes she realized that she was naked. She didn't know how she'd missed this major detail of her captivity, but for some reason it had eluded her. No one said that fear, cold, and hopelessness granted much clarity, but now she was looking down at her breasts, and the floor—which seemed to be several feet below her.

Why would they hang me higher? she thought, and that was when she noticed that she was alone. Her head was no longer hurting and she regained some feeling in her limbs, which would have been good if not for the pain that came along with the recovery.

The room was extremely quiet, the only sound being the oxygen blowing through the vents. There was no mist like the other room, and when she studied the ground she saw no footprints in the dust. In her arms ran several tubes, and when she followed them they went to a device which held a vat of red liquid.

They're feeding me, she thought, *keeping me alive for who knows what.*

She tried to move but her body wouldn't respond. Either she was still in stasis or her limbs were too weak. It frightened her that she couldn't tell which. It was as if they managed to separate her mind from her body.

The door slid open, and when she heard the noise, her body tensed at the thought of the Geralos coming back. When she summoned the courage to look, she saw a slender spacer that could have been Cilas Mec. He came up to her, pulled out the tubes, and then undid something above her that caused her to fall.

Despite the lower gravity of the settlement, the fall hurt worse than anything she'd felt in a long time. All of the nerves and feelings of her body came back like a flood. The spacer pulled her up violently and handed her a uniform. When she studied it she saw that it was her 3B XO-suit.

"Who are you?" she whispered, her throat too dry to say more.

"Can you see, Ate? It's me, Cilas. Get the suit on fast, and hurry it up. We only have a few minutes before this place is toast."

"What do you mean?" Helga said, struggling to pull on the suit. She was trying not to panic as she went. Her legs were so slender, and her nails had grown into ghastly talons. How long had she been locked up here, and how had Cilas gotten out? This and many more questions flooded her mind as she slipped into her XO-suit and stood in front of Cilas.

"The Louines got my SOS. They've come in and are giving the lizards hell. One of their commandos rescued me and Sol, but I came back for you," he said. "Still, I don't know if there are lizards in this building hiding and waiting for an opportunity. Can you walk, Ate? You don't look good." He reached around the back of her head and then exhaled with relief. "They didn't bite you. That's good, but you do have a nasty scar."

He led her out in the hallway, cradling a gun and limping as if he'd been injured. "Where's our armor?" Helga said, but Cilas merely shrugged. He opened the door to a closet lined with the settler's IEVA gear. He took out a small mask with a clear glass front and threw it into her hands.

She pulled it on but regretted it instantly. It reeked of vomit and something else. Minutes later they were back in the hallway, dressed in their 3B XO-suits. Helga could already feel the alien material trying to heal her wounds.

She understood now why Cilas insisted that they wear it whenever they intended to don the PAS armor. It was an extra life, a second chance if the armor failed you, but she wondered how well it would heal a body weak from malnutrition.

The hallways they traveled were lined with an organic growth that was so thick it hid all traces of the original metal paneling. "What is this stuff?" she said to Cilas, curious if he could hear her through the IEVA helmet.

"Lizards were terraforming, converting this to their home. They dropped spores that reacted with the oxygen in the vents, making an atmosphere similar to Geral. Any longer here and we would have suffocated, but the growth is too new to bother us," he said.

They stepped outside of the building, where Helga saw leagues of Geralos being marched toward the hatch of a Louine ship. All around her were the dead bodies of her captors, along with a few blue-skinned Louines.

A tall Louine came over to them and Cilas walked out to meet him. Helga saw an old crate half buried in the surface, and she limped over to it and sat down. She felt as if she'd just run a marathon, and would kill for something cold to drink.

Cilas and the spacer talked at length while she studied their big, sleek, silver dropship. She had always heard about Louine's advanced technology, but never thought she would see or experience it. Now as she gazed upon the shiny behemoth, she wondered what would happen if the Louines joined the war.

She felt a deep sort of pain that gave the impression that it was inside her bones. When she concentrated on it, the pain grew worse, and she noticed that her breathing was labored—and not from the musty helmet. She wanted to know what day it was, and the time. They had been under for so long that she had begun to confuse her dreams with reality.

Where was Brise Sol? She looked around to find him, and finally found him sitting near the drop ship with a man in white attending to him. Cilas Mec walked over and sat next to her, and she could tell from his face that he had something grave to tell her. He reached down for her wrist, and she let him have it. He slipped on a bracelet comms, and synched it to his own.

"Can you hear me, Ate?" he said when he was finished, and Helga nodded affirmatively. "Well, we're out of the bad part, but we're on our own. These Louines are a paramilitary group, as unofficial as they come. That's their leader, Amatu Vlax. He intercepted my signal and came in to help us. He told me that the Louines would have ignored it, since they want no part of this war. Lucky for us, he hates lizards just like we do." He laughed. "So we gave him an opportunity to try out his troops."

"How did they do?" Helga said, smiling. She thought he looked handsome beneath the light of his helmet.

"They are the truth, and I'm not being generous, Ate. They took on over a hundred lizards with thirty untested men. Apparently the simulations they trained on is top of the line amazing. They couldn't do it on their planet; they would have been arrested and locked up forever. So they stole a ship, modded it out for stealth, and used it as a training grounds for their men."

"So, what do they do exactly, if they aren't a part of the war?" Helga said.

"They want to be, Ate. This is why they came for us. We were the flair that lit up the sky for them, and now they're ready to join the war. I told Amatu that when we make it back to the Alliance, I would inform them about what he did. Hopefully we can recruit them into our corps and get them the hell out of this system. The longer they stay the more they risk discovery, and their ship is too small and underpowered to defend against a Geralos destroyer."

"Yeah, and if the Louines come to arrest them, they won't be able to stop that, either. I understand, Lieutenant ... wow. I want to give Amatu a hug," Helga said.

"How are you feeling, Ate? Please answer me honestly. I need to know. What did they do to you? You know you can tell me. What do you remember from when they isolated you?"

Helga struggled to remember the few times when she was conscious in that room. Nothing came, just a big black gap, and the painful memory of Lamia going rogue. "If I remembered, I would happily tell you, Lieutenant, but they kept me frozen the entire time. My body hurts though, like my bones have cracks in them. Do you know what I mean? It's pretty intense."

Cilas shifted and sat forward, placing his elbows on his thighs. He seemed to be watching Brise as the doctor examined him, and then he began to wring his hands. "I feel it too," he said finally. "If I stop to think, it's the absolute worst. Deep pains throughout my body, my guts feel like they are on fire, and the wound from the ship ... well, it's taking some real effort to ignore it. Helga, I feel like I'm already dead."

Without thinking better of it, Helga embraced him, and she felt him surrender in her arms. He'd done everything he could to get them to safety, and she wanted him to know that he wasn't alone. This went beyond protocol or appearances because she saw him as a friend. Cilas would not admit weakness to just anyone, so she felt honored that it was her.

Her eyes grew heavy while she hugged him, as if she hadn't slept in days. She fought to stay conscious, but she was losing, and eventually the darkness won.

12

Helga came out of her dreams to pressure on her eyes, an annoying beeping sound, and the smell of chemicals. She tried to open her eyes but they remained closed, and she struggled against the panic building up inside of her.

Okay, eyes are sealed, she thought, and then tried to move. Nothing, but she did manage to wiggle her toes and fingers. *Good, now let's see what's going on with these eyes.*

When she tried to open them she felt a bit of pain. Her mind then dipped into the realm of the absurd. She imagined that the Geralos had bound her to a bed, cut her scalp open, and sewed her eyes shut.

It's okay, she thought, *eyes can be replaced.* She lifted her right arm to try and reach up to her face. Something stopped her movement halfway up, and with two tugs she assumed that it was belt restraints. *Should I say something—could I say something?* she thought, then opened her mouth and tried.

"Lieutenant," she said, but it came out as a croak. "Lieutenant, are you there? Sol?"

"I'm here, Ate," a voice said. "We're both here in beds next to you."

It was Brise Sol, but where was Cilas? She tried to figure out where she was. The last time she was awake, she was hanging from a wall, but now she could tell that she was lying in a bed. There was also the beeping, and the strong chemical smell. They had to be in a hospital, which meant—"Hey, are we back on the *Rendron*?" she said.

Brise laughed. "No. Is something wrong with your eyes?"

Her memory was fuzzy, but she remembered them being rescued. For a while there had been a lot of darkness broken up by confusing dreams. Either she was flying into battle or reliving a scene from her past, so now that she was finally awake, she struggled to make sense of her location.

Brise was still talking. "It's just this cream they put over your eyes. It stings a little, but not for long. Try to open your eyes."

Helga did as he said and opened her eyes, slamming them shut from an assault of bright fluorescent light. When she opened them again, she saw computers all around her. On one monitor it showed a star map, which told her that they were leaving Dyn.

Her thoughts went to Varnes, Cage, and Wyatt. She wondered if the Louines had recovered their bodies from the crater. Cilas wouldn't leave without them, she knew he wouldn't, so either the full team was on the ship or the lieutenant had stayed behind.

She adjusted her body to look to the side, and that's when she saw the other beds. Cilas was in bandages, unconscious or asleep, and on the bed near the wall sat Brise. She had somehow managed to forget about him, but she was pleased that he had made it.

He pounded his chest in the Alliance's universal salute, and Helga wondered why. Maybe he'd forgiven her, now that they were out. They had been thrown into a blender, ground up to bits, and then dumped into a fire on that moon. Yet here they were, alive and rescued. That had to mean something, didn't it?

Suddenly Helga felt guilty and sick, unworthy of her life. Brise saluting her made it seem worse. Why did they make it and the others didn't? But Brise looked lost, just as lost as she was, as if he really needed a friend. Why should she leave him out in the cold? Because he'd yelled at her when they were captured?

She realized that it was like Cilas said, and they would need each other now more than ever. So she summoned some strength and made a fist, then touched her chest in a salute.

"So what happens now?" Helga said, as she studied the patterns on the grey overhang. The Louine ship's infirmary was different from any that she had seen before. Everything seemed so alien, from the stark white bulkhead to the odd, holographic numerals that floated in and out of the readout monitors.

Brise was sitting up with his legs hanging off the side of his bed, but Cilas was still unconscious. This placed a nagging pinch of worry in the back of Helga's mind. Cilas had been injured badly, then patched up in the worst of conditions. Not to mention she had no clue if he'd been hurt during their escape.

After a lengthy bout of silence, Helga wondered if Brise was having difficulties after the trauma at the settlement. He hadn't responded to her question and had a stare that seemed to penetrate walls. She'd heard that it happened to everyone, even legends like Cilas, and she had to admit that she was having difficulty herself.

Would there be a time when she didn't think about the things that had happened down on Dyn? Would she be able to function during quiet times like this, and not miss the high of being a key part of combat? Talking helped to calm her mind—she no longer trusted herself—but Brise was making it impossible. Why hadn't he answered her yet?

"I think that the lieutenant's injuries are significant. But our rescuers are going to make sure that he's back in working condition," Brise finally said. "I don't know any Louines but I've seen enough to know that they don't do anything halfway. Don't worry, Ate, we're in good hands. We'll be back on the *Rendron* in no time."

His cheerful tone sounded forced, but Helga was happy that he gave an answer. "Well, that's a relief, but I meant the three of us," she said. "How do we intend to get home? Are the Louines able to send a message out to the *Rendron*? I feel great, but I don't know how long we've been here. Do you?"

Brise shook his head. "I woke up and the two of you were still unconscious. I got bored sitting here so I pulled out my tubes, grabbed some clothes, and explored. This ship is huge, but from what I can tell, it's all medical facilities on this deck. There's even a gym for rehabilitation. When you're feeling better you should take a walk.

"This place is really wild, Ate. I wish the *Rendron* had some of their flair. As for getting home, I wouldn't worry about it. The Louines are neutral in the war and want no part of it. Keeping us here compromises their position, so they will want to get rid of us as quickly as possible."

"That makes sense, but how will they do it? I don't see them loaning three strangers a ship with an FTL drive," Helga said.

"Me either, but I'm not going to worry about it. At least we're no longer frozen meat waiting to be eaten. Why don't you take a walk or something? You're only going to drive yourself crazy stressing over things you can't control."

Helga took his advice and decided to get up. She reached over to pull the feeding tube out of her arm. It was painful, but it didn't last, though she expected an alarm to go off. After removing her tube, she looked over at Cilas and saw that he had several running to each one of his limbs.

She made to sit up, and placed her feet on the floor. "There's a robe above your head, there," Brise said. Helga grabbed the robe and pulled it on, testing her ability to walk. The gravity was strange. It was lower than she was used to, and it took an entire second for her feet to touch the deck.

With bare feet on the cold surface, she made it to the door and stared out through the transparent portal. "Touch it," Brise said, "and try not to panic." Was that amusement she was hearing in his tone?

She reached forward, hesitantly, and touched the glass surface. It was cold and wet, as if it was a pool of water standing vertically in front of her. She felt something grip her wrist and begin to pull her through. The whole thing sent her heart racing. She wasn't expecting any of it.

Helga found herself standing in the center of a long passageway, with the watery portal standing undisturbed behind her. On her right were giant bay windows revealing a spectacular view of Dyn. It was so vivid and the glass was so clean that Helga panicked, thinking she would be sucked out into space.

When she got her bearings, she felt embarrassed and studied the overhang for cameras. "I bet someone is laughing," she said to herself, as she stopped to look out at the moon.

Helga tried to imagine herself as a refugee, looking out through the glass at her future home. Would it give her excitement? Real land to live on, grow a family, and help develop a community? She felt nothing of it. Dyn was a cruel mass of grey, with wicked secrets like the dredge and the sneaky Geralos.

It was not meant to be a refuge for Vestalians, but no one had bothered to warn them. This last thought made her angry when she remembered the ruins on the surface.

Brise had made the comment that they were sent out there as food. The implications bothered her, though he refused to discuss it further. Was there something to the Geralos being so entrenched on Dyn? And what about the evidence of a former colony?

"Hello." The voice startled her and she glanced quickly to her left, where a tall Louine was hovering with a somewhat awkward smile. He was dressed in white and carried a tablet, which he used to scan her as his fingers slid along its surface. She didn't know how long it took for her to answer him, but when she finally did it felt like a long time.

It was as if her body and mind went through separate processes to allow her mouth the freedom to answer. First there was shock, since she hadn't seen the door open, and then there was acknowledgement.

Here was one of her rescuers, and he was tall, handsome, and apparently polite. "Oh, hello," she said, leaning away as he stepped in closer. She glanced around to see if he was alone. "You speak common Vestalian?"

"How are you feeling?" he said, looking her over as if she was a newly finished statue that he had sculpted for days.

"Are you a doctor?" she said, amused by their game of questions.

"Can you understand me?" He reached up to touch her ears.

Helga stepped back beyond his reach. She didn't like him touching her, despite his office. "Yes, but did you understand my question?" she said, still feeling his fingers on her lobes.

"Ah," the man said. "Introductions. Yes! My name is Jien, and I am third of the committee in charge of this, our Sick Bay. You can call me Doctor, if it's easier. I imagine our Louine tongue is difficult for the military-class."

"Military-class?" Helga said, before realizing that Jien's grasp on the language was probably not perfect. *Class, and questioning my ability ... are the Louines so elitist that they think spacers are dumb?* "Isn't this ship stolen? That would make you a pirate, right? Where does a pirate get off questioning my intelligence?" she said.

Jien looked frightened and covered his mouth. "No. No, I meant no offense. It's just, I haven't met many humans," he said.

"And the ones that you met were Alliance military, and probably too dumb to get past the fact that you're Louine," Helga said. "I can pronounce your name just fine, Jien. I am Helga Ate, and the men that you rescued with me are Brise Sol and Cilas Mec. Brise is—the red-haired one." She gestured to her hair for the emphasis. "The other man, Cilas Mec, he's our lieutenant, our leader."

"I met both men, and I remember Cilas. He is the hero who made contact with us. I had a chance to speak with him prior to our departure. He has great constitution, considering the injuries he had. He is the most impressive patient I've had. Humans are quite resilient. Perhaps I should make a recommendation for integrating the blood."

Helga wondered if it was a language thing, or if he truly meant what he just said. "Integrate the blood, huh? Would your government allow that? I thought you Louines didn't want any part of us, which is why you let us fight the lizards alone."

"Some of us disagree with that stance," he said, walking up to look out at the moon. "It is why I am here. I believe in Amatu Vlax. We must join the fight, or risk invasion. Your Cilas has told us that he will help us to get an audience with your Alliance. But he is not healthy, Helga. His body was ravaged, and he needs time to recover before anything happens."

It was as bad as Helga had feared. Cilas was hurt, yet had managed to rescue them somehow. They were fortunate to be rescued by the Louines, since their medical procedures were so advanced. If not for Jien, then Cilas would die, and she felt bad about being short with him.

"What about me, Jien? How am I looking?" she said, noticing his fingers tapping something on the tablet.

"Well, Helga Ate, you seem well enough, but don't overdo it. You need lots of rest. You were in poor shape when we brought you in. If you knew what they attempted, your sanity would wane. I've heard of these Geralos, and the cruelty they inflict, but what they did to you goes beyond—I'm sorry. I get carried away. I just meant to say, don't overexert yourself."

"I won't, Doc. I'll just be standing here, looking out at that muted ball of death," she said. *What the thype did they do to me for him to say that?* she thought, biting her tongue to prevent herself from asking him for details.

But what if it's permanent and hinders my flying?

She couldn't take the mystery anymore. She needed to know. "Eh, Doc ... could you tell me what the Geralos tried?" she said finally.

"They attempted a dangerous blood transfusion. Draining out yours and replacing it with another's. You must be very special for them to go through the trouble. They wanted to use you, but there's something about your blood. Is it because you're Casanian?"

"That's what I've been told," Helga said, still stuck on the fact that she had the *Seeker blood.* That had to be it. The lizards wanted her brain. She was one of the rare women that they slaughtered hundreds to find. *What are the chances*, she thought to herself, but she hadn't experienced anything to allude to this gift.

Seekers were said to be somewhat prescient, having the ability to see into the future. She had always known that there was something different about her that went beyond just being part Casanian. But a seeker? It seemed absurd. Maybe the lizards had kept her for another reason.

"Could you do me a favor and keep this to yourself, Doc?" she said. "The only person I can trust is Cilas Mec. Do you have it in your notes there? Them trying to experiment on me? If you do, can I ask that you wipe it out?"

"What experiment?" he said, giving her a wink, and Helga gave him a rare smile.

"Thank you," she said, and he touched her shoulder.

"Don't stay out here long," he said. "Please, get some rest."

13

"How long do you think it will be before the *Rendron* sends help?" Helga said to Cilas as they sat in the crew's mess hall, eating. It had taken a week for him to recover from his injuries, and another few days to be released by Jien Tor.

"If I could predict that, Ate, you and Sol would be the first to know," he said. "As it stands my guess is about as good as yours. We sent the message through the Louine's communicator, and it will take several days to reach. Their FTL comms is better than ours, but it's still up to Captain Sho to send for us when he gets it."

Helga sighed. She was really hoping that Cilas would have an exact date and time.

"He'll send help. Don't you worry about that," he said. "Do you really think they would leave us out here if they knew we were alive?"

She didn't want to answer that truthfully. The mission had been sketchy from the start, and she was beginning to believe Brise's assertion that they had been set up.

"How do we know that they received it?" she said, and Cilas gave her an impatient look. The question was stupid. He was a lieutenant, and an ESO leader. Officers were required to memorize the *Rendron's* codes in order to make contact at any time.

Seeing a signal coming from him would be received without any question. But the *Rendron* would not reply to the Louines, since that would reveal their location. Helga knew this, and Cilas knew that she knew this, so he took her question as a slight. When she saw his face, she looked down at her plate, realizing she had gone too far.

"The first thing I'm going to do when I get back is find some real food and gorge myself," Brise said. To emphasize the point, he lifted his spoon out of his bowl, leaving a long line of white goop stuck to the contents below. It was only when he had it over his head that the line finally broke and splashed liquid all over the table, causing Helga to flinch.

"What is that?" she said, laughing, and Brise made a face. "Can't be that bad, considering you've had several bowls. What does it taste like? Can I try it?"

He slid the bowl over, and she used her finger to get a little off the edge. It tasted like cheese—if cheese was sweet—and had a peppery aftertaste. "That's exotic," she remarked, "but I could get used to eating it. Back home we have processed bars and rations. At least here they have actual food to eat."

"They're not military," Cilas reminded her, but to Helga it was beside the point.

"The last time I had real food was after BLAST," she said.

"I remember that," said Brise. "It was that huge buffet after graduation. Damn it, Ate, why did you have to remind me? I can taste those eggs as if it was yesterday. Folded sandwiches, all kinds of steaks, and the liquor ... Man, I was so glad I made it."

Cilas laughed, and it gave them pause. "Sol, you really love food, don't you?" he said. "So now that we're together, and doing well enough to joke about the quality of the *Rendron's* food, I have good news and bad news to share with you," he said. "Good news is, we're going to be getting a ship. Amatu's engineers have been working on getting it space-ready. Bad news is it has no FTL drive, and only has enough storage for one year of rations."

"Sounds like we're being air locked politely," Brise said, and the flush in his cheeks revealed his disappointment.

"This is a paramilitary group on a stolen ship, Sol. Do you think they can afford to hang around over Dyn? How long before the lizards jump in to check on the settlement that's gone dark? What about our saviors, waiting around for the *Rendron*? How long before a Louine security vessel picks up their beacon? Amatu's a saint as far as I'm concerned. He gave us help when the entire planet ignored our call. Not to mention afterwards he risked discovery to orbit the moon while allowing us to heal. What more do you want, Sol?"

"Nothing, Lieutenant. I was just having a whine. Nothing personal," he said quickly.

"This isn't the time. We need to make moves. They're giving us our own vessel. It's a good thing. What do you think, Ate?" the lieutenant said, but Helga was stunned and didn't know what to say. She knew time was limited, but they were being made to leave, now? Like Brise, she'd expected to be with the Louines until the *Rendron* came for them.

"How big is this vessel?" she finally said.

"They're telling me it's a little bigger than this ship's infirmary. It's really an escape pod, but they fashioned it to be a ship—so that it's able to be maneuvered in deep space. Amatu is wary of the lizards. He's expecting that they will be jumping in sometime this week."

"Then we only have one chance, as far as I see it," Helga said. "We will need to wait out the Geralos and hope that they concentrate on Dyn. It's a shot in the dark but we're out of options, and hopefully Sol can get the Britz back online. We go down there, fix our ship, then leave again to jump back home."

"That sounds insane. Besides, how do you know that the lizards left the ship intact when they found it?" Cilas said.

"I don't know, Lieutenant, but would you rather we try, or stay floating up here in an escape pod, counting the days till our rescue? The *Rendron* will get the message, but how long before they come? You said you didn't know the answer to that. A part of me wonders whether they'll even answer. We've been gone a really long time. What if they assume that it's a Geralos trick to get more victims to come out to this system?"

Cilas seemed to think for a very long time, and then looked at her and shook his head. "It's too risky, Ate. Remember our last attempt at entry? We were shot down immediately by Geralos drones. Who's to say that they don't have more waiting for us? We wouldn't make it, not in a rigged escape pod."

Helga found herself having conflicting feelings. It felt as if they were being placed in a predicament worse than before. A part of her wished that she hadn't woken up, that she'd passed away after the last time she'd lost consciousness.

They weren't supposed to be alive; this was how she felt. This brief bit of happiness fooled her into thinking that they would be okay. Never again would she let her guard down. Not for the Louines, and not for Cilas. "Whatever you say, Lieutenant. I'm ready to go," she said.

Cilas shot her a peculiar glance. "Are you upset, Ate? We're all friends here, and I want to know your thoughts. Why don't you speak your mind?" he said.

"It's just so unexpected. I like to be prepared," she said. "We were just captured, and now we're having to go back again."

"Go back where, to Dyn?" Cilas said. "No, we're going to be safe inside of a ship. It's no different from being here, Nighthawks, except it will be just us. I think there is something else that is really bothering you. Why don't you come forward with it?"

"There isn't, Lieutenant. I think I'm just tired. I'm ready to go. I honestly mean that."

When they were dressed and ready, Amatu met them in the passageway outside of the infirmary. "I apologize for this," he said. "If it were up to me, you all would remain on *The San* until your people came for you. Jien has informed me that you are fully recovered. This has done wonderful things to my heart. From warrior to warrior, I bid you luck and clarity, Cilas. If only I could make you a part of my crew."

Cilas grinned. He knew it was a compliment, and the two men clasped hands and touched each other's shoulders. "Don't stress it, Amatu. You need to stay moving. Don't worry for us, we know how to survive. When the *Rendron* comes, I will inform them of your heroics, and set up a meeting between you and Captain Sho."

"I hope that you find these spacesuits helpful in your travels," he said, and handed them each a bundle. "They are made from adaptable Traxis material, impervious to fire and unfriendly conditions. Most of the pilots on Louine wear them. So when you go, know that we go with you."

He had come in with four spacers, and they all saluted in unison, and then he was gone through the watery door. Helga went back to the infirmary and slipped into her suit. It was as tight as her old 3B XO-suit, but easier to slip on and get comfortable in.

When she rejoined Brise and Cilas, they were wearing theirs as well. They said their goodbyes to the medical crew, then gathered their bundles to begin their walk. They were taken through a series of long passageways, with rebels saluting them as they went.

After a number of elevators and narrow passageways, they finally reached the flight deck. Helga was surprised to find it empty, but reminded herself that the ship was stolen and undermanned. The skeleton crew was busy on maintenance, and the majority were crew, not fighter jocks.

It also surprised her that the escape pods were on the dock when most Alliance ships had them near the bridge. She recalled the day one of the cadets had snuck into a pod on a dare, but couldn't deploy it without the captain's key. That same cadet was now one of the *Rendron's* dockhands, permanently grounded for pulling that stunt.

The memory of the cadet commander ripping into him almost brought a smile to Helga's face. She hated that cadet; he was one of the many who bullied her. Prior to his failed deployment, he made her young years a living hell.

The Louines led them to a hatch, which opened up to the interior of their escape ship. Brise, who hadn't said anything in an hour, climbed inside without looking back. Helga followed him in, curious about the controls, but Cilas lingered behind to speak to the men.

They were loaded up with boxes of rations, military equipment, and words of encouragement. Helga, too focused to be concerned with supplies, looked over the controls to make sure she could handle them. "Controls are in basic, and the layout is familiar," she said, more to herself than to the men.

She contemplated defiance, flying them towards the moon despite Cilas's plans. Before the Geralos jumped in, she could get them to the Britz. But how far would she make it before Cilas commandeered the controls? It was a foolish thought, best left abandoned, so she focused on her job and examined the console.

"How old is this piece of junk?" she whispered, looking around to see what else was out of place.

Cilas came inside and strapped himself in. "You want to get in position, Ate?" he said, "*The San* is about to launch us, and you don't want to be in that seat when the gravity drops."

Helga got up from the chair and walked over to a launch station. She strapped herself in and waited for *The San*. Cilas kept his eyes on her as if he expected her to speak, but Helga was too busy fighting her inner doubts to notice.

The voice of the captain came over the comms, and he said a few words in his strange Louine language. "Lieutenant Cilas and crew, we apologize for having to do this, but wish for the gods to guide you back to your home," he said. "When you are out on your own, keep an eye on your radar, and try to stay hidden from the Geralos warships."

"I don't understand why they can't just bring us back once the lizards are gone," Brise said.

Helga couldn't believe Brise. *Is he really this thick, or does he know something we don't?* she wondered. "They've risked their lives to save us, Sol. Isn't that enough? They gave us a chance, and now we need to act like Nighthawks. Stop looking for a break; we've already been given that. Whatever comes when they let us go is entirely up to us. I know you're frustrated, but suggesting impossible things will not help any of us."

"Prepare for launch," the captain said, and the cockpit turned red as an alarm began to blare.

Helga closed her eyes and thought about her brother. She wondered where he was and what he was doing. Did he have a family? Was he happy? Was she as dead to him as he made it seem?

She hoped that he was somewhere successful and far away. Maybe he was on Casan, living amongst their mother's people. If he was, then it was likely that he was an artist. Casanians more than anyone held creativity in high regard.

She decided that she didn't care what he did for a living, as long as it had nothing to do with the war. Their father, Algo had been a career spacer, and had fought against the Geralos since he was in his teens. His father before him had done the same, as well as his mother, and their parents before them.

Helga was the legacy, becoming a cadet, and now a member of the elite Nighthawks. She wanted to know that if she died on this ship, Rolph with a family would carry on their name. Unlike him, she had nothing to lose. No one would miss her if she never returned. She smiled sadly, allowing it to sink in. She was a "nobody," that no one would mourn.

This admission led her to the ultimate acceptance of her fate. It was as if she had died inside of that Geralos prison. She felt a freedom that she'd never experienced before. The happy, ambitious Helga Ate had died, survived by this hollow woman with pain in her heart.

She opened her eyes and saw Cilas watching her, and it was then that she realized that she was clutching her chest. "We're going to make it, Ate. Can you trust me, at least with this?" he said.

She met his eyes, too shaken to respond. *Why is he trying to make me feel better?* she thought. *Me, the dead woman, on a doomed escape ship.* The look that he gave her made her feel sick. She didn't want his pity or whatever it was he felt.

"It doesn't matter, does it?" she whispered, releasing the fabric on her chest.

The vessel shook violently, and the lights went off, followed by the blast doors ascending to shield their launch. They watched *The San* as it faded in the distance, along with Dyn where everything had been lost.

We have to make it, Helga thought suddenly, not liking the idea of the Nighthawks' sacrifice being in vain. Who would know what they had done if none of them made it to tell their tale? Varnes especially deserved better, and she wanted to make sure that his family knew.

The vessel shook and they slowed to a halt as the computers blinked to life. The lights came up and the air cooled, and the restraints on their stations loosened. Helga exhaled and unclipped her straps, then floated over to the pilot's seat where she strapped herself in.

"I don't know how long we're going to be out here," she said. "But we need to be prepared for anything. We can't die. I'll do my part to make sure of it. I expect that you Nighthawks will do the same."

14

Helga stood in front of one of the giant glass blast windows staring out at Vestalia. It hovered before her like a bright blue ball submerged in jet-black ink. The other cadets were having fun, dancing, laughing, and having a good time. Several boys had taken turns asking her to dance, but she had happily sent them on their way.

She wore a long black dress that accentuated her athletic form, and her hair was up to reveal the Casanian spots on the side of her head. It had taken her a long time to feel proud of her non-human heritage, but now that she did, she wanted all of her critics to see.

"Something told me that I would find you here," someone said, "standing apart from the others."

It was the captain of the *Rendron*, Retzo Sho—a man who she never thought she'd have the honor of meeting. Why would she? She was just another orphaned Navy cadet, and Retzo's office was the highest on the ship.

"Captain Sho." Helga gulped, bowing deeply.

"Relax, Cadet Ate, there's no need for formalities. This is your graduation, after all. Second class, isn't that right?"

Helga nodded, smiling proudly. "The first one in five years," she said. "I still find it hard to believe."

"To believe what, that you're special, or that you're the first in five years?" he said. "Cilas Mec was the last cadet to break past tier-three. Before him there was me, and only twenty other *Rendron* cadets. It's a tremendous feat, Helga, there's no need to be modest. You're in a small fraternity of leaders now, one of the five percent. I heard your father served, so I looked him up. First Sergeant, Algo Ate, a Marine."

"Yes sir, Dad was a career spacer, just like all the Ates before him," she said.

"Algo gave up a lot to fight for the Alliance," he said reflectively. "He was impressive. I'm surprised he didn't try for BLAST. The things they did on Meluvia, Traxis, and Casan." He whistled. "Men and women of his generation were made from different stuff. Anyway, I've held you up too long, and I'm sure you'd rather be celebrating. Keep up the good work, Helga, and like your father Algo, great things will be coming your way."

With that, he touched her shoulder in the standard gesture of support. He then took his leave, and was joined by a host of guards as he exited the graduation party.

Did that just happen? Helga thought. She couldn't believe that she had met Retzo Sho. She let out a sigh and returned to staring at the planet floating outside of the window. There was a difference in what reflected back at her now, taking her focus off the planet. She was seated in a vessel, and directly behind her, two men were playing on their handheld devices.

Helga realized that she had been dreaming, and she was strapped into the cockpit of the escape ship. It had been two months since they'd left *The San* and a set of Geralos ships were now orbiting Dyn. The Louine ship had jumped, leaving them stranded, and they were stuck, doing whatever they could to pass the time.

Helga spent most of her days fiddling with the ship's computer. She had grown comfortable with its interface and had begun a procedure of tweaking it to perfection. When she wasn't doing that, she was talking to Cilas and Brise. Most of their time was spent swapping stories, and other times joking around.

A few times during the week, they would don EVA suits and crawl through the airlock outside. The tiny ship may have started out as an escape pod, but as an interplanetary vessel, it had everything a traveler would need.

It was Brise who found the EVA suits, and it was he who took the first venture outside. What they found was that time in the vacuum of space was a therapeutic activity. Outside the ship, Helga found peace from the "trapped in a tin can" feeling that occupied her mind. Their prison wasn't a terrible one, but she had trouble getting accustomed to it.

Cilas—who was quiet all the time—was not the best conversationalist, and Brise, with his lack of couth, had the worst opinions to share. Helga wished that Loray Qu, the cadet commander, was on the ship with them, or Casein Varnes with his stories of Virulia, or Lamia with his spy adventures.

When they weren't lazing around or taking turns in the EVA suits, Cilas tried to make contact with the *Rendron*. Brise stayed on his personal device—Helga assumed he was playing games—and she would study the galaxy map, trying to come up with options to get home.

"You've been staring at that monitor for a few hours now, Ate. What are the lizards doing that can keep your attention like that?" Brise said.

"Nothing, they're doing nothing," she said. "I was actually asleep. Had a dream about a day, back in the cadet academy, when I had my first meeting with the Captain."

"You met Retzo Sho?" he said, and she could hear the skepticism in his voice.

"I met him and we spoke about my dad. It was one of the best days of my life, to be honest. I know that you think I'm full of schtill, Sol, and I want you to know that you don't have to believe me. It's just nice to finally dream about something positive for once. I've been cycling nightmares nonstop about being inside of that Geralos hell."

"You and me both," he said. "They haven't stopped for me either. What about you, Lieutenant, you still having nightmares?" he said.

Cilas looked up from his personal device, and regarded each of them carefully. "I've seen a lot of schtill, Brise. Too much to count, really. It isn't easy to brush off and forget the type of things we've seen. You keep some of it with you for the rest of your life. That is, unless you're one of those rare freaks who can push it down until you forget it. Every time I close my eyes I see Lamia coming at us the way he did."

"Did you ever think about a psych treatment, Lieutenant?" Brise said. "They say the doctors on the *Rendron* can black out whole chunks of your past if they deem it unhealthy for you to keep remembering."

"That would be great, Sol, but officers need their memory. We have to live with past mistakes so that we don't make them again, and use that knowledge to educate our future ESOs. You and Ate are new, and unfortunately you've been through something worse than I have had to deal with in over ten years of active service. I am recommending that you both see the psych doctor as soon as we hit the *Rendron*, and it will be totally your prerogative whether to wipe the memory or not."

"No thanks," Helga said, thinking about being strapped to a hospital bed and going through the same confusion she did being chained to the wall. "I am an officer, so like the lieutenant I'll keep my nightmares and learn to live with them."

"I'll remember that little speech when you airlock yourself and the council brings us forward for questioning," Brise said.

"Were you always this dull an instrument, or did it take some effort?" Helga said. But Brise didn't seem to take offense. Instead he made a face and went back to his device.

She wondered how long it would take before they all wanted to kill one another on the ship. There was a tension growing between Cilas and Brise, and she could no longer pretend to ignore it. Brise was annoying, and he seemed to be getting worse. When he would ask Cilas a question, the answer would be brief. That is, if he chose to answer him at all.

Brise was in trouble, and she wondered why he didn't see it. The constant insubordination that he displayed would either get him reprimanded or transferred off the *Rendron*. That seemed harsh, but Cilas was as serious as they came, and Brise had crossed the line several times.

She had thought about talking to him when Cilas was outside. Just a brief suggestion for him to apologize, and reassure their leader that he was loyal. But Brise was immature, and had proven this time after time. She didn't know whether he'd take her advice or turn it into another accusation of her being the favorite child.

It was exhausting, but she recognized that it was inevitable when you lock two men together who were so drastically different. The only reason Cilas hadn't killed him by now was due to them having the EVA to allow him to blow off some steam.

Helga tried to imagine if they couldn't get out and all she could see was Cilas choking Brise and swearing her to secrecy. Would she have to become the wall that separated the two? It would be a full-time job and not one that she particularly wanted.

"Hey, Ate, I'm sorry," Brise said, and when her eyes met his she was surprised to read sincerity. "You got it a lot worse than we did, and I know that you're going through your own *schtill*. That joke I made earlier about the airlock, I'm sorry, it wasn't funny."

"Thank you," she said, not knowing what else to say. The apology had come so unexpectedly that Helga was stunned. When she looked over at Cilas, she caught him looking, and he too seemed surprised with Brise's apology. "We're stuck together for a long time, Brise, and we don't have the luxury of retiring to our own bunks when we're upset. I can't afford to get offended over the things you say or it will be really hard to keep my head."

"I agree," he said. "Thanks for being so cool about it." She knew that his words were meant for Cilas to hear, but she accepted his gratitude regardless.

With the ship being an escape pod it wasn't outfitted with the gravity simulation that commercial ships had. This forced them to stay in perpetual zero gravity within the tube-like chamber. There was the pilot's station—or cockpit if you were keeping the ship façade—which was a caged in console with a giant monitor, and several "rest stations," which were padded recesses along the sides.

It was apparent that it was a rushed solution since comfort wasn't easy for the Nighthawks. But the temperature was regulated, and they were stocked with supplies, and enough power to keep their personal devices going strong. The devices were good for watching vids, listening to music, and playing games. Brise found a way to connect his with the ship's computer, so that if anything went wrong, he would know immediately.

Helga's pastime was watching the distant moon, and the odd colored "stars" that were really Geralos destroyers. They had jumped in soon after they'd left *The San*, and had been there for over a Vestalian week. She watched them daily, wondering what they would find, and what they would do once they found it.

The most pressing part of her worry was that they would probe the space near Louine. There would be starships orbiting to the planet, and more than likely they would be ignored. If the Louines were as meticulous with their cleanup as Cilas had said, then the lizards wouldn't suspect their involvement.

Their escape ship was Louine, but it was an obvious anomaly, and the cloak that they used was a hack discovered by Brise. It utilized mirror technology and would reflect back any visual shots, but if the Geralos did a deep probe then they were bound to be discovered.

It would only take one shot to burn a hole through the hull that would kill them instantly. So Helga watched them daily, preparing for when they would start their investigation. If they so much as moved, she would take them farther away from Dyn. The downside to her plan, however, was that they relied on its gravity.

Drift too far out and there would be no rescue. Stay put and they risked being picked up by a Geralos tractor beam. After being a captive to the terrible lizards, she wasn't looking forward to doing it again. She would rather die than be taken alive, and she knew that her fellow Nighthawks felt the same way.

"I'm going outside for a walk," she announced, and the two men grunted their approval. She floated down to the door that separated them from the makeshift locker room.

She grabbed the wheel with both her hands and hooked her toes into the ladder on the bulkhead. Spinning it counter clockwise she pulled it open and caught a loose helmet as it tried to escape. "Brise, you're such a slob," she whined, but he didn't seem to hear her. "Put schtill back where you got it from. Why is that so hard for you to do?"

"Did you say something, Ate?" he said after a while.

"Nope, go back to your games," she said, rolling her eyes. She slipped into the compartment and resealed the door, then floated over to a locker and pulled out an EVA suit.

After getting dressed, she floated out of the door, used the wheel to lock it behind her. Cilas floated over to where she was and took her helmet, then got behind her back and screwed it on. Several checks and she was ready to go, and he manned the airlock as she stepped outside.

"How long do you think you'll be this time?" he said, but it was almost impossible to hear without comms.

She held up two fingers to indicate two hours, and he nodded and made the signal for comms. Helga floated to the other end of the ship, near what would be considered the nose. She typed in the password on the panel and pulled open the heavy door.

Inside was a small compartment, immaculately white, with a circular blue door on the far end. Helga sealed the door that she had come through by punching in her code again.

"Can you hear me, Ate?" Cilas said through her comms.

"Loud and clear," she said. "I have door one sealed, just need you to release door two." The circular door began to spin and then finally opened out. Helga floated through this one and turned to watch it close automatically. "Attaching line," she said, then hooked one end of a safety tether to her belt. She then wiped off a screen that had a lot of condensation, typed in the password, and waited. Another panel slid open to reveal a stack of equipment, and she grabbed a pair of magnetic soles and attached them to the bottom of her boots. "Ready to walk," she said.

"Okay, Ate, be careful," Cilas said. "Pressure door is now unlocked. Don't forget yourself out there."

"I won't, Lieutenant. I'll see you all in a couple of hours."

15

The silent battle between Cilas and Brise continued for several days. Each of them stuck to their respective corners, working on ways to cure their boredom.

Cilas, the warrior, tried to keep himself in shape by eating the protein-heavy rations while finding ways to work out in the null gravity. Brise, the defiant, worked on schematics for the ship and shared with Helga his plans for making the interior more livable.

Helga wasn't too thrilled with these plans since it involved stripping metal from the storage area, but Brise knew what he was doing, so she hesitantly gave her support. She pointed out problems that could occur if that area of the ship got ruptured, but Brise adjusted for it and came back with more ideas, and these new plans seemed feasible.

They had gone over the plans for hours the day before, and Helga showed them to Cilas to get his approval. By rank, he was the de facto captain on their little ship, and she wouldn't want to be moving things without his blessing.

When she had finished with Brise, she went back to the pilot's seat and fell asleep almost immediately. Her nightmares returned in remarkable detail, bringing her back to their captivity. She was hooked up against the wall but her consciousness stayed, and she was forced to watch the Geralos biting into the settlers. When it was her time to be bitten, she tried to scream, but she found that her mouth had been sealed shut.

A drilling sound came to her ears as they cut open her skull, and though it should have been painful, she couldn't feel anything. But she knew what they were doing. A chill wind found her scalp and she knew that her brain was exposed. Then there was the hot breath, followed by the teeth, violating her brain as they began to sink in.

The thought of the Geralos eating her alive was too much for Helga to take. She forced open her lips, tearing the skin apart, and screamed so hard that it brought her out of the dream.

She was strapped in the pilot's seat with her head resting on her arm, and she could feel her heart beating as she tried to get her bearings. *That was a bad one,* she thought, as she wiped her mouth with the back of her arm. *Did I scream out for real? No, if I did, one of them would be over here.*

In front of her loomed Dyn, magnified several times to show the Geralos destroyer. There were a number of dropships leaving it now, but nothing to cause her concern. The nightmare was still vivid in her memory, and the appearance of the moon did not help her to forget. Helga closed her eyes and focused on their space. That was when she heard the commotion behind her.

Cilas and Brise were in the middle of a stiff conversation, with the latter seeming to have forgotten all protocol in lieu of an emotional outburst. Cilas remained as calm as humanly possible, but Helga could tell he was on the verge of losing his temper.

She sat still and listened, pretending to still be asleep. She wanted to see what they were arguing about before deciding whether or not to step in.

"You let us still come out here without questioning it, and that's why I'm upset," Brise was saying. "We should have smelled a rat the moment we were sent out to AO-9, but nobody said anything and look what it got us."

"This is hardly the time for conspiracy theories," Cilas said. "Not to mention your accusations are against the captain of our ship. You know the price for treason is the airlock."

"Then airlock me now and get it over with," Brise said. "It would be leagues better than rotting away in this schtill hole. We were dead the moment you sent us off to Dyn."

"That's not fair," Cilas said, "but you're allowed an opinion. Just don't expect me to be sold by it. When you got out of BLAST, your life belonged to the Alliance. This was what you agreed to when you became a Nighthawk. I'm just sick of your negativity; you're only making things worse. You've gone from blaming Ate to blaming me, and now you've upgraded to Captain Retzo Sho. Who will you be blaming once we get back on the *Rendron*? The Galactic Alliance? Are we that important, Brise?"

Helga waited for a retort, expecting an explosion from Brise, who seemed to be seething from something Cilas had said. No response came, and she hoped that it was over, but something told her that it was about to get worse. She opened her eyes and touched the controls gently, darkening the monitor to see their reflection.

Cilas was at his station, strapped in with his legs kicking. She assumed that this odd bit of movement was a form of exercise. Brise was near the other end, looking through of one of the windows. He was holding onto a ladder with one of his hands, but the other was balled up into a fist.

"How do you feel about what Brise said, Ate?" Cilas said suddenly, and Helga was surprised that he had known she was awake.

"This is my first mission," she said. "That doesn't give me enough experience to have an opinion, Lieutenant. I know that Kyden Ahmad died—that was how I got this slot—but no one has told me his cause of death. I find the silence odd, considering the closeness that I saw with this squad. Did he do something disgraceful, or was it just something that you agreed to keep from me?"

"Nighthawk missions are classified. We try not to bring up the past. Talking and reminiscing invites loose tongues, and the wrong person hearing something can get us into trouble," Cilas said. "But we've been out here a long time, Ate, and the future is uncertain." She waited for him to say more, but it was as if he was still considering it.

"Did Ahmad get corrupted the way Lamia Brafa did?" Helga said.

"No," Brise said quickly. "He lost his life in an ambush. We flew into a trap, but he was one hell of a pilot. He got us to the LZ, but when we exited the Britz, he was shot in the throat and died. A Geralos sniper hit him in the one area where his armor wasn't sealed. How's that for coincidence? The lizards knowing where to shoot us. He died and we didn't even know he was shot until Wyatt pointed out that his vitals were red."

"Only the best shooters tend to become snipers," Cilas said. "Spotting a vulnerability doesn't mean there's foul play."

"Yeah, but him being sniped on that sort of mission does," Brise mumbled.

"What sort of mission?" Helga said. "Everyone keeps talking in riddles. I know you're upset, and being trapped here doesn't help, but could you tell me about it in detail? What I know so far is that it was a bit of a messy mission, and that none of you were exactly thrilled to do it. Outside of those points, I have no clue what it was about, or who Ahmad was, and why he had to die."

"It was my first mission with this squad," Brise said reflectively. His carrot-colored hair was a stark contrast against the off white bulkhead. "An Alliance vessel had gone dark somewhere in Seryac space, and just like this trip, everything came off the rails. Now that I'm talking about it, there's been a lot of similarities. From the ambush on approach, to our pilot getting sniped." He looked over at Cilas, but the lieutenant didn't seem to be listening.

"I met the new team, got the treatment, same as you, and we were on the Britz flying out when the rest of the *Rendron* was asleep. This was exciting stuff. An elite team, and I was one of them. I wanted nothing else but to prove myself, to get past the treatment to call myself a Nighthawk. So we drop out of FTL, and Ahmad isn't seeing schtill on the radar. We're all confused, but the *Rendron* confirmed the dead ship's location, so we stay for weeks ... scanning and looking. Some of us began to think that the intel we got was bad.

"Then a warbird uncloaks and we're in a fight for our lives, but Ahmad knew how to fly so we didn't go down like we were supposed to. No disrespect to you or Cruser, Ate, because you were both pretty good, but the things Ahmad did – man, it was impressive, and the warbird had to run. Eventually it jumped away, and we were left with the Britz in poor shape. We should have gone home then, but we had a mission to complete, so we continued searching for our target."

Helga didn't know what to think. Everything she was hearing sounded like a setup. Coordinates were given to Seryac space, and there just happened to be a warbird waiting for them? The Geralos warbird was a sleek fighter, built to slip in and assassinate targets. It had an FTL drive, but rarely was it ever seen without a destroyer or fleet in tow.

If there was a warbird, it wasn't accidental. It was there to kill a target, which meant that it had been sent. Helga's mind was racing. Had she joined a squad that was marked for death? It made no sense; they were at war with the Geralos. What human in his right mind would be in league with those planet-stealing aliens?

"When did you find the target?" she said finally, wanting him to continue.

"A few days later Cruser spotted an anomaly, and Ahmad takes us over to investigate. There, floating as if it had been dead for ages, is an old busted up destroyer. None of us could tell if it was Alliance or

Geralos. So I did some digging in the records to see which of our destroyers were missing. Turned out this ship was neither Alliance nor Louine. It was something else, alien, a model we hadn't seen before.

"Ahmad took a shot in the throat as soon as we were off the Britz. It was ... thyping awful, Ate. Next thing you know, we were on our guns, shooting it out with the lizards. Turns out they had beat us there and were stripping this thing for parts. Lamia Brafa found their sniper and cut off his head." This memory seemed to please Brise as he stopped to grin, remembering it.

An alien ship that they didn't recognize, Helga thought. *But there are records of every sentient being within the Anstractor galaxy. Is there another alien race that we haven't heard about?* The thought of aliens made the hairs on her arms stand up. What if they were discovered by these visitors, and imprisoned anew? At least they understood the Geralos, but what would this new race want with them?

"I swear it was beautiful," Brise said after a pause. "He took off that lizard's head and started cutting the rest to threads. You would have thought that Ahmad was his family the way he went off. Varnes pulled me back to the Britz to help, but Ahmad was gone ... there was nothing we could do to save him. That was the day when I felt really lucky to be a part of the Nighthawks. We'd lost a brother, but the way those men answered, it showed me just how much they cared. This was the type of unit I wanted to be in since cadet academy—"

"Who didn't want to be a Nighthawk?" Helga said. "If you didn't want to be a Nighthawk, then you wanted to be a Ranger. Just listening to your story reminds me of the cadet academy. Graduating wasn't enough; we wanted to get invited to the BLAST tryouts. It wasn't just you, it was every cadet. We're both very lucky to be here."

"I'm sorry that we let you down, Brise," Cilas said, and they both turned to face him, shocked that he had been listening. "Before losing Ahmad we did a lot of good work. Not a day goes by that I don't feel guilty. He was a busy guy, that one. Had children on several ships. Three on Meluvia, I think, where two of his wives lived, and one on Geral, if Wyatt was to be believed," he said, laughing somewhat hysterically. Helga wondered what had gotten into him.

"Get off it, Lieutenant," she said. "That's physically impossible, not to mention gross. If the guy was that hard up, I doubt that he would go so far as to sleep with a lizard. Then again, you mentioned

Wyatt ... the biggest fibber in the known galaxy. So I'll settle on the fact that Ahmad may have children on Meluvia."

Cilas kept on laughing, and she saw that she had been set up. It made her feel naïve, and she gave him a look of impatience. It was an odd time to joke when the mood was one of dark remembrance. But maybe that was the point. Cilas's motivations weren't always clear.

Brise, on the other hand, seemed undeterred by Cilas's joke. He waited for his superior to stop laughing, and then continued talking about the mission. "You are right about us being lucky to be here, Ate. My recommendation came from Ahmad. I know his family well."

"I joined this team under the assumption that I'd be making a difference. That's why we all tried out for BLAST, right? To do great things for the Alliance? All the ads they show on our vids, about 'the chosen' being the tip of the spear," he scoffed. "I thought that I'd be blowing up starships and killing lizard commanders, not being hung out to dry by the very council that created us."

"That's enough, Brise," Cilas said, and the ship grew deathly quiet. Helga could hear the hum of the reactor pumping oxygen into the air. There was a clanging sound that occurred every few seconds, and she hadn't noticed it before. Something was loose, or in need of replacing, and she wondered if Brise had noticed it too.

She tried to meet his eyes but he was in another zone, his blue eyes staring forward as if they could see through the hull. When Cilas shut the conversation down, it was in a tone that Helga hadn't heard before. It had a finality in it that sent shivers down her spine.

What the heck just happened? she wondered as she looked at them both, but Brise was no longer willing to talk. She found this dynamic between the two men to be so interesting, though she sided with Cilas more than Brise.

"Sol, how about you blow off some steam by starting those enhancements we spoke about?" she said.

The engineer looked up at her. "You mean the plans from earlier?"

"Yeah. No time like the present to get started on it, I think," she said. "This way we can have a bit more privacy. Even more, it will be good to get us working again."

16

Being the captain of a starship as large and important as the *Rendron* meant that above all else, trust was the most important asset that Retzo Sho could rely on. Retzo trusted his officers implicitly. This trust having come from decades of issuing commands, seeing them carried out, staying on top of all aspects of the ship, and making sure that the right people were assigned whenever there was a replacement needed.

It was this trust that had the young captain confused when he received word that a distress signal had been sent from the Nighthawks several Vestalian days ago.

Standing at the head of the large octagonal table that dominated his cabin, he moved the reports around, reading and rereading them. His disbelief turned to anger when he read the time and date they had been received. Why had he not been told immediately, and why had his CAG, Adan Viles, not bothered to bring it up the numerous times he'd seen him since?

He picked up his comms and called the operator, leaning into it as if it could support his 80kg frame. "Tell Mr. Viles that I need to see him in my cabin, immediately," he said as soon as there was an answer. The operator, a fresh-faced ensign named Cyulan Ore, confirmed quickly, but Retzo had already disconnected the channel.

It took Adan Viles less than ten minutes to get to the cavernous compartment, which was impressive considering the *Rendron's* enormous size. His punctuality didn't serve to belay Retzo's anger, however, as he stood in front of the giant table, watching him as he walked in and saluted.

Retzo didn't return the salute. He knew that his anger was obfuscating any chance at reason, but it was too far gone to check. He couldn't imagine Viles saying anything that would make the situation excusable. What could he say? Eight highly trained *Rendron* servicemen were missing in action. This did not happen on Retzo Sho's watch, not when it was the Nighthawks.

When the door slid shut, he lit into Viles, sparing no expletives in his attack. For as long as he and the CAG had been working together, he was comfortable with talking to him like this. The position was a privilege, and Retzo Sho was the *Rendron* in every single way. Losing Special Forces personnel reflected badly on the ship. It would lead to other captains talking about his leadership, and questioning whether or not he knew what he was doing.

Beyond this, the years and money pumped into building warriors the likes of Cilas Mec, Cage Hem, and Lamia Brafa, made the team irreplaceable. He had lost sleep over the Nighthawks' silence, and as a captain, sleep was the rarest form of currency.

It didn't help that Viles wore a look of guilt as he berated him. He didn't try to object, and he didn't seem surprised. He just stood there, looking pathetic. "So what do you have to say for yourself, Mr. Viles? What could possibly be the reason that news of this weight and importance gets to me, the captain of this ship, 89 hours after it was received?"

"I apologize, Captain," he said, looking directly at Retzo Sho. "As you know, the enemy likes to falsify messages to the *Rendron* in order to draw us out for ambush. When we received the distress code, it came from a Louine transmission—which didn't make any sense. I had it analyzed immediately and it was determined that it was a Geralos trick."

"This report in front of me has Lieutenant Cilas Mec's personal passcode, Adan. Under no circumstance would that code be used unless it is a call for help. You know this as well as I do," Retzo said, steadying his breath.

"I do, sir. But, the thing is, it came from the Louines. What if Lieutenant Mec gave up the code under duress, and this is a Geralos trap? We could be risking even more lives by responding to it, and at this point, sir, can we really afford to do that?"

Retzo sat down in his chair and looked over his notes again. He knew it was Cilas, not by the notes but by a deep intuition telling him that it was indeed legit. But he could not deny that Adan Viles was right about the potential risk for the would-be rescuers. He read the notes several times, and then looked up at Viles.

"The Louines have never shown themselves to be hostile against the Alliance. Why would they start now? That was no fresh out of camp troop of rookies that went out to that moon. Those were Nighthawks. Are you to have me believe that the pacifist Louines were able to capture Cilas Mec and force him to send a coded message to us?" he said, laughing.

Adan Viles seemed to think it over, then his face made an expression of doubt. "No, I wouldn't believe it either, but the strangeness of the message and its source is why it has taken us some time to act," he said.

"89 hours, Mr. Viles. If Cilas Mec put this out while they were dying, then they are definitely dead now. Every second we wait results in days for the Nighthawks, who probably think we've forgotten about them."

"I know, sir," Adan said, then looked off to the side as if something had caught his eye. He was very much the icon of an officer, tall of stature, and everything about him was neat. Even his slick green hair complied with his appearance, allowing only one section to reveal his grey hairs. Adan was impressive in both look and action, and this was the only reason Retzo was talking to him.

"Could we assemble a team similar to the Nighthawks to jump out there, and see if they can make contact with Cilas Mec?" he said. "If it's a trap, they will be expecting a destroyer, or at the very least a small fleet. The lizards know that we value our people, so an interceptor won't trigger an immediate response. Our team can scope it out, jump back here if it's an ambush, or stage a rescue if it is legitimate."

Retzo thought about what he was saying, and did the calculations in his head. "I want you to get a note out to Commander Lang of the *Inginus*. He is to infiltrate the space above the Louine moon of Dyn. He and his Marines are to eliminate all Geralos threats and investigate the missing Nighthawks. Adan, I want this to be executed immediately," he said, and watched Adan's face to see how he received the orders.

"I'll have it done, Captain," Adan said, his face revealing nothing. "May I take my leave now to get to it?"

"Just a minute," Retzo said. "This Dyn mission. Do you know the original source of this intelligence, Commander?"

Adan Viles seemed offended that the captain would ask, and the normally responsive Meluvian hesitated before answering. Retzo Sho took note of this, and listened keenly as he spoke. "The Dyn situation was reported by Commander Lang, sir. His Marines picked up on a lot of liz—I mean, Geralos activity in the Louine sector, and when he reported it to us we reached out to the Virulian Spy Network."

This was yet another bit of information they had kept him in the dark on, but Retzo kept himself calm, choosing to remain stoic as he listened. "The Jumpers?"

"Yes sir. The Virulian Jumpers."

"What did the Jumpers report once you reached out to them?" Retzo said.

"They put out feelers on that sector and learned of the Colony of Abarion, and the fact that the Geralos were eyeing their settlement as a possible feeding farm. From what I was told, they reached out to several ships, but no one was willing to commit to the rescue," Adan said.

"Do you blame them, now that you see what it has cost us?" Retzo said. He couldn't help but turn this into a teaching moment. Adan Viles was smart, and had done a lot of good for the *Rendron* in terms of strategy and recruitment, but he was idealistic, and Retzo saw this as a flaw.

Whenever things like this would happen, he wanted to make sure that Adan learned from it. He could become a captain of his own ship one day, and when he did, people would remember that he learned from Retzo Sho.

"I understand sir. I do. But we are fighting to save our people as much as we are fighting to kill the enemy. Leaving those settlers on the moon would only lead to more lizards, let alone a new headquarters for them right under the sleeping Louine."

"Right on both counts, Commander, but Nighthawks?" Retzo said.

"This was what was recommended from the manual, sir," Adan said. "Special missions require Special Forces. It's unfortunate that we're in this position, but everything was done to the letter."

Retzo thought about his words. He was right but it didn't make it easier. He wanted his Nighthawks home safely, and he wondered if he was being unnecessarily short with his CAG. It wasn't because he thought that the settlers weren't worth it; it was because he'd dropped the ball on protecting his men and women.

From the time he was granted the captaincy of the ship, Retzo had overseen every aspect of their military efforts. He was there for space fighter operations, strategic meetings, and graduations—not limited to the cadet academy. Besides that, he knew everything about his ship, and did all the things a good captain was supposed to do. But he was human, and humans needed sleep. There was no way he could be everywhere at all times, and so he hired men like Adan Viles to make key decisions that weren't on his level.

The Nighthawks was an experiment started by him and his Executive Officer, Lester Cruz. Together they had handpicked Lieutenant Cilas Mec to be the lead of the company, which comprised the top graduates from the grueling BLAST Training. Cruz had been killed—an unfortunate accident with his service weapon—and Retzo saw the Nighthawks as part of his legacy.

If it were up to him, he would direct and oversee everything to do with that unit, but the war was at a fever pitch, and his attention was needed on bigger things. He had left Adan to handle the Nighthawks direction, but asked to be involved on the initial planning. Now he was missing his chosen lieutenant, and it brought into question Adan's leadership.

"You can go, Commander," he said, forcing a smile. "Let me know if you get any pushback from the *Inginus*."

Adan bowed deeply, then exited quickly, and Retzo watched the door for a long time after it slid shut. He wanted to flip the table over, he was so upset. How had things gone so awry, and under his watch, at that? For everything he'd done, it took this one act of trust to get valuable assets killed.

All the years of meticulous micro-managing had led to the *Rendron's* operations being as well-oiled as you could get. The Marines both onboard and on the satellite interceptors were lauded as some of the most professional and effective in the entire Alliance.

Yet now as he sat staring down at the table, he felt helpless and betrayed. As a former pilot and BLAST graduate, he wanted to handle it himself. All he would need was an FTL drive and five seasoned Marines. He would jump out there, knock some heads, and bring back Cilas Mec.

Why couldn't Adan Viles do this? he thought. *There has to be something else going on.* He touched his comms and flipped the line to private. "Miss Ore," he said, when the operator answered. "I need all correspondence that you have on record for Commander Adan Viles."

"Crossing the line with him is only going to land you in hot water once we get on an Alliance ship," Helga said, as she sat watching Brise screw out a portion of the bulkhead and replace it with a section of tarp.

"I don't care. This unit's finished anyway, and I've been biting my tongue for over a year. Someone has to do something, and it won't be Lieutenant Protocol out there. It may end up being you, Ate, now that I think about it. If I get booted, they will silence me, and they will have gotten away with it," Brise said.

"See, this is exactly what I'm talking about. You aren't making any sense, Sol. Who will get away with what, and what proof do you have that it's true?"

"I don't have any proof yet, but I aim to get it as soon as we are back on the *Rendron*. I'm going to ask the Captain, right to his face, whether or not he knew that the lizards were out here. If he lies, I'll know it, Ate, and then no one will be able to stop me. They got our people killed, and I need to know why. Isn't that worth fighting for?" he said.

Helga decided to let him vent. Considering the two missions that he had been on, she couldn't blame him for being angry with their leaders. In the span of months this young recruit had lost friends without any explanation.

BLAST was a tough, grueling course that only a handful of already special spacers survived. It taught you perseverance above all things, regardless of the losses you suffer. What Brise was doing exemplified this, though it made him a very bad ESO.

He believed that there was a conspiracy against the Nighthawks, perpetuated by someone inside. This placed the three of them in danger, along with any future recruits that were coming. In his mind, he was out of options now that his lieutenant had silenced him.

Helga wondered about Cilas. Was he of the same mind? If the stories she'd heard from both of them were correct, he had to have some feelings towards what Brise was saying.

"What do you think?" he said suddenly, drifting back so she could examine his handiwork.

"I think that we'd better start hoping even more that a Geralos blast doesn't find our hull," she said. "That's a lot of metal, but do you think it will be enough?"

"It will," he said, flashing her a boyish smile. "You'll thank me when you're able to get a little privacy."

"Do you hear that?" Helga said, and Brise closed his eyes to listen.

"What am I supposed to hear?" he said.

"The knocking. It sounds like it's coming from the bulkhead to the right of us," Helga said.

Brise turned to his right, holding up a hand for her to stay quiet. For a second she wondered if he wouldn't hear it. Perhaps it was something inside of her head, and this would only end up with him questioning her sanity. She had been tortured, frozen, and gone through trauma, only to be stuck in a tube for months.

Maybe she was going crazy, and the knocking was only the beginning of her descent. When the noise came again, she stared at him, hoping, but then she saw him raise his eyebrows and open up his eyes. "Sounds like something's loose," he said. "What do you think? We may as well investigate since we're here."

Helga nodded quickly as she exhaled with relief. Her mind was still in place—for now. She helped him pry the panel off, and they attached a tether to his belt, just in case he went into the framing and became stuck behind a web of wires.

"Are you sure I shouldn't come with you?" she said, but Brise shook his head firmly.

"This is my jurisdiction, Ate. You would only be in the way. Plus, I'm guessing that it's just a loose wire, moving around whenever the air mobilizes it."

Helga nodded and watched as he pulled himself into the small hole, kicking as if he was swimming against the zero-gravity. When he was all the way through, she tied the end of his tether to the ladder, then floated over, inverted herself, and peered into it to see where he was.

The space was black, and it was a wonder that he could see, but she could make out his white spacesuit, deep inside the engine. Her comms crackled, and then she could hear him breathing. "We have a problem," he said, as soon as he could catch his breath. "There appears to be some sort of tracker that was installed near the fusion drive."

"A tracker? But why?" Helga said, her mind racing through the various possibilities.

"I don't know, but we're cloaked, and I think that's why we haven't been discovered," he said. "I'm coming back out. We need to show it to the lieutenant. This is Louine tech, Ate. My hands are literally shaking."

17

Cilas Mec rotated the strange device over and over in his hands, working through the reasons why their Louine rescuers would track them.

There was the positive spin, which was that they needed to know where they were in case the *Rendron* never came. When their resources dwindled, they would come back, pull them in, and restock them. It would be a noble gesture, and they could even allow them to spend some more time on the ship, to get a proper shower and a good night's sleep.

Amatu was a brilliant man—he had learned as much talking to him on the very day of their rescue—and he would understand that they needed rescuing after such a long time stuck out in space together. But what was in it for the Louine rebel? The Nighthawks had nothing to give as payment for their rescue. Why would he want to give them more after losing an escape ship, medical resources, and rations?

The negative and yet pragmatic spin, however, was that Amatu and his ship, *The San*, were not what they appeared to be. They said that they were a paramilitary unit, formed for the sole reason of killing Geralos, despite being part of a neutral planet. Due to this, their attacks had to be top secret, with no chance of discovery.

This whole story about being rebels, hiding out from both the Louine government and the lizards ... it was a romantic fallacy, and Cilas had always known. They were too well-supplied for it to be true.

So what was *The San*? Louine Special Forces? That wouldn't make sense, considering the things he saw onboard. Their fighters were good, but not Special Forces good. They fought like seasoned warriors, but their methods were extremely sloppy.

"Pirates," he whispered, as the word came to his mind. They were pirates who did the rescue for some sort of monetary gain. They had rescued them and healed them, holding them as they brokered another deal. Then when the deal was done, they prepped a pod with a tracker, leaving them to drift until the buyer came to pick them up.

So, who was the buyer? That was the million-credit question, and now as he played with the device, he thought about all the different factions in the war. They were Nighthawk Special Forces personnel, valuable enough for ransom. But outside of the Alliance and the Geralos lizards, who would risk bartering with Retzo Sho?

He looked down at where Helga and Brise stood, waiting for his decision. "Ate," he said, "how are we looking on fuel?"

"Our stores are good for about four Vestalian months," she said. "If we have to run, though, it will deplete us quickly. What are you thinking, Lieutenant?"

"I'm thinking of building a floater and attaching this to it. If whoever was looking for us is blind to Brise's cloak, then we could keep it on and watch when they pick up the tracker. This way we can know who our enemy is. Right now, I don't know what to think. What I do know is that someone is coming, and since this was hidden, I know that it isn't someone friendly."

"If it's the lizards you may as well airlock me now," Brise said. "There is no way I'm going back on ice for those things."

"You won't," Cilas said. "None of us will, I promise you. But time is running out for us, Sol. Can you build a floater for the tracker?"

"We just pulled off a pile of metal from the bulkhead. We can use it to make something that can get picked up on radar," Brise said. "I'll build us a buoy, but in order for it to work, I'm going to need one of the rocket packs from the EVA suits."

"No way," Helga said. "We only have three and—"

"Use it," Cilas said. "If there comes a time when we need to escape, and we're short a suit, we'll figure it out then. But for now we need that floater."

He tossed the tracker to Brise, who floated up to catch it, then went back into the locker room to begin working on the floater. Helga stood watching Cilas, but he couldn't read what was on her face. Then she too went into the locker room and sealed the door behind her.

It had been too long since he sent the signal to the *Rendron* from *The San*. Amatu had let him do it, and Cilas saw the message deploy. *Why would he allow such a thing?* he thought. *Hmm, he probably knew that he would be long gone before our rescue. It would be bad news for the buyer, but Amatu, as a pirate, wouldn't care. It would only cover the fact that he had sold us out.* Cilas had to admit that it was brilliant.

But the *Rendron* hadn't come, and he was beginning to worry. Was the ship in trouble, or had something happened to the message? Cilas went over the protocol to see who could have dropped the ball. The comms officer was Genevieve Aria, and though they had history, they remained friends. She would have eagerly passed it on to the CAG, Adan Viles.

Cilas had never liked the man, not since graduating from the academy. Viles was the son of rich settlers that had property on Traxis, and Cilas believed that he bought his commission. Outside of talent like Helga Ate, Adan Cruser, and Kyden Ahmad, the space power of the *Rendron* was the weakest in the Alliance.

The infiltrator wings were developed because of this weakness, housing an elite group of pilots, each independent of Viles' blundering. The Marines were exemplary only because their commander wasn't Viles, but it was one of those things that only officers at his level had noticed.

Now that he thought about it, Cilas began to wonder. If Viles had somehow forgotten to send them help—he closed his eyes and bit his fist. "Thype me," he whispered. "Thyping Viles."

He didn't have a personal grudge against the man, and had only ever done what he was ordered to do. If Viles meant to keep them out here alone, it would have little to do with how he felt about them. So it made no sense to speculate on his actions. The CAG would have sent the message up to Retzo Sho.

Would the captain leave them stranded? Brise Sol seemed to think that he would. But Cilas had broken bread with his leader on many occasions. Sho was beyond proud of the work that they did. This meant that the message had to have been intercepted or lost.

"I need to send another SOS," he said, looking around at the equipment. "Can't do it from here, though; there's no FTL communication."

He sighed and ran his hand through his thick crop of black hair, annoyed at how much it had grown. He liked to keep it high and tight, but now it just looked like a mess. There were no shears on the ship, and nothing remotely close to a pair of scissors.

Weapons, he thought suddenly, remembering the predicament that they were in. If they got boarded by whomever was tracking them, they would need something with which to fight.

The auto rifles and starguns they had brought with them to Dyn were still in that crater along with the bodies of his men. *Maybe I should have listened to Ate*, he thought, regretting their situation. *We would be down on the surface, with shelter, weapons, and supplies. Plus we'd have Cage and the guys to take back to the Rendron for a burial.*

He marveled at how smart the young recruit had been, and he chided himself for being so trusting of Amatu. *Maybe it isn't too late*, he thought. *We could probably still make it down to the surface.* But they had no armor, and the ship had no weapons. One direct hit and they would disintegrate.

I need to get us repositioned, he thought. The feeling of helplessness had run its course. *Weapons, what can we do about weapons?* With the Geralos parked above Dyn, going back to the moon was impossible. The Louines had only given them clothes, and not even the ship had a cannon to defend itself with.

He looked down at his hands. They were calloused and strong, despite the malnourished period he'd spent with the Geralos. On board the *Rendron*, they had all been trained for combat in any situation. If a time were to come when he needed his fists, he was beyond confident that he would be fine. But against projectile weapons and Geralos swords, those fists were as useful as fighting fire with paper.

He needed a plan, and he needed it fast, so he strapped himself in to concentrate.

✳

It took an entire week of focused work for Brise to complete the decoy buoy. Cilas expected him to build something reminiscent of a tiny ship, but what he produced was crude and ugly.

It was boxy and lacked any specific shape, but regardless of what he and Helga thought, the engineer was proud of his creation. He assured them that it would do the job, and that the thrown together aesthetic was part of it.

"The trick is to fool their radar that old *Deborah* here has a lot more mass than she does," he said.

"*Deborah?*" Cilas said, unable to get past the fact that he had named it.

"Yeah, I had to give her a name. *Deborah Score*, the human boomer, who gave her life to liberate Casan. The idea was mine, but the name came from Ate. Says *Deborah's* face is on the coins in the capital of her mother's old country. Thought it would be an honor to name our little ship after her."

Cilas nodded. "It's an excellent choice. Continue telling me your plans."

"When she's out in the vacuum, the radio inside of her will pulse," Helga said. "On a radar the blip will look big – just like our ship would, and they will only know the truth when they try to approach. By then, we will be scanning their vessel to know who it is that is coming for us. I will keep us out of range, and with the ship cloaked, there's a good chance they will ignore us. Once we learn who it is that came after the tracker, I will fly us out farther where we cannot be picked up."

"Good job, you two," Cilas said, but he was feeling worried for their fate. Once Helga flew them out further, they would lose Dyn's gravity. They would drift out into deep space, where no one would be able to find them. That would be the end of their eventful journey, and eventually their lives.

"An adjustment to the plan, Nighthawks," he said. "We're running low on everything. Whatever that vessel is that comes for us is bound to have things that we need to get home. If it's as small as *The San* was, I say we board it and take it over."

Brise and Helga exchanged looks as if Cilas had lost his mind, but he kept his composure as they processed it. "That could be suicide," Brise said.

"I'm well aware of it, Sol. But what are our options, considering the state of this ship? If Ate takes us out of range, we will be adrift and far from the beacon we sent. Our rescue could come and not locate us. Then we'd really be trapped in here forever. At least with attacking them we give ourselves a chance. Their ship could have an FTL communicator, and we could contact the *Rendron* again. Better yet, it will have an FTL drive, and we could plot a course and go home. What do you say, Nighthawks, does it still sound crazy?"

"It does, but it's what we were trained to do," Helga said. "Cloaked I can get us close, and we could use our EVA suits to slip through the shields. With a torch we can crack a bay window, and slip in before the blast doors, shut us out. It will be risky, but it's possible. I just don't like that we're going in blind."

"What if it's a warship with hundreds of troops?" Brise said.

"Then we stick with Plan A, and get the heck out of this sector," Cilas said. "My plan would only be valid if it's a ship of thirty or less. We are Nighthawks; we can take those odds. But a warship is too much, even for us."

"Do we have weapons?" Helga said.

"We have blowtorches, knives, and our fists. Once we're on board we'll need to make quick decisions, but as a small unit it will be easy. We take one out, and relieve him of his weapons, then a second and a third will give us all the weapons we need. Once we have that, we can lock down compartment after compartment. We move to the bridge and relieve the captain of his command. After the mission is complete, we'll officially have a ship. We can call in to the *Rendron* and get ourselves rescued."

"Sounds like a plan, Lt," Brise said, surprisingly, but it was good to see the old fire reflected in his eyes.

Once they finished talking things over, he placed the tracker inside of *Deborah*, then released it into the center of their space where it floated to the bulkhead and stopped.

Helga went over to her station and strapped herself in, then picked up her tablet and began working at something. Brise mumbled something to her, and she grunted in approval. Cilas watched them do this without bothering to ask.

When *Deborah* began to fly around the compartment, he quickly understood. Brise had built a program for Helga to control the vessel. He had built one for himself, too, so that they both had access, but for now it was Helga that had control of it.

She flew it down into the locker room, and Brise followed behind. On his command, Cilas did his part, with opening and closing the airlocks. When *Deborah Score* was gone, Helga pinned her tablet to the side of the giant navigation monitor, and flew *Deborah* away from them, until it was barely visible on their radar.

"Now we just have to wait to see who comes in to collect," she said. "I'm turning us around, with preparations for a quick exit. This is exciting and scary, I cannot lie, but it feels good to make some sort of progress."

"I wish I shared your thoughts, Ate, but I'm still shaken up," Cilas said. "There's a chance that our Louine friends were not who they claimed to be. All I know is that captivity is not an option for me—not anymore—and whoever comes for that tracker is in for a world of hurt."

"We're right there with you, Lieutenant," Helga said. She looked at Brise, who nodded his head. "I hope that they're a small team of losers so that we can board them and take their ship. I want to be inside a real cockpit again, with some sort of control over my life."

"Damn right, Ate. I am right there with you," Cilas said. "But I just hope it isn't what I think it is."

"And what would that be?" Brise said, raising an eyebrow.

"Vestalian pirates," Cilas said. "The lowest form of life."

18

Days passed as Helga watched the throbbing blip of the *Deborah Score*. The gravity of Dyn had already taken it on as one of its own, adding it to the loose debris that orbited the moon.

At first she thought the Geralos would spot it, and either take it inside their ship to investigate or blast it to clear up their radar. But nothing happened as it continued its journey, and she began to wonder if Cilas had been wrong.

The bickering between him and Brise had ceased, and this at least was a positive. They both kept to themselves, prepping for what was to come, and when they weren't doing that, they were talking to her.

Nobody used the EVA suits while they waited, and Helga appreciated this more than they would ever know. The time it took to reel someone in was over fifteen minutes. If they were discovered and had to go, that delay would be the end of them.

As she made to push herself away from the monitor, she saw a flash of light and a brand new warship appeared. This new ship she recognized, and her lips began to quiver before she could manage to get the words out.

"Ci-Ci-Cilas, I mean, Lieutenant – you are going to want to see this," she said.

Cilas and Brise floated over from their respective corners to see what had gotten her so excited. Brise reacted first, his laughter sounding as if he bordered on insanity. Cilas, ever the stoic, pumped his fist and patted Helga on her shoulder. "Faith, Ate, I told you to have faith. Now we get to watch that bird make mincemeat of those lizards."

The warship, *Inginus*—one of the *Rendron's* two deadly infiltrators—loomed before them like a titan: angry, beautiful, and ready to vanquish its enemy. It was already firing on the smaller Geralos ships, tearing one in half and crippling one of the others.

For Helga, it was a thing of beauty watching this warship fight. Where the *Rendron* was parked in deep space, they remained hidden from the Geralos. Due to this, things stayed quiet, and fights occurred away from the gigantic battleship.

Helga had only experienced an attack once, but she'd been so young that all she remembered were the flashing lights and noise. She had forgotten that the *Rendron* was built for war, and witnessing one of its smaller ships made her respect its strength.

The Geralos ships were trying to fight back, but the gunners on the *Inginus* were accurate and deadly. They swapped blasts for a while—with the Geralos feeling the bulk of it—then the *Inginus* launched a warhead that set the dark space on fire.

"Ate!" Cilas shouted behind her, and gestured towards the larger monitor. A new ship had appeared and was moving to intercept *Deborah*. With the *Inginus* distracted with the Geralos, this predator sought to capture its prey right underneath their noses.

Cilas and Brise both came over for a closer look, and the three of them tried to decipher the make and model of this new ship. From what Helga could see, it was a repurposed dropship, large enough to hold up to forty-five spacers. But if the interior was anything like the hull that they witnessed, it would be a wonder if it sustained any life.

"I'm getting chills," Helga said, watching it as it loomed, surprised that it hadn't noticed that their decoy was just a toy.

"Lieutenant, do you see that?" Brise said, pointing at the ship.

"Good eyes," Cilas said, touching the panel and zooming in on a porthole near the rear. It sat apart from the rest, which meant that there was a chance that it was an unused compartment. "That will be our entry point. This is the moment we've all been waiting for," he said. "There are two EVA suits, and I am occupying one of them. As commanding officer and the man with the communication codes, I don't get a choice in the matter.

"Now, the second EVA suit will need to be either one of you—who gets the honor, I don't care. But the person who stays will need to be ready for our contact. We're going to take that ship and evaluate the threat. If we deem it to be hostile, we will eliminate its occupants."

"What happens to the escape ship?" Helga said, looking at Brise.

"Once we have the controls we will open a channel and then guide whomever into its dock. Once we're reunited we will hail the *Inginus*—"

"That's if it's still space-worthy after what I'm seeing there," Brise said. "Those lizards are giving it one hell of a go, but *Inginus* doesn't want to back down."

"It's an infiltrator, Sol, it's fought battleships and survived. What you're seeing is Commander Lang merely playing with his food. The lizards have already lost, trust me. The *Inginus* lives on lizard meat. Now, the two of you decide, and make it fast. Who stays and who comes with me?"

"Brise is the senior, so I should stay," Helga said. "Although I want nothing more than to get off this ship. When you get things under control, I will fly her onboard, and then I'll take a good look at those controls."

She saw doubt in Brise's eyes and wondered if he wanted to stay. It made her feel bad for opening her mouth. If the man was scared, he would never admit it to them, and now that she'd volunteered, he was forced to go along. *Thype me*, she thought, it was as if she could never get anything right.

"Sorry, Sol, I just realized what I did. How about we flip for it? Would you be okay with that?" she said.

"I'm good with whatever, Ate, but we can flip for it, sure," he said. "Lieutenant, please guess a number between one and thirty. The person who gets the closest will accompany you on the ship."

"Alright, but make it snappy," Cilas said. "That floating piece of junk is moving slow, but we don't know how long before it picks up on our trap. A part of me thinks they have been hailed by *Inginus*, and are now forced to produce identification stating that they're friendly. Failure to do so will turn the infiltrator on them, so again I have to remind you two to hurry it the hell up."

"My number is 21," said Helga, quickly, citing her favorite number.

"I'll say 19," Brise said, and then looked to Cilas for confirmation.

"The number was 30, so you're it, Ate," Cilas said. "Sol, are you comfortable flying this thing?"

"I can practically build it, Lieutenant, of course I'm comfortable. I may not be able to have it do tricks, but I can park the damned thing."

They hustled to the locker room to put on their EVA suits, and Cilas handed Helga a knife. "Don't let them take you alive," he said, and when she saw his hard brown eyes, she saw a deep concern reflected there.

It was hard to miss it, and she struggled to understand what it was. Cilas never spoke of his past, but it was obvious that he had an interesting history. People like the lieutenant always came with a special history—perseverance through tragedy, an unqualified parent, or a sibling who needed him to play the role.

Maybe that was it. He had a sister, and Helga reminded him of her somehow. This was what she accepted with the look that he gave her, because she dared not hope that he was attracted to her.

She took the knife and slipped it under her glove. "I'll bury it into one of them and then myself if I have to," she said. They were all on the same page, and it was fully understood. She would gladly face death over captivity.

When they were both fully dressed in their EVA suits, Cilas took the lead and opened up the first of the three airlocks. The comms connected them to Brise, who opened the far doors on command. But when they reached the final airlock, Cilas stopped and turned to face her.

She heard the comms click to private and he grabbed the airlock's wheel, steadied himself, and then reached out and took her hand. "Helga," he said suddenly, startling her with the informal way that he addressed her. "What we're about to do will probably get us killed. I am only having us do this because I believe that we can win. But belief isn't reality, and the odds are stacked against us. That being said, I just want you to know that I'm glad that I'll be doing it with you. From BLAST until now you've been a real five percenter, and I'm more than proud to call you a Nighthawk."

"Thanks Cilas, I love you too," she said, letting her smile shine despite the situation. He reacted the way she expected: confused, but too awkward to call her bluff. It was one of those jokes where she would accept either reaction, but since he merely froze, she laughed it off.

"Always with the jokes," he said, and then released her hand. He switched over the comms and then commanded Brise to release the final door. When they heard the click, he snapped a tether to her belt, then attached the other end to his. He then looped the rest around his arm and pulled it up and over his shoulder.

In a manner of seconds they were out in the black of space, with nothing but their packs to keep them from floating off. The EVAs had small rockets to help in emergency situations, but using them for flight was never a good idea.

The pull of the numerous ships in the area, along with the gravity from the moon, made it much of a challenge for the tiny packs to handle. But Cilas and Helga had been through BLAST, which had prepared them for this method of boarding a spacecraft. It was all about the shields, and exploiting the magnetic pull, so they angled their trajectory to reach the pirate ship.

Cilas flew at full throttle towards the rusty hull, and Helga stayed on his heels as close as she could. Taking a chance to glance back at their ship, she saw how well the cloak had been working. There was distortion around its shape, but at a glance you couldn't see it, though she knew that they would still register as a tiny blip on the radar.

They were at the shields now, and her helmet's alarms began to scream. They had to pass through it slowly, fooling the generator that they were tiny pieces of debris, or else it would pulse and send them flying off into oblivion.

Cilas motioned to the tether. "Unclip your end," he said through comms. Helga complied immediately, without understanding why he'd want to detach. Without the tether, she kept up as best she could, using their rockets to stay in position.

Suddenly Cilas was nudging himself inside the shields, passing the translucent barrier to reach the hull. Seeing him do this, Helga tried the same maneuver, but she must have moved too quickly since the shield rejected her.

She was pushed away violently, forcing her to max the rockets in order to slow down. It was a brief moment of panic but she focused on not going into a wicked spin. Once that occurred it would be the end for her, so she remembered her training and got herself under control. Once she was good, she flew back towards the ship, but there was now a huge boulder lodged inside her throat.

Thype me, she thought. *I came in too fast like an idiot.* She could barely breathe from the panic that invaded her body, but she focused on her job and found a way to push it down. On the second approach, she saw on the HUD that her fuel was all but depleted. *One last shot*, she thought, seeing Cilas climbing along the hull. *If I miss again, it will be death. A long, lonely, drifting death.*

Biting down hard and slowing her breathing, she flew near the shields and pulsed her rockets. Relaxing a bit, she closed her eyes, believed in herself, and nudged inside. A part of her expected to be rejected again, her luck run short and demise inevitable.

Don't panic, she thought, and then something grabbed her arm. She opened her eyes and saw the large gloved hand of Cilas from within the shield.

He had attached the tether to the ship and was now using it as an anchor. He pulled her in slowly and she grabbed the tether, still worried that rejection was inevitable. Within a few minutes she was next to him, and he put his arm around her waist.

They stood breathing heavily against the hull, and she shifted her position to fully embrace him. If they didn't have helmets she would have kissed him then and there. She no longer cared, now that she had been so close to death. She saw him gesture upwards, then freed the rest of the tether from his waist. Now he hooked that to her belt so that they were both anchored to the ship.

When he motioned to his back, Helga remembered the attachments for their magnetic boots. She reached inside his pack and pulled them out, and he reached into hers and did the same.

Though her heart was still beating thunderously in her ears, Helga knew that the time for hesitation was long gone. Now it was move or die, and Cilas would be relying on her to do more than watch his back. They clumsily aided each other in attaching the magnetic soles. When they both had them on, they activated the grips and started the walk towards their target.

They found the small porthole after a few minutes of searching, and Cilas knelt down to peer inside. He held this position for what seemed like an eternity, then looked up at her and gave her the thumbs up.

Pulling out torches, they went to work on the glass, melting away screws to loosen the exterior aesthetic. This work took a long time, and Helga worried that they would be discovered. The ship should recognize the intrusion and alert it to the bridge. Though with the *Inginus* pressing them for identification, she hoped that their pilot would be distracted.

The frame came off, and then the first layer of glass, revealing the reinforced crystal pane that would be the real challenge to dislodge. Cilas unhooked the tether from their waists, and then attached the frame to one end. He welded the other to the grill of the crystal pane, working as if he had done this before.

"Give it some room," he said, and Helga backed away. After a count of three, he heaved the frame out past the shield, leaving the tether in its wake. When the tether was taut, he reeled it back in, and that was when Helga realized his plan.

As soon as the metal frame came in contact with the outer shield, it rejected it violently and threw it out into space. Cilas barely got out of the way as the inertia yanked the crystal pane free, leaving a hole inside the hull where the porthole had once been.

Two figures flew out, ejected violently into the vacuum of space, and Helga stared at Cilas with horror. She wondered if he'd known that they were inside. She had been under the impression that it was empty!

"Now it's clear," he said with a smile. "We need to get in and ditch these suits, immediately. Security protocol will seal the doors, giving us about ten minutes to prep for combat."

"I know the drill," she said, still stunned by the death of those two unfortunate souls.

Cilas gripped an edge and then pulled himself inside, powering down his magnetic boots. Helga did the same, but her EVA was too bulky. She was struggling to be fast, but got stuck halfway inside the hole. Every ship had the means to repair itself, and portholes had metal panels to seal the glass.

She feared that she would be in the way once the processes began, but she got inside through sheer force of will and scrambled away from the hole. Once inside, she saw that they were in one of the crew quarters, with rows of bunks lined up on the wall.

Cilas was already out of his EVA suit, and holding on to what appeared to be a table. Helga didn't know how he'd done it—removing that bulky suit so fast—but she understood the need for speed at this point. An alarm was going off, and as expected, a section of the hull slid shut, covering the porthole. The alarms went silent when the vacuum sealed, but she could hear men on the other side of the door.

"Ten minutes," Cilas had said, and they had already expended several. Helga threw off the helmet and struggled out of the bulky material, making sure to grab her knife and wrist comms from the pack. This ship had oxygen to breathe, and an atmosphere with gravity, allowing them to move around freely.

This is definitely Alliance, she thought. *No, human, but not one of ours. This is a militia, possibly pirate, in league with Amatu.*

She felt a rage coming on as she realized that they had been sold. The Louines had helped but at the price of selling them off to human gangsters. When she saw Cilas's face, she recognized the same rage reflected in it. She joined him by the door with her knife raised, staying on his hip the way she was trained.

"Less than a minute," he whispered, and she nodded, ready for action. Whoever was coming in would get the biggest surprise of their life.

19

If one was to draft up a book on Cilas Mec's life, each chapter would begin with a situation just like this: Desperate measures, no advantage, and waiting by a door for an unknown enemy. Somehow, the lieutenant and former Second Class Cadet always made it through, and much of it had to do with a natural instinct for survival.

"If you want to be a thinker, you stay on the bridge," an old instructor once told him. "In the field your brain is a liability. Shut it off and rely on your instinct and training. This is why we have you out here freezing and dying. You must learn to trust your team, suffocate your weaknesses, and defeat the enemy."

These words—or some variation of them—were drilled into recruits during the grueling days of BLAST. It was this training that kept Cilas calm as he waited. The ticking numbers of an invisible clock counting down inside his head.

There was a hiss, and the sound of metal against metal as the door turned counter-clockwise and swung in towards him and Helga. He held his breath for just a moment, needing to confirm the target before unleashing his tools.

A slender form slipped in wearing an EVA suit, and toting a flobot loaded with a welder and other tools. Helga was on her before he could assess who she was, and that was when he was forced into action. Behind the first woman—who was now on the ground—were two armed men, bearded and grizzled.

Cilas hopped over his partner and put a shoulder into the first while slamming his knife into the thigh of the second. The space beyond the door was a long passageway, but Cilas recognized that they would have sealed the next door in case of a loss of atmosphere. This meant that their screams would not bring reinforcements, so he let his knife sing in a splendid display of stabbing.

By the time he was done the place looked like a slaughterhouse, with blood smeared on the bulkhead, deck, and his person. He turned to check on Helga, and was surprised to find that she had the first woman unconscious on the floor.

This made him happy, since they needed answers, and the Ensign had enough foresight to keep her victim alive. Besides having a hostage, they now had weapons. Cilas relieved the corpses of their pistols and tossed one over to Helga.

"Point of no return," he said, breathing heavily. "I hope that we're right about them being pirates."

"We were right," Helga said, motioning him over to look at the woman. Cilas walked over and knelt next to the unconscious body. Helga had shredded the EVA with her knife so he could easily remove the topmost portion.

She was young and obviously Vestalian, with light brown skin, freckles on her shoulders, and long, auburn hair. He brushed her hair to the side to reveal her neck, and there at the nape was a slave's tattoo.

"How did you know not to kill this woman?" Cilas said.

"When I jumped her, the eyes told me that something was wrong," Helga said. "I still hurt her pretty badly, but it couldn't be avoided. Those EVAs are pretty thick, and there were three of them. You know how it is, Lieutenant ... I just reacted."

Cilas wondered about Helga's answer. It wasn't that he doubted she could read someone's intentions, but as a person new to killing, he wondered if she was being honest. There had been plenty of situations in the past when a recruit would freeze on a kill.

Most of the time—due to the war—it was a Geralos commando that was the target. From their days as cadets they were taught to hate the lizards, so when it came time to act, most were able to do it.

Cilas had known too many recruits who had lost their lives due to hesitating. Geralos looked different from humans in every way, and they were violently aggressive. Convincing an ESO to kill one for the first time was a lot easier than asking them to take a human's life. Helga had killed on the moon of Dyn, but that was a Geralos running away from her.

He looked into her eyes to see if she was lying, but what he saw looking back was something indecipherable. Was it anger, fear, or something new? The only thing he was sure of was that it was different—she was different. Here in front of him was a woman he no longer recognized. She seemed older, tired, and hard.

"You and that knife, Lieutenant," she said, her eyes now wide with wonder. "I don't want to ever be on the business side of that thing."

Same humor, Cilas thought, then smiled and got to his feet. "She's your responsibility now, Ate. We need to move. I think that door on the far end there is going to be locked. Now, this is the crew's quarters, so there are bound to be stragglers once we get past it. This woman is the only hostage we can afford to take."

"I got it, Lieutenant. I'll kill anything that moves," Helga said. He could tell from the look on her face that she wasn't thrilled with the plan. "Wait," she said. "I have an idea. Maybe we don't have to keep moving blindly through the ship. If we could get her to talk, she could probably help us."

"Or she could trigger an alarm and get us swarmed within the hour," Cilas said.

"No disrespect, Lieutenant, but I disagree" Helga said. "If her tattoo tells us anything, she'll be happy we came onboard."

Cilas weighed the odds and decided to take a chance on her idea. The faster they were able to take the ship, the greater their chances of survival. A long battle would have them winded and prone to making mistakes, and not knowing the layout of the ship made that almost guaranteed. Then there was Brise Sol, cloaked and by himself. He would be found and eliminated if they did not succeed.

"Okay, wake her up," he said, "But make it fast. Whoever is captain will be waiting to hear a report on the breach. When these three don't answer their comms, they will send spacers to investigate. Then we will be forced to do what we have to do."

Helga woke the woman up, then covered her mouth to stifle the scream before it could occur. She mounted her in such a way that all Cilas could see was her back, and from the way the woman was kicking her legs, he made to step in and help.

"Ate?" he started, but she held her forefinger up to tell him to wait. Cilas started to object—now he knew what the look was that she had on her face.

Obviously Helga had lost her mind and was torturing this woman unnecessarily. This too was something that Cilas had seen before. When violence happened at the scale that they'd seen, some recruits were prone to become the very thing they feared.

Cilas started forward, but Helga shifted her weight, and now he could see the woman's face as she allowed her to sit up. He saw her expression change from fear to surprise, and then she did the strangest thing and hugged Helga Ate.

She was definitely Vestalian but spoke an unknown language that Helga seemed to understand. As she spoke, she kept looking back at him, her eyes like a frightened child's. Helga looked back at him once, then spoke something soft and harmonic. This caused the woman to start crying, and then they hugged again.

"Lieutenant," Helga said after a time, "This is Ina Reysor, a Meluvian pilot, formerly of the *Aqnaqak*."

"Meluvian?" Cilas said, confused by the woman's human features. Her freckles were plentiful, like a Meluvian's, but it didn't explain her dark complexion. *Is there a region of Meluvia with people like this*, he wondered. *If there is, I'm definitely going to have to take my shore leave there.*

Helga grunted. "Well, I mean she's obviously human, but she's a Meluvian citizen that was kidnapped and enslaved by these pirates."

"So they are pirates," Cilas said, feeling the weight fall from his shoulders. He had done what he had to do in killing the two men, but he wanted to be sure they weren't Alliance. They had come aboard the ship, knowing that it was hostile, but there was always the chance that they were wrong.

"It gets deeper," Helga continued. "They have clearance codes which gives them access to Alliance space. They have others like her, spacers, stamped and reclaimed as slaves. She said that they were given jobs around the ship. Hers is to handle various repairs."

"How many of them are actually on this ship?" Cilas said. "Pirates, I mean, not slaves."

"She doesn't know, but she estimates about thirty or so," Helga said.

"She doesn't speak basic?"

"She does," Helga said, "but for some reason, she chooses not to use it. She speaks a few languages from Meluvia, and that's what we've been communicating in."

"So she understands me then. Good," Cilas said. "She will help us take the ship, but I will need to know who among the captives is trustworthy. A ship run by slaves, jumping around Alliance space unchecked – it defies belief, do you know what I mean? If most of them are former spacers like this one, there should have been a mutiny by now."

"We tried to mutiny once before and eleven of us lost our lives," the woman said. "They have the weapons, and we have our marks." She brushed her hair to the side to show her slave's tattoo. "There is something inside of us, something they can use. If we are defiant, or deemed worthless, they can kill us, just like this!" She snapped her finger for emphasis, and the sound echoed throughout the passageway.

"What's with the language games?" Cilas said.

"I do it to prevent them from making small talk with me," she said. "I don't have to tell you what we deal with here, but each of us deals with it in our own way. If I don't talk to them, I don't have to understand them. They are animals—"

"Got it, I got it," Cilas said, not wanting to know more. "You were on the *Aqnaqak*. How long ago was that? Who was your captain, and what was your rank?"

"I don't know times or dates. They don't tell us anything. But my captain was Tara Cor, and I was an Ensign. Ensign Reysor," she said, smiling.

"Good to meet you, Ensign Reysor. I am Lieutenant Cilas Mec, and if you're willing to help us take this ship, we'll have you back with your *Aqnaqak* family. I'm going to need you to hang back and listen to Ensign Ate. If we play this wrong it can go south fast, and we all will be dead or back in shackles."

Ina nodded but then she knitted her brow and let out a scream before covering her mouth. Cilas spun and dropped to a knee, firing off a round that struck the bulkhead near the door. It ricocheted into the chest of a pirate, who had come in while they were talking.

Helga fired her own pistol and dropped the second pirate behind the one Cilas shot. It happened so fast that he stood frozen, waiting to see if more would emerge. But the door was open and they could see through it to the compartment beyond. They were alone again, with the exception of the two corpses.

Cilas stared at his handgun. "Freaking kinetic rounds? That first shot went wide, but thank the planets that the ammo wasn't frangible. Did you see what happened? They use kinetic rounds. If we're not careful, we can actually put a hole through the hull."

"Yeah, bullets that ricochet means that we cannot afford a shootout," Helga said.

"And that was the reinforcements. We're officially out of time," Cilas said. "Get her up and let's get moving, and be careful with your aim. Use your knife when you can. It's move or die from here on out."

He led them through the next compartment, checking the areas below the bunks. The ship was dark, darker than he was accustomed to, but this was the living area. A small ship that had little access to power reserves would conserve energy by moving it around. The crew slept here, so in the living hours they would shunt the power to the other areas.

They crept past a bay window with a breathtaking view of the *Inginus* locked in combat with the Geralos ships. Cilas spared a glance back to see how Ina was doing, and in her eyes he saw longing and hope. Helga nudged past him, ignoring the window, then got to the door and posted up.

He saw her lean over and place her ear against it, then close her eyes to see what she could hear. Cilas stepped up to the other side and listened for himself, but he could hear nothing except the humming sounds of an oxygen generator.

When they opened the door, they expected a fight, but all they found was a ladderwell leading down. Cilas motioned them away from it, sealing it anew. He then took them back to the second door and knelt behind a bunk. "There's a ladder leading down," he said, looking at Ina. "Is this the topmost deck?"

"Yes, the bridge is actually two decks down," Ina said. "The next deck is where they briefed me about fixing the porthole. It is the main deck for them, and it will be covered with armed men."

Cilas looked at Helga. "The bridge is on the bottom floor? That's mighty odd," he said. "We have sleep quarters up here, and the next one is the main deck. Probably where the galley, chow hall, and entertainment is housed. Below that is, what? Control room, bridge, and captain's quarters? Whose ship is this? The layout baffles my understanding."

Helga shrugged, and Ina's face was blank; it was hard to read what was going through her mind. Cilas tried to imagine himself in her shoes, using the days on Dyn as a comparison for how she felt.

When those Louines had come in, he didn't question their motives. They weren't Geralos and that was good enough for him. Here they were, Alliance, and Helga would have told her the quick version of their story. Would she trust them to be who they claimed to be, and did she think that they could pull it off?

Any hesitation would get him and Helga killed, or worse; she could turn on them and lead them to her captors. These things happened, and he couldn't read her mind to know if she was an enemy playing possum. "Ina," he said. "What can we expect, now that we've killed the reinforcements?"

"They all have vitality Nanos that report their location and health back to the central CPU. The captain knows they're dead, and is wondering if it is me, since I am the only one registering alive in the two parties that he's sent up here. To be honest, Lieutenant Cilas, I am not understanding why they haven't killed me by now."

"You say they have it inside your body. Some sort of chip to kill you when they want. Is there a way to cut it out?" Helga said, and to Cilas's surprise Ina nodded her head.

"It would need to be fast, or they'll know what you're doing," she said. "It's below the skin where they place our tattoos. They told us that removing it would kill us instantly. But I've seen someone do it, I can show you how. It is painful, but what is pain? I can—"

"I'll leave you two to it," Cilas said. "I'm going to secure that ladder. When you have it out, Ate, I'll be below deck waiting."

He got up from the floor, walked back to the door, and placed his ear against it to listen again. After a minute, he eased it open, stepped through, and closed it behind him. The ladder led down into darkness, and he descended it slowly, keeping the pistol high and ready.

There was a door at the base, but no pressure lock like the ones before. He listened for a few minutes, then pulled down the handle, easing it open to take a peek inside. His heart stopped cold as someone walked by, barely missing the fact that the door had opened.

It was a big muscular spacer who reminded him of Cage Hem, but the man was so intent on his destination that he didn't turn around. Cilas watched him for a second, then looked the other way. There was another armed man—not quite as big—walking in the opposite direction.

One of these men was bound to turn around, so Cilas slipped in quickly and stalked after Cage's twin. On quiet soles, he catwalked behind the man. When they walked past a cracked door, Cilas stopped and slipped inside. If luck was with him when he descended the ladder, he had exhausted it in the passageway.

This new compartment was the galley, and it was filled with pirates who regarded him curiously. The first man who saw him swung a knife towards his abdomen, but Cilas was ready, and spun into his attacker to avoid the knife. When he was belly to belly with the man, he trapped his knife hand with his arm.

Using his free hand—which held his pistol—Cilas reached over the man's shoulder and shot another in the face. He finished breaking the arm that he had trapped, which caused the man to drop the knife. When he started screaming, Cilas dropped to a knee, using his body as a shield.

Two more shots from this position put another pair of pirates down, but not before several of their own shots hit Cilas's human shield in the back. He dove out from the dead man's body and landed on his side, squeezing off two more rounds to kill a fourth man.

Shots from behind him brought him around, but he saw that it was Helga, walking in like the angel of death. He didn't know how she'd manage to get past the men in the passageway, but she was there—and there was no alarm—so he didn't bother to worry about it.

"Where's Reysor?" he said.

"Here," she replied, and held up a bloody patch of flesh. "That's Ina as they see her, but ours is on the ladder. We need to move," she said, flashing a cruel grin, and for the first time since they had boarded the ship, Cilas felt confident that they would make it.

"That's my line," he said, then followed her out, where Ina was waiting in the passageway. Cilas froze when he saw her and lifted the pistol. She was armed with a handgun, and he didn't know what to think. "Ina?" he said.

"What? I'm helping out, or am I to be your slave now?" she said. It was a different attitude than the mouse she had been earlier, and he saw that she had a makeshift bandage wrapped around her neck.

"Okay," he said slowly and lifted up a hand. "Just remember that these weapons have—"

"Kinetic rounds, I got it," she said. She lifted up the pistol, ejected the clip, dropped while spinning, catching the clip, and slamming it back inside. "I've been through basics, Lieutenant. I am trained. *Aqnaqak*, remember? We've been through a battle or two."

Cilas laughed. It was the biggest understatement. The *Aqnaqak* was the deadliest battleship in the entire Alliance fleet. Even their bridge crew would be dangerous, and Ina's stunt reminded him of this.

"Go easy, Ensign Reysor, I remember who you are," he said. "Still, this is highly unconventional. It goes against everything I know about infiltration. You and Ate take that side, and I will continue in this direction. Clear the floor, kill every last one of them. I don't want phantoms creeping when this ship is ours."

"Aye aye, sir," Ina said, giving him an Alliance salute.

"Let's go, Reysor," Helga said, and Cilas watched the two women disappear through the door. He reminded himself that Helga was a professional, and that she wouldn't have armed their captive without confirming that she could be trusted.

"I don't like this," he whispered to himself, but he put the thought far from his mind. He then lifted the pistol, stepped over Cage's twin, and made his way down the passageway.

20

Retzo Sho sat back in his large, soft leather chair and sighed. It had been four long hours of focused study on the past mission details of the Nighthawks. Many hands had been involved in the planning of their missions, and it was the same people involved every time. This made it difficult to pinpoint a single change that had led to them being on the mission to Dyn.

Due to this he took all of their names down and asked the reporter, Cyulan Ore, to provide him with their details. The young woman did as she was asked and dug up everything about them. Nothing was spared due to his level of access as the captain.

Cyulan's notes showed him everything, from their daily routines, to job history, and the projects they were involved in. He could even see who their significant others were, since the ship's computer kept track of such things.

Retzo used all of this to look for any changes that happened prior to the mission where Kyden Ahmad was killed. Nothing stuck out, even after hours of studying the lives of all of his officers. He had become somewhat obsessed, drawing out a matrix on his special interface. Now he leaned forward and touched an icon to expand a hologram in the center of the compartment.

The captain stood up, stretched his legs, and then studied the diagram intensely, trying to see if he'd missed anything. Three council members had received the mission details, then sent them to the Alliance to see who would execute the job. On both of the missions in question, his own *Rendron* had volunteered for the assignment. Retzo crossed out the council members as potential suspects.

This left him with his Adan Viles, but there was nothing out of place to make him a suspect. Outside of being slow on informing him about the state of his Nighthawks, the man led a stellar career and conducted himself as an officer should.

Retzo walked over to the cabinet and poured himself a drink. So much time had been spent on looking into these people, he wondered if he was wasting his time. *No, never that*, he thought. *I started this search for a reason. I need an answer in order for this to mean something.*

He lifted the glass to his lips and held it there, then grimaced when the hot liquor touched his throat. It was a harsh drink, hard to get accustomed to, and Retzo wasn't much of a drinker outside of times like this.

"A long line of kill missions, carried out without incident. The last target was a captain: General Uhr Raja of the Geralos ship, *Kha-jurn*. Infiltration and execution, all successful missions. Operators were Cilas Mec, Cage Hem, Lamia Brafa, Casein Varnes, Horne Wyatt, Adan Cruser, and Kyden Ahmad."

As he said their names, he tried to remember each of their faces, what sort of crewmen they were, and how he remembered them from the past. His comms chirped, but he hesitated to answer it, not wanting to break the thought process out of fear that it would be lost. It had taken him hours to reach this point, where he had narrowed it back down to Adan Viles.

"I'm chasing my tail," he said with disgust, and touched his wrist to answer.

It was his communications officer, Genevieve Aria, and he couldn't miss the excitement in her voice, "Sorry for the disturbance, but am I speaking with Captain Sho?" she said.

"This is Sho, Miss Aria, what's the situation?" Retzo said. He expected bad news and had prepared himself to receive it, but even now he tensed as he waited for her answer.

He knew her well enough to recognize her tone, and that was how he knew that something was wrong. If the Nighthawks were finished, there was no reason to rebuild. Not without Cruz by his side, and with a potential spy in the ranks.

Even if he was wrong about Adan or whomever ordered the last two missions, he didn't have another Cilas Mec to start a brand new team.

"Sorry to disturb you, Captain, but you have a call from Commander Jit Nam, of the *Soulspur*."

"Patch him through," Retzo said, ready for the horror. He placed the glass down on the table.

"Captain," came a gravelly voice on the other end of the line.

Retzo touched his earpiece so that he could use his personal comms. "Jit, what's going on?"

"Sir, we have a situation above Meluvia. Five, C-class Geralos warships have just come out of FTL. We were forced to retreat when they drained our shields, and reports are coming in that they've sent raiders to the surface. The Meluvian government has been alerted of the invasion, but they've just lost a destroyer and are in a critical state. I am requesting the help of our sister ship, the *Inginus*, but we may need the *Rendron's* supreme firepower."

Retzo froze where he stood. This made no sense. How could five Geralos warships of that size coordinate a strike without the Alliance spies being aware of it? This was the second major news that he hadn't been given, and now he began to wonder if faulting Adan was premature.

"Hold tight, Jit, the *Rendron* is coming," Retzo said. "The *Inginus* is not enough to drive them out of the system. I need to make some calls, and then I will make a decision. Hold together and stay clear, my friend. I will call you back to tell you how we plan to answer."

"Thank you, Captain," Jit said quickly, and he could hear the uncertainty in his voice. The man sounded concerned, which struck Retzo as odd. A warrior like Jit Nam was not one that was easily rattled. Whatever these Geralos ships were, they had made quite an impression on him. Not to mention they had secured the space to allow for raiders to be sent to the planet.

Retzo stormed out of the cabin and made his way to Communications. The walk wasn't too long, but he purposefully avoided the bridge, walking quickly so that no one could stop him.

When he opened the door to the tiny compartment, the entire room froze and stared at him. Cyulan Ore looked up from her station, surprised, but when the shock wore off, she rose and shouted, "Captain on the deck!"

The six members of the communications team rose in unison, bowing and saluting their captain. It wasn't often that they got to see Retzo Sho without the COMMO, Genevieve Aria in tow. Like most good captains, Retzo made routine visits to all the areas of his ship, but normally he would talk through Genevieve.

To see him come in to engage Cyulan Ore must have been both exhilarating and confusing to them. But Retzo didn't notice—though most days he definitely would—he had questions that demanded answers, and his blind focus took him to Cyulan's station.

"What is going on with our communications?" he said, ignoring the formalities. "We have a Geralos attack and one of our interceptors was forced into retreat. News like this should have come my way the moment our ship made contact. Do you know why this is happening?" he said, kneeling down next to her seat.

"I'm not sure, Captain," she said so that only he could hear. "Does Lieutenant Aria know—"?

"Where is Adan Viles?" he said.

"I'm sorry, Captain, but I've been trying to locate the commander for thirty minutes now."

"Why were you looking for him?"

"Lieutenant Aria asked me to inform him about our current situation, sir," she said.

So, that means that Genevieve is clueless to Adan's whereabouts. If she's having Cyulan hail him, then she's hardly in the know, he thought. "Where's the *Inginus*?" he said softly, looking into her eyes. Retzo was a handsome man, and he was well aware of this. Between his looks and his rank, there weren't many that could resist him.

He knew how Cyulan Ore would react with him so close to where she sat, and he intensified her discomfort when he looked into her eyes.

"They were sent to Louine space, Captain," she said. "Ha-haven't you been told?"

"No," he said, laughing. "When were they sent there, Miss Ore?"

"Five days ago, sir, on Commander Viles' order," she said, her hand coming up to her mouth.

Retzo could see now that she understood why he was asking her these questions. He could read it in her eyes, and it made him happy that he didn't have to spell it out. She would be his eyes and ears whenever he needed it now. This was the type of loyalty he was used to.

"They should have arrived by now, but we haven't received a message confirming this," she said, her voice trailing off as she sat up and stared at her screen.

There was some new commotion and Retzo looked over to find Genevieve Aria at the door. "Captain Sho," she said. "I apologize for not being in place. Has Ensign Ore been able to answer your questions? I'll be happy to brief you on anything." Her voice wavered in a way that he hadn't heard before, and Retzo realized that the woman was scared to death.

He stood up and gave Cyulan a wide-toothed grin. "Thank you, Ensign Ore, you've been a tremendous help," he said. He walked out with Genevieve Aria, who fell in a few steps behind him. Retzo walked slowly this time so that she could keep up, but waited until they were past the bridge before he chose to speak. "Did Viles leave with the *Inginus?*" he said without looking back at her.

"If he did, I haven't heard about it," she said, her voice so small that he could barely hear her.

When they got back to his cabin, Retzo turned and regarded his communication's officer. "We're being called in to war and I don't have my CAG," he said. "He didn't tell me where he went, and you don't seem to know where he is. So if he isn't dead—which I pray he isn't—we need to find out where he is. There has been a lot of things slipping through the cracks and I suspect that it isn't accidental.

"As communications officer, I need you to find me an explanation, Genevieve. I need to know why the *Soulspur* was engaged by five destroyers, and why we didn't hear about it until after they were ambushed. I would also like to know why the message from Lieutenant Mec was purposefully delayed for 89 hours. Oh, and one more thing –the whereabouts of Commander Adan Viles."

"Immediately sir, I will get to the bottom of all of this," she said. Her face reflected fear, which he really didn't like. Reverence was okay, as well as respect or adoration, but fear was for the enemy, and he liked Genevieve Aria.

"At ease, Genevieve, you are not in trouble," he said. "Just find me some answers, and prep the crew for a jump. If Viles is not on this ship I need to know immediately, since we have to scramble our fighters as soon as we come out of light speed."

"What's going on, Captain Sho?" she said, and he realized that he hadn't given details.

"Our Meluvian allies are being invaded by the lizards, and the *Soulspur* is the only thing out there trying to fend them off. I need you to call the Central Alliance Cabinet and get me an immediate audience, and then I need you to find me Viles, wherever he has gone. Once that is done, call my comms so that we can discuss any further action. Do you have what you need?"

"I do, Captain Sho. I will call your comms as soon as everything has been taken care of," she said.

Retzo stepped into the compartment and paused as he looked around. *To think that just an hour ago, my biggest concern was finding Cilas*, he thought. *Now, as usual, the lizards strike when we're at our weakest, and the officer in charge is nowhere to be found.* "This isn't coincidence," he whispered. "Something really stinks." He sat at the table, touched his comms, and waited for Cyulan's voice.

"Hello again, Miss Ore," he said as soon as she answered. "I need you to patch me through to Commander Jit Nam of the *Soulspur*." He was leaning into the table, feeling weak, and it was only then that he understood why. He hadn't eaten since he had started his research and now the hunger was taking its toll. "After you make the call, Cyulan, could you please tell the chef to send up some lunch? Anything will do, but I will take a lot of coffee, as well."

"Aye aye, Captain, I will get that ordered. If it's okay with you I can now connect you with Commander Lam," she said.

"Excellent, Miss Ore. Please put him through," he said. He then sat back and closed his eyes, preparing himself for more bad news.

"Captain," Jit said. "It is good to hear from you. We eagerly await your orders."

"*Inginus* is out, Jit, so we'll be coming ourselves. Stay out of contact with the enemy until you hear from us. I will be talking to the council about enlisting another battleship, and then we'll be coming in to liberate the planet. What's the situation there, have you heard anything more?"

"No sir, not since we last spoke, but the Meluvians have reported contact. The lizards are on the planet, Captain, and they have managed to set up a beachhead."

"They have done what? How long have they been there, Jit? How is it that they've made so much progress in so short a time?" Retzo said.

"That's the thing, Captain. All of this happened just like that. We were here, they appeared, and we're running to save our hides. My contact on Meluvia told me that the Virulian spies went dark. There were lizards on the surface, waiting for this to happen. I cannot explain how the Meluvians stayed blind to lizards being on their planet, sir, but when the dropships broke the atmosphere, they were ready to spring their trap."

Retzo felt a headache coming on. This wasn't the Alliance that he knew. They had been ahead of the game for well over a decade, and things had been hopeful for once in this war. Prior to the disappearance of his Nighthawks, he had successfully removed a number of key Geralos. The Alliance was looking at Geral—in terms of taking the fight to their planet—thinking that with one key strike, they could bring an end to it all.

Now it seemed they had been asleep, and the lizards had put enough things in play to cause this chain of events. His Nighthawks were gone, and his infiltrators spread out to separate systems. He wondered if the other Alliance warships were going through the same scrambling that they were going through now.

"Stay strong, Commander Jit, and look out for my signal," he said. "When I come, I come to conquer, and I need men like you by my side."

"I'll be here, Captain. If there's anything, please don't hesitate," he said.

"You're a good man, Jit, and your Marines are lucky to have you. Just sit tight and stay alert until I tell you when to come in."

When he got off the call, he saw a message from Genevieve, stating that the Alliance Council was ready to speak to him. Retzo got up from his chair and leaned over to swap the interfaces. The hologram display of the Nighthawks vanished, and in its stead hovered the Alliance symbol.

With just one touch he would be in front of the twelve most important beings in the Anstractor Universe. They would ask questions that he couldn't answer, and force him to answer for Meluvia. The big blue planet was under his jurisdiction, and this Geralos invasion would be deemed inexcusable.

Due to this, Retzo hesitated. *Am I really ready to talk?* The way he felt at this point, he wouldn't be able to stay respectful. A chime echoed throughout the compartment, pulling him out of his thoughts, and it was only after the fifth time that he realized it was the door. He touched an area of his bracelet which was connected to the ship, leaned into his comms, and said, "Come in, the door is open."

A young cadet in dress blues wheeled a cart of food inside, and to Retzo it was the most beautiful thing he had ever seen. The scolding would have to wait, as well as the strategy needed for the Geralos. With food inside his stomach—and a momentary break—he would be ready for the Alliance.

"Bring it in, Cadet," he said. "You can set the food up here."

"Immediately sir," the young man said, and Retzo watched him intently as he went. He laid out the food and a heated container full of

Vestalian coffee. He then set a place for the captain as if he was the most important person in the universe.

The entire time he worked, he averted his gaze, but Retzo watched him closely with interest. "How did you come by this station?" he said when the young man was finally finished.

"Yes sir. Sure. I made high marks on my physical examination," he said. "Part of my reward is that I get to work for the officers, sir. There was an emergency, so they asked me to serve you your lunch. I hope that it's okay, sir."

"It is, young man. What is your name?" Retzo said as he sat in front of the food and spooned some meat into a bowl.

"My name is Markus Hem, sir. My father is Master Chief, Cage Hem," he said. Retzo felt his heart sink when he recognized the name.

"You must miss your father," Retzo said, feeling lower than he'd felt in days.

"I do, sir, but he has an important job," he said. "I'd like to have a similar job someday."

"There's a bright future ahead of you, Markus. You're a credit to our cadets," Cilas said. "Keep it up. You did an excellent job here. I will not forget to thank your commander when I see him later today."

21

By the time Cilas, Helga, and Ina were at the door to the bridge, the ship had been on full alert that there were intruders on board. Several men and women had been sent to shut them down, but they hadn't realized the caliber of enemy they were up against.

Cilas, who had been through just about every disaster that could be thrown against an ESO, stacked bodies up in the passageway as they came. The pirates were just not skilled enough to take on the veteran, or his understudy, Helga Ate. So eventually they retreated to the bridge and barricaded themselves inside.

Now it was a war of attrition as Cilas, Helga, Ina, and several former slaves stood outside the bridge's door. The captain—which Cilas assumed he was due to his loud threats—was on the intercom shouting. He repeatedly asked who they were, demanding they stand down and telling them what he was capable of.

"They will have either killed the captives servicing the bridge or kept them as hostages in hopes of negotiation," Cilas said. "Anyone who conducts the business of selling flesh is looking out for themselves and themselves alone. This means they will do whatever they can to survive. So we must be willing to take advantage of that."

"Why haven't they sealed the doors and dropped the atmosphere for the majority of the ship?" Helga said, looking at Ina. "It's what I would do if I was trapped on a bridge. Seal everything off, remove the gravity, and make the atmosphere difficult for anyone to move around."

"I don't know," Ina said. "Maybe there's precious cargo onboard that requires the atmosphere? I'm also not sure if they can lock the ship down from the bridge. The last situation we had on board, it was the engineers that isolated the threat, and you've cleared that compartment and killed them all. I don't think they can do much inside there."

"Atmosphere and sealed doors would not stop the Geralos," Cilas said. "We've been good about taking out the surveillance on this ship, so there is a good chance they don't know who we are. Tell you what, Reysor, take Ate to engineering and see if you can find a way to open this door. If not, there's bound to be a way to do some proper damage."

"What are you going to do, Lieutenant?" Helga said.

"I'm going to speak to their fool of a captain," Cilas said. "All of this noise over the intercom is desperation, so I'll give him an audience while you do your thing. When you find something useful, let me know, and then we can flush him out."

"Engineering is right down here," Ina said, before leading her down the passageway to one of the many compartments that had been cleared.

"We're going to need the men now," Helga said. "You can tell them to come up and hold the door."

Ina complied, leaving her side, though Cilas wanted to object. *Maybe we can use them*, he thought, remembering that they were former Alliance spacers. Throughout the ordeal of getting there, he had managed to liberate more people like Ina. He assigned them to her, with only one instruction: *keep them out of our way as we do our thing.*

The Nighthawks had done what they could to make sure that each deck was clear. But there was no way to search every nook and cranny, so Ina suggested they leave the former captives to do it. They were to lock down the crew deck and prepare for anything. This included sealing all the doors and clearing every livable compartment.

Once this had been done, they were to await instruction and help the Nighthawks if it was needed. Cilas and company left them to handle these things while they rushed off to clear the bridge deck. But the captain and crew had locked themselves inside, and the door to the bridge could not be breached.

As Helga and Ina went about their business, Cilas searched for a way to communicate with the captain. He found it quickly—a phone installed on the bulkhead near the captain's cabin. He lifted the receiver and touched the icon for the bridge, then waited to see if he would answer.

"Who are you?" came the harsh voice that he recognized from the intercom.

"A friend of Amatu Vlax," said Cilas sarcastically, and he smiled when his response was met with a long bout of silence. There had to be some confusion at the mention of Amatu's name, and the man was probably wondering if he had been betrayed.

"You lie," he said finally, his voice taking on a new level of irritability.

"We set the beacon, you came for it, and now I must ask you to surrender your ship, Captain," Cilas said. "Open the door and let my team in, and we will spare your life. Keep us out, stalling the way you are, and we will kill your engines and leave you here for the lizards or the Alliance infiltrator. It's your choice."

"You are in no position to make threats, worm. I will deal with you just like I dealt with the traitor that allowed you on this ship. Amatu is not your friend, and you have no team. I'm guessing that you are either an assassin or one of those Alliance jumpers. Either way you will not gain access to my bridge. We will flush you out and then you will suffer for the loss of life that you have caused."

Cilas's comms came on, so he hung up the phone. "We found a computer with some limited options," Helga said. "Apparently the Louines built fail safes for situations just like this. We can cripple the ship by detaching the fuel supply, or dropping the shields—which should cause him to panic. Another option would be killing the lights, though I'm sure the bridge has an auxiliary back-up."

"There's no controls to affect the bridge door then?" Cilas said.

"No, sir, just the ship as a whole," Helga said.

"Blind them with their surveillance system. He all but indicated that he's able to see me on this deck. Disable the engines and their FTL. I don't want them to have the ability to run. Oh, and shunt all power to the external shields. Burn up as much resources as you can, force this thing into a state of paralysis. Once you do that, get out here and be prepared to fight. Once he knows we have him, he'll send out his men, and we will need to drop them before he can escape."

"What do you mean, escape?" Helga said.

"It's the bridge of a deck ship, Ate ... they are bound to have escape pods. Look to see if you can disable those too," Cilas said.

"*Thype!* You're right. Copy that, I'm on it," she said, before clicking off the comms.

Cilas reached over and grabbed the phone, then dialed the captain again. "You have five minutes," he said once the man answered, but he didn't bother to wait for a reply. He hung it up and walked back to the locked door leading to the bridge.

Out of habit, he checked his weapon's heat gauge and saw that it was at the lowest point. With the amount of shooting he had done, this meant that he had been waiting a really long time. The captain was back on the intercom again. He was so angry that his words were incoherent. By now, their surveillance would have gone dark, and he could no longer see where Cilas was waiting.

Cilas touched his wristband and connected to the comms that they'd taken off a pirate and given to Ina Reysor. "How's our team holding up on the crew deck, Ina?" he said, trying to remain cryptic in case the man on the bridge was listening.

"Scared, excited, wanting to help," she said. "But mostly they are scared. We have had rescue attempts before."

"We always finish our missions, Ina. They don't have anything to worry about," Cilas said. He touched his wristband again. "Ate, what's your status?"

"I'm about to shunt the shields, sir. It took longer than I thought. This engine room is unlike any I've seen. I had to call Brise for help, since I was out of my league." He heard her laugh. "It was a bit of a challenge, but I think that we can finally get it done. Sorry... rambling... I'm moving the slide. Any minute now and the power will switch," she said.

Cilas adjusted the grip on his pistol and waited, listening for a change. It was the grumbling threats over the intercom that took on a new life, and he could understand some of his words. He made out, "what are you doing?" and something about compromise, but there was no way Cilas Mec was going back to that phone.

Any minute now he expected the door to open, followed by an outpouring of angry, armed pirates. They wouldn't be open for conversation, so he had to be ready to meet them. A noise from behind him forced him to dip low and spin with the pistol raised, ready for action.

It was Helga and Ina, followed by a man and a woman they had freed. These former spacers weren't armed with weapons, but their eyes were all fury.

Cilas turned back to the door and raised his free hand, signing to Helga for them to wait and cover him at a distance. There was a clang, the door was moving, and his heart began to pound. He tried to relax his muscles as he waited, not knowing what to expect.

Then something inside of him told him to retreat, to get away from the door as fast as he could. Cilas listened and backed away, keeping his pistol raised as he did. The next few seconds were a blur, and he would never be able to remember it in its entirety. There was white light, and the ship shook violently, throwing him into the air where he struck the overhang.

Consciousness waned, but there was white smoke, and dark figures barely visible within it. For a second he thought that he was in the crater on Dyn again, but there was no room to run in this passageway, and in his ears was a muted ringing sound.

Getting his bearings, Cilas recognized that the pistol was still in his right hand. He rolled up to a knee and began firing, realizing now that there were shots coming from behind him.

Oh yeah, that's Helga, he remembered ... his head feeling heavy. *It was a bomb. They blew off their own door,* he thought. *Of course they did. When they had surveillance, they saw me lingering outside.*

Helga and the rest cleared the passageway as the smoke dissipated, leaving several corpses riddled with holes on top of the charred black door. In front of Cilas stood the open portal leading to the bridge he aimed to take. But what was waiting for him? A high powered rifle, or another bomb rigged to some sort of tripwire?

If this was an Alliance or Geralos ship, all he needed was a superior force. Firepower and strategy would gain the bridge, and the people in charge would surrender. This wasn't dishonorable, and both sides felt this way. Standing down preserved the lives of the men and women who were your responsibility. The captain would negotiate and step aside, but these were pirates who knew no honor.

Helga came forward and hunched down next to him. "Are you alright, Lieutenant?" she said, and he nodded quickly. "What are you thinking is in there? Another booby trap?" she whispered.

"Not sure, but be ready for anything," he said. "We cannot afford to hesitate on this one. They rigged that door and put everyone on that bridge in danger, not to mention the poor fools who ran out, looking to overrun us. The time for mercy has passed, Ate. Inside is a very desperate man who will be looking to take us out by any means necessary."

"Desperate man? More like a cornered rat," Helga mumbled, and turned back to Ina to say something in Meluvian. She then got up, touched Cilas on his shoulder, and crept toward the smoking doorway while keeping her shoulder tight against the bulkhead.

She knows I'm injured, Cilas thought, annoyed at her for not staying back. *I need to take point. She's going to get herself killed.* He got up and followed her, struggling against the pain, his arms holding the pistol above her left shoulder.

When Helga was a meter from the door, he slid past her to take point, hesitating now that he was about to roll the dice. Glancing down at the pirates who had rushed out and died, he noticed that the door they lay upon was not as thick as he'd thought.

Squatting down, he grabbed a corner and pulled it out from under the bodies. This took some effort, since one of the men decided to come with it, but Cilas was stubborn and managed to move it several meters. He could hear shouting coming from inside the smoky bridge but it was hard to tell how many were in there.

Cilas reached down and grabbed a rifle from one of the dead men at his feet. He checked it quickly, making sure that it was serviceable, and then threw its strap over his shoulder before rolling the corpse off the door. Once his makeshift barrier was clear, he hoisted it and walked back to the doorway. Placing it on its side, he slid it across the opening, making sure to do it in a way that didn't expose his limbs.

He now had a barrier on the lower half of the doorway, and he spared no time in sliding behind it and coming up in a crouch. Instantly, shots came from the bridge, slamming into the door loud and frightening. Some shots flew over his head, striking the bulkhead behind him, and a number of these ricocheted and came dangerously close to where he crouched.

It was so loud that his ears began to ring again, but luckily none of them punched their way through the thick metal. When he finally got his bearings, he noticed that Helga was squatting next to him. She was bobbing back and forth, firing at the enemy, and it was a wonder she hadn't been shot.

"These are amateurs, Lieutenant. They're all exposed inside that space," she said. Her voice was so confident, as if they'd already won.

"Stay down," Cilas ordered. "We don't know this ship or its people well enough to come to that conclusion. You're exposing yourself firing, Ate. Stop being impatient. You're our only pilot. As in, the most important person for getting these people home!"

The reminder of her role seemed to have worked on the Nighthawk, as she slid to the deck with her back to the door. Cilas saw

Ina inching up and signaled for her to stop. It was at these critical moments that his leadership was needed, since impatience would lead to unnecessary casualties.

He thought about Cage Hem, his long lost Nighthawk brother. In situations like this they never needed to speak. They had been through so much together, they could practically read each other's minds. Cage would've given him cover, and he would pop up and put a round in the captain's chest.

It would have been an easy takeover, unlike this, which had become complicated after freeing Ina Reysor. *This is who you have, Cilas, and you're their leader. Tell them what to do, Nighthawk,* he thought. *Do your thyping job.*

More shots punched the door, and it almost fell over, so he quickly removed the rifle and handed it to Helga Ate. "Do like you were doing before, but let your arms do the suppressing," he said. "Remember your training foremost. Give me the time to clear that space."

Helga seemed to inhale a prayer, then shifted her weight onto one knee. She then took an awkward seat and lifted the rifle above her head. With only her hands exposed, she fired off several shots. Cilas could hear the bullets ricocheting and the shouts of panic that it caused.

He got up on his knees, and several shots flew by his head. But he didn't let this delay his actions as he looked to mark his targets. It was still smoky from the explosion, but he could see movement through the smoke. "Just like old times, brother," he whispered, a quiet prayer to his friend, Cage Hem.

One by one he put bullets into these shadows, the same way he'd done on the numerous missions he'd survived. When three men went down, Helga stood up and started firing with precision. Cilas allowed the door to fall but hesitated to enter for fear of a tripwire. When all movement was stopped and the counter fire ceased, he touched the muzzle of Helga's rifle and brought it slowly down.

The smoke was gone, though the bridge remained hazy, and he could smell the heated metal of their weapons. "Don't shoot," came a voice inside that Cilas recognized as the captain's. "We're standing down. Please ... mercy ... we're standing down," he said, and Cilas looked over at Helga Ate and exhaled a sigh of relief.

22

After taking the bridge, Helga saw another side of Cilas Mec that she hadn't known existed. It was as if he'd stepped aside—the charismatic, caring Cilas that she knew—and let his evil twin take over. Now she stood near the doorway with Ina watching in horror as he tortured the ship's captain for information.

He hadn't given them any orders once the man surrendered, and with the things that he was doing, Helga wasn't sure if she wanted him to. *Do your job,* she thought when the man's screams rose an octave, and became enough to snap her out of her frozen state.

"Ina," she said. "Ask your comrades to collect the bodies and place them near the airlock on every deck. We won't be able to do much with the *Inginus* while they're swapping blows with the Geralos. Can you imagine the smell in here if we leave it the way it is?"

"Uh, right – let me go talk to them," the tall woman said, and it took some effort for her to turn away from Cilas's interrogation. The lieutenant had the man tied to a chair and was punching him repeatedly. He would stop once in a while to ask a question, and then punch him again if he didn't like the answer.

Helga walked over to the cockpit area where the dead pilot was slumped in his seat. She pushed him off, where Ina's men could see him, and sat down in his place. Her throat constricted; it had been so long since she'd been at the helm of an actual ship.

During those long hours of staring at a monitor, inside of their escape pod ... she had wondered if that was it, if she would die in the tube with Cilas and Brise. Now she was here, and though it was an alien ship, it was a ship, and as she wiped her hand across the console, she recognized the controls.

"Definitely Louine," she said to herself, as she took in the complex layout. She placed the pilot's communication device on her ear, opened up comms, and synched communication to the ship's radar. After locating the tiny dot that was their cloaked escape ship, she sent a signal to its radio and waited for it to be received.

All of a sudden, she remembered what they had done: crippled the ship and maxed the shields at the cost of everything. *This bird is going to be stuck in recharge mode for several Vestalian days*, she thought.

"Lieutenant?" came a familiar voice in her ear, and she knew that it was Brise.

"Sol, this is Helga Ate. How're you holding up?" she said.

"Ate! I'm here, alive, but worried out of my mind. Are you and the lieutenant okay?"

"We have the bridge, and we will be pulling you in, but we have a few technical items to take care of first. Hold tight for a few hours and then wait for my hail. I'll work as fast as I can, alright?" Helga said.

"As long as it takes, Ate. I'm just glad to hear your voice. Were you able to shunt power to the shields? You never called me back, and I thought ... Oh, never mind." He laughed. "I'll get all the details when you have me on board."

"I will, and I'm sorry for not calling you back," she said. "That had to be terrifying, but we have the ship. Anyway, let's talk when you're on board. I'll call you when we're ready to bring you in."

She rose from the chair and looked over at Cilas, who was wiping his knuckles on the unconscious man's shirt. "What did you find out?" she said, and he shot her a look of annoyance, causing her to flinch and avert her gaze. "Are you alright, Lieutenant?" she said, hoping that the real Cilas would return.

"I'm alright now," he said, still looking at the captain. "Got a lot of information that I have to work out. Either way, it can wait. Our first priority is to get this ship back to working form. Then we need to collect our man and dispose of the deceased through the airlocks."

"I've already spoken to Sol, Lieutenant. We need to pull him onboard, and then with your permission, I'll put the crew to cleaning up the place," Helga said.

"The ship is yours, Ate. You should use Ensign Reysor to help you with the bridge. As to the cleanup and what we do with the dead, let me worry about that. Get Brise here so that he can right the damage we did in engineering. Then I need to hail *Inginus* and convince them that we are who we say we are. Once we've done all of those things, we need to be off this ship."

"Can you tell me why, Lieutenant?" Helga said, confused as to why they'd do all this work just to ditch the ship.

"This vessel is a slave galley, just like *The San*, and I'm guessing several others all over Anstractor. They are unified, Ate, and comprise crews with people from all over the galaxy. Meluvians, Casanians, Vestalians, and Louines are capturing our people and forcing them into labor. There's a chance that through a corrupted source, they are selling us to the lizards."

Helga couldn't believe her ears. It was the most absurd thing that she'd ever heard. How was it that they were communicating with the lizards, let alone selling humans to them? "I don't get it, Lieutenant. Wouldn't the lizards capture the pirates themselves? What could they possibly gain by playing nice with people like that?" she said.

"We were all on Dyn, Ate. We saw enough to corroborate what I'm telling you. There is a language barrier with the lizards, and to them we're nothing but food. But what if a select group of food can open a pipeline to human resources? They have spies in our Alliance, Ate. Spies that are helping to feed their camps."

It was as if all the life had been drained from her face, as the weight of the flesh pushed Helga down to the deck. She remembered Lamia, how he'd turned on them so quickly, and she remembered how good of a person he was before he became corrupt. Couldn't the Geralos do the same to people in power on the Alliance council?

Warship commanders, operators on the ground. Why were they even fighting when the enemy's advantage was so thorough? She hadn't realized that she was now seated on the deck, too weak to move and too proud to admit that she was frightened. "Were we sent here as lizard food, Cilas?" she said, knowing the answer already.

"That's what I aim to find out, now that I understand this whole pirate network," he said. "I have no proof that the *Rendron* has a lizard onboard, but I'll know sooner or later. *The San* is the main contact for the network, and Amatu is a dangerous traitor to our cause. Those ruins you saw on Dyn were old settlements, ones he liberated the way he did ours. See, he has a conscience, and he's playing the Geralos for whatever profit they're giving him. He steals their prisoners from their camps and then sells them to ships like this."

"No wonder he could play the nice, caring liberator. His hands aren't directly linked to the Geralos," Helga said. "He figures we're dead anyway once we're captured by the lizards, and so we become goods to trade, with traitorous pieces of schtill like him!" She spat at the captain's unconscious body. "Now I want to give him some blows of my own. I want to punch him so hard that he'll never wake up and then find Amatu and—"

"Go easy, Ate," Cilas said, offering her a hand and helping her to her feet. "I shared this with you because you're my only friend in this thing. Do not say anything to Brise or anyone on the Alliance ships. You and I can look into things until we're sure who we can trust. Do you understand me, and are you willing to do it?"

"You can rely on me, Lieutenant," she said, and saluted awkwardly. As soon as she touched her chest, she was confused as to why she was saluting. She had called him Cilas, he had shared an intimate secret, and he was actually addressing her now the way he would a peer. She expected him to roll his eyes, shake his head, or something else negative, but he smiled reassuringly and returned her salute.

"Had I known that I was taking you into a mess, I would have delayed your joining another year, Helga," he said. "I never thought that things would get this thyped up, let alone lose the friends that have been with me my entire career."

She wondered if that was the reason for the brutality that he'd unleashed on the captain. Maybe it was the pent-up anger over the betrayal that he was hearing caused them to be where they were now. How could she blame him when she felt the same? At least Cilas had enough self-control to stop.

Were it her or Brise administering the torture, they would have definitely killed him, knowing that the orgasm of hurt was only able to come when the pain you caused robbed the target of its life.

"I don't think you should regret me being here, Lieutenant," she said. "I knew what I was getting into even as far back as when I was just a teenage cadet. If I wanted it easy, I would have stayed on the *Rendron*."

It took a lot of time but when the ship was in order, it was hard to believe that it was once owned by pirates. Ina stepped up in an impressive way and led her fellow ex-captives to clean and scour the decks.

When all hope had been lost for the ship's captain, he had ordered that the slaves be put to death. One by one the chips inside their flesh corrupted, causing their bodies to be wracked with pain until it found their hearts.

The five people who survived had cut theirs out as soon as they were rescued. Seeing the bodies of the pirates gave them hope, and they had considered themselves liberated. There were others who weren't so sure, and chose to leave their chips in longer. They hedged their bets because they knew, that the penalty of removing one's chip was the airlock.

Had the Nighthawks failed to take the ship, they would have been recaptured and made to answer. It was an intelligent choice, to hold on to it till the end, but they gambled wrong on the captain's cruelty, and for that they ended up dead.

Two of the surviving five were on the bridge now, a former Marine named Noli Dawn, and a Phantom pilot named Pavlid Rif. The former being a Meluvian, served on the battleship, *Uman Roo*, and the latter came from *Helysian*, another floating city like the *Rendron*.

Every last one of these spacers were hard, which made Helga wonder how they wound up on the pirate ship. She couldn't stop thinking about betrayal, and the leaders that could be corrupted by the Geralos. What if Pavlid had been given a special mission, one in which the pirates were waiting to capture him?

It wasn't dissimilar to what she and Cilas had gone through. Why did it have to be spacers? Did they need naval experts to man their stolen ship? Cilas had mentioned ransom; were civilian hostages worth too little? Ina had told her that every captive she'd talk to on the ship was a former Alliance spacer. Were there more ships like this floating around the worlds, looking for warriors to fall into their web?

Helga touched the interface and thrummed her fingers on several icons, which told the ship to close a rather large hatch. Once it complied, she increased their shields a hair and then set the rest of the focus on the internal power supply.

"Lieutenant, Petty Officer Brise Sol has come aboard successfully," she said.

It seemed like ages since she had spoken to Brise, and even longer since they had become friends. He had been so nasty to her when they were captured, but she had learned that it was his defense mechanism, to lash out when he felt helpless. But she had forgiven him on *The San*, and over their month in the escape pod, she had learned to like him.

He was a brilliant engineer and a bad ESO, but she knew that the reason he was bad was because he cared too much. This made him the antithesis of everything that Cilas was, which forced her to be the shield between them. She didn't agree much with Brise, but she felt drawn to him regardless. This was due to the fact that she couldn't see that he was everything her brother Rolph was.

She watched the monitor showing the *Inginus*, still locked in a fight with the Geralos destroyer. Though she wanted to help, it wasn't possible, not in this old ship whose weapons hadn't been fired in several years.

The *Inginus* was strong, but it needed time against a ship of its size, and there was nothing that an old pirate ship could do to assist them.

Even if she turned them around to approach the Geralos destroyer, their own *Inginus* would see it as a sign of aggression. They were in an old Louine ship, whose model was a relative unknown for any Alliance spacer. The *Inginus* could assume that they were Geralos and cut them in half with a trace laser.

If this happened, then everything they had done to take the ship would have been for nothing—since they would be dead and forgotten.

Helga felt a presence behind her and the hairs on her neck stood erect. Deep down she knew it had to be Cilas or one of the former captives, but that did nothing for her nerves, which were still on edge in this strange new ship.

It was Ina, who looked as if she had spent some time going through the captain's wardrobe. She had changed into the clothes and leathers of a pirate, and somehow it worked with her fiery hair and muscular frame.

Cilas was in charge, but Ina looked the part, and Helga caught herself staring as the tall woman came up and placed her hands on the back of the chair. "You seem worried. Isn't that ship one of ours?" she said, pointing to the *Inginus*.

She said ours. Welcome back to the Alliance, Ensign Reysor, Helga thought. "It is, but we've been gone so long, I dare not hope that we will be rescued," Helga said. "Every time we catch a break, things only seem to get worse. And though I recognize that ship, it doesn't mean they're ready to take us in."

Ina sat in the chair next to hers and placed her feet up on the console. She still wore the bloody bandage around her neck, but it too complemented her ensemble.

"Just imagine how we feel. We, the forgotten children of the Alliance. Most of us abandoned hope until we saw you and the lieutenant killing Rax's men," she said. "Now he's in the brig, unconscious, and probably dying, and I'm on his bridge, sitting in his chair... free. Think this is real life for me, Helga? I'm still struggling with believing it."

Helga smiled. Ina had a point. There was no use complaining to someone who had it just as bad as she did. Yes, the Geralos were much worse, but they had survived them and had wound up with their own ship. So she decided to change the subject to something more positive.

"What will be the first thing you do when you're back on *Aqnaqak*, Ina?" she said.

Ina looked lost, but Helga could tell that she was giving her question some serious thought. "I've been doing a lot of thinking, Helga. And after what we've done today, I'm done being an ESO. I've seen enough blood to convince me of that. Plus, I'm disappointed in our Alliance. Look how many spacers were held captive on this ship. Am I to believe that they came looking for us, or did they just sign us off as missing in action?

"It makes me angry, to be honest, but I don't know what to say about it. I don't know. Maybe my first move will be to find a bar that serves cheap drinks. I'll flirt with a fighter jock who is too far gone to get attached and make it weird. Then maybe I'll wake up next to that stranger and realize that my nightmare is truly over. I do know that I don't plan to serve on that infiltrator, or the *Aqnaqak*. Maybe I'll go back home to Meluvia, and help my father with his business."

"Whatever you choose, you earned it," Helga said. She couldn't help but admire Ina's spirit. She seemed so strong now that everything was evening out, and it was obvious that the Alliance had lost an asset. "I don't know what I'll do, but I'm too angry to become a civilian. I want to find out who sent us here, and why, and I want to make them feel everything I felt in that Geralos prison."

A tone from the console broke her train of thought, and she looked at Ina's boots to see if she had accidentally triggered something. "The *Inginus* is hailing us," Ina said, as she kicked her feet up and off the console. She seemed to know communications, and proved this by patching it through. She then turned around to Cilas to see what he wanted to do.

"It's okay, Ensign Reysor," he said as he straightened his spacesuit, then stood at attention. Ina connected the ship's communications, and the hologram of an older Alliance commander appeared in the center of the bridge.

23

The conversation between Lieutenant Cilas Mec and the *Inginus* went on for a short time before Cilas switched it to his comms so that he could speak privately. By that time, Helga had heard enough to know why they had come.

The *Inginus* had been sent to Louine space in order to rescue the Nighthawks. But they had no intention of bringing aboard what they called refugees, even though these people were Alliance military. Hearing this commander take such a hard stance made Helga consider staying with Ina Reysor.

Ina took it well, as if she had expected it, but Helga wondered if this was just a façade. She had come so close to being rescued, and the *Inginus* had the means to get her back to the *Aqnaqak*. Was it enough that the pirates were dead? Helga couldn't believe that Retzo Sho would agree with what the commander was demanding.

After what seemed like an hour of discussion, Cilas called a meeting on the bridge. Everyone took the chairs around the perimeter, and he stood in the center near the captain's console. "I'm sure most of you heard that," he said, meeting their gazes. "The *Inginus* only intends to take the Nighthawks. We were given no choice. Either we come, or they will take us, aggressively. Most of you have served, so you know it's not a bluff."

"Are we seriously going to leave these people behind?" Brise said, and Helga was surprised that he managed to keep himself composed.

"Yes and no," Cilas said as he walked around the chair. "I reminded them of the oath they took when they became officers in this Alliance. *No spacer left behind.* What they are demanding violates that oath. I also told them that as Special Operations they have little say over my crew, and if I chose to remain on this ship, aggression would be seen as an act of treason."

"Wow, Lieutenant, you said that to the commander? I really don't know what to say," Helga said.

"I know you all think that I'm some sort of Alliance robot," he said. "I'm a spacer first, yes, but I have a heart, and everyone here risked their lives to liberate this ship. Do you honestly think that gets lost on me? Just because another man issues a threat? I have a ship here, with an FTL drive, and they don't want me jumping back to speak directly to our captain."

Helga had to smile at the thought of Cilas Mec playing the part of the headstrong lieutenant. It was out of character, but pleasantly surprising, and raised him higher in terms of her admiration. "So what was their compromise?" she said, knowing that there had to be something or he would still be on the call.

"We're going to dock on the *Inginus* as soon as the lizards are done, and they will repair this ship and make her jump-ready. Everyone will be fed and given appropriate accommodations. Those who want to contact their ship will be given the opportunity. Once the ship is ready, it will be yours to captain, Ina. Whatever you choose to do with it is entirely up to you and your crew.

"Is everyone okay with this?" Ina said to the former captives. "I never asked to be your captain, but I will accept it if everyone's onboard."

Each of the men and women gave their blessing, and Noli Dawn reminded her that without her they'd still be slaves. They were in agreement that the *Inginus* was a place that they didn't want to be, since their commander had originally intended to leave them stranded.

Helga leaned over towards Ina and whispered in her ear. "Captain Ina Reysor sounds really good to me." She didn't realize that her whisper was still heard, and Cilas cleared his throat to snap her back to attention. "Sorry," she said, forcing a smile and looking around, embarrassed.

"I am dressed the part," Ina said, laughing, and the rest of her would-be crew laughed as well. "I don't know what to say, but I will do right by everyone. I will get us out of this system and back to our families," she said. "Many of you have told me that you want to get back to the fight, and it will be my first priority to reunite you with your ships. For those who are done with the war and people like this *Inginus* commander, this is a large ship, and I will need a crew. Anyway, Lieutenant, sorry – I didn't mean to interrupt," she said.

"It's your ship, Captain," Cilas said. "In all seriousness, Ina Reysor, these men and women are lucky to have you."

He then looked at Helga and Brise directly, and she could see his shoulders dip, as if he was about to deliver some bad news. "For us, the uncertainty of our future will continue," he said. "First we have to wait out this battle, and stay clear of the warheads fired from that Geralos destroyer. Next we will have to dock, and at that point, I assume we will be interviewed by Commander Lang. When it comes to that part, Sol, let me do the talking," he said, staring at the young engineer until he nodded in agreement.

"I can tell you that while they jumped all the way out here to find us, they are not exactly happy to be here. Expect a hostile commander and an even more hostile crew, but keep in mind that we'll be amongst the brothers and sisters of the Alliance military. We'll be expected to serve if the time for combat arises. Sol, you and I will be with the Marines, and Ate, you will be with the pilots."

"Will they separate us, or will we live with one another?" Brise said, his face a mask of stoic resignation.

"We will probably be together, but separate during operations. Even if we aren't, I'll be available. You're my team, and that will never change," Cilas said.

Helga turned around and stared through the window at the battle being waged between the two ships. She didn't know how to feel about this rescue. Shouldn't their return be a positive thing?

"Lieutenant," she shouted, gesturing towards the ship, and Cilas ran over to see for himself. The last remaining Geralos ship had just jumped away, and the *Inginus* was alone, victorious.

"Are we able to dock this thing?" he said, and Helga got up and rushed over to the pilot's chair.

"We should have enough power to dock," she said, doing the math in her head. "It's going to be tight though ... Ina what do you think?"

Ina walked over and stood behind Helga's chair. She reached over her shoulder and swept her hand across the HUD. A display of gauges replaced the radar, and she gestured to enlarge one of them. "This is more than enough," she said to Helga, who looked in awe at her mastery of the interface.

Strapping herself in, Helga grabbed the controls and applied a bit of thrust to see how responsive it was. "Please find the closest station to strap yourself in," she said over her comms. Her voice echoed over the intercom, and she didn't like how it sounded. *I have the voice of a frightened child*, she mused. *I am going to have to work on that.*

When she felt how the ship moved, she put more power in the thrusters and aimed the fore towards the massive *Inginus*. It felt like an eternity since she'd last flown anything, and though they'd been in space the entire time, it could not compare to the way she felt now.

It wasn't a feeling of relief, or excitement for getting rescued after so many days. Helga wanted to be excited, but she couldn't, not after Cilas's speech. Their return would be a somber one, mostly due to the things that they had been through. Not to mention she was lonely; the type of loneliness one feels when you can't be open with anyone.

During the long months of being secluded with the two men, she'd come to realize just how lonely she was. Loneliness could be masked with work and war, two things that awaited her on the giant infiltrator. Piloting was one of the most difficult jobs, and she took it more seriously than most. And due to its difficulty it always sufficed to keep the loneliness at bay.

The thrusters came to life and they began to heat up, so Helga found the link to the *Inginus* and sent a signal requesting communication. The air crackled and the link activated, and then a stern human voice came over the comms. "This is Ensign Elan Nix of the *Inginus*. Trade ship, what is the intent of this call?" he said.

"This is Helga Ate, a Nighthawk of the *Rendron*. We have spoken to your commander, who gave us permission to dock. We have injured and deceased onboard, and seek entry to your hangar."

There was a very long break and Helga glanced over at Cilas expectedly. The lieutenant was strapped in out of reach, but he merely shrugged when their eyes met. "Patience, Ate. They're just running their scans," he said. "Making sure that we don't have Geralos onboard trying to gain access to the ship."

"Permission has been granted, Nighthawk Ate," the voice on the comms said. "Welcome home, we are happy to see you. Please use aft bay 15-45."

Helga took the ship in steadily, which was a lengthy ordeal. The thrusters could only push them so fast, and she had to navigate to the aft of the *Inginus*. The infiltrator was so big that it was a looming endless wall, but Helga took her time and found the hangar bay.

There was something surreal about docking now, after everything that they'd gone through. She wanted to rub her eyes to see if she was dreaming, but feared that she actually was. Maybe they had died a few weeks back, and this was the illusion of a torturous afterlife. A part of her expected to dock the ship, only to find that it was overrun with lizards.

When the bay doors opened the shields rippled a bit before a hole materialized to grant them entry. Helga shook off her thoughts, steadied the ship, and slowed down their thrust. She brought them to a stop, and then waited patiently for the *Inginus* computer to take over her controls.

After ten minutes of waiting, they were pulled in slowly, and then a small transport ship appeared. It flew up to the same doors which had granted Brise entry. Then a bridge was extended to attach itself to their ship.

"Attention everyone, we have a transport ship waiting at the aft bay doors," Helga said. "Please make your way to the dock, and keep in mind that it may be some time before you can return. If you have anything personal, bring it with you, but do so fast since we're on limited time."

It was the standard exit protocol, and Helga hadn't given much thought to the fact that these were slaves without any possessions. Some brought weapons that they had lifted from the bodies of the pirates, but most merely walked to the bridge and stepped into the transport ship empty-handed.

The ship was shaped like a rectangular box and comprised of nothing but seats around the perimeter. It had one purpose, which was to bring people on and off the *Inginus*. The seats were an eggshell color, soft, clean, and comfortable, and all around it were tall bay windows allowing them to see out in space.

Once they were all seated onboard, Helga found the controls and withdrew the bridge. She gave one final glance at the old pirate ship and then approved the return to the *Inginus*. They glided slowly into a bright hangar bay and landed in an empty area away from the fighters.

Upon touchdown, everyone jumped up and quickly filed off the vessel. But it took Helga a long time to find the courage to follow them out.

When she finally emerged, she was quite surprised. There were a host of men in hazard suits standing below the ramp. They rushed her and the others into a large decontamination room. There they had to strip out of their clothes and stand facing the bulkhead while gripping an iron bar.

Helga thought about the equipment that had been lost on the mission: Eight PAS suits, the Britz SPZ, and one Louine multi-featured escape ship. This still paled to the loss of her comrades, those veterans she had looked up to. You could replace equipment, but life was different. There was no replacing years of combat experience.

A cold mist came from the vents, which reminded her of the Geralos prison, and she closed her eyes unconsciously, expecting it to put her to sleep. But it was over just as quickly as it had started, and then the doors opened up to several men and women dressed like masters-at-arms.

One handed her a bundle of clothes and pointed to a corner, where she saw Ina pulling on some coveralls. Helga joined her and dressed quickly, not liking the fact that she was naked around all these men. When she was fully dressed, she looked up, only to see Ina and the former captives being escorted out.

"Excuse me, but where are you taking them?" she said, worried that she had freed their chains only to lead them to new ones.

"The Commander wants an audience with the Nighthawks only," said one of the men, as he nodded to the others to continue leading the captives out. As Ina fell in, she gave Helga a smile. It was the reassuring kind that said, "We will be okay."

"So they go from a pirate's prison to an Alliance one," Brise said. "I wonder what their supposed crime is." His face had the look of someone who was beyond his limit, so Helga remained silent to respect Cilas's wishes.

It wasn't long before the door slid open and Commander Tyrell Lang walked in. Next to him were a number of officers, but they hung back as he approached. The three survivors stood in unison and saluted him with respect. Helga was still mulling over Brise's words, and she began to worry for their future.

"First of all, let me say that the fact that you're here is a testament to your bravery," he said. "We sent you out to help people compromised by the lizards. Yet here you are, the ones being rescued. How does an elite team wind up on a Louine ship?"

Cilas, who Helga reasoned had the patience of a saint, ignored the offensive question to relay the information to him mechanically. He left out the details about his injury and more importantly, Lamia Brafa's corruption. It was shocking to see him not be forthcoming with the commander, and when she glanced over at Brise, she saw that he was smiling.

Outside of the capture and rescue on Dyn, Cilas got creative with the rest. He spun a tale about a pirate rescue, which ended in a mutiny that got most of the crew killed. As he told his lie, Helga remembered that they had left the captain unconscious in a cell on the ship. His wickedness had been absolute, but to die in pain, hungry ... it seemed too much. But Cilas knew what he was doing—at least she hoped—so she bit her tongue and listened.

Tyrell seemed satisfied with what he was told; they had been ambushed, then kidnapped upon entry. Nowhere in the details did Cilas mention the dredge, the thopter that they'd commandeered, or the truth of how Cage had died. He spun the story to make it seem that the mission was doomed upon entry. They had flown in hot, crash landed on the moon, and became prisoners to the Geralos until the pirates showed up.

"And the others?" Tyrell said, jabbing a finger at the door that Ina and company had been escorted through.

"Fellow captives that were there before us," Cilas said. "They freed us from our cells, and we did our thing to take over the ship. Our plans before you showed up, Commander, was to jump back to Alliance space."

"What a mess," Tyrell said, as he scanned their faces. "I'm especially impressed with you, young lady. How the hell are you not bitten?"

Helga realized that the commander was addressing her directly, but her tongue felt thick and it took some time for her to answer. "I don't know why, sir. They had plenty of chances to bite me," she said.

"Casanian blood is extremely toxic to the Geralos," he said, running a finger through her hair. This violation was to reveal her spots, but Helga knew that his touch meant more.

"They found this out when they invaded the planet a year after taking Vestalia," he continued. "You probably confused them, but they dared not try you. Count your blessings, *shrak cy*. Your racial background saved your life."

Helga felt sick to her stomach; first from his touch, then his use of one of the older Casanian dialects. "Shrak cy," meant "pretty girl," and it annoyed her that he was addressing her this way. She felt her cheeks get hot as she struggled with her anger, and she wondered if Brise and Cilas had noticed.

"Now, you all are probably ready for a proper meal, and we have just that waiting for you in the chow hall," he said. But Helga stared at the floor, angry and embarrassed, too unsure to look up at him.

"Thank you, Commander," Cilas said. He saluted again, and the older man returned it. Helga forced herself to follow suit, and was quite relieved when he and his officers exited the compartment. As they followed them through another door, Helga touched Cilas's arm to get his attention.

"What in the worlds was that?" she whispered, looking up at his face. She hadn't seen him so angry since the time when he was beating the captain to death.

"What, Ate, did I leave something out?" he said, giving her a hard look that forced her to remove her hand.

"No, I think you managed to cover all of it, Lieutenant," she said, realizing that this wasn't the time or place.

"Good," he said. "We'll talk later." And he quickened his pace to get ahead of her.

24

With the *Rendron* being light years away and the *Inginus* patrolling the far side of the moon of Dyn, the dead warriors of the *Rendron* Nighthawks did not get the sendoff that Helga expected. Instead of a speech from Retzo Sho, their beloved captain, they received one from Commander Tyrell Lang, which fell embarrassingly short.

The ceremony culminated with a speech from Cilas, expressing his sorrow and gratitude. The entire thing lasted a little over thirty minutes and then the Nighthawks were allowed to slam Alliance pins into the coffins that represented their fallen comrades.

It would have been understandable for them to hold a grudge against Lamia Brafa, since it was his sword that had sent the other men to their deaths. But they knew that he had been corrupted, and loved him all the same, so Helga placed a pin on his coffin and slammed it home with her fist.

Cruser's coffin hurt the most, and seeing his name in gold on that black shiny obelisk brought a pain to her heart that she could no longer hide. It seemed so long ago since he had helped her into her first armor, and she recalled how much of a child she'd been then. Despite all of her faults and bad off-color humor, he had been a friend, teaching and protecting her.

Now she remembered that she would never see him again. She would no longer feel the warmth of his hugs, or here his loud obnoxious laugh from the other end of the barracks. When her fist touched the pin she lost it all together, and as she leaned over, crying, it was Brise who came to console her.

So much had happened since Lamia's mind had been invaded. So much that it felt to Helga as though she'd lived several different lives. There was the past that she held onto, the one with her parents, and Rolph, her brother. Then there was the Dyn mission, which felt surreal. *Did I really pilot a Geralos thopter on that moon?* she thought.

The lapse in consciousness during her imprisonment ran into the memory of the Louine rescue. She recalled white walls and kind blue faces, but all of it faded away to the long month aboard the pod. Her eyes found Ina Reysor, who seemed regal in civilian clothes. She stood with her men, her eyes strong but sympathetic. It was enough to remind Helga where she was, and she stood up tall and collected herself.

She watched as the coffins were ejected from the airlock, and the men's names, ranks, and accolades were announced to the ship. A moment of silence ended this painful show of remembrance, and then everything went back to normal.

Helga, who had been upset since the beginning, felt angry and helpless over the way things had turned out. She went back to the compartment that she had been given and sat on the bunk with her head in her hands.

Varnes was gone without his family being there, and somehow it just felt wrong. Since their arrival they had been given accommodations, and time to heal, but this brought back everything in a painful force.

Helga got up from the bunk and walked over to a floor-length mirror. She'd lost so much weight that she thought she looked sickly. Her skin was thinner, and her spots stood out in stark contrast against a complexion that was beyond pale.

I wonder if I'll ever look normal again, she thought, and reached up and touched the cheekbones jutting out from her skin. She traced fingertips across the dark bags below eyes that were puffy from crying. "I look like schtill," she said, and kissed her teeth.

A loud jingle came from the door and she wondered who it could be. Adjusting her uniform and fixing her hair, she crossed the compartment to see who it was. On the vid's monitor, she saw Cilas Mec standing outside the door. Helga quickly unlocked it and slid it open to see what the lieutenant wanted.

Cilas walked in and took a seat at the table in the center of the compartment. When Helga locked the door he motioned for her to take a seat across from him. *I wonder what I've done now*, she thought, trying to remember if she'd done anything disrespectful during the funeral.

"What's going on, Lieutenant?" she said, steeling herself for the bad news that was about to come.

"Nothing much. I came to check in on you. See how you're settling in. And I wanted to talk to you about our situation here. Do you have time to talk … off the record?"

"Always," she said, happy to learn that it wasn't about the funeral.

Cilas seemed pained as he sat staring at the table, his hands wringing so hard that she became concerned for him. Eventually he looked up at her, but his eyes danced around as if he struggled to see her. "Lots of things have happened since you joined our team and I haven't had a chance to sit down with you," he said.

"I'm alive, I have food, and a bunk to rest my head on. Considering where we've been in the last few months, I am doing extremely well," she said, smiling. "To be honest with you, Cilas, I've been wondering when my luck's going to run out. Let me see, both you and Cruser were hit when we entered Dyn, yet I was the one in the front.

"Then Wyatt saved me from the dredge and Cage from the Geralos in the thopters. We get captured and somehow I managed to not get bitten. Then we're rescued and we took over a ship, and still managed to make it back here. If luck was a resource I should be scraping the bottom right now. For me to complain would make me a bit of an ass."

Cilas smiled and mussed his hair. It was obvious that something was on his mind. "Just now, Sol asked me if he could put in for a transfer off the *Rendron*," he said. "As his superior, he asked me to sign off on it. Toughest thing I've had to do as a leader, Ate. Looks like he's had it for some time. He admitted he had it drafted after his first mission."

"He doesn't like being a Nighthawk?" Helga said, surprised.

"Oh, he does. He said as much. But he doesn't like being a spacer in a Navy that doesn't give a *thype* about him. See on *Rendron*, had he handed me that thing, I would have had him thrown in the brig for cowardice during a time of war. When you're a Nighthawk, you can't quit. It said it right there when we all signed up."

"But?" Helga said, watching his discomfort and wishing that she could help him somehow.

"But on that ship we confirmed his fear, Helga. So I understand why Sol would want to run. I just want to see if you're still in, or, I don't know, maybe you feel the same. You've always been respectful, and I appreciate it more than you know."

"I'm here to stay, Lieutenant, you don't have to ask," she said. "I remember what I signed, and beyond even that, I don't think I have anything to give to the civilian world. What am I going to do when the lizards own the galaxy? Hole up in some hub, hoping and praying that our military gets a major win? If I can have it my way, I will be a part of that major win. Corruption or not, I don't want to be helpless, not as long as I have the ability to fly."

"That's what I thought you'd say, Helga, and for the record, I never doubted you. But Ina Reysor needs help, and I know that you two grew close, so I figured I'd ask you now before she and her crew are off the ship," Cilas said.

"Is Brise going to join her?"

"No, he's hitching a ride to the nearest hub. I think that funeral did something to him, or maybe it was the pod. Either way, he's finished. Signing that paper felt more like accepting defeat than the day we surrendered to those Geralos," Cilas said. "We knew that Sol was skeptical of our leadership. How could he not be skeptical? His own father was corrupted years ago."

"I didn't know that," Helga said.

"When I signed his paperwork, he said some things to me, things that made me look past my cynicism towards his agenda. I came in here to see what you think. I want to hear from you, where your thoughts are on everything. I want to move forward and rejoin the fight, but I cannot pretend that five of my men aren't dead."

Helga started playing with the ring on her right hand, it was the one she'd been given for graduating from the Cadet Academy. She was about to ask about the commander, but thought better of it. If Cilas didn't trust him to tell the truth about what they had gone through, then the last thing he wanted to do was talk about it.

She also knew that he didn't trust him, and she suspected that they were being watched and recorded. The fact that there were accommodations ready for them on their arrival led her to believe that each of their compartments had probably been bugged.

Helga thought about inviting Cilas out for a walk so that they could talk openly about the Alliance, but they were dressed in clothes that had been given to them. Bugs were small enough to be woven into the lapels. The entire ship would be under surveillance – making it impossible to hide for long.

"We're being watched, aren't we?" she said after a time, and Cilas smiled, which meant the answer was a yes. "I should talk to Brise before he leaves. We've barely spoken since he joined us on the pirate ship, and I don't think I'll get the chance to see him again."

"You okay, Helga? I don't mean to keep asking, but earlier at the funeral ... I can't just ignore that. We've been together long enough for me to know a bit about you, and what I saw at the service struck me as the truth leaking out. Have you been to the sick—?"

"It was a funeral. I got emotional, Cilas," she said, feeling cornered. "I'm not weak or out of my mind, alright? Brise may not be able to take it, but trust me, I can."

"Helga ..."

"No. Cilas, please, just – just leave it alone," she said. The pain was back, like a burning wound in the back of her throat, and it was becoming increasingly hard to keep it all together.

Cilas didn't seem convinced but he didn't say anything more. He scooted back his chair, stood up suddenly, then turned and walked over to the door. Helga assumed he was upset, but so was she, and he was prying beyond what she needed. If only he could just listen, and be there for her – it was all she really needed.

"I may seem to have it together, Helga, but that's just my training," he said, without turning to face her. "A part of me died when that lassword robbed me of my best friend. You're all I have left, and I don't take that lightly." There was a painful silence that passed between them as a tear broke free and rolled down Helga's cheek. "Don't forget to eat," he finally said, and then he was gone. Just like that.

Helga walked to the door. She needed to say something, but he was too far and she didn't know what to say. It was obvious that he had a lot on his mind, yet he was worried more about her. Why wouldn't he be? He was Cilas Mec, a model ESO in every way, skilled, experienced, and loyal to a fault.

This stalwart and icon of the Alliance military had been told that his superiors had a hand in Lamia's corruption. This led him to lie to a superior officer and pretend that he was still oblivious to the facts. *It's probably eating him up inside and he wanted to talk*, Helga thought. *Can't talk here, will need to figure it out later.*

If the lizards could corrupt people on shielded warships, Helga didn't know what they'd be able to do. At any time one of her fellow pilots could become corrupt and fire on her. A dockhand could sabotage their entire fleet and stall them out when they were engaged with the enemy. She was also an Alliance officer, sworn to carry out commands. What if she was ordered to cripple one of their starships?

Helga wished that she had something stiff to drink. She'd give anything to take the edge off the paranoia she felt. It had her in that doorway staring after Cilas like a concerned lover seeing her man off. She caught a few Marines watching her with piqued interest, so she snapped out of her stupor and stepped back inside.

As the door slid shut, she stood with her back against the bulkhead, staring up at the dirty vent above the table.

The Geralos had been sneaky and precise in their scheming. Lamia, for all his spectacular gifts, had not been able to stop the mind control, she thought. *He was supposed to kill us all, and then the Geralos were supposed to kill him. No one would have known that we died down there.*

The Nighthawks had been a unit for several years. They were the unit every cadet dreamed of joining after graduation. She had been given the privilege, then proved herself alongside them. Now Brise was out, and she was left with their leader.

"We need to get off this ship," she whispered. "It's not safe here for any of us."

The words repeated themselves in her head, and she understood why Brise had decided to quit. She tried to think of an excuse but none came to mind. She was stuck on the *Inginus*, just like the lieutenant. "We must do what we need to honor our fallen brothers," he had said, which meant that she would face death if that was what it meant for justice.

"I died back on Dyn," she reminded herself, and closed her eyes to accept this truth. She would play along with whatever the *Inginus* offered, but when it came time to act, she would be ready.

Brise Sol was in the hangar, seated on the deck near the transport ship, his back to the bulkhead. He didn't seem to notice Helga as she walked beneath a Phantom's wing, and it was only when she hovered over him did he acknowledge her presence.

"How long did it take you to find me?" he said without looking up at her.

"Was this a game that you were playing, Sol? See how long it will take for Helga to find me?" she said.

He cracked a smile, and she kicked him in the leg, not hard but with enough strength to let him know she wasn't amused. "You think sitting next to this thing will make the time go by faster?" she said. "You're stuck with us until the commander decides that you can leave."

"So he told you then," he said with disgust. "I don't know how you can follow that guy after everything we've been through."

"You mean the lieutenant?"

"Who else would I be talking about?" he said.

Helga slid down next to him and drew her knees up so she could hug them. "Cilas ain't so bad. You two are just ... different. Is it because of him that you're leaving us to go play adventure with the pretty redhead?" she said.

"Oh, get off it, Ate, she has nothing to do with this," he said.

"Doesn't hurt that she's hot, right? You think that you're her type?"

"Look, just because we have the same color hair doesn't mean that I've lost my mind. She's a good-looking woman, yes, but I'm hardly her type, and again it has nothing to do with me leaving the Alliance. Seriously, Ate, have you walked around this ship? Have you seen the way they look at us? We, the so-called elite bunch. They were sent out here to collect us but they hate our guts. Makes sense considering that their very leaders—"

"Stow it and don't repeat it," Helga snapped. "Lest you want to leave this ship through an airlock. We can't talk about that, but know that we aren't far from where you stand on the topic. Are you understanding me, Sol? The time for talking about that is over. The people who run this ship and its crew are made of different stuff than Cilas. Yes they hate our guts. I'm hardly blind, but you know what? We're better than them."

"Go on."

"How many of these brush cuts have been up close and personal with the lizards? How many of them can boast about that, or anything that you've done? They see us as a threat, a reminder that they're not as bad as we are. So they give us mean looks and talk behind our backs. You know what, Sol, thype them. They're the same caliber of losers I beat back in the academy," Helga said.

"Are you okay, Ate? You seem ... angrier than normal," he said.

"Oh, not you too," she said, and ran her fingers through her hair.

"You've been through a lot, Helga. This was your first mission and we put you through it. I joke around, but I want you to know that I see you as a sister in many ways. When we voted to go with the lieutenant, I know that you spoke up to cut me a break. I...." He stopped talking so suddenly that Helga looked around to see if someone had startled him.

"It's okay, Sol, you know that you can talk to me. I hold no judgment on you," she said.

Brise Sol was hunched over, his shoulders resting on his knees as he toyed with his laces in a way that reminded her of a child. "After the camp something changed, Ate. I lost the urge to go on. There was a time when I woke up and saw all those bodies hanging near me, and I knew it was over. I knew that my life was done. But then the lieutenant saves me and calls me a coward in the same breath. From that moment I hated him, because deep down I knew he was right."

"The Brise Sol I know is no coward, do you hear me?" Helga said. "You saved Cilas's ass when we were hemmed up in that cave. You didn't balk at the dredge, and you were there with us fighting the lizards. He was unconscious so he couldn't appreciate all that you'd done. I'm not making any excuses for Cilas, but you aren't a coward, Brise."

"That's the thing. I wasn't a coward, but then I was caught and something changed. Even now I can still feel the cold of the mist inside that room. This is why I have to leave, Ate. I'm going to get you killed. There will be a time when you need me and I am going to let you down. No, don't talk me out of it, please. Just ... just let me go and salvage what's left of my life."

"I was just going to say that I love you, Brise. Like a brother, of course, so don't get any ideas," she said, laughing.

Brise grew quiet as he stared forward, and she knew he'd drawn into himself. It was his defense mechanism when his mouth no longer worked for him and he knew that he was about to break. Helga reached out with one arm and pulled him in, and his shoulders loosened just enough for him to rest his head on her shoulder. "Wherever you go, if you get into trouble, know that you have a friend on the inside," she said.

"I know, Ate. If I get in trouble, I know you'll be here. I could never admit this when I was in uniform, but you're the strongest spacer I know."

25

Since the rescue and the departure of Ina Reysor from the *Inginus*, Helga found that she had a hard time sleeping. Her insomnia had started before that, really, but in the past, it was sporadic, not persistent like it was now. Her sleep had come in spurts while floating around within their escape ship. She recalled Brise having the same issue, but Cilas would pass out for hours.

Now as she became acclimated to the new ship, she found herself restless—a circumstance of staying constantly on guard. It wasn't that she felt threatened being inside her compartment or that she had little voices inside her head convincing her that "they" were coming for her. It was something else, a more subtle nagging that refused to let her sleep.

She had started running with Cilas every morning to keep herself in shape. But even this strenuous exercise didn't urge her body to rest. Nothing worked, and though they had good conversation during their runs, she had begun to have trouble focusing.

When she wasn't running she'd explore the ship and stand at the windows, staring out into space. This was how she knew the *Inginus* was at full thrust, traveling at the speed of light. Helga didn't know what they were chasing, but the ship was an inflator so she assumed that this was standard.

Several days after Ina left with Brise and her crew, Helga agreed to meet Cilas at the gun range to practice a bit of shooting. She had stumbled back to her compartment after their run. She showered and dressed, but fell asleep while eating a ration bar.

As it always did when sleep finally came, the darkness took her into an elaborate nightmare. She didn't know when she had fallen out of reality, but she found herself in a line with over fifty men and women. She recognized the setting as one from her past, when they were ready to take on the final test of BLAST.

When her eyes came open, she was confused and frantically looked around to assess where she was. A long line of drool stuck to her arm as she lifted her head to see. *Blaargh!* A horn blared over the intercom, so loud that she could barely think. *What is that noise?* she thought. *Is that an alarm? We better not be under attack.*

She wiped her mouth with the back of her hand and rubbed at her eyes. It felt as if she'd slept for days. Her limbs were sore, but in a good way. The dream of that memory was still fresh in her mind, so vivid and real that she wanted to go back.

Blaargh! The alarm startled her again. It was making her angry. "Planets! Will someone shut that thyping thing off," she shouted.

She put her hands on the table and pushed back her chair, standing up on rubbery legs and trying to steady herself. "Oh man, Cilas," she whispered, remembering the range. She had showered and dressed—that part she remembered—but how had she fallen asleep all of a sudden?

She tasted powdery chocolate in her mouth, thick and beyond disgusting, and she saw the half-finished protein ration laying on the table. "Wow, I fell asleep eating," she said. "Well, on the bright side, I got some sleep despite doing it with my mouth full. Cilas is probably done with me."

She reached down amidst her clothes and located her communicator. When she found it there were several messages ready for her to open, and the one from Cilas simply read, "You probably fell out. I'm glad. We'll go shooting later on."

The message made her smile, and she thought of his kind eyes— *wait*, she thought. *He's your lieutenant, silly girl.* She tried to put him out of her mind and grew upset with herself for thinking ... *It's been months since I got any, so obviously I'm hard up,* she thought. *Stars, what is wrong with me? I'm such a thyping wreck.*

Fumbling with the communicator, she opened a message from an unknown source. It addressed her as "Ensign Ate," and bore the official seal of the Alliance.

It was a formal summons to come to the hangar to meet her new squadron. It had to be a mistake. She read it one more time. *"Thype, we are under attack,"* she said, and then walked to the far end of the compartment where her operating system stood in stasis.

Waving her hand across the node, a vid screen appeared on the bulkhead. It showed a view of all the main areas of the ship, and she waved her hand again to show the exterior. That was when she saw what was going on. The *Inginus* had caught up to the Geralos destroyer that had jumped away.

Helga placed the communicator on her wrist and quickly threw on some clothes. She took off running down the passageway, looking to gain the hangar. The run helped to melt the stray cobwebs from her brain, and by the time she arrived she was wide-awake.

She waded into the company of Aces and Marines. Most of them gave her questioning looks, as if she had walked in on the wrong house party. Self-consciously, Helga took inventory of what she was wearing: a long t-shirt, sweatpants, and soft running shoes. All of the *Inginus* Marines were in uniform, which were blue flight suits—coveralls—branded with the ship's insignia.

Helga looked over at a raised platform where a woman was prepping them for combat. She was petite, but her voice was deep and strong enough to carry throughout the hangar. Helga was surprised to see how young she was, since she was obviously the flight commander. This made her smile, and she felt proud somehow. Seeing someone like her in that high a position was both refreshing and inspiring.

The woman was telling them the status: they were to deploy immediately. The *Inginus* had disabled the Geralos's FTL drive and it had launched a fleet of fighters to return the favor. They were to wipe out these fighters, then attack the destroyer itself, forcing it into defensive maneuvers while the *Inginus* primed a torpedo.

Her speech was short and sweet, and it was loaded with phrases meant to pump them up. Phrases like, "they took our planet," and, "we are not their food." Even Helga found her blood running hot, ready to be part of the fight.

When the speech was over, Helga pushed her way to the front and stood in front of the woman to get her attention. "I came as ordered. I am ready to fight," she said.

The woman, whose rank read lieutenant, looked Helga up and down with what appeared to be extreme annoyance. "You're the stray from the *Rendron* that's supposed to be hot schtill, right?" she said. "Well, since you're too badass to dress in uniform, you can fly the VC parked over there."

"Yes ma'am," Helga said, fighting the urge to roll her eyes. She saluted and made to leave, but the lieutenant ordered her to stop.

"Name's Joy Valance, but you refer to me as Lieutenant," she said. "I don't know how they do it on the *Rendron*, skinny, but we wear our uniforms to battle, not ... what is that? Workout gear?" She covered her face, as if Helga's clothes offended her. "Get out of my face and get mounted," she said.

Helga bit her lip and marched over to the ship. It was a Vestalian Classic, a once popular model before the phantom took its place. This one seemed particularly old, and she wondered if it would fly. A dockhand came up and handed her a helmet resting on a bundle. She saw that it was the uniform, and looked up to find the lieutenant staring daggers at her.

"You can shove those ugly rompers up queen cruta's rear," she said to him, then pulled on the helmet and ascended the ladder.

The Vestalian Classic was built very much like an interplanetary aircraft, in that the cockpit was at the top allowing for a 360-degree view through the glass. It didn't hover like a phantom since it rested on wheels, which was an obsolete carry-over from the air force back on Vestalia.

The Classic was once popular for its multifunctional capabilities, allowing it to break atmosphere and land outside of a starship. It sprouted six wings, three on each side, an aesthetic that was abandoned when the phantom was developed.

Helga was sure that the lieutenant had given her the Classic as a form of punishment, but it was a model that she knew from the *Rendron*'s simulations.

She started on her preliminary checks as the dockhand looked over her weapons. When he was satisfied, he gave her a thumbs up, and she returned it with a smile. Helga regretted that she'd been short with him when he didn't deserve it, so she mouthed a "thank you" to let him know he was appreciated.

The lieutenant, Joy Valance, came over the comms, shouting out the call signs of the pilots she wanted to deploy. One by one the sleek phantoms lifted up and shot through the tunnel leading to the bay doors. When Helga heard her say *"Rendron"* she drove the Classic forward, lined the nose up with the tunnel, and acknowledged that she was ready to take off.

She overcharged her thrusters until the gauge was glowing red and then released the brakes while slamming the thrust forward. The tiny ship shook violently as it shot past several phantoms, and she pulled back on the stick before it crashed into the bulkhead.

Though she couldn't hear her gasp, Helga knew that she'd frightened the lieutenant, but she banked hard to the side as the Classic found air. This maneuver was dangerous, but it was one she'd mastered in the simulation. On the *Rendron* she would have been reprimanded, but on this strange new ship she could feign ignorance.

She performed a roll above the frightened pilots to test how responsive it was, and flew around the hangar once before locating the tunnel and taking it at top speed.

When she flew out into space she was immediately assaulted by a Geralos ship. He'd timed her exit and evaporated her shields, causing the interface to scream warnings into her helmet. "You've got this," she whispered, and forced herself to remain calm.

The bogey was on her now and she took defensive maneuvers, but a shot had clipped her wing and she saw death flash before her eyes. "Okay, now I'm mad," she said, as she flew at the *Inginus* to shake off her pursuer.

If she hit the infiltrator's shields, it would be like flying into a wall, but she pulled up in time, skimming the bottom of the Classic. The Geralos copied her maneuver but pulled up before she did, which bought her enough time to counter.

Helga reached down towards the console to adjust her power reserves. Although her shields needed to be repaired, she transferred 70% of the power to her thrusters. The other 30% she poured into her cannons, then pulled back on the stick to arc the Classic away from the *Inginus.*

When the Geralos was in her crosshairs, she fired twice and then dipped towards the infiltrator again. Her shots hit home, frying the shields, but instead of him pursuing her like she'd hoped, he flew away to repair.

"No, you don't," she announced when she saw what he was doing. She took the power from the cannons and put all 100% into the thrusters.

She was on him in seconds, flying so close that the system screamed. But she was smelling blood now, and nothing was going to stop her from destroying him. As she grew close she shifted the reserves again to a balanced ratio of cannons, thrust, shields, and controls. The Geralos pilot tried to shake her, but Helga Ate was too good.

She waited for him to panic, then took advantage of his mistake. When he was reduced to debris she flew back around to find the *Inginus* again. All around the two warships were Geralos and Alliance aces dogfighting. She would have been in awe at the sight—this was what she'd always dreamed of—but she was too focused to appreciate it.

The fever of battle took over, followed by something akin to predatory instinct. 2400 hours in simulation paid off as a second Geralos went down from her guns.

Helga hugged the *Inginus*, relying on the proximity to keep the enemy from surrounding her. But when she found a line of cannons that were firing on the Geralos destroyer, she smiled cruelly from the cockpit, knowing she'd struck gold.

She timed their fire and stayed between their shots. "Who's the psycho in the Vestalian Classic?" someone said over comms.

"I don't know, but whoever it is won't be around long for us to find out," another one said.

"That's because you all have no imagination," Helga said, as she watched a careless Geralos die trying to get through the cannon fire. Several more broke off when they saw what she was doing, but this allowed her to take the offensive, frying their aft thrusters as they made to escape.

Four of the Geralos went down like this before the rest avoided her altogether. The *Inginus* fighters were winning now, and the Geralos scrambled back to their destroyer. One of the phantoms followed them inside and sacrificed his life to wreak havoc on their hangar.

"That was Corporal Eddie Zyn. Remember his name," the lieutenant said, and there was a moment of silence over the normally chaotic comms.

"Lieutenant, this is *Inginus* command, do you copy?" someone said.

"This is Lieutenant Valance of Revenant Squadron, over. I copy you loud and clear, command," said Joy.

"Good job, Lieutenant. That was an ace display of defense. We are now cleared to launch a torpedo, so clear the area and come on home," he said.

"You heard him, Revenants, let's find that dock and get cover," Joy said.

Helga didn't know what this meant, so she flew away from the destroyer towards a triad of phantoms. They had formed a triangle near the deployment hatch and were taking turns to enter it. The comms were eerily silent, and Helga didn't know what to think. It felt as if something devastating was about to happen.

She joined the back of the line and waited, feeling goose pimples on her arms. *How in the world did I survive just now?* she thought, her mind running calculations on how lucky she had been. The word "instinct" surfaced but it was more than that. She had employed large strategy, tricks she'd seen accomplished by the aces of her father's time.

Helga felt a smile come across her face as the stress fall away from her mind. It was such a good feeling that she wanted to scream. Not just scream to herself, but into the comms to let everybody know. But she merely laughed to herself, a deep, freeing laugh. She laughed in a way that made her feel better than she'd felt in ages.

The *Inginus* pilots were seasoned aces, yet several of them had died. Helga had come through it alive and sent several of the lizards to their graves. She grabbed one of her dog tags and pointed it towards the Geralos destroyer. "Thank you," she whispered. "Thank you, whoever is out there looking out for me. Thank you," she said again, and kept on saying it until a noise brought her back to the present.

The next few moments were a blur as the Geralos ship began to disintegrate. The torpedo had been deployed and the explosion was so bright that Helga had to shield her eyes.

Helga had seen ships take each other apart in feeds from the old war, but to see it live and up close was something she'd never forget. Her comms chirped loudly, and it was so unexpected that it caused her to jump.

She saw that it was the lieutenant, so she didn't answer immediately. How was she going to talk with her beating heart lodged somewhere inside her throat? She accepted the call, then exhaled evenly, guiding her ship down to the open bay doors.

"Finished watching the show out there, Rendron? Do you want to join us inside the *Inginus*?" the lieutenant said, and Helga realized that she was the last one left.

"Coming in," she said through her teeth. She was so upset that she wanted to slap herself. Extra attention was the last thing she wanted, especially after the euphoria she'd experienced from the victory.

What do they call you, Rendron?" the lieutenant said.

"The name's Helga Ate—but Rendron is fine, Lieutenant." *You're about to give me some thyped up nickname either way, aren't you?* she thought.

There was a bit of a pause, and then the lieutenant came back on the comms. "You dress like schtill, but you're alright, Ate," she said. "You can fly wing with me any time."

Helga didn't know what to say. She didn't expect friendliness from the lieutenant, especially after she'd given her this rusty old ship. What was she supposed to think of a woman like this? A woman who knew nothing of her skills, yet had her deploy in a junky fighter.

She shut off her comms and let out a scream, then glanced over at the lieutenant's phantom. She had landed and was now close enough to see into her cockpit. "It's a pleasure to meet you, Lieutenant Joy," she said in a mocking voice. "I cannot wait to make you pay for trying to get me killed."

She switched back on the comms and took a breath, composed herself, and said, "My pleasure, Lieutenant. Glad I could impress you. I bet you didn't think I'd do much inside of this old ship." *Except die and be out of your hair,* she thought as she maintained a false smile.

"Oh, that," Joy said, laughing hysterically. "I seriously didn't expect you to know how to fly it! My plan was for you to stay stuck inside the hangar, but you showed me up, didn't you? I should have your wings for that stunt inside my hangar. Anyway, that was good flying, Ate. You should let me buy you a beer. You can tell me who taught you how to fly that thing, and I'll formally welcome you to the Revenant squad."

26

"So, were you born on Casan or are you just another Boomer like the rest of us hopeless humans?" Lieutenant Joy Valance asked, as she hovered over her beer like a dragon perched above a chest of gold.

Helga shrugged. She hated the term "Boomer." It was a derogatory word that meant "One who was not born on a planet." The way she saw it, the term originated from the bored minds of the Vestalian elite, those lucky refugees whose ancestors fled the planet with enough credits to buy property on a moon.

Being rich and safe allowed such boredom and gave them the time it took to judge the Vestalians who were fighting the enemy. What bothered her more than these hateful elite was that the term was adopted by the Boomers themselves.

"I am," she finally said, studying the woman's face. She had those smiling eyes that made it appear as if everything was a joke. "I spent some of my childhood years on Casan with my brother and my mom. What about you, Lieutenant, what planets have you visited?"

"Genese, and Traxis," she said, as if she'd anticipated being asked. "Never been to Casan, but it's definitely on the list for next time I get some shore leave."

Helga forced a smile and then sipped her beer. She decided that she didn't hate the lieutenant, despite the tension in the hangar. It helped that Joy Valance had gone out of her way to get her into the bar, starting with giving her a locker on the dock and signing the classic over to her, officially.

There had been no apology after the sortie, but every one of the pilots had introduced themselves to her. This she knew was the lieutenant's doing, and it made her feel good that her flying had impressed her this much. "Shore leave, what is that?" Helga said with a wink, and they both started laughing hysterically.

"So, Cilas Mec ... care to dish?" she said, running her forefinger around the mouth of her mug.

There it is, Helga thought. *I knew this couldn't just be about my flying.* "You mean Lieutenant Cilas? My Lieutenant Cilas?" Helga said.

Joy Valance sat up suddenly, as if something had lodged itself inside her throat. Her brown eyes widened. "Oh, I didn't realize," she said, quietly. "I was just curious. Y'know how it is."

Helga tilted her head unconsciously, trying to read the lieutenant's face. "What just happened there, Lieutenant?" she said. "Are you—oh." It finally dawned on her what had made the lieutenant react the way she did. "My Lieutenant," Helga whispered, thinking. "No, Lieutenant Cilas and I aren't ... no, not like that. We're just friends," she said, quickly taking another sip of her beer.

She wanted to disappear. Why had she taken this woman up on her offer of a drink? It had to look bad: the words she'd used, her reaction now—

"Good!" the lieutenant said. "Girl, I was about to say ... oops," She spat out beer as she burst out laughing. "Awkward, right? Because if you and he were a thing, you wouldn't like me right now. Let me just leave it at that."

Is this woman drunk? Helga thought. "So you and Lieutenant Cilas are...?"

The lieutenant lowered her eyes and sipped at her beer. That was all the answer Helga needed for her feelings to get involved. She felt confused. No—more like hurt. *But that isn't fair*, she reasoned. Cilas didn't know how she felt, plus it wasn't allowed, and he was so much older.

Excuse after excuse went through her brain as Lieutenant Joy Valance talked on. Helga was no longer hearing her, only the thoughts in her head, the thoughts that let her know that Cilas was now out of her reach.

Joy Valance was no beauty, but she had good bone structure and a pretty pair of light brown eyes. She was intelligent, and an officer, not to mention the top ace on an Alliance interceptor. The woman also had the sort of confidence that was irresistible to men like Cilas Mec.

"...this is why I called you out for the drink to explain," Joy said. "It was Cilas's idea all along."

"I'm sorry, could you repeat what you just said?" Helga said, hopeful that the lieutenant was saying that the whole romance with Cilas was a prank that he was pulling on her.

"I was letting you know that the Vestalian Classic thing was Cilas's fault. He suggested that model when he heard you would be on my squadron," she said. "He told me that you were an ace in the making, and that all of your simulations were done in a Classic. I said, Cilas, you are going to get your girl killed, but he was like, no, Helga is the best. So I owe him a few things, and I owe you an apology," she said.

Helga wanted to hate her now more than ever, but she was being too honest and it made her even more likeable. She felt her brows knitting as she stared at her face. Then she shut her eyes defiantly and nodded. "How are you so cool?" she said, pushing back the hurt to change the subject to something else.

"Cool?"

"Yes, cool as in relaxed. Just look at you. I want to be you when I grow up," Helga said.

Joy started to laugh again and Helga joined her, letting it all hang out. The beer helped her heal, and she drank more to make herself numb. She forced herself to be happy for Cilas, no matter how absurd it was. They had been out in space forever, and he would be just as lonely as she was. Being together was never an option so why should she begrudge him for finding happiness with this woman?

"You're really funny, do you know that?" the lieutenant said. She was on her fifth mug and it had become obvious that the alcohol was taking its toll. "You wanting to be me. Girl, if I could fly half as well as you, I would not be here on this raggedy ship," she said, and started laughing again.

Helga didn't know what to say. It was drunken honesty, but it was honesty nonetheless. The lieutenant had given her one of the greatest compliments. Her words managed to push off the sadness she felt for not having Cilas while pulling in a want to get back to action.

"Thank you, Lieutenant," she said, reaching forward to touch her hand. "Thank you, but I mean it. Cilas is a very lucky man."

Since winning the fight with the Geralos destroyer, the *Inginus* began salvaging parts from the debris. This was common practice for Alliance warships, considering the lack of resources coming in from the planets.

It had been days since the excitement, and Helga was doing better – well, better in that she was sleeping more, and had left her compartment for more than eating and taking a shower. She had kept to herself, but no one bothered her and somehow she knew this was due to Joy. The *Inginus* Marines had heard about her skills so she was no longer treated like an unwanted refugee.

This thawing of her icy comrades did not serve to make her friendly. She still saw them as dangerous, and kept her back to the bulkhead whenever she passed a crowd. This was what she was doing now as she waited by the range for Cilas to arrive. They had agreed on a time to shoot and she wanted to pick his brain about the Alliance conspiracy.

The lieutenant showed up with Joy in tow, and she saw that they were pretending that they weren't an item. She wondered just how many people were actually fooled since Cilas had a hard time not looking at her.

Joy gave her a wave and a knowing look, and Helga quickly returned the gesture. They hadn't spoken much since that night at the bar, but she still felt a deep connection with the woman. Something in the way they bonded went beyond words. It was when their eyes met; there was an understanding there that went unsaid.

Joy spoke to Cilas briefly and stepped in to kiss him before she left him to walk back down the passageway. He looked ready to go after her—a man that couldn't get enough. But he was strong and resisted, walking to Helga with a forced smile.

"Ready to work on that dead eye?" he said, cheerfully.

"I'm ready now." Helga forced a smile. "Turns out sleep can be a good thing."

He stopped in front of her with his hands on his hips, looking past her face at the closed door. "Surprising, isn't it?" he said. "But I do have to warn you that the men who run the range are a bit ... closed-minded? The idea of an alien woman fighting on our side ... well, they have their own opinions, and it isn't very nice."

"I can handle a bunch of racists. Are you saying that they won't let me shoot?" she said.

"Well, they're still Marines, and if you're with me then they will leave you alone."

Helga thought about the cold reception she'd received when she first got on the ship. Now she understood why they took to Brise and not her.

"When Vestalia was invaded, the Casanian military answered the call," she said. "They bled to protect their allies instead of turning their backs like the Louine. Humble civilians put down their tools and picked up guns for the cause. Many of them lost their lives, Cilas, leaving the planet filled with widows and orphans. I won't be treated badly for my lineage. Not here on this ship nor back home on the *Rendron*."

"Hello, Ate, this is me you're talking to," Cilas said, looking a bit offended. "Nothing you're saying is news to me. Just keep your head and let me handle them."

Helga wasn't so sure about Cilas's promise. He wasn't the one who had grown up with humans that made every alien out to be the enemy. Her spots were a target, and many had taken aim, using her as the avatar for the cause of their suffering.

"They can't help themselves," she said, defiantly. "But if they start with me, they will learn quickly why I made second class."

"Let's go kill some virtual lizards," Cilas said, his jaw jutting out as if he expected a fight. Stepping past Helga, he pushed open the door, and she followed him inside to an extremely cold passageway. The walls were reinforced Louine glass, impenetrable to laser and ballistic weapons.

Helga stumbled on a ramp that seemed to come from out of nowhere. She looked around, embarrassed, hoping that no one saw, but when she made to follow Cilas again, she saw that he was watching her.

"Are you okay?" he said.

"I'll live," she said, biting down the urge to tell him off. The one thing that always annoyed her about Cilas was his incessant need to play the guardian. She didn't know if it was just because she was a woman or if he saw her as a younger sibling. Either of those realities did not make her feel good. She was a *Rendron* warfighter, trained to bring death to the Geralos scourge.

How dare he pretend that a mere stumble could have hurt ... she wasn't his girlfriend, and she damn sure wasn't helpless.

She reached forward and pushed him as he walked up the ramp, and he stumbled and caught the railing, stopping in his tracks. She hadn't meant to hurt him; it was just frustration leading to action. But he was her superior, and she froze when she realized what she had done.

Cilas turned around slowly and regarded her curiously. "Did you do that on purpose, Ate?" he said.

"Okay, Lieutenant, I did push you, but I swear I did it respectfully," she said, adding a grin and hoping that it would diffuse the offense somehow.

"You're a little schtill, do you know that?" he said. "Always with the jokes and the messing around. I'll be ready next time, just remember that. You'll be surprised how fast I am. You don't want to test me, Helga."

The utterance of her first name came with mysterious undertones, and as he turned to continue walking she wondered if it was part of the threat. Either way she felt stupid. Why had she pushed him like that? Children pushed each other playfully, not grown up Alliance spacers.

When they got to the top there was an open lobby. The bulkhead was lined with all manner of weapons. There were auto rifles, pulse rifles, starguns, and pistols. In front of these weapons were several Marines with long beards and muscles corded like rope. One took off his shades to eye her up and down, and she shot him a glance that could melt a glacier.

Cilas introduced himself and placed his hand over the identification scanner. The computer chimed, then displayed all of his information, from his place of birth to his numerous combat accolades. "Welcome, Lieutenant," said the beard, and saluted him sharply. The rest of the men did the same, and Helga would have rolled her eyes if she wasn't used to it.

Cilas was a big deal wherever he went, and being so close to him made it easy to forget. For the first time she was confident that this boy's club wouldn't give her trouble. And she glared at one menacingly, daring him to say something now that he knew who she was.

They picked out a variety of ballistics weapons and went inside one of the private ranges. These were tight passageways built to be impenetrable by the bullets, and would display virtual targets picked out by the computer.

"They can't hear us in here," Cilas said, "and I doubt they thought to bug all of their gun ranges. This is why I suggested it, but let me hear what you think. I'll hover close so I can listen, but keep firing – just in case they're watching."

Helga did as he said, and began to shoot at her targets. She found that her aim was much better than she thought. She was proficient with the handguns and above average with the pulse, but the auto rifle was a lot for her frame, so that was the weapon she decided to focus on.

"I've been wondering something," she said, as she aimed down the sights. She put two bullets in the hologram, shattering it immediately. A diagram of the body appeared on the screen to her right, showing that she had put both rounds near the creature's heart.

"How is it that our Alliance leaders missed the fact that this moon was a trap? Why did they choose to send us in alone when they could have jumped in *Inginus* from the start? Wouldn't saving human lives be enough to warrant an *Inginus*-led strike? Yet they send in the Nighthawks—assassins, not rescuers. Then they add two rookies to a six-man team of seasoned veterans. It's a very confusing oversight, wouldn't you agree?"

Cilas stepped up next to her and triggered his own set of targets. One by one he dropped them with precise shots to their vitals. Helga wondered if he was human, his aim was so immaculate, and he did it all so easily that it was over as soon as it started. He didn't even bother to check where his bullets had registered. It was as if he knew, and didn't need the computer to tell him.

"You said a mouthful," he said, "but I can explain why you're here. We needed a pilot and I made them choose you. Brise, on the other hand, was a good engineer. He won the lottery over several other people so he got the chance to join us. There's no conspiracy about you two, but Lamia Brafa is another thing. He's been on missions with us before but he isn't an ESO so his motivations were outside of my scope."

Cilas inhaled a deep breath and placed his weapon down on the table. He then picked up a pulse rifle that looked like a toy. "Bottom line for me, Helga, is that my men are dead at the hands of an ally. No matter how much I want to chalk that up to schtill luck, it still bothers me that they could corrupt a Jumper. You saw Brafa's skills, and he's talked to you about his order. Jumpers train their minds to prevent exactly what happened to him."

"Are you saying that Lamia Brafa's order is behind what happened to us?" Helga said.

"I've been doing a lot of thinking, and I think that we're in danger for surviving Dyn. The Alliance military sees this as a botched mission but I have a deep feeling that someone orchestrated this entire thing. This someone would be a part of Captain Sho's circle of trust, and this is why I kept the details from Lang."

"I get it now, Lieutenant, but what are we to do? I don't know this ship, and they obviously don't want us here."

"Just keep your mouth shut about what really happened on Dyn, even if you're pressed to contradict me," he said. "We're on this ship for a while; they won't be jumping until they're ready. Adapt and excel, the way you were trained. When the time arises I will pull you to the side and tell you our next move. Until then, stay cold and keep a set of eyes on your six."

"Yes, sir," she said. He wasn't giving her any ideas that she hadn't had before, especially when it came to watching her back. Brise had left, leaving the two of them, and she wondered if he'd wind up dead on a hub orbiting Vestalia. "What will happen to Brise?" she said, finding his eyes.

"He's going to have one hell of an adjustment fitting into civilian life. He was new military, so he'll have no commission, and *Rendron* is a war machine. Civilians aren't welcome on there. Plus, he wouldn't want to be on there when he'll be seen as a coward the rest of his life. I think that he'll find a hub, get himself some shelter, and live out the rest of his years in poverty and peace."

Helga couldn't believe what she was hearing, but she knew that civilians had it the hardest. It was why parents sent their children to war fleets like the *Rendron*. They would become cadets, cared for and trained well into their teens, and then they'd join the formal military where food and shelter were provided.

This beat the alternative of the disgusting hubs, where humans preyed on each other in an overpopulated space. "I can't believe Brise would choose this reality over being here with us," she said. "No matter his reasoning then, he'll be seen as a coward. It's unfortunate. He lost a lot for the military but no one will believe us about him, will they? You don't have to worry about me, Cilas, I won't say anything. I'll just keep my head down and do my part."

"I know you will, Ate, that's why I have you here. It's just the two of us now. We're the last of the Nighthawks," Cilas said.

After three hours of shooting, Helga was sore but better, and the lieutenant walked her to her compartment after they agreed to meet again. "Those hard legs in there won't give you trouble," he said, "just in case you want to come back without me. We'll be fighting again soon, Ate. Me, you, and some good recruits. We'll rebuild the Nighthawks, and you will help me make it a great unit again."

"I will," she said, as they clasped wrists in the standard gesture of friendship within their unit. Then he was gone, back to Joy Valance, and she was left in that doorway feeling lonely again. Helga had mixed and conflicting feelings about Cilas but made it her own personal battle to suppress them. The world had been so dark and unfriendly after the horrific time on Dyn, and she had reached that point where life itself was becoming a painful thing.

Every waking moment was a reminder that she didn't belong. She should have been shot or bitten down on that moon, yet she had been spared to return to ... what? Even the silence that the *Inginus* afforded when she was on her cot in the compartment was torture. She craved the sound of something, anything.

Helga grabbed her head. It was happening again. She didn't understand why this was happening to her. The doubt and the severe feeling of ... *blah*, whenever she was alone. Her mind went to the bar where she had shared the drinks with Joy, and the feeling she had afterwards when the liquor took hold of her mind.

It was one of the only nights she had managed to fall asleep, and as she'd traded stories with that stranger, she felt a bit like she belonged. Her body craved that feeling again. No—her body craved companionship. It had been too long. She needed something to escape from her doubtful mind. So she took a transport out of the common quarters and stepped off in front of the bar.

27

The life of an Alliance spacer was one of extreme discipline, and love for humanity that dipped within the waters of fanaticism. To make it onto a squad you had to care about your people; anything less and you were forced onto a hub to live out the war that wouldn't end.

Cilas Mec cared, but it wasn't because he had to. The young man cared because he had been raised on one of those hubs. There was something about seeing people feed on each other like rats that became so much a part of him that he was never able to shake it. Gangsters ran the hubs, and his father—a discharged, former Marine—had developed a gambling habit that made him into their slave.

Young Cilas remembered how his father would go missing for days, only to return with new wounds and knuckles bruised and swollen. He was a proud man despite his disease, and his gambling cost them everything. It eventually cost him his life to get his son to the *Rendron*, when the top gangster began to eye the boy for recruitment.

Sitting up now on his cot, Cilas thought about the look in his mother's eyes that fateful day he boarded the transport ship. It wasn't a look of sorrow, regret, or failure; it was a look of triumph. That look stayed with him. It was the last time he would see her, and though much of his youth was forgotten or recessed, he could still remember her eyes.

A light above the door came to life and a vid screen appeared a few meters in front of him. It showed a shot of the chow hall and Marines having supper, before Joy Valance's face appeared in front of it.

"You there?" she said, and he touched his wrist comms, granting her access to his compartment's cameras.

"I'm here," he said.

"Just confirming that you did watch the vid I sent to your quarters," Joy said.

"Your joust with the lizards?" he said. "No need, I saw it when it happened. You know that the entire ship is on watch when you all are out there fighting. Are you calling just to gloat?"

"No. I'm wondering if you saw your girl in action."

"Ate? Of course. She was the star of the show," he said, smiling. "Pretty hard to miss a Vestalian Classic among all those Phantom fighters."

"Good call on the ship, love, but I'm thinking about keeping her here with us. I could use another ace, and she's wasting her time on the *Rendron*," she said. "Don't be upset with me. I know that you two are close, but if you saw her in action, then you have to admit I am right," she said.

Cilas stood up and stretched, not caring that he was fully nude. He walked over to his locker and fumbled for a fresh set of clothes. "I'm glad she impressed you, Joy, but she's still a Nighthawk. You can borrow her while we're here, but when we jump, she will have work to do. I'm not downplaying the importance of your Revenants, but her skills go way beyond shooting down lizard ships."

"We'll see about that, I think she enjoyed flying with us," she said, and from her tone, Cilas knew there was more to what she was telling him. Helga and Joy had become drinking buddies, and he wondered what the Nighthawk had told her.

"You're a planet-buster ... recon," she was saying. "With you, all she'll ever fly is a dropship. Don't be selfish, let me have her. The girl should have been born with wings. You would have her crawling through mud and playing infantry with the rest of you frogs. She's a bird, Cilas, don't clip her wings. Do I need to come over there to convince you?"

"Now you're just playing dirty," Cilas said, though he wouldn't mind her coming over despite the fact that his mind was set. He thought about it for a minute, and though he agreed with what Joy was saying, he couldn't imagine facing Retzo Sho as the last survivor of the Nighthawks.

He needed Helga, at least for now, until he was back on the *Rendron* and able to rebuild. "After we get back to the *Rendron*," he said flatly as he walked over to the sink. "Once we've been interviewed and given the all-clear, Helga is free to decide where she wants to be."

"Thank you," Joy Valance said, exhaling as if it had taken a lot for her to ask. "I'm all worked up looking at you walk around like that. There's something to say about your body, despite those ugly scars. What are you about to do?"

"I have another date with Ate at the range," he said.

"Is that a no to me coming over?"

"Of course not. Get over here. We have less than half an hour," he said, turning on the water to let it pool into his palms. The vid powered down and he found himself excited. It would happen just about any time he heard her voice. From the first time he met her—a day after they were rescued—he'd had an unhealthy obsession with Joy Valance.

It wasn't that she looked any different from the other well-conditioned military women, but she set his blood to boiling, and there was only one way to tame it. Love at first sight? No, it wasn't love, more like something physically magnetic. They had left the hangar together—she the driver, he the willing vehicle—and went straight to her compartment to have sex.

As Cilas washed his face thoroughly and slipped into a robe, his mind went back to Helga's reaction when she'd learned that the Vestalian Classic was his idea. She had come to his compartment in a drunken rage and told him in so many words that she didn't need his help. She had been more honest than she normally was, and he had seen something in her eyes.

He knew the look, but it wasn't one that he wanted to confirm. She was young, and they had been through the worst conditions together ... of course there were feelings, but he had Joy, and Helga was a member of his team. The image of her drunk and flipping out caused him to laugh. "Go get some sleep, Ate," he had said, and that had somehow calmed her down.

She had hovered in his doorway, her eyes begging to be invited in, but he had fought his urges, and though he regretted it, he was happy that she'd taken the hint. This struggle with his feelings was more complicated than anything he'd ever felt.

Even thinking about her now—the way she'd looked when she'd confronted him—made him want to do right by her. He knew that playing with Helga's heart would destroy what was left of her soul. But he was only human, and he had read what was in those eyes.

The door's chime snapped him to attention and he stepped off the padded mat and onto the cold metal deck to see who it was. A part of him worried that it would be Helga again. She had popped up before unannounced, and could do so now to catch him undressed and vulnerable.

When he saw that it was Joy, he exhaled with relief, and cracked the door wide enough for her to slip inside. She came to him then, hot and ready—the way she always did—grabbing him by the throat before the door was fully sealed.

She pressed her lips to his and backed him into the table, her breath hot and sweet from what he recognized as liquor. She was always rough like this, but it was what she liked and he could take it. He fell back into a chair and she was on him like a spider.

Long limbs and muscles rippling comprised the picture they made. He didn't know when she'd lost her pants, but she was on him before he could react. United, she loosened her grip and hugged him even closer, nails in the back of his neck and hips bucking in rhythmic thrusts.

It was all Cilas could do to hold on as his aggressive partner rocked his world. He wanted her to slow down, but she was strong and it felt amazing, so he closed his eyes and enjoyed the ride until her legs tensed and she froze, groaning.

Seeing an opening in her grip, he stood up and carried her over to the cot. There he lay between her legs and put her arms above her head. He interlocked his fingers with hers and she surrendered to his control. The aggression had passed, and she was his sweet Joy again. He took it slowly, enjoying every bit of her until it was too much to stand and he finished.

"Wow," he whispered as he rolled to the side. He lay on his back looking up at the overhang. "What was that about?"

"I'm sorry, did I break skin this time?" she said.

"Well your nails got longer," he said, laughing, "But the choking ... that was new."

"You have a big bull neck. I just wanted to feel it," she said, standing up and making her way over to the sink. He took a good look at her then, all long brown legs and confidence. Even the way she flicked hair off her shoulder seemed to be practiced with precision.

"Were you a cadet on the *Rendron*, Joy?" he said, still watching her as she went about her business.

"We're swapping histories now? I must have been really good," she said, giggling. It annoyed him that she was never serious, and he really wanted to know. Yes, she had blown his mind, along with giving him some minor injuries, but if she was his girl—and she was his girl—shouldn't he know a bit about her life?

"I was raised on a hub, somewhere over Vestalia. I got brought into the academy later than what they accepted," he said. "But Retzo Sho took a liking to me. He made them take a chance on me, this teenage hoodlum from the bottom. That was a hard time back then, but I'd like to think that I made him proud."

"Cilas, there is nothing about you that hints at an easy childhood," Joy said over the running water. "You're scary good and hard, but only to those outside of your heart. I would be an idiot if I didn't notice that about you. Look, love, I know what you're doing, and it makes sense, but ... you don't want me for that. Trust me. I'm a thyping mess that will just end up disappointing you."

"So this is enough for you? All physical, and nothing else?" he said, sitting up.

"I'd be full of schtill if I said that it was all physical," she said. "I just want you to be sure, that's all."

Cilas didn't know what to say. What could he say to something like that? It was more than physical but not so intimate that they needed to know each other's lives? "Are you scared, Joy? Is that what this is?" he said, and she stopped pulling on her boots to face him.

"I wouldn't call it scared," she said. "I just know what I am, and I know that I like you, and I don't want to thype this up."

He thought about her words, and wondered why it was that she would be so guarded about her life. It made him instantly suspicious, and somewhat tired. It felt as if everyone had lost their minds after he and the Nighthawks were rescued from Dyn.

Had the lizards frozen them and pushed them into another reality? A reality where a man can sleep with a woman, anytime, but he dared not ask her about her childhood. "It's okay, Joy," he said. "We can keep this purely physical. You don't need to worry about me asking again."

"That sounds awfully harsh. Let me try again to explain what I mean," Joy said.

"Nah, save it, I'm running late, and I need to get to the range in five minutes," he said. "We'll talk later if you want, but if you don't mind, I need to get going."

Joy Valance walked to the door, then stopped and turned around to face him. "You're upset. I don't want to leave you upset," she said, and then placed her back to the door.

"I'm a Boomer; my mothership was the *Sairon*. As you know it was destroyed over Geral, and the debris of it and my parents still orbit the planet today." She smiled when she said this, and he could see the pain in this mask she presented. It made him feel guilty for pressing her, now that he understood. "I was a cadet there but got transferred to the *Rendron* after graduation. Had a talent for flying, so they stationed me on this infiltrator. Met some good people ... and bad. Let's just say I got a really quick education. And then I became the lizard-killing machine that's in front of you."

"I'm sorry," Cilas said. "If I'd known, I would have let you tell me on your own time."

"How could you know? Cilas, I just want you to understand that I am not here to use you, but you're a guest on my ship, love. What do you think will happen once we're back in Alliance space? Wait, no, let me tell you what will happen. You will leave this ship, and me, with a ton of promises, and then I'll be one of those pathetic girls sitting around hurt and wondering if you're still alive."

"So, you're worried that I'll get myself killed?" he said.

"No, not worried, just aware that what we have is going to be temporary. But we don't have to be jerks about it, or act like machines because we're afraid of our feelings. We both need this, Cilas, and I know that you're big enough to accept it for what it really is. Aren't you?"

He nodded, though he didn't agree with her. They could make a relationship work, even across ships. He would have to convince her, but he would never push again. Her sad story had struck him in a way that made him feel low.

"Will I see you later?" he said as he approached her.

"Of course," she said, and hugged him. He held her for a long time, until he felt the tension leave from her shoulders. "Thank you," she whispered into his ear, and then she opened the door and was gone.

28

It was the smell that led to the complaint, which led to the panic, which led to the discovery. And this discovery was a new one for Retzo Sho. As he walked through the officer's quarters, past the doors of the privileged few that answered only to him, he saw a crowd gathered in front of Adan Viles' compartment.

His heart did a curtsy—this could not be good. The last thing he needed on the way to a battle was panic within his crew. When they saw him approaching, they cleared a path, some slinking away in the opposite direction. They knew they would be scolded for leaving their posts, but whatever was there made them risk it. This made Retzo even more concerned as he walked towards the door.

Covered noses and downcast eyes were the masks on all their faces, and when he finally reached the doorway, the smell punched him in the nose. Grabbing a handkerchief from his pocket, he covered his mouth and stepped inside. There, in the corner, and surrounded by the masters-at-arms, was his long lost CAG, Adan Viles, hanging from his neck.

He had taken a length of cable and thrown it up over the grill on his vent. He then fashioned a noose, donned it, and kicked the chair out from under him. It had been years since the *Rendron* had a suicide, but it had never been one of his officers. Here was Viles, technically royalty on his ship, and a committed family man, dead in his compartment.

Retzo couldn't understand the motive. *Was it the way I spoke to him?* he thought. He couldn't kick the guilt he felt for playing a part in this.

"It's not safe to be here, Captain Sho. We need to secure and clean the compartment, sir," one of the MA's said, and he recognized him as Misa Chase, the *Rendron's* chief master-at-arms. It seemed like ages since he'd last seen the man, but he was still the same intimidating presence. Bigger than most, with a hawk nose and sharp eyes that seemed to pierce your very soul.

Misa stood at attention in front of him, refusing to move despite his station. "Alright," Retzo said. "But leave it to your people. You're coming with me. I have a lot of questions and I need quick answers. Do you understand?"

"Yes sir," the man said, and followed the captain out of the compartment.

"You all have jobs to do and this ship is on the way to a warzone," Retzo said to the people still gathered in the passageway. "I caution you all to keep this to yourselves. Anyone found spreading rumors will be dealt with. Do you understand? Adan Viles was an officer who served his post well. I will not have his name in the dirt because of misinformation. Move out!"

They scattered like roaches when he stamped his foot, and he was left with the master-at-arms. He walked a ways down the passageway before turning to face the man, his hands in his pockets and his chin held high.

"Why didn't you block off that compartment to keep the people out?" he said.

"When we received the call, Captain, they were all there by the time we arrived. You came a little after we did, and I had just made the call for reinforcements. Did the Commander say anything recently about wanting to take his life, sir? Anything you can tell me will speed things up in terms of finding a motive."

"No, Sergeant, he didn't. I had a stiff conversation with him a few days back. Nothing out of the order, really. We've had stiff discussions before. He seemed to have it together, do you know what I mean? He was the sharpest of all of us, and he was the same way when last we spoke. No, this has to be something else, something... sinister."

"Sinister, Captain?" he said, pulling out his tablet to take notes.

"Well, think about it, Sergeant. We're on our way to a fight, a time when I'll need my CAG more than anything else. This is literally the worst thing that could happen to us. It forces me to replace him with someone that might not be ready. That stiff conversation I mentioned was due to Viles withholding information from me. He was up to something regarding the Nighthawks, and that is what I need to learn."

"Anything we find, you will be the first to know, Captain Sho," the big man said, and Retzo released him back to his duties. What he'd seen in that compartment had sent shockwaves through his body. Adan Viles, dead, when he had assumed he'd snuck off with the *Inginus*.

Why would Viles take his own life? he thought. *Could someone else had done this? Someone that feared that he would talk?* Every sign had pointed back to Viles as the cause of the Nighthawks' disaster on Dyn. Now that he was dead, he could search his compartment, look through his personal device, and more.

He dared not speculate any farther. He was at full light speed racing towards Meluvia. The last thing he needed was a ship in panic over their dead CAG. The people needed him to be a captain now, not an armchair detective looking for a villain. Maybe this was the plan, to take him off the trail. He couldn't go into battle like this.

"Who knows," he grumbled, angry and annoyed. *It's time to get smart and get ahead of this thing.* He touched his wrist and brought it up to his mouth, talking as he continued to walk. "Genevieve," he said. "We have a situation. Get the captain of the *Aqnaqak* on my comms."

"I think I've figured out what's wrong with me," Helga said as she aimed down the sights of a laser-powered auto rifle. Two Geralos ran across her path and she shot them both, shattering their holograms.

"Nice shot," Cilas said. "But what do you mean, you've figured it out? Trauma is trauma, and you refuse to go to sickbay, so naturally your moods are going to be all over the place."

There he goes again, thinking he has all the answers, Helga thought. "Nope. It's this ship. I need to be back in action, not sitting around waiting for Joy Valance to call on me. On the *Rendron* we had routines, drills, and actual jobs. Here, outside of our runs, and this, I'm bored out of my mind."

Cilas nodded when she said this, then nudged her out of the way and brought up a large handgun. He fired off several rounds, putting nine Geralos down, then moved to the table where he ejected the clip.

"You make a good point there," he said as he reached for another weapon. "How do you think I feel? I'm never grounded for this long. I'm hearing that the Geralos are in Meluvian space, and there's a real chance we'll make the jump to give aid to our allies. That happens, Ate, and we're off this thing. Just be prepared. Once we start it's going to move like light."

"Not looking forward to cryo, but Meluvia is worth it," Helga said. "Plus that's only a few light years away from the *Rendron*. We can help the Meluvians and then hitch a ride on one of their ships... that's unless the *Inginus* decides to rendezvous with the big ship."

"Good. You sound ready, but until then, Ate, you need to start taking care of yourself. Get out of that compartment of yours, and meet some Marines. Kick the schtill a bit and socialize. The longer you stew, waiting for the *Rendron*, the more your mind is going to convince you that you're messed up. Listen, since coming out of that coma, I've seen nothing but impressive action out of you. None of this is your fault. Brafa got corrupted. He was our best warrior, but it happens.

"Even if you had tried to stop him, he would have wiped you out in less than a second. Something tells me that when he got flipped, there was enough of him left inside to spare you. Earn the chance he gave you, Ate. Kill so many of those thypes that they start calling you the angel of death. Let them learn who you are and what they did to you. They will realize that it would have been better to let us rescue that colony, since now they have the attention of Helga Ate."

Helga felt herself smiling. It was like fuel for her rage, and now more than anything else, she wanted to fight. Grabbing the auto rifle, she leaned over the barrier and began to drop one target after another. It felt good, but she wanted the real thing, though she didn't know when it would happen.

A few days later she got her wish. The *Inginus* was to jump to Meluvian space to help to remove the Geralos from the planet. The announcement came over the comms as well as the computer system in her compartment. Everyone on board was to report to the deck level E, which was where the cryogenic units were housed.

Helga met up with Joy on her way to the transport, and they fell in with the rest of the squadron. Joy and her aces called themselves the Revenants, and had little spirit icons on their helmets. She assumed that these were used to keep track of their kills.

It wasn't possible to look at a pilot and immediately know her skill. The icons on the helmet did that, and from a glance you could tell that Joy was an ace. As Helga looked them over, she noticed a trend: not one of these pilots had more than ten. Joy Valance had the most, eight spirits in a line at the base, which made sense to Helga, since being elected flight leader meant that you were one of the best.

"Looks like we got some more excitement," Joy said as Helga fell in beside her. "Good news for you is that we'll be jumping in next to your old ship." She was smiling as if she was the luckiest woman in the world. Helga wondered if this was due to Cilas or her being excited to fight the Geralos.

"You're just happy that I'm going to be gone soon," she said, smirking. "This way you can remain flight leader and I won't be a threat."

Joy nudged her violently, causing her to run into an ace named Wynter Sol—no relation to Brise. She was surprised when Sol didn't shrug her off, but Helga straightened up quickly and stifled a laugh. "Truth hurts—I know, Lieutenant. But even with a Vestalian Classic I'd be coming for your spot."

When they were back walking together, Joy touched her arm again, but this time it was gentle, no shoving or punching. She pointed at her helmet. "Do you know why we didn't hand you any boos for your kills?" she said, and from her tone Helga could tell that she was about to get schooled.

"Because I'm not a part of your squadron? I don't know. Not that it matters that much to me, anyway. I just want to fly," she said. "And you call them boos? What in the worlds is that? It's so childish and cute. Not very scary for infiltration pilots."

Cilas Mec came up quietly on the other side of Joy, and Helga was surprised that they didn't kiss. Their coupling was no longer a secret on the ship, but they seemed determined to keep on pretending.

"First of all, the 'boo' got its name from Commander Lang's baby girl. You go tell Gloria Lang that her boos are too childish for us," Joy said.

"Well, when you put it that way," Helga started, but Joy held up her hand to continue her explanation.

"Second of all, these boos are for lizard warships that we helped destroy. For every sortie that we fly and survive, we hand out a boo. Now that you know their meaning, big mouth, I want to give you this."

She reached under her helmet and produced a sticker, which she handed to Helga with a wink.

The aces stopped walking and surrounded her, and then they began a series of cheers. Helga realized that she had been set up, and that this all had been planned. She took the sticker, peeled off the back, and stuck it to the top of her helmet. When she held it up, the cheers intensified, and a genuine smile came to her face. "Thank you, Lieutenant," she said under her breath. "This is the nicest surprise. I don't know what to say."

"Say you'll formally join us. Earn yourself more boos. Try to take my position, Ate. If you're as good as I think, it's bound to be yours anyway," Joy said. But when Helga looked at her, she burst out laughing, and that was when she realized that she wasn't being serious. "I have eight boos, cruta, you're not catching up," she said. "But that doesn't mean that you can't give me a run."

Helga thought about the offer. If wrecking warships gained you boos, then Joy would always be ahead of her. Only sickness and death would close that gap. On the *Rendron* they had no boos, but she would be building the Nighthawks with Cilas.

The choice seemed obvious, since she was ambitious and wanted it to matter. If it was a month before she'd gone to Dyn, she would have jumped on this opportunity without question. But she needed to find who set them up and make them answer for Varnes and Cruser.

"I appreciate the offer, Lieutenant, but I'll always be a Nighthawk. After the things we went through down there on that moon, I have a score to settle with the lizards. You're my girl, though," she said, and the two women touched fists. It was something they started doing when they were out drinking.

"We'll fly together ... whenever you wish, Lieutenant," Helga said. "Whenever you need me, I'm your cruta."

Joy looked over at Cilas who was beaming with pride. She gave him her customary violent shove, and that forced the laugh out of him. "I told you that Helga was loyal, Joy," he said. "She isn't on my team by accident."

The three continued to joke until they reached the cryo bay, then they went their separate ways to their assigned pods.

On infiltrators like the *Inginus*, the cryogenic chamber took up an entire deck. It had enough pods to accommodate three times the ship's crew, since it was assumed that they would capture prisoners. There were hundreds of pods, lined up in long rows near the bulkhead, and over fifteen levels, with additional pods stacked on top of them.

Helga's assigned pod was on the third rack, so she would only have to climb up a few steps. There was a locker near the pod to store her clothes during the jump, and dividers installed for privacy.

She stripped down and threw her clothes inside of the locker, using the mirror on its door to look at herself. There was nothing worse than bringing a foreign object into the pod, since the sensors would literally scream at you—which was the most embarrassing thing ever.

Tyrell Lang's deep voice came over the system. "Thirty minutes till faster than light speed, Marines. Get into your pods and prepare for the jump. Officers run a head count, we don't want to miss anyone."

Helga touched the small square on the side of her cryo-pod, and the system read her vitals and confirmed. "Welcome, Ensign Helga Ate of the *Rendron*," it said. "Please step inside, make yourself comfortable, and touch the yellow icon when you're ready."

Taking a moment to look around at her comrades, Helga thought about everything that she had been through. She was a veteran now, there was nothing green left. The next time she stepped on the *Rendron*, she would be afforded the respect of a true Alliance ESO.

She remembered being a teenager and seeing the reaction on the cadets' faces when Cilas Mec came in to talk to them. "That is going to be me," she said, smiling at the thought. "I went through hell, and I made it, and now I'm going home."

This was the first time since deployment that she allowed herself some praise, and she knew it was due to Cilas, who all but drilled it into her head. *Thank you, Lieutenant,* was her final thought as she placed her back against the cushion.

29

Sirens, loud sirens, and shouting everywhere. This was all that Helga could hear as she opened her eyes to darkness. The pod did its standard checkups to make sure that she was intact, and then the glass dropped its tint, bringing in the brightness of the chamber.

Helga rubbed her dry eyes when they began to hurt, remembering where she was. All around her pod were Marines scrambling, and she wondered what was going on. A number of commands came over the system, and the officers on her level barked orders at the Marines. A half-naked, older man ran in front of her pod, then stopped and backpedaled to look hard at her.

"You need to get out of there," he said. "We got lizards up our rear. Get ready and get going, spacer. Get up and come on."

He took off running as Helga sat up in a daze. *Did that just happen?* she thought. *Oh, never mind.* She threw herself into motion, pushing open the cryo pod's glass and stepping out to locate her locker. Pulling on her underwear—they were so cold that it was almost painful—she found the Revenant branded coveralls and dressed in them quickly.

There would be no time to find Cilas and Joy, so she ran along with the rest of the Marines. Her intuition warned her that she would be trampled—there were just too many of them running through the narrow passageway. She pushed past the few Marines, keeping track of where she stepped, until she gained the door that led out to the main hangar.

The place was in chaos with pilots sprinting for their ships. It was obvious that there would be no speeches or well wishes for them. The *Inginus* had come out of FTL into a sweltering situation, and the ship was being torn apart by a Geralos battleship.

"Get out there and take the heat off mother," she heard Joy say over the intercom.

When she saw several phantoms take off through the deployment tunnel, Helga stopped and looked around. "Are we seriously doing this without prep?" she said to no one in particular. *There will be a lot of people dying today*, she thought, and felt saddened at the fact that there would be no goodbyes. She put it out of her mind and sprinted towards her Classic. There, she pulled her helmet on and climbed into the cockpit.

Once she was given a runway, she launched up and through the tunnel. There was a phantom in her way but she squeezed past it and shot out into space. It looked like a maelstrom of destruction when she emerged, black with splotches of bright sparks, lasers, and ballistics.

There were fighters everywhere, pepper and salt in this mélange of metal and science. Even for a woman like Helga, with countless hours of time in the cockpit, she couldn't help but worry that this would be her end. Nothing simulated or real could replicate what she was seeing, and no inventive cadet weaving tales of glory could come up with a lie this complex.

Flying anywhere between the battling warships was suicide, and she knew it. Unlike the former destroyer that the *Inginus* had beaten, this new ship was bigger and had someone at the helm that could fight.

Beyond the battle loomed the mighty *Aqnaqak*, the deadliest battleship of the Alliance. Its presence gave Helga hope, despite the reality that Meluvia was in trouble. Next to it was the *Soulspur*, the *Rendron's* other Infiltrator.

Helga saw that the *Aqnaqak* was shielding the *Soulspur*, but the Geralos battleship was firing on them both. While the big boys fought it out, the smaller fighters were trading blows. Some were dogfighting with the Geralos while others destroyed gun batteries and whittled down the shields.

Two bright flashes came from the *Inginus* then, and a torpedo shot out towards the battleship. A number of Geralos zip ships cut in front of it, giving up their lives to defend the bigger ship.

"Revenant squadron, what are you doing?" said Tyrell Lang, his authoritative voice a gavel on the comms. "Get those damned lizards off our guns."

Several phantoms took up the charge, flying towards the Geralos attacking the *Inginus*, but a trace laser—like a yellow line of death—sliced through their numbers and destroyed them. "This is flight leader, Lancer. Revenants, we need to be smart," said Joy Valance. Her voice was firm but pained, impressive for someone who'd just lost a handful of friends.

Tyrell Lang is an idiot, Helga thought after seeing what had happened. She maximized her thrust, circling to the safer side of the *Inginus*. Two Geralos ships followed her away from the trio of warships, firing on the Classic and depleting its shields.

Helga ignored the alarms coming from her computer and flew out into open space. Here she could get them by themselves without retaliation from the battleship. They were good, but she was better, and they went quickly to their deaths.

Maybe I can lure them out here one by one, she thought as she flew back to the *Inginus*. That was when her comms came alive again, as an out of breath Joy began to speak.

"Revenants, the Meluvians are in trouble on the surface. Our Marines just dropped, but they have zero air support. Break atmosphere and rendezvous at my coordinates. Let's show our allies some support and catch the lizards with their pants down."

Helga quickly did the math on how long it would take for her to get to Meluvia. There was enough fuel to get down there and back, but she knew that it still wouldn't be enough. *Thype it*, she thought. *I'll figure it out*. She put all resources into the thrust and then switched velocity from *Wave* to light speed.

The Vestalian Classic transformed itself by collapsing the wings into the side. Then the cannons rolled to the bottom of the ship, where they slid up into compartments. Once in this mode, the ship was defenseless, but it would allow for faster travel around the system.

Helga located Meluvia and punched in the coordinates, then closed her eyes and touched the activation link. As the countdown towards light speed ticked, Helga chanced a glance at her radar. To become combat-ready took a cooling down period, and she no longer had shields after committing them to thrust.

"Fifteen seconds," the computer said, but it felt more like fifteen minutes. Helga saw a blip on the edge of the radar, a Geralos zip ship seeking her out. *If that lizard shunts his thrusters, I'll be toast in less than ten seconds*, she thought.

"Please, not like this," she whispered to any deity or entity that would listen. It was a silly thing, she assumed, but that did not stop her from praying.

A shrill sound caught her ears and then everything went white as the Vestalian Classic shot towards the planet of Meluvia. When it had reached the coordinates, Helga retched inside her mask, coughing as orange liquid obscured her vision and breathing.

Pulling off the mask, she gasped for air, then took the time to take in her surroundings. All she could see was Meluvia. Several shades of blue and green, broken up by clouds, and debris. She was close enough to break atmosphere but there was no one else in her vicinity. *Where's everyone?* she thought, checking the location to make sure she was in the right place.

Unzipping her flight suit, Helga pulled off her shirt and used it to wipe the vomit from out of her helmet. The smell was so strong that she retched again, this time into the shirt. When she was done dry heaving, she triggered the artificial air. It blew cold and smelled of the Classic's engine, respite from the stench of her undigested breakfast.

Frustrated, Helga slammed her fist down into her thigh. *How did I forget how much traveling in light sucks?* She placed the helmet off to the side and pushed her thruster forward. When the ship didn't move, she made to panic—checking the fuel gauge—but then a message flashed across the HUD: Cooldown initiated. PLEASE STANDBY.

The system had given everything to get her to this position and had forced itself into a state of self-repair. Flipping through the information screens, Helga found the timer and saw that she had an hour before her thrusters would be online.

"Perfect," she whispered, then reached up and wiped her mouth. "There's got to be something that can remove this thyping smell."

She spent the next hour scrubbing her helmet clean, and by the time the system was ready, she was able to wear it again. "This is Rendron, breaking atmosphere," she said into her comms, hoping that the lieutenant would pick up her voice.

"It's about time," she heard Joy Valance say. "Get down here, Rendron, you're late to the party."

The Meluvian region that was under attack was off the coast of a country known as Dwax. Joy's coordinates took Helga to a colorful mountain range, where the pastel giants spread out for as far as the eye could see.

The Meluvians, not wanting to defy this natural phenomenon by ripping up the surface with architecture, chose to use floating cities that hovered between the valleys. Many of these cities had been attacked and were burning as they floated. This ugly sight brought Helga back to reality.

Below her like a swarm of insects were the Marines from the *Inginus*. She wondered if Cilas was with them, leading, taking the fight to the Geralos.

As she flew the Classic to join the phantoms, her comms came alive with their chatter. They were speaking in code, calling out locations and kills. There was so much going on that it was hard to keep up. Helga waited to announce herself. "VC Rendron here to assist," she said.

"Got three and four, east," said Valus Rho, one of the handful of Revenants in their squadron.

"Light them up," said Joy.

"Moving in to assist," said Millicent Ral, a girl Helga remembered from the bar.

When Helga saw a Geralos zip ship, she made to pursue, until another appeared out of thin air. *I'm losing my mind*, she thought. *No way did that just happen.* "Got a bogey south," she said into the comms.

"That's four. Be careful," said Valus. "He has the ability to cloak."

"Splash one," Darius Ghea said excitedly.

"Splash two," said Will Haws. Then, "Three just cloaked."

Helga opened up her cannons on the ship in front of her, but his shields were strong so she had to pursue. "Stalking four," she announced, but then the ship vanished again. Helga cursed, and rolled the vessel before shooting out over the water.

Her computer began to scream, and she knew what it was without having to look. The Geralos ace had uncloaked and was now bearing down on her. "I knew it!" she shouted, and dipped the Classic so low that its underside touched the sea.

There was something about Geralos missiles that the Alliance pilots knew well. Being near water confused their sensors and made it impossible to track. The missiles that trailed her began to dip into the water, but the lasers were tearing into her shields as the Geralos took to her rear.

"On four," Valus said.

"I got it," Helga replied. "I'm baiting, so back off me. I have him right where I want him to be."

Helga scanned her shields as she held the Classic steady and saw that they were at 15%. She bit down hard and pulled back on the stick while slamming the thrust forward with the palm of her hand. This pushed the Classic into an upward loop that took her above her pursuer's position. But the Geralos ace recognized the maneuver and slowed down to cloak in front of her.

Instead of completing the loop, Helga rolled the Classic upright and let loose a barrage of missiles into the oncoming ship. There was no way to avoid the exploding debris, so she closed her eyes tightly as the two ships collided.

The only thing that saved her was the shields she had left, but it still felt as if she'd flown into a wall. Helga tasted blood from where she bit into her tongue, and the pain forced tears into her eyes.

The computer screamed loudly to protest the damage to its hull and moved into a state of self-repair. "Splash four," Helga said with relief, but there was only silence on the comms, and she wondered if she'd damaged her equipment.

"Hey, idiot, get your ship repaired and fly like you've got some thyping sense," Joy said. She was on a private channel, but her words still stung. "If you have one on your six, then someone is going to peel it off. Don't tell us that you 'got it,' you arrogant cruta."

"Sorry, Joy—I mean, Lieutenant. I got caught up, you know how it is," Helga said. There was no immediate reply, and that stung even more. So much had happened and she was still making rookie mistakes.

She found a narrow valley away from the others and flew the Classic inside, staying so close to the ground that she could make out a camp. She recognized their flag as the Meluvian military. They had been fighting the Geralos for weeks before the *Inginus* had been called.

They were in really bad shape and were about to lose the land, which meant that the Geralos would set up a base on the planet. She knew that this was how the humans had lost Vestalia. They'd been unprepared for the lizards, who set up beachheads everywhere. Eventually the death toll became too much, and they were forced to escape their home planet.

The Alliance battle cry was "never again," yet here they were about to lose Meluvia. She kept the Classic flying low until her shields were fully replenished, then she pulled up and out of the valley.

As she made the climb, Helga narrowly missed a warbird that had found the hidden valley and was cruising with ill intent. The two ships had almost collided and she wondered how her computer had missed it. It still wasn't on her radar now that it was in plain view.

"Got a bogey here that's not on my radar," she announced, but the comms were still quiet. She climbed up to the clouds, then descended on the warbird, which was doing its own maneuvers to try and locate her.

They almost collided again, but Helga banked hard and brought the Classic around to try and flank it. She squeezed the trigger of her laser cannon as if she wanted it to break. But her shots merely tickled its impenetrable shields, and it maneuvered itself to return fire.

"Anyone have five?" said Millicent suddenly.

"We all got five," said the lieutenant. "Light it up."

Several phantoms appeared from the clouds above and fired on the warbird. First its shields depleted quickly and then it buckled as it tried to escape, but the Revenants were relentless and it crashed into the ground.

For thirty minutes they fought like this, fending off the Geralos. Then reinforcements arrived, and the lizards began to escape. Several jumped recklessly into space to try and preserve their lives, while the others fled across the sea to find another country to harass.

When things were under control, Joy gave the coordinates to an air and space station where they could refuel. Helga couldn't wait to stretch her legs and breathe fresh air without the need of a mask. She followed the Revenants—who flew in a tight formation—only breaking off to land when they finally found the strip.

After coming to a halt, she slid open the glass, appreciating the sweet fresh air after what she'd been smelling in her helmet. It was raining, but she didn't care. The water felt amazing on her skin and she opened her mouth, flicked out her tongue and tasted the refreshing droplets.

As she sat in her cockpit licking raindrops, a rumbling sound forced her eyes open. There was a truck pulling up with a tank on the back, and Helga realized that it was their fuel. She didn't know how long they'd have this break so she climbed down from the cockpit and unzipped her suit. The water was cold but it was welcome, and in her excitement she forgot that she'd taken off her shirt.

Whistles and cheers came from the truck as Helga unknowingly gave them a show. When she realized what they were looking at, she covered herself, embarrassed. Then Joy Valance walked towards her with a cross look on her face.

All of the happiness she'd felt since landing melted away in an instant. "Do I need to say it?" Joy said as she walked up, and Helga shook her head and sighed.

"I could use a break," she said, and the lieutenant's features softened.

"We all could, Ate, but time and place, girl. Zip up your suit and pretend you're one of us," she said.

Helga turned around and zipped up her front before giving her admirers an obscene gesture. She looked down at the helmet, remembering the vomit. The rain was really coming down now, and she watched as the men ran for the cover of the station.

The lieutenant was still standing in front of her when she came out of her daze, and she saw that she was waiting patiently. "Are you good, Ate?" she said, looking concerned.

"Where's Cilas?" Helga said, suddenly feeling confused. For a split second her mind drifted off and a deep depression settled in.

"The lieutenant is with the 110th, Ate. They dropped out early before anyone else. I'm sure we'll see him when this is all over, but we have a job. Are you able to do it?" she said.

Helga regarded her through bloodshot eyes, then nodded despite what she felt. Deep tiredness and depression had become her reality, and all she wanted to do was get drunk. "I'm good, Lieutenant," she said, saluting stiffly. "I just need a few minutes to catch my breath."

30

When the *Rendron* came out of light speed to join the fight, Retzo Sho saw that their delay had in fact been devastating. The *Inginus* was in bad shape, and the *Soulspur* was the only thing stopping it from becoming scrap. Both infiltrators—for all their might—could not withstand the power of the Geralos battleship, even with the *Aqnaqak* taking most of the heat.

The *Soulspur* had flown ahead of them at the behest of Captain Retzo Sho, but now as it fought alongside its twin, Retzo could see just how futile it was. They looked like two bull terriers and a Great Dane trying to take down a velociraptor.

When he recognized the Geralos vessel, his heart sunk at the reality of what they were up against. This was *Nian*, a battleship, and the Geralos' indomitable planet killer. *Nian* had turned enough warships into salvage to make its very presence frightening. What Retzo Sho was witnessing was the shape of death itself.

He thought about his crew, and the thousands that called the *Rendron* home. They were a warship first, but this did not take away the fact that they were also a floating city. He, their captain, was meant to keep them safe, so it made him reconsider his actions.

"*Inginus* is not going to make it," Genevieve said, her hand over her mouth as she leaned against her console. She had family on that infiltrator—most of the crew did—and seeing it buckle against this giant warship sent tendrils of fire down Retzo's throat.

As he picked up the communicator and made to give his orders, a bright light appeared as a smaller Geralos ship—a destroyer—jumped in to assist the *Nian*. "Mr. Riles," Retzo said. "Intercept the new vessel and put us in between it and that battleship. *Rendron* fighters are cleared to engage the enemy. Focus on the cannons. Give the *Inginus* a chance."

He shifted the channel to speak over the PA system so that everyone onboard could hear. "*Rendron*, this is your captain speaking. We've come out of light speed to quite the situation. We have a Class-A Battleship dropping lizards onto the planet Meluvia. We remember how that went last time, don't we? Never again. You have been well trained and now it's time to show and prove.

"Over ten billion Meluvians will be relying on us, *Rendron*. I will not let them down, and neither will you. File your fangs, sharpen your claws, and let loose that fury you've honed on my ship. We are the last defense, my friends. Now get to your jobs and let's give them hell."

Retzo looked over at Genevieve Aria and saw fire in her eyes. He hoped to have inspired the same fire in his pilots, who would be running to the hangar to deploy. He nodded at her then, and she picked up where he left off, speaking to the ship while he got up to pace the bridge.

"All hands man battle stations," Genevieve shouted, her voice taking on an octave that Retzo didn't recognize.

It's been too long. We're not prepared for this, he thought. *We've let the infiltrators get hard while we softened in the shadows.* "Listen to me," he said, addressing the crew on the bridge. "Everyone here and the officers below deck are the only thing that will get us through this alive. Mistakes will happen, but we must make up for them, instantly. There is no time for regret or chagrin. We're all together now, a fist, and we need to take that ship out of the fight."

They echoed their acknowledgement, but he wasn't so sure. Most of these officers were very young and hadn't seen combat past simulations. It put a lot of pressure on him, but he was Captain Retzo Sho. He won this role by commanding the *Soulspur* and by sending over eight warships to a fiery grave.

They would look to him now to be the legend that he was. The commander who knew where to hit the lizards, to exploit their weaknesses. He stopped behind his captain's chair, his hands gripping the back as if he meant to break it.

Retzo watched the screen showing a simulation of their flight as they moved to intercept the new destroyer. But the *Nian* saw their intentions and turned its batteries on them. *Good, you thyping idiots, fire on us and not the Inginus*, he thought. He grabbed his communicator and contacted the *Soulspur*.

"Jit," he said when the commander was on the line. "What happened? I thought I asked you to stay out until we jumped in."

"The *Aqnaqak* contacted us to help with the defense," Jit said. He didn't sound well, and Retzo began to worry. "We came in with them but this ship must have unlimited shields. I'm sorry, Captain for disobeying your orders, but I truly believed the *Aqnaqak* had gotten your clearance."

More communication issues, he thought, *but who am I to blame?* "Captain Cor loves a fight," he said. "I'm not surprised to find *Aqnaqak* here. Don't apologize old friend, you've done the *Soulspur* proud. Now I am going to have to order you to jump."

"I can't Captain Sho, our FTL is offline. A chunk of our aft was blown out from a torpedo. We're crippled, sir. Our cannons are just about the only thing left functioning."

"How's your crew holding up?"

"I sent my Marines to the planet to aid the effort. Lang has done the same, though his ship is in worse shape than mine. Our pilots are out their fighting, whatever's left of them. We don't expect to live out the night, Captain. Those that stayed have accepted their fate. We—"

"Stow it, Jit. No last rites. Not now. Your first priority is to get your engine repaired while we and the *Aqnaqak* attract the heat. What I need you to do is to get enough thrust to break off and leave when you can."

He didn't wait for a response as he clicked off the communicator and patched a call through to Tyrell Lang. The *Inginus* was in the worst shape of them all, yet it was being aggressive and moving out from the cover of the *Aqnaqak*.

"Commander Lang," Retzo said. "What you are doing is literally suicide. Disengage from that battleship and put your focus on repairing your shields." *What are you doing Lang, you dolt?* he thought, as he hung up to contact the *Aqnaqak*.

"Captain Cor," he began. "What's your situation?"

"Strut, thank the planets," said Tara Cor, and he smiled at the nickname and the sound of her voice. It was one of the many things he'd loved about her back when they were pilots sharing bunks. She would call him strut because of the way he walked. He knew it was a compliment so it would always make him smile.

"I don't know what this thing is made of, Strut, but we're at a bit of a stalemate, trading shots. Get your infiltrators out of here, man, and you and I, we'll crush this thing. Whatever you do though, make it quick. I'm running out of resources."

"Hold tight, Tara, I'm on it," he said. "Call you back in a bit."

He stepped forward and touched the glass, looking out at the *Aqnaqak* and trying in vain to gauge her condition. Two of the gun batteries were badly damaged, but the other thirty-eight were firing. The shields seemed to be holding up against the missiles from the *Nian*, and the ship had enough bulk to provide cover for the infiltrators.

"Captain," came a voice from his right, and Retzo looked over to see who it was. Toro Hanes, one of the ship's navigators, had stood up from his station and was beckoning him over. He was one of the newest members of the bridge, and Retzo didn't recognize him. Short of stature, hair dyed green like a Meluvian's, but his bushy mustache revealed the fact that he was very much Vestalian.

"Mr. Hanes," Retzo said. *This had better be good.*

"Sir, I think that you're going to want to see this," he said, motioning to his console. Retzo saw that there were a set of translucent ships in front of him, hovering over a semi-circle on a hologram display.

"*Rendron* shields at ninety-five percent," announced the computer. They were beginning to take a beating from the *Nian's* main cannon.

"Put some fighters on that destroyer," he growled. "CHENG, I'll take what you can give me. Where are my fighters, Genevieve? I want that destroyer put on ice." *If Viles was alive, there would be no need to ask*, he thought. He marched across the bridge to Toro Hanes. "What is it?" he said impatiently.

"A destroyer just jumped in, cloaked," Toro said excitedly. "See the distortion? I can tell from the size. He jumped in at this location and will attempt to flank the *Inginus*, sir."

"Two destroyers, what are the chances? You have to be thyping kidding me," Retzo whispered. It was the last thing they needed. They could actually lose Meluvia. He leaned over the hologram display which showed their ships above the planet.

From what he was seeing the *Rendron* was flying to the far side of the *Nian*. On the other side—the business side—was the *Aqnaqak* taking it on. Behind the *Aqnaqak* was the crippled *Soulspur*, with the *Inginus* above it all, with just enough gap above the *Aqnaqak* to fire on the *Nian*.

On the far side of the *Soulspur's* location was a distorted oblong shape. He knew this was the cloaked destroyer, and his heart began to race.

"CHENG," Retzo shouted into his comms.

"Captain," Chief Engineer Dino Centuri replied in an exasperated voice.

"Cloaked Geralos ships. You did some study on them, correct?"

"Yes, sir. Well not officially; they were a bit of a personal obsession, really," he said. "What makes you ask, Skip? You thinking about investing in Geralos tech?"

The sarcasm annoyed him but he forced a smile. He would often do this when he felt stressed, to take the edge from his response. Leave it up to Dino to crack a joke at the worst times, but the Chief Engineer was one of his best men.

"I know that the way those things operate are completely alien to our own," Retzo said, "but what about cloaking? Is the technology similar to ours? Specifically what I am asking is... can they be shielding while they're cloaked?"

"That's a new one, Skip. I'm not sure," Dino said. "Give me a minute and I will find out."

Retzo considered the layout. "Rendron prime," he said to the computer. "Give me simulations of positive outcomes with no casualties from the enemy."

Immediately the computer presented several holographic screens with different situations played out on each, running on a loop. There were too many to study, and he didn't have the time, so he narrowed it down even further until he had an idea of what to do.

He reminded himself that it wasn't just their lives at stake, but the lives of the billions living on their allied planet. The Meluvian people were kind, and one of the first to aid Vestalia during the invasion. Meluvians were a major presence in the Alliance, and many members of his crew had family there.

"Never again," he muttered, not realizing that his elbow rested on a live communicator. Genevieve had accidentally left it on when she made the announcement to the ship. "Never again," came his voice over the *Rendron's* PA system, his thoughts now becoming a battle cry.

All across the bridge, the crew stood up and shouted, "Never again," some saluting, some looking at him with what he could only read as determination. It carried on throughout the entire ship, from the bridge to the wounded in sickbay.

Retzo eased off the communicator, tempted to throw it at the deck. It had startled him. *What if I was up here spreading grave news?* he thought. "I'm so sorry, Captain," Genevieve whispered from her chair, and grabbed the communicator and placed it in its dock.

He looked at her, disappointed, but his comms buzzed in his ear. It was a private call from Dino Centuri. "CHENG," he said. "What did you find out?"

"They're just like us, Skip. The lizards have no defenses, not while their ships are cloaked."

"Mr. Ranks," Retzo said, shouting. "Slow us down and arm torpedoes." He waited for the crew to comply with his commands. He nodded at Hanes to send the coordinates to the Tactical Action Officers. "Let me know when we have a lock on that destroyer playing hide-and-seek."

"Target locked, Captain. On your command," Lieutenant Noe Ranks said.

"Let fly," Retzo said, not sparing a second's delay, and moved to a window where he could observe the end results.

Four flashes of light flew past the *Aqnaqak* and struck an invisible force that was the destroyer. The cloak was obliterated. Then the salvo shook the ship, and as it came into view, Retzo could see that it was severely damaged.

"Direct hit, Captain," shouted Noe Ranks.

As Retzo made to order another salvo, the *Inginus* moved on the destroyer. Its batteries poured forth a streamer of death, splitting the vessel in half.

Seeing an opening, the other destroyer retaliated and fired missiles into the *Inginus's* freshly exposed hull. Retzo grabbed his ear where the comms was clipped and called Tyrell Lang to give him a piece of his mind. "Are you mad? I gave you an order. Charge your shields, that's what I said. You are going to die, Lang, do you understand? You're thyping exposed, you bloody fool."

As the remaining Geralos destroyer turned its firepower on the *Inginus*, *Soulspur* tried to intercept by moving between the two ships. Retzo watched in horror as the destroyer shifted location. Its aim was to break the *Inginus* no matter what.

"Jit," said Retzo, standing up straight and brushing off his uniform. "How are your engines? Are you still stalled or can you move?"

There was a pause on the line as the commander consulted his crew. "Thrust is online, Captain, and our shields are at forty percent," he said.

"I want you to shunt your shields and drive into that destroyer," Retzo said. "Push it past the reach of the battleship's batteries. We'll have to take it out with phantoms if you can't get Marines on board."

"Yes, my captain," said Jit Nam, bitterly. It was to be expected since he was being asked to disable his ship. The collision would damage the *Soulspur* badly, but would do more to the Geralos ship. If they punched a hole in her hull, then Marines could board and bring the pain internally.

The least that could happen was the shields would drop to critical condition, and then a squadron of fighters could finish it off easily. Retzo contacted Tara Cor. "Captain, I am going to attempt to come about that battleship to rescue my infiltrator. We will be in your line of fire, just behind that thing, but I doubt that it will last long between two Alliance warships."

"Do it, Strut. This is getting hairy, and Alliance central is taking their time on reinforcements for this ship," she said. "They mentioned the *Scythe* and I was like, 'seriously, an old warship? Never mind if that's all you have, Strut and I will handle this ourselves.'"

"Thype them," he whispered. "Our Marines are enough." He could almost see the smile that crossed her face when he spoke those words. Tara Cor was a great captain, and loved the idea of leading men. But even more than leading, she loved glory, and the greater the odds, the better.

"I'm going to buy you some time, Strut. Don't let me down," she said.

"Have I ever?" he said, and got off the comms before she could answer.

"Mr. Hanes," Retzo called as he stepped quickly over to navigation. "I need us here," he said, placing his finger near the damaged destroyer.

"Listen up, TAO. When we come about, I want that destroyer vaporized. Then I want to focus our batteries on the aft region of that battleship. Genevieve, contact Commander Lang and tell him that he is to prepare his ship to dock with *Rendron*. Commander Nam is to do the same once that destroyer is a debris field. Am I clear?"

"Aye aye, Captain," she said, and jumped back on her comms.

"Captain!" Noe Ranks shouted, and Retzo spun to see what he wanted. On the large monitor above the window was a close shot of the *Inginus*. The infiltrator had been split in half and was drifting in two separate pieces.

"No!" Retzo shouted. "What happened there just now?"

"Trace laser from that destroyer, sir. They didn't have a chance."

The emotions that shook Retzo Sho's very core had a source that he couldn't pinpoint. Was it the deaths of all the spacers that called the *Inginus* home, or was it the rage from losing a part of their fleet? "Commander Lang, what is your status?" he said into his comms, and he stood there waiting for him to answer. "Lang, come on, just answer your comms," he whispered.

"Captain, I'm here," Lang said, and then the connection died.

"Change of plans," Retzo announced to the bridge as he walked towards the center. "That ship has shields to hold us off until more reinforcements show up. It showed its hands just now by trying to sneak in destroyers when we were sleeping. Two Alliance warships aren't enough, and we're uncertain if another warship will make it here in time to help us. *Aqnaqak* is in bad shape, and our shields are at eighty percent.

"This is new for most of you. I've kept us out of the heat for too long. But this isn't new to our infiltrators who are now being taken apart. I know it probably seems hopeless, and some of you will want us to jump away. But that's Meluvia down there, and she carries billions of good people, just like Vestalia did. Now, I don't intend to sit here while we slowly lose shields. I need support and strength from everyone to make the right decisions for us to win."

The chants of "never again" started as Retzo walked off the bridge. He needed to think, and the passageway was a welcome respite, but as he stepped through the doorway his eye caught a glimpse of one of the screens.

As he had ordered, the *Soulspur* rammed the destroyer with tremendous results. It not only killed the shields, but put a hole in its hull, and the damage to the infiltrator seemed minimal. "Hell yes, Jit. Hell yes," he growled. It was a little slice of hope, and it was what he needed as he stepped into the passageway and closed the door.

31

Long hours of fighting followed for Helga Ate and the Revenant squadron, as the Geralos seemed determined to take the country. After a day of fighting, they parked their ships outside of a Meluvian Army bunker near a space station. There, they set up camp with individual tents pitched in a line and a bonfire built on the side farthest away from their spacecraft.

It was a quick setup that impressed Helga, since the teamwork was focused and effortless. They had started at sunset, and by the time it was nighttime they had everything prepared to accommodate them for the night.

The final touch was for a few of the aces to borrow crates from the bunker. These they used as chairs, forming a jagged circle around the fire.

As they sat around joking, Helga took note of all their faces. They were twelve survivors of the original twenty-six that comprised the Revenant squadron. Most had died when the *Inginus* came out of light speed, but there had been no more casualties on the planet's surface.

She noticed that they all had what Cilas would call "the stare of death." On the escape ship during one of their frequent bouts with boredom, he had confided some things with Brise and herself. He told them that officers were trained to notice that look because it was a turning point in a spacer's career. They would monitor the afflicted to see how they'd changed, to know whether or not they could go on.

Helga knew that she had gained the look after their first fight on Dyn. She knew because she'd noticed Cage Hem giving her looks. Now as she took in these aces, she felt a deep sense of pride. Every one of them had seen friends die, yet here they were after a day of combat, joking around like brothers and sisters.

She found herself missing Cruser and the rest of the Nighthawks. She remembered that their camps were very much like this. The dumb questions she would ask, and Cage kindly brushing them off to save her from Wyatt's wrath. The thought made her smile. They had been her big brothers.

Thinking about them now brought a familiar pain to her throat, but she had cried enough to wash their bodies a hundred times in the afterlife. Now it was just a numbing throb that, left unchecked, would drive her to the darkest place. On *Inginus*, the cure had been lots of alcohol and joking around with Joy, her would-be twin.

She looked around for the lieutenant, and found her by the ships, squatted down, hand to her ear, speaking on her comms. *I bet she's talking to Cilas*, Helga thought.

She glanced up into the sky to see what colors would be there now. Meluvia was the most colorful place, and its sky was something that fascinated her. Sunset had been a painter's palette, blues spilling over into red, but now it was black as night had come, and with it the sounds of the forest.

The sky was clear enough for her to see clusters of stars, and the battle going on between the warships. When she'd jumped to Meluvia, things had looked bad for the *Inginus*, but she reasoned that all the lights that she saw meant that the fight was still going on.

When she lost her focus, she could hear Millicent talking. She was saying something about Commander Lang, and the rest of the Revenants were laughing. "I am not joking," she said, "He has a family here. That's not the scandalous part though, from what I hear, he has a really big house, with servants and everything."

"Did he tell you that before or after you thyped him in his cabin?" Jessica Orda said. She was one of the better aces, short and stocky, just like her temper, and possibly the bluntest woman Helga had ever known. She watched Millicent's face, gauging her reaction, but the pretty mask that she presented to Jessica stayed surprisingly aloof.

"Gross," she whispered, her face still unchanged. "Don't put your fantasies on me, you hard up cruta."

Here we go, thought Helga, wondering how ugly the fight would get. But Jessica laughed, then threw some dirt at Millicent, who in turn began to smile and shake her head.

One of the men, Darius Gan, did not seem to like what he was hearing. "That's bogus," he said. "He's the commander of an infiltrator. The man can't have a life outside of what the Alliance gives him. When would he have been able to come down here on his own, marry a Meluvian, have a bunch of children, and purchase a mansion and land? Come on. The man paces a warship that stays at war, constantly. I've heard some ridiculous rumors in my time, but this one? This is the king."

"Commander Lang takes shore leave every year at the same time, and he has been doing it since he took over the helm," Jessica said. "Who here wouldn't choose to be a commander and devote your life to a ship if you were promised a family and home for two happy months out of every year?"

The aces grew quiet as they considered her words, even though it was both a dream and an impossibility. There was no way they could get enough credits to afford a family, and real planet property. They all looked stunned, some perplexed, and others outright jealous. Being the commander was a big deal, and though they laughed at the joke about him having no life, they all could agree that the position had its perks.

The commander having a life on Meluvia, with an alien woman? It was feasible; he liked women—a bit too much, if you asked enough of his crew. He was also a powerful man who could use his influence to befriend powerful Meluvians.

Meluvians that were landowners, with so much money that a house was nothing to gift. They would give him a home, this powerful Vestalian commander, who would in turn patronize their planet and live there once he retired.

Meluvian tourism would benefit, since this powerful commander would invite all of his starship flying friends. Helga imagined that they were doing something like this. Something that made sense as an answer for why he'd have these things.

For some reason her mind went to Ina Reysor, the Louine rescue, and the pirate ship. *Would Tyrell Lang be involved with selling off soldiers to pirates?* she thought. *Was it a lucrative venture? No, it just wouldn't make any sense.*

As she racked her brain for an explanation, Helga saw something out of the corner of her eye. It turned out to be Joy Valance, walking up to take her seat. It was dark except for the fire, but she could see that the lieutenant was crying. It wasn't tears or a grimace that gave her away, it was the way her eyes seemed so unsettling.

"Everything okay?" Helga asked where only Joy could hear, and scooted in close to be next to her friend.

"Cilas is on the *Inginus*. Can you believe it?" she said. "That thyping jerk ordered him to stay."

"You good over there, Lieutenant?" said one of the other girls.

"Great. Just going over things with Ate," Joy lied.

They went back to gossiping once Joy had gone quiet, but Helga did notice that Lang was no longer the subject.

"What jerk?" Helga whispered.

Joy shot her an impatient look. "Lang of course. Who else? He did it on purpose, Ate, I know he did."

Helga listened to her go on about how Tyrell Lang had it out for Cilas. She didn't give a reason why, but from the way she spoke, she really didn't have to. Joy had either slept with the commander or there had been a relationship. Either way, he was jealous, and was using his position to punish the man she loved.

On top of this, Tyrell Lang hated outsiders, and though they were from the *Rendron*, it didn't matter. Neither she nor Cilas had been visited by the commander; not even a quick call to check on their condition. He had given Cilas a hard time, and now he was stopping him from doing what he was commissioned to do.

"That's pretty selfish of him," Helga said under her breath.

"Oh, it gets better. That call that I just made? Cilas couldn't stay on for long because half the ship was drifting away from where the Geralos split them. They are struggling up there, but they haven't called for us. You would think that we'd be needed up there," she said.

"Oh, no, Joy, I'm so sorry. Is Cilas injured?" Helga said. "I tried to reach him earlier, but he wasn't answering his comms."

"He says they're good but the place is in shambles. He would never admit it but I know he's feeling helpless and alone up there," Joy said. "He says the *Rendron* disabled a destroyer using torpedoes, and Captain Sho ordered the *Soulspur* to ram into another," she said.

"Ram a destroyer. Are you serious?" Helga said, taken aback. The Retzo Sho she remembered didn't seem the type to order such a move. It made him even more attractive, now that he had an air of mystery.

Who was this man? He had always seemed like a by-the-book sort of officer, but ordering a ram? It was hard to believe. "Way to go, Captain," she whispered. "When the admiral finds out, he is going to flip. Heh, I bet our captain was a bad boy back in the day, pulling pranks in his Vestalian Classic."

"Can you imagine it? I can't see it," Joy said, and they both began to laugh. It was the first rule in their textbooks: do not use your ship as a blunt instrument. Doing it with a fighter was suicide—though many aces claimed to have pulled it off successfully—but an infiltrator filled with people? It was positively unheard of. Not only was it illegal, but Retzo could also be court marshaled if the crew complained.

She placed her hand on Joy's knee, and then took her hand. It was cold despite the fire, but Helga knew that the temperature had little to do with how she felt. "Joy, Cilas is a freak. There's literally nothing that can defeat that man. I saw him take a shot in his chest from a Geralos drone, and he was back shooting it out with us less than eight hours later. We're talking about someone who singlehandedly took over a pirate ship."

"You were with him throughout that whole thing—at least in his version of the story," Joy said.

"Well, yeah I was, but it was Cilas who was doing everything," she said. "What I'm telling you is that he's a survivor. He was before he met you; it's how he's wired. So don't worry. No matter the odds, the lieutenant will always find a way out."

"You love him, don't you?" Joy said with a smile, and Helga snatched back her hand.

"What?"

"It's okay, sister, I can see it in your face. I knew it from our first drink in the bar when you sat there and lied about how you felt," she said.

"Thype you, cruta," Helga said dismissively, but it wasn't enough to hide her embarrassment from Joy.

The others were still swapping stories over the fire, but Helga didn't trust that some weren't listening to their conversation. It was human nature to be nosy, and they had been whispering to each other for a while. She pointed towards the phantoms. "I think we should take a walk to my ship," she said.

"Wait a second, Helga ... I meant nothing by it. We're sisters, remember? I just thought you should know that I know," Joy said, looking frightened.

"Planets, you're actually serious. Joy, come on, I just want to talk. All ESOs aren't psychopaths, despite what they told you in cadet academy," she said. "What am I going to do, anyway? Lead you over there, kill you, and then hide your body inside of your phantom? Even if I could get away with it, I wouldn't want to. You're my friend, even if you're wrong about me crushing on your boyfriend."

When they were far enough from the campsite, Helga felt safe enough to talk freely. She glanced back at the fire, hoping that her voice wouldn't carry when she spoke. "They were saying that there is a rumor about your Commander Lang," she said. "They say that he has family, and property on this planet."

"That sounds ridiculous," Joy Valance said, hissing through her teeth. She touched the top of her cornrowed hair, using her forefinger to scratch an itch. "Those talking heads back there, I love them to death, but they drive me crazy when they're not in a cockpit. All they do is gossip the most ridiculous schtill. When would Tyrell Lang have time to establish a family on Meluvia? Are you saying that you believe it, Helga? How does that even work? I just don't see it being possible. We're in different systems throughout the year."

"They say he takes two months shore leave, same time every year, and that is when he stays with his family down here."

Joy Valance stopped walking and closed her eyes. She looked like a child that was about to have a tantrum. Her face reflected anger as she stood frozen beneath the spotlight. "He does take that time off, but ... I don't like to talk about this, Ate," she said, opening her eyes to regard her friend. "It makes me question my commander's motives, and if I do that then how can I lead?"

"You're right," Helga said. "And you are smart enough to realize this. He needs you in his corner to carry out his commands. The minute you start to question them, you'll freeze and get yourself killed. Even if it's true is it really any of our business? The man has a family, so what? I'm sorry, Joy, I don't know what I was thinking. I feel bad for putting it in your head now."

"Don't be," Joy said, her breath visible in the cold air. "I mean, none of us get paid enough to afford a Meluvian home. What I'm trying to understand is, how he could afford property on a planet? Property and a family on Meluvia, the most expensive planet in the galaxy."

"Not in the galaxy. None of us have been to Louine but I'm betting that if they allowed us to live there, it would cost way more than here," Helga said. "Plus, couldn't he have saved up enough credits over the time he's been an officer? I imagine that after twenty years, his credits could be substantial. Plus, he's a commander. They have to pay him enough to afford the accommodations wherever he's needed."

"I'm a step below him, and I save my credits. Cilas could be a commander soon, and even he isn't making that kind of money," she said, seeming disgusted. "Anyway, let's head back before they send a spy down here to see if we're thyping. If those bored Revenants of mine run out of topics to squawk about, we will be the subjects of interest."

"Who cares?" Helga said. "Let them talk their schtill. Besides, they already think we're thyping. They just won't come out and say it."

As they made their way back in silence, she thought about Tyrell Lang. He had been given command of the *Inginus* after Lester Cruz moved up to be Retzo's XO. Sho had commanded the *Soulspur*, but beat out Cruz for the top position, and since Lang was Cruz's first mate, he won the command of the *Inginus* while the *Soulspur* was given to Jit Nam.

Not much had been known about Lang before his promotion, but the *Inginus* had gone on to have successes against the Geralos. They barely docked with the *Rendron*, so Helga knew nothing about him or his ship. What she did know was that on the day they were rescued, she'd seen something in his eyes that had frightened her.

They walked back to the fire and sat down with the rest, who were now singing old Vestalian songs. Helga knew the one they were singing; it was a folk song from one of the main continents. So she picked up the tune, humming at first, and then singing along, despite the look she received from Joy.

It had been ages since she sung anything, and she had been known to have a good singing voice. The others heard her above them, and met her with smiles. This emboldened her to sing even louder.

The song was about perseverance and eternal love. A woman who had been taken from her home by bandits was eventually rescued by her family. As she sang the lyrics, she appreciated them now more than ever. Her mind went to Cilas on that fractured ship. What was going on up there, she wondered, and would there be an *Inginus* left when they flew up to rejoin the fight tomorrow?

For the longest time her only dream was to get back to her tiny compartment on the *Rendron*. She wanted to see her mother's face, and kiss the frame that held her image. She even missed her lumpy cot and the mildewed smell that wouldn't go away. Most of all—more than anything else—she wanted to get back to being herself. This hard woman who sung with the Revenants felt like a machine that she was trapped inside of.

Going home was still a mystery with the conflict in space. Were they winning, were they losing? Not even Joy Valance could know.

Tomorrow, Helga thought, *tomorrow we will find out*. She looked up at the stars, her voice bellowing out the tune, wondering if she'd ever see her crummy compartment again.

32

The damage the *Soulspur* caused to the destroyer was monumental in scale. This didn't stop the Geralos from retaliating, however, and with the infiltrator stuck, they focused all of their gun batteries on its hull.

Everything I do seems to turn into disaster, Retzo thought. "Genevieve, tell Commander Nam to brace for impact," he said. "There are shield reserves on the *Soulspur*, and he will need to use them now."

As he made to get up to walk around, he noticed that a young girl—who couldn't be older than thirteen years of age—had come onto the bridge to stand next to his chair. She had hair so blonde that it shone like silver, but it held traces of green which hinted at a Meluvian heritage.

She wore the full sun of a colonel—cadets had their own ranks emulating the military—and handed him a cup of tea. *What is this now?* he thought, as he looked around to see who was responsible. It had to be a practical joke, right? Why would there be a cadet on his bridge?

He forced himself to smile at her as he tried to imagine her commanding her classmates. *She's so little, but the rank says it all. Kid must be something special if she's on my bridge*, he thought. "Won a contest to get in some bridge time?" he said when she met his eyes, and her cheeks immediately turned red.

She seemed so frightened that he touched her shoulder reassuringly. "It's okay, Colonel. Thank you," he said, and lifted the tea for effect.

"Commander Nam says they are shielded now, Captain," Genevieve said, and then looked past him to shake her head negatively at the young cadet. The girl, getting the message, retreated quickly after a strong salute. *How cute*, Retzo thought. *She must be one of Genevieve's relatives.*

"Mr. Ranks, put a torpedo on the aft of that destroyer," he said. "We need only one, and for the love of humanity, do not hit our infiltrator."

He sipped at the tea. It was his favorite flavor, and the temperature was absolutely perfect. It had to be Genevieve's doing, sending over this cadet. They had worked together long enough for her to know what he needed.

"This tea is excellent," he said to her, and looked back at the cadet and winked.

"She's a good kid," said Genevieve. "I apologize for her timing. That tea was supposed to be given to you during a time of inaction." She touched her ear where the comms was attached, and looked up at him suddenly, her eyes widening. "Skipper, it's Captain Tara Cor," she said.

"Patch her through," Retzo said.

He got up and walked to one of the large bay windows, taking the teacup with him. The torpedo was a direct hit on the aft of the destroyer, and with its shields failing, it shattered around the *Soulspur*. More cheers went up, but Retzo wouldn't join in since he knew his decision had crippled the infiltrator.

"I'm going out in the passageway to take this call," he said to Genevieve, and she gave him a look of understanding.

He walked past his tactical action team and flashed them a confident smile, and patted the cadet on her head as he made his way out the door.

"You okay?" he said to Tara Cor, after connecting the comms to his earpiece.

"Still here trading blows, but shields are dwindling. There'll be more coming in if we don't hurry this up."

"I'm taking the *Rendron* around to the broadside of that beast, and together we will wear it down to nothing," he said. "If we can kill the FTL drive as soon as the shields go dead, we can take down a battleship. How's that for your record, beautiful?"

"I won't get my hopes up. The lizard's captain is smart. They will jump out of the system before we get a chance to disable anything. Okay, so we're sandwiching the bastard then. What do you need for me to do?" she said.

"Just keep pumping out those cannons. The rest is entirely up to me," he said. "Keep giving it to them, Tara. It will all be over soon."

"I hope you're right," she said. "When I'm at twenty percent, I'm getting my ship out. I miss you, Strut. It's been too long since we caught up. Let's win and fix that, what say you?"

"Sounds wonderful, just like you," he said, and then switched off his comms. He exhaled the stress and placed his back against the bulkhead. He could talk a good game but he was unsure. The Geralos battleship was something out of his worst nightmare, and words wouldn't be enough to kill it.

He looked down the passageway with its ugly aesthetic of exposed pipes and wires. It was supposed to have been repaired over two months ago, but here it was still, as if the crew didn't want it repaired.

The *Rendron* wasn't the oldest ship, but it was old in many ways. A direct hit from that battleship would kill many of his Marines, and exposed pipes and wires made this certain.

He thought about the cadet who had served him the tea and imagined her getting thrown from a collision with the hull. It was the worst kind of thought but he couldn't seem to shake it. At any moment he knew that he could literally lose it all.

An alarm started to blare and he glanced at his wrist pad. Another ship had jumped into the system and the computer was letting him know. He exhaled, shaking. This would be it for them. Another Geralos destroyer or even a battleship would be enough to take them out.

He closed his eyes to regulate his anxiety, cautious to not jump to conclusions before knowing the truth. His eyes opened, and he brought up his hand, reading the message on his wrist pad that had come in from Genevieve.

"New ship is Alliance, Captain. A battlecruiser known as the *Scythe*."

Retzo gestured with his fingers across the wrist pad's interface, syncing to his station on the bridge. Once established, a hologram appeared, showing the details of the new ship.

Seeing the *Scythe* hovering above his wrist pad gave Retzo Sho a sliver of hope. The *Scythe* was the last of the Vestalian battlecruisers. It was one of the few that took on the Geralos back when Vestalia was filled with humans.

The fact that the other battlecruisers were now extinct spoke volumes of the hardiness of the *Scythe*. It looked like a wraith, freshly come from the grave. It was bigger than an infiltrator, but still much smaller than the Geralos battleship. To call the vessel ugly was an understatement. Calling it frightening was closer to what he felt. In that hologram was a metal golem that seemed comprised of salvaged parts.

Like all the originals, the *Scythe* had been built when shield technology was in its infant stages. To compensate, the captains of these vessels would layer the hull in salvaged scraps. The *Scythe's* strength, however, was that it was a mystery. The Geralos would be in for quite a surprise.

Shield management was optimum in modern spatial warfare, but the *Scythe* was from a different time when it was about brute strength. Beyond the ability of the old warship, Retzo knew who was at the helm. It was Gerald Hal, Admiral of the Vestalian fleet. He hadn't announced his arrival, but Retzo knew it was him.

He contacted his communications officer to put him through to the admiral. Ten painstaking minutes of waiting followed before Genevieve confirmed a link. "Retzo Sho," said a gruff voice, sounding annoyed and distracted. "Why are you playing with this reptilian thing instead of using your weapons to kill it?"

Retzo rolled his eyes at the old man's tone. It was the standard *I know better than you* attitude of an Alliance Admiral. Gerald Hal especially, who was a legend across the galaxy, and it wasn't as if he could offer up any kind of retort.

"Admiral Hal, with respect," he said, "this enemy has proven difficult due to its shields. It is stalling us purposefully while they run amuck on the planet. Every time we get some traction, a new set of ships jump in. If you have some wisdom, sir, I would love to hear what you think."

The comms went silent and Retzo stared at his feet, noticing that the one on the right had a small white mark that stood out. Grabbing his handkerchief he dropped to a knee and cleaned it off methodically. *Why isn't he replying? He must be gloating*, he thought, annoyed at the fact that the admiral was even there.

"It sounds to me that they know us very well," Gerald Hal finally said. "They know that we're spread thin, and that communication is a joke. They can keep throwing warships at us, and in time the planet will be lost. It's how they got our ancestors, Captain. It's why I'm here now."

"If I knew you were coming, sir, I would have—"

"What? Put out fireworks?" he said. "You wouldn't have known, Retzo. That's how we will win. Don't you know that we are compromised on every level in this Alliance? Even this chat of ours, and that Genevieve girl. How do you know that she doesn't have family under the gun from some traitor?

"The lizards have mind control, son. Why would I announce myself? Now, stay your course and wait for me to hail you before you do anything else. You've already lost an infiltrator, and the other one seems eager to join. Pull them out now, then watch and observe. Today's lesson will be a course on removing lizards that hide behind shields."

This is something I have to see, thought Retzo as he opened the door to the bridge. He'd be lying if he said that the admiral's words had no impact, as he mulled over the loyalty of Genevieve Aria.

Hal was completely right in his assertion that there could be a spy. Viles had committed suicide after sending the Nighthawks to their deaths. Even now he was clueless about his former CAG's involvement. *Did he have family under the gun? Was that what drove him to kill himself?*

"Captain on the bridge," Genevieve announced as he walked back to his chair and took a seat. He depressed two buttons and a vid screen materialized, with a shot from the fore of the *Rendron*. He saw that the *Scythe* was now descending on the *Nian*, who shot a torpedo in response.

Retzo's breath caught in his throat when it struck the *Scythe's* hull, but the payload merely dissipated. "What in the worlds?" Retzo whispered as he looked at Dino for an answer.

"Absorption shields, Captain. Photon weapons get absorbed. It's a rare feature of beautiful science, really. Admiral's privilege, eh?"

"Yeah, no kidding," Retzo said. *No wonder the old man's cocky.*

The *Scythe* moved in front of the *Aqnaqak's* position, absorbing all the shots that the battleship pumped out. After a time the firing ceased, and the *Nian* jumped out of the system before the *Scythe* could retaliate.

That was anticlimactic, Retzo thought, but the bridge seemed to disagree. Every one of the crew began to cheer, offering up hugs and shaking hands. Even Genevieve was on her feet, applauding, and Retzo Sho felt pressured to join in. It was just like the admiral to show up late and steal the show, but the battleship was gone, and the Geralos on Meluvia would be without support.

As they congratulated one another, Retzo got a new message on his wrist pad. He closed the channel and shut down the vid, then took a close look and saw that it was private. Getting up quietly, he slipped into the passageway, noticing that there were cheers coming from every corner of the ship.

He walked to his cabin, not stopping even when hailed. "Good job, Admiral Hal," he muttered. "You can now tell stories about the time you saved our skin."

33

Retzo's cabin was very posh, way too posh for someone as humble as he was. He'd inherited it from his predecessor, who was a man with a taste for the finer things. Retzo had never been comfortable with the fact that his cabin was nearly as big as the bridge. It was resplendent with whites and golds, plush carpeting, and even a couch.

A large glass window showed the *Soulspur* in self-repair, floating between the *Scythe* and the *Aqnaqak*. Retzo walked past the king-sized bed to a large desk in front of the window. He sat in the chair and pulled up the message. It was from Misa Chase, his master-at-arms.

"Captain Sho," it began. "I am sending you this message in confidence. There's a surveillance video attached. It was the last one taken of Commander Viles. I don't know how to put this easily, sir, but the commander's suicide was staged. The man on the video is a corporal named Ozie Arl. He is a Marine from the *Inginus* who we now have in custody.

"Captain, we questioned him, and he is willing to talk, but he wants a guarantee—from you—that he will be absolved of the crime. Please watch the video, sir, and call my comms when you're ready. I will await your word on what to do next."

Retzo read the message three more times in disbelief. "They committed murder on my ship?" he whispered, "They murdered one of my officers?" In all his years as captain, there had been three murders that he could remember.

Two were from a lover's spat, where a crewman found his woman with another man. The third was a teenager, a cadet, who killed another that had bullied him. They were unfortunate deaths, but he understood them. This one was still a mystery.

His fingers found his temples, massaging gently as he read the words over and over. *The man on the video is a corporal named Ozie Arl. He is a Marine from the Inginus,* the message had read.

"Why would an *Inginus* Marine be on my ship when his infiltrator is off on duty?" Retzo mused. His mind began to work. *If this is Lang's doing...* but he quickly removed it from his mind.

The surveillance showed a passageway where Adan Viles was walking. Nothing seemed out of the ordinary until the scene switched to another angle. This time he was at the fore of the ship, walking towards the ladderwell.

After a minute went by, a Marine caught up to him, and then the door to an elevator slid open. The two men got on the elevator and the door closed after them, and then the video blinked off ... finished.

What in the worlds was that? Retzo thought. *Where is the footage from the officer's deck? Were the cameras in the elevators offline? What about the footage of him walking to his compartment?*

He touched his comms to try and reach the master-at-arms (MA), but there was no answer on the line. Retzo twisted his lips, "What is going on?" he said. *When you got a call from the ship's captain, you drop everything to take it.* Either his MA had fallen into trouble, or something was interfering with their communication.

Annoyed, he leaned over and triggered the video again, this time playing the footage back at a quarter of its speed. There were more details that popped out, the man who joined Viles was speaking to him – no, speaking was an understatement, he was obviously upset and shouting.

Without audio or additional footage, it was hard to determine his intent. Still, something didn't feel right about this exchange. Adan Viles was a commander, and the crew knew to afford him respect no matter how they felt.

If that angry man was one of the Inginus's Marines, then he was out of line, Retzo thought. *But Adan's face seemed so calm.* "Planets," he exclaimed and stood up suddenly. *Had Adan been aware that he was about to be murdered, or coerced into suicide by this piece of schtill?*

The admiral's words echoed in his head. *Don't you know that we are compromised on every level in this Alliance?* Retzo reached into his desk and took out a large silver handgun. It was oiled, brilliant in the light, immaculate in its appearance.

He slid the weapon under his coat, checking the mirror to make sure that it was hidden. Then he stepped out into the passageway, feeling a mixture of anger and fear. Several officers walked by, smiling and saluting as they went. They had probably been celebrating the *Scythe's* victory over the battleship, ignorant of what was really going on.

Retzo forced a smile when their eyes met, then scanned the passageway on both sides. Misa hadn't called, and this more than anything was troubling. "You got this," he whispered, willing strength into his legs.

As he placed one foot in front of the other, he thought of everything that had happened with Viles. The compromised mission that the Nighthawks had been given, and the withholding of information when Cilas had called.

Adan Viles had been a good officer, and a candidate for being his next XO. He had kept the position vacant for way too long, and the Alliance was pressuring him to appoint another officer. Jit Nam had been his first choice, but Viles had been his second. He hadn't bothered to tell either, waiting for the right time to announce the promotion.

Then all of this happened, with Viles, the most straight-edged of his officers, disappointing him at every turn. It was almost as if he was being made to fail. Retzo stopped and stood staring into the bulkhead. *Made to fail.* The word brought some clarity to his mind. *Made to fail by someone with ambition.*

His comms buzzed and he saw Misa Chase's face. "Where have you been, sergeant? I was about to come down there, ready," Retzo said.

"My apologies, Captain, I had an emergency but—"

"Very good, Mr. Chase, I watched the surveillance video," Retzo said. "I am on my way down to see this man you have in custody. What has he told you so far about Viles and his reason for killing him?"

"That's the thing sir. He hasn't admitted to it, but we have fingerprints and video that place him inside the commander's compartment. He claimed that they had a drink together, and were discussing his transfer to our ship," Misa said.

"Nonsense," Retzo said. "Adan Viles doesn't drink, and he knows how I feel about rates in the officer's quarters. This innuendo in your tone, is it meant to hint at something else? I don't have much time—as you very well know—and I'd appreciate it if you speak to me straight. Is there any evidence that this was a relationship of some sort? Was Viles the reason that man was on my ship?"

"No, Captain, there was no evidence of that, and the officers on Commander Viles' deck said they didn't recognize Ozie Arl," he said.

Damn you, Adan. Why couldn't you talk to me? Retzo thought as he got off the comms and picked up the pace to reach the large metal door for the brig. His fingers registered positively when he placed them on its surface, and the door slid open to reveal a cavernous compartment.

Several cells sat against the bulkhead, their transparent walls facing out. In the first two were a pair of crewmen who averted their eyes when they saw him. Their faces were nicked with bumps and bruises, as if they had been in a brawl.

All the other cells were empty except for one, where Ozie Arl watched him like a hawk. Retzo didn't notice the other MAs, or Misa getting up from his desk. All he saw was the murderer and the way he stared out at him.

"That man isn't who he says he is," Retzo said, staring into his eyes. "I can tell a Marine anywhere, and what I see in front of me isn't it."

Misa walked up next to the captain and looked at Ozie Arl, who was now on his feet. It was as if he had been waiting to perform, and the curtains had been opened. "Did you tell him my stipulations?" he said to Misa Chase, and the MA looked at Retzo to see what he would say.

"Give me all the details of your involvement with Commander Viles, as well as your accomplices, beneficiaries, and partners. Lie to me and I walk out of here, and you can sit in this cell and rot," Retzo said. "But if you confess to me now, I will allow you to leave my ship."

The man—who spoke in a thick Meluvian accent—seemed to consider his words, then walked back to the bed and sat down. "I've heard about you, Captain Sho. They say that you're a man of your word. What happened to the commander was unfortunate, but in my line of work, we have no choice." He exhaled heavily and ran his hand through his hair, a thick crop of dark green locks with the sides shaved in the military standard.

"I am originally from Meluvia. I am what you call a professional. My organization lends safety to the citizens of a city called Senel. Some people would call us gangsters, but we are much bigger than that. We have land, influence, but we—"

"Speed it up, Mr. Arl, I have a ship awaiting my command," Retzo said. "Skip to the part where you were paid to kill my man."

"It wasn't like that, you see," Ozie said, gesturing with his hands. "It started when the commander came to the city."

"Viles went to Meluvia? When?" Retzo said, growing impatient.

"No, the other commander, Tyrell Lang. You see?" Ozie said, and Retzo felt his strength give out at the mention of his commander's name. "Commander Lang visited our city every year, so we knew who he was. He fell in love with the daughter of San Patren, a local magistrate. Master Patren was a kind man, a very polite man, you see ... but he was also a nationalist, and hated Vestalians more than anything."

Ozie Arl sat forward and placed his elbows on his knees. He stared through the cell wall as if the scene played out there. "You can imagine how he felt when he learned his beloved Liza was with this commander. We saw an opportunity, so we approached Lang, and in exchange for Patren, uh, playing nice," he said, smiling at the memory. "He promised us credits, and influence in your organization, if—"

"How did this end up costing Viles his life?" Retzo said, already annoyed with the story.

"We got the information for your Viles' family, and sent him a warning to do what we asked," he said. "At first he complied with our demands, the details I'm not at the liberty to discuss. But Mr. Viles became defiant overnight, as if something had changed and he no longer feared us. We spoke to Lang about this complication, and he offered up someone else, but we didn't trust that Viles would keep quiet about our arrangement."

"When did you bastards murder his wife?" Retzo said, understanding now why Viles had slipped in the execution of his duties.

"Not long before we killed him," Ozie Arl admitted. "He had confronted Lang and threatened to tell you about our arrangement."

"I've heard enough," Retzo said. "One more question and I'll be on my way. Are there any more of you 'professionals' on my ship?"

"Only I," said Ozie Arl, resigned now that he had told.

"Master-at-arms," Retzo said, and then turned to exit the compartment.

It was all he could do to get out of the vicinity before his emotions got the better of him. He wanted to pull his weapon and shoot the

Meluvian, and then send for Lang and shoot him too. But this was an Alliance vessel with Alliance rules, and shooting a prisoner—no matter who it was—would have him in front of the admiral.

There would be a hearing, and the gangster would be charged, even though he'd lied and told him that he would be exonerated. That is if the council didn't want to hear more. He reasoned that Ozie Arl would be shipped off to stand before them. They weren't held to the same rules that he was, and would find a way to get the full story out of him.

He had murdered a commander inside of his own cabin, and that would be seen as the worst kind of offense. Lang would get worse, much worse than he could imagine, and he couldn't wait to be there, to see him come to justice.

Retzo felt numb, and his jaw hurt something terrible, as if he'd punched himself while listening to the treachery. As he walked the length of the *Rendron*, he could no longer see. His mind was dominated with the tale he had just heard.

Lang had betrayed them all for a Meluvian woman on the surface. It was something he couldn't understand. The worst part of it all was the guilt he now felt for the way that he'd treated Viles. Yes, he had sent the Nighthawks on a doomed mission to—what? Get abducted by the Geralos? That part he didn't know, since Ozie Arl had kept it to himself, but he expected to have a long talk with Lieutenant Cilas Mec when he saw him.

He opened the door to the bridge and walked over to Genevieve Aria. Hovering over her as she sat looking concerned, he stared into her large hazel eyes. "Are you still with me, Jenny?" he said, using her nickname. "Look me in my eyes and tell me that you're still with me and this ship."

"Always, Skip. I am with you, always," she whispered. Her eyes spoke truth, so he relaxed and knelt down next to her. He hadn't felt this angry in what felt like forever, and he needed justice to quench his thirst. The job had taken its toll and he felt older than his years, but the betrayal was beyond unsettling, and he was shaking with rage.

"I need you to get an officer from the *Inginus* on the line," he said, speaking quietly so that only she could hear. "It needs to be someone you trust, someone who can keep things quiet. I want Commander Tyrell Lang to be placed in an escape pod and brought to this ship for questioning. Whomever does it, I give permission to use force—that is, if they feel it's necessary," he said. "This is a can't-fail mission, Jenny. Do you understand me?"

"Explicitly, Skip," she said, nodding. "I will have it done."

34

It had been well over a year since the last time Cilas Mec heard from Genevieve Aria. It wasn't due to malice or hurt feelings on their part, but more to do with moving on and respecting each other's space.

Cilas had a hard time remembering what it was that had pulled them apart. They had grown up together on the *Rendron*, and had each turned out to become exactly what everyone predicted. He, the superstar cadet, was now an ESO leader, and she, the studious academic, was now an officer on the bridge.

He recalled making fun of her for being a part of the captain's "fist," but a joke wouldn't have done it; it would have been something about their different roles. Maybe he'd run her off when he became a Nighthawk. It sounded like him, brains before heart, but Genevieve wouldn't have let him go so easily.

Still, when he received her comms, he remembered how much he loved her. The sound of her voice—the pitch high yet breathy—brought him back to long days of hearing her talk about her dreams.

There was something hypnotic about the way she spoke, and he recalled long periods of time sitting with her in his arms. The *Rendron* had a large window next to the hangar, which served as a backdrop for a small meeting area. No one used it for what it was intended, so they'd sneak out there together to sit and talk.

Genevieve was the dreamer, and he the stoic warrior. They had something together, and as he listened to her talk, he knew that his feelings for her had never truly left. Anything she asked, he would happily do it, even when it involved an action that could get him killed.

When she asked him to take the commander and force him into a pod, he did not think to question her, since it would have come from the captain himself. Plus, he knew the rules. She would never tell him the source of the order, not when their comms could be hacked and intercepted.

"I will do my best," was his reply, though he struggled against the urge to say more. He wanted to know how she was doing, and if the captain treated her well. Was there someone in her life—someone like him? Someone who would nip her nose just to see that smile?

He didn't know he still had those feelings for her, not after all this time. It made him feel foolish and ridiculous, since he believed—incorrectly—that she no longer felt love for him.

Their conversation ended abruptly. She closed the comms and left him with dead air. He didn't take offense. It wasn't a casual call, and now he had his orders. He focused on Tyrell Lang, and how good it felt to have this mission. He hated the man, hated the fact that he was grounded on a ship commanded by him.

Being on the *Inginus* while the craziness went on gave him enough time to cement his feelings on Lang. Serving a lunatic like this was his worst nightmare, and he counted his blessings that he had been privileged enough to be stationed on the *Rendron*.

Retzo Sho knew honor and was a man of the people. Tyrell Lang was sloppy and cared little for their lives. This became evident a few hours back when he ordered an attack instead of repairing the ship. Cilas had wanted off when they came out of FTL, but was ordered to stay on by Lang.

Being the only ESO onboard, Lang wanted him close for protection, just in case they were boarded and needed to fight. It was a selfish command, which had burned Cilas up, but he had no choice but to comply.

Now he was being ordered to get off the ship and to take Commander Lang along with him. *What were her words?* "If you need force, you're cleared to use it." He couldn't help but feel giddy at the prospect of sticking it to Lang.

After Genevieve hung up, he found his way to the bridge. Since Lang had given him clearance, none of the crewmen stopped him or gave him grief. He surveyed the bridge to see who would pose a problem, and that was when he noticed that the commander was missing.

"Where's Commander Lang?" he said to Rennie Jos, who was Lang's yeoman.

"Haven't seen him in a while, sir," the bubbly ensign said. "He said something about taking a private call with Captain Sho from the *Rendron*."

What a lying sack of schtill, Cilas thought as he thanked the man and walked off the bridge. He had a brief thought that he was about to walk in on Lang, between the legs of an older cadet. It was his modus operandi—though he hoped that he was wrong—he hoped to find the man seated at his desk.

All through the passageway, lights were flashing. The ship was so damaged that nothing wanted to work. The atmosphere of the *Inginus* was absolute chaos as men and women ran about, trying to repair what they could.

He would have to use his head to isolate the old man, unless he wanted a scene when he dragged him off the ship. The other problem he faced was that no escape pod would work, not without permission from the bridge.

He's the commander, Cilas thought. *There has to be an override on those pods.*

He didn't have time to think it through as he found the ladderwell leading up to the officer's deck. Halfway up and the ship jerked violently, forcing him to use both hands to prevent himself from falling. He wasn't sure what could have shaken the ship like that, but he really wasn't interested in finding out.

All he wanted to do was get Lang and then get off this vessel. More crewmen passed him by when he gained the top and looked around for the commander's cabin. It wasn't hard to miss; it was as brazen as Lang himself. A set of double doors, in polished black and gold, sat at the end of the wide passageway.

When Cilas found himself alone walking to this door, he was very surprised considering the panic of the ship. The poor crewmen of the *Inginus* had been given no updates on a rescue. None of them knew whether they should evacuate or if help was on its way.

The *Scythe* had come in and the Geralos were gone, but they were split in half and immobile. Joy had told him that she would be on her way back now that the battle was over. He wanted to see her more than anything, and Ate he missed more than he'd ever admit.

Cilas got to the door and checked the passageway behind him. He could hear people around the ladderwell but none were on the deck. He pulled out his sidearm and checked its charge to make sure that it was ready. "Commander Lang," he said. He was met with silence, but he could hear noises coming from inside.

When he reached to pull open the doors, he was surprised to find them unlocked. *Well that's a mistake,* he thought as he slid them open. *Didn't think anyone would be bold enough to come inside, huh?* What he saw inside was a cabin bigger than any other compartment in the ship, but where it once was stately it now looked like it had been tossed.

Crouched behind the desk, stuffing items in a case, was none other than Commander Tyrell Lang. Cilas closed the doors behind him and hid the pistol behind his leg. He didn't think that Lang had noticed him yet, so he eased over to the side to see what he was doing.

As he suspected, the commander was leaving the ship, but had stopped by his cabin to empty out his drawers. When Lang finally saw him, his eyes were angry and confused. *He doesn't know what I want,* he thought. *I can see the gears turning in his head.*

"What are you doing, Commander?" he said, breaking the silence. "Are you really about to abandon the ship? Did I miss your announcement? The one where you tell everyone onboard to evacuate? I somehow missed that command, and from what I just saw on the bridge ... it looks like everyone else missed it too."

Tyrell Lang made a sudden move, and Cilas leveled the pistol at his head. "Commander, I'm relieving you of command of this ship," he started, but then Lang did the strangest thing. He knelt on the deck with his hands on his knees and began to laugh hysterically.

"I relieve you, sir, under the authority of Retzo Sho, and the Galactic Alliance of Anstractor. For your reckless hazarding of your command, your drunkenness, and placing the lives of your crew in jeopardy. I assume full responsibility with this, and will report to Captain Sho with what I have witnessed. There will be others to corroborate my claims, whenever the time comes that you will be tried. You will accompany me to an escape pod, where we will launch from the *Inginus* and dock on the *Rendron*."

"Planets, you're actually serious," he said, his face flushed with anger. He got up from his knees and placed the case on the desk, and spread his arms for effect. "You relieve me of my command of the scrap that once was *Inginus*. Great, the wreckage is all yours, son. May she serve you well."

"Over a hundred crewmen lost their lives due to your terrible leadership," Cilas said. "You chose to be aggressive when we were badly in need of repair, against a superior power with a high-powered shield. Did you think that doing this would somehow impress Captain Sho?" Now it was Cilas's turn to laugh.

"One hundred thousand credits are yours. Just, let me go, Lieutenant," he said.

"One hundred thousand credits? I don't want to know how you came by that, sir," Cilas said. "Tell you what we're going to do. We're going to take that case you packed and the two of us will find an escape pod. You can explain everything to Captain Sho."

"The captain ordered you to do this?" he said, looking disappointed. "Look, I can't—"

"Oh, yes, you can," Cilas said, stepping forward to detain him. But Lang feigned at the last minute and swung a fist into Cilas's face. It caught him in the nose with blinding success, forcing him to kneel on the deck. For a split second he couldn't see, but he could hear Lang scrambling out.

When the pain allowed for his eyes to open, Cilas noticed that Lang was gone. He got to his feet and was out of the cabin instantly, running so fast that if anyone got in his way, they would have been bowled over by 80kg of pure adrenaline.

Though he was upset with himself for letting Lang get away, he could no longer think clearly enough to dwell on it as a failure. His mind went to the times when he was running with Helga, right below the very deck that he was now sprinting down. He recalled seeing the hatches attached to the escape pods, and he knew that if Lang made it down the ladder, he would never see him again.

As he reached the ladderwell, he leapt down several flights. Luckily he didn't twist an ankle as he turned and pushed a crewman out of the way. He gained the main passageway—the one he used to jog with Helga—and beyond the crewmen milling about, he could see the back of the commander.

Pushing past anyone in his way, he picked up the pace after Lang. A few tough-guy Marines took issue with his pushing, but Cilas had no time for confrontation. In his mind he was on a Nighthawk mission, tracking down his prey, and like the many Geralos he'd put to death, Lang would learn that he was quite efficient.

The commander glanced back and saw Cilas coming, so he too began to run. This was disaster in that passageway, despite it being wider than any on the ship. But he was the commander so nobody dared stop him from fleeing.

At one point when the path was clear, Cilas got a good view of his back. He was already frustrated and wanted to take a shot. But was he good enough to hit him? And if he hit him, could he be certain that it wouldn't be fatal?

It would lead to insanity; the already stressed out crew would rally around their leader, and he would be arrested or killed. It was bad enough that he was actively chasing their commander through this crowded passageway. The instant he brought up the pistol, or made any aggressive moves, an MA would be alerted and they would never hear reason.

Lang didn't stop at the escape pods, but instead ran into the officer's wardroom. *He's going to lock that door*, Cilas thought with frustration, *and then he will be trapped inside.* He tried to speed up to catch the door before it shut, but by the time he made it there it was too late.

Pulling up short to pace in front of the door, Cilas thought about how he could enter. The door was built to keep the unwanted out, and was as smooth as the bulkhead that held it. There would be no prying it off or kicking it in. He would only be able to enter with an override.

He touched his comms and picked up his pacing, mostly because his adrenaline was still up. "Genevieve," he said. "Patch me through to Captain Sho."

"Are you on your way with the commander?" she said.

"No, he gave me the slip and ran. Jenny, can you believe this man? He offered me a hundred thousand credits to let him go. What is going on?"

"I wish I knew, but the captain does. Hold on, I'm patching you through to him right now."

"I heard," said Retzo Sho almost immediately, and Cilas didn't know what to say. "It's okay, Lieutenant, he can run for now; that is, if you think that the Nighthawks can find him," he said.

"Sir, he's still on the ship, but has locked himself inside the wardroom. Is there any way you can speak to the *Inginus* and get the crew safely off, sir? Commander Lang should have done that, but no announcement has been made. Bringing him to the *Rendron* will be very difficult, sir, if the Marines are under the impression that I mean to harm their commander."

"Hold that thought," said Retzo Sho, and then the comms went dead.

Did I lose him? Cilas thought, looking at his wrist pad. A drip of sweat smeared its surface, and he lifted his arm to wipe his face. He was sweating profusely from running so hard, harder than he'd run in months. The runs with Helga had just been jogs, light enough to avoid running into the crewmen that they passed.

He checked the time on his pad, and saw that a whole minute had passed. He tried Genevieve again, but even she wasn't picking up now. "Thype!" he exclaimed, and slammed his fist into the door. What was he supposed to do now?

There was a commotion behind him as a group of Marines approached, led by a large man who Cilas assumed was the *Inginus* master-at-arms. He recognized him from the range but he didn't know his name. He saw that they were armed, and his eyes scanned the area for an advantage.

"Is there something I can help you with, Lieutenant?" the man said, his hand hovering over the sidearm that was strapped across his chest.

Cilas was stuck; this was the end. Nothing he could say would be a sufficient explanation for chasing their commander across the ship. Someone had called and reported the disturbance, and he was thinking it was Lang himself.

As he made to rush at the crowd of men, a jingle played across the system. Cilas recognized the tune. It was from the *Rendron*. It would play when the Captain was about to speak.

"This is Captain Retzo Sho of the *Rendron*. Commander Tyrell Lang has been relieved of his command by Lieutenant Cilas Mec. He is to be afforded the respect of a commander of an Alliance vessel. Lieutenant Mec will see to your repairs and proper evacuation protocol. *Inginus Prime*, you've done us proud, so hold your heads high. Lieutenant Mec will see you through this as I await you on the *Rendron*."

The jingle played once more and then there was an unsettling silence followed by a loud commotion in the passageway. The MA dropped his hands, and saluted Cilas briskly, followed by the Marines, who seemed stunned by the announcement.

"First order of business, master-at-arms. I need you to get this door open," Cilas said.

He moved out of the way, but then there was a sound, like an explosion from the inside. The MA moved quickly, overriding the controls and pulling open the door to the wardroom.

Inside was a long table with chairs all around it, but the glasses and plates had shifted during the fight. Some were on the ground, shattered into pieces, while others were intact and remained in place.

It wasn't the sight of these broken dishes, however, that made Cilas exhale with frustration.

Commander Tyrell Lang sat at the head of the table, his mouth stuck open as if he was about to sing. They could see the hole where the bullet had passed: through his mouth, the chair, and the bulkhead. From his gaping maw the smoke still lingered, and a smell like sulfur permeated the air.

35

The reality of the last few months did not settle in until Helga Ate was back aboard the *Rendron*. She had been given a formal request to return to the ship, along with Joy Valance and her Revenant squadron.

It didn't really matter, since Joy had committed to return the morning after she'd spoken to Cilas. During the night sometime he had spoken to her again, and she learned the bad news about the *Inginus* and Commander Lang.

In the morning during breakfast, she had informed them about everything. Millicent had taken it the hardest, since her husband was killed when the ship got split. It had been a quiet launch home in the wake of that revelation, but Helga was excited to be finally returning home.

As she left the hangar with the Revenants in tow, she noticed the lingering looks and the gaping mouths. She had thought herself skinny after the events of Dyn and the pirate ship, but the way the crew regarded her made her think there was something more.

Is it that bad? she thought, trying to remember how she appeared before setting out with Cilas. She had less hair, and a little more weight, but that was about it... not counting the PAS armor that she wore. A smile crossed her face when she recalled how good it felt to slip into the armor for the first time. She had been so happy that nothing could bother her, not even the things that Wyatt had said.

She wished she still had her armor; then none of these stares would even bother her. Seeing the HUD readouts about your health and stability, and the fuel gauge that never seemed to dip lower than 50%. That pulse it would do when you walked too fast, like a bird flapping its wings to get ahead a little faster. Oh, how she missed that suit. She felt naked now without it.

It was surreal for someone who had grown up being bullied to now have the same people looking on as if she'd risen from the dead. *Maybe it's something else?* she thought. *Maybe they are in awe of me.* She glanced back at Joy, who was still on her comms, talking to Cilas and smiling. It had started before she docked, and now she lingered back, chatting away as if nothing else mattered.

Helga had expected to have her by her side as she walked these familiar passageways. It would have been an excuse to talk, to play guide while she avoided those staring. With Joy she wouldn't have to notice the looks and relive old memories that she'd suppressed. Now with every step she felt the darkness coming on, and she was once again cold and alone.

Maybe I should have stayed on Meluvia, she thought.

When Joy saw Helga looking, she gave her a wink and sped up to join her, taking her hand. "You're a bit of a celebrity, Ate. I feel like one of your handmaidens," she said. They were passing through the Merchant Center, with its kiosks stacked against the bulkheads. Everywhere they went had clumps of crewmen, however, and most of them looked on as their squadron walked past.

"Celebrity?" Helga said. "Most of these people don't even know me. It's Cilas who's the celebrity. They're just gawking at my cheekbones."

Although she spoke what she felt, Joy Valance laughed it off and went back to being a schoolgirl on her comms. The other Revenants were strangely stoic, and it reminded Helga of her first night on the *Inginus*. She, Cilas and Brise didn't know who to trust—least of all the commander—so they had made an effort to keep to themselves. But then Joy Valance happened, and they got integrated quickly. That was their Joy, the irresistible extrovert. No one was allowed to hide.

Helga found herself alone and stopped to see what had happened. When she looked back, she saw the Revenants huddled in front of one of the screens. "We'll catch up later, Ate," Joy said, waving her off. "Cilas says that they are waiting, and that you should take the elevator."

Elevator access. It must be serious, Helga thought, remembering what Joy had told her about Cilas going after Commander Lang. It was big news now, the disgraced officer, and the brave lieutenant hunting him down amidst a hostile ship.

The idea of meeting Retzo Sho to talk about Dyn gave Helga butterflies, and nausea. She didn't want to relive the trauma. *Inginus* and Joy had felt like therapy after everything she'd been through, not to mention her daily runs and range visits with Cilas.

She was so much happier now than she had been when they were in that escape ship. The door to those memories had been sealed— outside of nightmares and times like this. Now they were going to make her talk and relive the pain of the past. It had crippled her psyche; didn't Cilas understand how hard this was for her? She reasoned that he was so in love that he no longer cared how she felt.

The familiarity of these *Rendron* compartments allowed her to move on, regardless. She toyed with remembering pieces of Dyn, but even the few that came made her angry. "Why are you all staring at me?" she said all of a sudden, fed up with the eyes.

She had been through too much to be patient with their antics. Not after everything, not after Dyn, not after finding true acceptance with the aces of the Revenant squadron. The first "spots," or "half-breed" that got thrown her way would be eating her fists and feet. She waited for it, she anticipated it, and she accepted that when it came, she would lose control.

"Hellgate," someone called, and she looked over at a group of women.

Here we go, she thought, feeling the fire in her chest. That was another nickname she hated. It was a gross mispronunciation of her name. Hellgate. The cadets had thought it clever to nickname her something evil like that.

As she spun on them to remind them that she was an ESO operator, they stood up in unison and saluted. Helga stood there, frozen, unable to process what was happening. It was respect, it was adoration... *was this what the stares were about?*

A year ago, she was one of these women when the Nighthawks would walk the ship. Seeing their PAS armor, knowing that they were deadly effective ... she'd wanted to be one of them, badly. Now she sucked in her emotions and returned the salute, then turned to continue her walk.

Helga Ate had returned, and she was not the little "half breed" that they had made fun of. For some reason she had thought that returning would renew feelings of happiness for her. It was her childhood home, after all, but the place seemed to be nothing but a reminder of her past, the painful past of being an outsider who was constantly jeered.

But here were crewmen saluting and smiling as she passed. They regarded her with a respect that normally came with a fleet-wide reputation. The same respect she'd seen given to Cilas no matter where he was.

Maybe this "Hellgate" had become more than a jeer. It had become legendary to those who knew.

I like this, she thought, grinning as she reached the elevator lobby. "I can get used to this treatment," she said as she touched the icon indicating up.

Made in the USA
Las Vegas, NV
19 November 2024

12092455R00163